BROKEN SYMMETRIES

Later that night the electronic disks and certain other partial records were recovered. Some evidence had been destroyed or distorted by electromagnetic pulse, but other recordings had been well preserved. To the testimony of these unbiased mechanical witnesses were added the impressions of seven human beings who had survived the destruction of Building W. The old man was not among them; he and seventeen others had died.

The evidence confirmed that the countdown had never been completed. The explosion had apparently occured inside the beam projector's ion source. . . .

"Paul Preuss has written a magnificent book . . . I admire his knowledge and artistry."

—Roger Zelazny

BROKEN SYMMETRIES

PAUL PREUSS

PUBLISHED BY POCKET BOOKS NEW YORK

Excerpts from *An Introduction to Haiku,* by Harold G. Henderson. Copyright © 1958 by Harold G. Henderson. Reprinted by permission of Doubleday & Company, Inc.

Excerpts from *Duino Elegies,* by Rainer Maria Rilke, with English translations by C. F. MacIntyre. Copyright © 1961 by C. F. MacIntyre. Reprinted by permission of University of California Press.

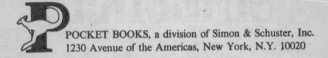

POCKET BOOKS, a division of Simon & Schuster, Inc.
1230 Avenue of the Americas, New York, N.Y. 10020

First Pocket Books Science Fiction printing August, 1984

10 9 8 7 6 5 4 3 2 1

POCKET and colophon are registered trademarks
of Simon & Schuster, Inc.

Printed in the U.S.A.

Acknowledgments

I am indebted to David Crommie and Karen Crommie, John Douglas, Joyce Frommer and Diana Price, Rebecca Kurland, Lee Mendelson, Bill Neil, Mark Preuss, Jerry Rasmussen, Michael Rogers and Janet Hopson, Michael Rosenthal, Rob Semper, and Chelsea Quinn Yarbro for help with research, location scouting, translations, and other valuable but unclassifiable assistance.

For wise editorial advice, thanks to Charles N. Brown, David Hartwell, and Marta Randall.

Special thanks to staff members and researchers at the Stanford Linear Accelerator Center and the Lawrence Berkeley Laboratory, especially to the generous staff of Berkeley's 88-inch cyclotron and its director, Robert Stokstad.

Errors of fact and interpretation are, of course, my own.

for Karen

The physics in this story is intended only to seem plausible, not to be predictive. Inside quarks don't exist, nor do I-particles, and there is no TERAC on Oahu or anywhere else. The characters and events are likewise wholly fictitious.

Since they could not actually create souls, after having evoked the souls of demons and angels, they introduced these into their idols by holy and divine rites, so that the idols had the power of doing good and evil.

—"HERMES TRISMEGISTUS,"
The Perfect Word

I ask myself just what scientists think they are up to.

—HIDEKI YUKAWA,
Creativity and Intuition

1

Three secretaries stared at him, prepared for anything. He crossed the carpet between their desks wordlessly, intent only on reaching his office door. The youngest, prettiest woman rose nervously: "Dr. Slater, Dr. Edovich asked me to remind you of the party this evening. . . ."

He nodded, avoiding her eyes. He'd never learned her name; he didn't want to, for she reminded him too much of Kathleen. He scooped a thick manifold of new computer printout from the corner of her desk as he went past—then he was inside his office, safely out of sight and hearing.

Briefly he imagined the glances they exchanged behind his back, the appalled and knowing looks; a week ago he'd left the pretty one in tears with some unfeeling remark, and Brownie Lasky, whose office was next door, had gently reproved him. He hadn't meant to make her unhappy. He just wanted to be left alone. Completely alone.

In fact, Peter Slater's mood was better than usual this fine spring morning. He'd slept well, a rare thing, and gotten up a half-hour late, filled with vague optimism. He looked forward to the day's work. He laid the new data on top of the stack on his desk and went to the window, opening the curtains to the morning sun. Pressing his fingertips gently to the cool glass, he stared down on blue green vistas from his eighth-floor window. Thirteen miles away, beyond Pearl Harbor, a silvery jetliner descended toward Honolulu International Airport. Within moments he had drifted into reverie.

Six weeks earlier Peter Slater had been shown to this office at Hawaii's Teravolt Accelerator Center for the first time. Its luxury was unsettling. Spacious, furnished with bleached oak and chrome and rough-woven wool in the latest style of the nineties, equipped with well-stocked shelves of reference works and its own state-of-the-art minicomputer, it posed a startling contrast to the cramped, cluttered working quarters he'd shared at the mathematics department at Berkeley. Soon he'd be spoiled for other potential employers, and he suspected this was precisely the intention of TERAC's administration. Slater was a man who appreciated good taste in material things.

Perhaps best of all was the view from Tomonaga Hall. Beyond the landscaped interior of the accelerator's main ring, broad pineapple and cane fields gently sloped toward a smear of suburbs; in the distance beyond them glittered the windows of downtown Honolulu. The purple silhouette of Diamond Head floated in the farthest background, like a cruise ship at anchor. The ocean lay blue and calm under the midmorning sun; lazy fat cumulus clouds drifted in the windless sky. Away to the south a cane field was burning, sending a column of gray brown smoke a mile into the air, where the warm rising moisture gave birth to a benign mushroom cap of cloudy vapor.

But though Peter Slater appreciated the panoramic view, he did not really see it. He didn't even see the airplane landing in the distance, the bright moving speck that had snagged his staring gaze. He didn't see the workmen directly below his window who were erecting a wide wooden platform on the broad green lawns, and setting up towers to hold television cameras, and poles from which to hang loudspeakers. Slater had forgotten all about the big invitational dedication ceremonies to begin on Monday, had forgotten that he'd agreed to play some part in the formalities. He was lost in a profound daydream of the sort that had become more and more seductive in past weeks, and the tranquil scene outside his window served merely as an aid to his concentration, just as a single chrysanthemum in a vase might serve as a suitable point of departure for a monk's meditative trance. The brain persists in the childish urge to show itself pictures, even when the mind is otherwise occupied.

Slater's distraction was of that class of creative narcolepsies that one's colleagues may recollect in their memoirs, fondly or otherwise, as the mark and affliction of young genius. The suspicion that Peter Slater was such a one, though his genius was far from proving itself beyond doubt, allowed him much forgiveness within the society of particles-and-fields physicists, a society rich in eccentricity. No one minded that he'd played the recluse since coming to TERAC, hardly bothering to introduce himself to his new associates unless he urgently needed to talk physics with one or another of them. His fearsome theoretical reputation helped keep the gregarious at bay, his chilling hauteur intimidated mere celebrity-collectors, and those who dealt in gossip quickly spread the word, more or less accurately, that he was recovering from a painful divorce, and was entitled to lick his wounds in private. Slater was oblivious to them all.

Years ago Peter Slater had learned to uncouple his thought processes from visualization. Without that peculiar skill he still would have been an extraordinary child, a preternaturally bright high school student who loved chess and was teaching himself Mandarin and Japanese so that he could read and write poetry in those languages, but who'd flunked Algebra II out of sheer inattention. But somewhere between his junior and senior year, not really

overnight but so quickly that it seemed so, he'd emerged
as a prodigy, producing a pair of papers at the frontier of
set theory. Part of that profound transition in modes of
thought had occurred to him as a mere trick during a
chess game with a friend, when instead of trying to picture
the elements of the strategy he was pursuing, he'd tried
to "hear" them instead, as if they were the melodic lines
of a fugue, each composed of individual notes woven into
chordal patterns. Researchers had long known that
human chess masters, and masters of other board games
like go, relied upon their unconscious store of recognizable
patterns to guide their play—unlike the winning computer
chess programs of the day, which won through linear ex-
trapolation and vast number-crunching power. Peter wondered what it would be like not to see the patterns as an
arrangement of differently valued tokens in a
two-dimensional matrix, but to hear them all at once like
symphonic chords—as if pawns were strings, castles brass,
knights percussion, bishops woodwinds, the king some
showy but fragile instrument like a harp, and the queen
a piece of immense range and depth, a piano. If he hadn't
already been winning the game he was playing when he
had the idea, he might have suppressed it—for he hated
to lose at anything, and he would never have taken the
chance of letting his concentration slip. But he tried
it—and it seemed to work, or at least not to get in the way
(he borrowed a chord from a Vaughn Williams piece that
was playing on the tape deck at the moment, to see how
it would resolve, and the solution was powerful, if not elegant; later he found Bach a much more fruitful source of
examples)—and he started habitually to coax his mind
into the rich but quirky path.

Once his obsession with sound symbols almost drove
him mad. His first doctorate was taken in astrophysics,
under Hawking at Cambridge; there one evening, during
one of those intense and extended discourses bright young
men are apt to pursue on the Nature of Mind, an English
friend who sought his approval quoted Lewis Thomas to

him: "If you want, as an experiment, to hear the whole mind working, all at once, put on the *St. Matthew Passion* and turn the volume up all the way."

Slater's English friend thought it an amusing conceit. He never dreamed Peter would set out to test the hypothesis. Slater abandoned his proper reading while questing fruitlessly for an isomorphic mapping of the structure of thought onto music. Weeks later, exhausted, confined to the infirmary with a raging fever and lungs teeming with pneumonia, he woke up in the middle of the night laughing. He was saved. He'd gotten the joke. Bach had tricked Thomas and the others who'd entertained similar notions, for only Bach could mimic the music of the neurons, through the elegant expedient of coaxing sensual beauty from abstraction. This was not the mind working, this was the mind alternating between opposite poles. Beethoven could not do it, nor even Mozart, not for long.

Nevertheless the compelling analogy stayed with Peter. He haunted the common rooms of the colleges along the Backs, playing pieces for the *Well-Tempered Clavier* on various ill-tuned pianos as the soft English evenings turned to cool spring nights, and he would mentally wrestle with, say, the quantum thermodynamics of black holes. One or two quite original papers resulted from this odd habit.

On Oahu, some years later, he was still at it. Where Kekulé had dreamed before the fire of a snake biting its own tail, and wakened to apprehend the ring shape of the benzene molecule, where Pauling, sick with the flu and shivering in his room, had entertained himself with folding a piece of paper doll-fashion and thus deciphered the alpha-helix structure of collagen protein, so Peter Slater dreamed of endlessly rising baroque canons, and woke to propose new arrangements of quarks and leptons. So far, however, none of Slater's schemes had proved to have anything like the practical importance of decoded benzene—or any necessary relationship to reality at all.

But he dreamed on. On this tropical spring day, while

his unseeing eyes stared out at the contours of TERAC and the bright island beyond, Peter Slater was hearing concertos, whole symphonies, joyful progressions of staggered chords, intricately woven melodies.

And somewhere in the midst of them, a persistent sour note.

2

The flight attendant collected the agricultural inspection forms, and a moment later Anne-Marie remembered the two apples in her shoulder bag she hadn't eaten and hadn't declared. It amused her to think she was smuggling apples into paradise.

She could see nothing of the islands through the window as yet, except for a telltale mass of blue white cumulus clouds throwing indigo shadows on the sea ahead of the plane. She felt Gardner Hey's eyes on her and knew that if she turned quickly she would find the chubby reporter trying to peer down the front of her dress. She wished she hadn't worn the thin, brightly printed sun dress. Hey's low-grade lechery wasn't entirely unprovoked, for she was deliberately dressed to kill, even to the point of overdoing the make-up. Nerves. Anticipation. Never had the interior of an airplane looked so exciting; even the fact that the connecting flight was two hours late leaving Los Angeles had made the whole trip that much more adventurous to her, who hadn't been away from home in five years. The quite ordinary tourists who filled the cramped interior of the DC-10 took on an air of romance, or at least of fresh hope.

After five hours in the air a sense of proportion had returned—the young lovers across the aisle had proceeded to become mildly squiffed on Mai Tais, and their increasingly loud conversation had made it plain that their relationship, while by no means Platonic, owed more to their mutual interest in scoring exportable quantities of Maui Wowee than it did to tender esteem—but Anne-Marie wasn't disappointed. This was freedom, if of a limited sort, and the fact that it was real—that her seat was hard and narrow, and that she had to go to the bathroom yet again, and that Gardner Hey had turned out to be rather homely and uncouth despite her secret hopes to the contrary—all this merely served to persuade her that she was a live creature again, that the world was a vivid and bustling and unpredictable place, once more filled with the possibility of adventure.

Restlessly Anne-Marie shifted her long tanned legs in the cramped space in front of her seat. She briefly considered making another trip to the toilet, but she decided she could wait until they reached the airport. It couldn't be long now. She sighed, gave Hey plenty of warning by first returning her gaze to the book in her lap—*Hermetic Hieroglyphs, Their Meaning for Today,* by Carla Mawson, Ph.D.—then looked up at him sharply. Hey was staring straight ahead, worrying the fuzz of one long sideburn with the nail-bitten fingers of his right hand, trying to appear lost in thought.

"How's the view, Gardner?" she asked sweetly. He seemed harmless, even if he was a bit of an oinker. He'd tried to do all the right things, opening doors and grabbing at her luggage and scurrying around to get between her and the curb, and while he was inept at what he apparently understood to be the social graces, Anne-Marie was truly grateful to him for his part in arranging her first real photo assignment in years.

"Hmm?" Hey was playing the innocent. "Oh, can you see anything yet?"

"Not me," she said dryly. At that moment the smooth whine of the DC-10's engines subtly altered in pitch, and the big plane began to lose altitude. "I'm surprised at myself," she said. "I'm actually getting excited all over again."

"Really? Hawaii's about as exotic as Hoboken. With ferns."

"I don't think so. But the only time I was ever here was on my honeymoon." She caught herself twisting her rings; the diamonds were just big enough to assert wealth without overstepping the bounds of good taste. How like Charlie.

No wonder he'd been irritable when he'd taken her to the San Diego airport this morning: it wasn't that she was going away, for the thought that she might leave him would never enter his bourgeois noggin. He saw it the other way around, saw her as a symbol and representation of himself, a woman whose task it was to be intelligent, cultured, attractive in a, well, *girdled* way; an excellent hostess, of course, and not least a competent mother, competent to produce genetically superior children and competent to provide them with the rich environment they required to flower into flawless specimens of investment-bankerhood some day. But headed for Hawaii with cameras in hand, Anne-Marie must have exuded a sexuality that struck Charlie as extravagant, loose-kneed, bikini-briefed, braless—rich, all right, but bordering on the vulgar. It bothered Charlie to think his wife might be mistaken for a member of the wrong class.

"Hawaii honeymoon, eh?" Hey scratched at his pink tummy between the buttons of his thrift-store aloha shirt. "Life's been good to you, hasn't it?"

"Because my husband always plays by the rules," said Anne-Marie, glancing at Hey. "I don't."

Her little boy was four now, innocent and demanding, and she could not imagine abandoning him; neither could she imagine wresting custody of Carlos from Charlie and the lawyers his family money would buy. For now she was merely grateful for the separate vacation, the working vacation of the next few days. It made no difference to her that *Science Weekly,* Gardner Hey's paper, was a cheap newsletter that used no color, paid only space rate for what photographs it did buy, and doled out minimal travel expenses—it didn't matter that she would lose money on the assignment. With Charlie's money she could have traveled first class. More valuable to her than money was the fact of a legitimate job, one that might lead to other photography jobs which paid decently, that might in turn lead, in the dim future, to some kind of independent career.

Perhaps her dream of freedom was silly. Still, photography was the only skill she had, not counting the ability to look and sound good behind a reception desk, say, or in a cocktail lounge.

Unconsciously she'd been working at the rings on her finger, twisting them over her knuckle; she was surprised to find them lying free in her right hand. Surreptitiously she slipped them into the pocket of her skirt before Hey saw what she was doing. It didn't occur to her to wonder why the simple, natural act should make her feel guilty, why she thought it needed hiding.

The thud and rumble of unfolding landing gear frightened her out of her distracted thoughts. The sound was always so unexpected, so inexplicably violent, as if something were being torn from the plane, as if some blunt object were beating against the fuselage. It was a reminder of mortality. "The-captain-has-turned-on-the-fastenseatbeltsign," a cabin attendant recited, slapdash, managing to sound less human than a recording. The plane banked and turned. The passengers in the crowded jumbo jet stared glumly at the seat backs in front of them, trying not to think about popped cargo doors or engines dropping suddenly into the sea.

Oahu appeared beneath Anne-Marie's window. The island's serrated green ridges were crowned with mist and rainbows, and creamy surf surged out of turquoise seas to collapse on golden beaches. Then the city appeared, a compressed conglomeration of cement and glass and wood and rusted tin and stone and stucco, crawling with cars and people, trapped, overflowing the narrow strip of land between the Koolaus and the sea. Sliding beneath the wing were stark towers of featureless glass and concrete, what surfers called "The Wall of Waikiki."

Again Anne-Marie sensed Gardner Hey leaning toward her; this time he really was looking out the window. "There's my baby," he whispered, sounding not at all like a proud parent, but very much like a safecracker contemplating a vault; she could hear him mentally sandpapering his fingertips. She followed his gaze toward the middle of the island, to the immense interlocking circles there traced out against the gray pineapple fields by grassy mounds of bright green, a giant bull's-eye in the center of Oahu—TERAC, the Teravolt Accelerator Center.

"The main ring's over six kilometers in diameter," Hey said. "But the tunnel is actually way below the surface—that mound, what they call the berm, is only landscaping."

Anne-Marie took a moment to assimilate just how much of central Oahu the Teravolt Accelerator Center subsumed beneath its tastefully sculpted surface. She knew nothing of this machine or its smaller cousins around the world; indeed, she knew no more of high-energy physics than any ordinary person, that it had to do with "atom smashing" and particles with odd names like "quark." Her response to TERAC was wholly aesthetic. She'd expected to see something that looked like an oil refinery and was pleasantly surprised to find herself mistaken.

Studding the earthen rings were clusters of buildings with the rough dark geometry of natural monoliths.

Within the largest ring meandered a serpentine lake. From high in the air the accelerator center looked like a miniature Zen garden of stones and moss. "It's beautiful," she said. "And much bigger than I'd imagined. It's huge."

"Oh, it's so huge—" Gardner Hey's eyes glistened. "You can't begin to imagine the fortunes that have been squandered on this overgrown peashooter, the political careers that have been made and wrecked, the *deals* . . . "

"It sounds like you could write a book," said Anne-Marie, smiling.

"That's what I'm doing, all right. I've been following this story for years—there couldn't be a better example of what really goes on behind the respectable ivy-covered walls of Big Science, Inc."

"But this is the first time you've ever been to see TERAC?"

Hey sniffed resentfully. "I don't work for *Science,* you know. Or one of those flashy pop-sci slicks. If there weren't so many big names coming to this dedication I'd probably be writing up some stringer's files instead of coming in person. But I twisted arms. This conference is a perfect excuse for me to get . . . " Hey glanced at Anne-Marie, breaking off his sentence. Then he leaned back, and when he spoke again, the topic had shifted. "I'm glad Chauncey put us in touch with each other, Anne-Marie. Even if *Science Weekly* doesn't use enough of your stuff to make it worth your while, I can help you find other markets. Good photos really help sell a book."

She thought he sounded peculiarly insincere, but it didn't matter; she'd do the best job she could, better than Hey and his newspaper deserved. She was working for herself. "I hope there'll be something more interesting than speeches," she said, watching the shapes of TERAC blend into the distant fields as the plane settled lower.

"I'll get something a hell of a lot better than speeches," said Hey complacently.

The plane dropped swiftly toward the Reef Runway, its multiple landing gear reaching like birds' claws for the asphalt-covered landfill.

3

Chauncey Tolliver sat on the couch in Matsuo Ishi's outer office, wordlessly humming an old drinking song he'd picked up in the Air Force: "Last to know, first to go, we are the troopers of the PIO."

On his lined yellow pad TERAC's public information officer had been scratching crude drawings of knives and spears, their points diametrically opposed. Now he moved his gold ballpoint to the bottom of the page and wrote "Anne-Marie" in his loopy vertical hand, and drew an elaborate picture frame around the name. If her plane hadn't been late, if Director Ishi hadn't asked him to stand by to help prepare a last-minute press release, if these Friday afternoon staff meetings didn't always run so interminably long while the director waited for everybody to agree with everybody else, Tolliver could have stolen forty-five minutes from his schedule to meet Anne-Marie at the airport.

Tolliver stretched his legs, studying the crease in his seersucker trousers critically, judging the shine of his per-

forated-wingtip oxfords. He rubbed his aching eyes. He
still had a thousand details of the dedication ceremonies
to attend to: the workmen were running behind schedule
with the speakers' platform, and his budget couldn't ab-
sorb much weekend overtime; somewhere he or one of his
staff had to get hold of a crate of salmon roe—Japanese
delicacy—to replace the shipment he'd had flown in from
Alaska, which had arrived spoiled; already writers and
dignitaries were arriving from all over the world, and Tolliver had to be sure the key people got their invitations
to Martin Edovich's lawn party this evening, or Martin
would chew his ass. Martin always preferred to do his
arm-twisting and cajoling in informal settings.

Through the polished oak double doors of the conference room, across the room from where he sat, Tolliver
could hear the muffled voices of the director's staff, familiar even when unintelligible: Edovich's jocular baritone,
laughing but insistent; Ilse Friedman's tart, superior con-
tralto, salted with an assumed working-class bluntness;
Lasky's soothing murmurs; Shigeki Yamamura's uninten-
tionally comic growls. By eavesdropping halfheartedly
Tolliver knew that Yamamura had already wound up his
standard speech of complaint, the one about "most important experiments awaiting to the adjusting of the
beams"—Yamamura's experiments—and "also interesting experiments but now going on for more than one
year"—Martin Edovich's. It seemed that Yamamura
could never get enough beam time to suit his purposes.

Anticipating adjournment, Tolliver got to his feet. The
doors opened abruptly. Martin Edovich, always in a
hurry, was the first out of the room. The red-haired Yugoslavian gave Tolliver a wink and a grin; "I'll see you in
a couple of hours, my friend." Then Edovich spun around
to snag Ilse Friedman by the elbow and lead her away before Yamamura could catch up. The other staff members
walked past Tolliver without acknowledging his presence.

From inside the empty conference room Ishi's secretary, Miss Sugibayashi, nodded to him: "Ishi-sama will

see you in his office, Tolliver-san," she murmured, closing the double doors.

Tolliver ripped the top sheet from his notepad, wadded it into a ball, and tossed it into the cylindrical leather wastebasket beside the couch. The door to Ishi's inner office was to his left; like a Maxwell's demon Miss Sugibayashi opened it from inside just as he approached. She bowed as he entered.

Matsuo Ishi was slowly crossing the room toward his desk. His severely malformed left foot, damaged at birth by a clumsy doctor, caused him to lurch precariously as he walked. Ishi was a tiny man, almost hairless except for his wiry brows and the equally wiry gray hair bordering his crown. His shiny skin was stretched smoothly over his large skull and over the delicate bones of his hands. Yet once he'd seated himself behind his desk he appeared perfectly proportioned. Stillness, not action, was appropriate to his nature. "I am very sorry to have kept you from your duties, Mr. Tolliver. Please be comfortable."

Tolliver bowed awkwardly—in his years at TERAC he'd never mastered the polite gesture—and sat stiffly on the hard chair facing the desk. "Whatever I can do, sir."

"It is a matter of timing. Of what to say when."

Isn't it always? thought Tolliver. "What's the situation, sir?"

"I will relate an experience. You are aware that the Japanese staff held a little gathering in my honor at the Akasaka last night?"

"I had heard of it, yes."

"Yamamura-san had instructed the management to serve all my favorite dishes. The hostesses were charming and adroit, as usual."

Tolliver smiled politely, tapping the point of his pen against his yellow pad.

"After dinner the younger men became quite relaxed. I don't mind telling you, the toasts and songs were somewhat hilarious! Watanabe Hiro did a little dance he claims to have learned from an old farmer in the mountain village where he and his family vacation." Ishi glanced up at Tolliver. "Jokingly I told him it seemed more likely he had learned it by dancing in the streets with the rioters who closed the university. From the confusion on his face I knew I had hit the mark without aiming. Even today the younger men retain their foolish admiration for Marxism. Those like Watanabe who have spent part of their careers in the United States seem no less susceptible."

Tolliver said nothing. Of course he knew all about Watanabe and the others, had known from the beginning. He twisted his strong fingers around the thin ribbed metal of his pen.

"Yamamura came to Watanabe's defense, as was to be expected," said Ishi. "I was inspired to do a bit of entertaining myself. I told the tale of how sensei Nishina lost the cyclotrons—the one he bought in your country in 1938, the one we made for him during the war. Are you familiar with the incident, Mr. Tolliver?"

"Vaguely, sir. . . . "

"I remember the *intensity* of my gratitude at being allowed to help with the project," said Ishi. "I, an insignificant lame boy—turned out of school like all the others, but saved from the army by my twisted foot and from the factories by my mathematical aptitude. And, as I learned only a few years ago, by mutual debts of honor between my father and my sensei. Oh, Nishina was a good man and a brave one. We kept the machines running through the firestorms, almost to the end. Once when a machine failed we repaired its rectifiers with parts taken from the wreck of a B-29, one of those planes which was bombing Tokyo to rubble and ashes over our heads."

On Ishi's desk was a tattered, paper-covered notebook Tolliver recognized as a volume of his diary. He must have been keeping it since childhood, like most Japanese of his generation. The old man carefully opened the book and took a yellowed scrap of newsprint from between its pages.

"An American colleague gave me this, Mr. Tolliver, when I was visiting the Institute for Advanced Studies in the year after the war. From this article the American scientists first learned what had become of our cyclotrons. It is from the *New York Times* of November twenty-fourth, 1945, a report from Tokyo." Ishi held up the bit of paper and read aloud: " 'Today, under orders to destroy them, engineers and ordnance men from Lieut. Gen. Robert L. Eichelberger's Eighth Army here and General Walter Kreuger's Sixth Army in Southern Japan, moved into the plants armed with welding torches, explosives and other equipment and began to take the machines apart. Parts of them will be loaded on barges, taken out to sea and sunk.' "

Tolliver sat very still. Was Ishi making some sort of personal reference with this outdated tale of military stupidity? There had been a good many mistakes on both sides; mistakes happen, when men are afraid. After all, Nishina had been using those cyclotrons in a pathetic attempt to build a Japanese uranium bomb. "How did the others respond to the story, sir?" he asked.

Ishi replaced the fragile newspaper clipping and closed the book, folding his hands carefully on its cover. "They understood me, I'm sure." He paused, then said, "Five years ago the Prime Minister managed to persuade me that my acceptance of the directorship would make the Trillion-electron-volt Accelerator Center project more attractive to your government. I will admit that for too long I shamefully resisted the honor."

"Your record is not only distinguished but scrupulously fair, sir," Tolliver said automatically.

"You are gracious," said Ishi. "Of course, I have made enemies; that could not be helped. Now, however"—as he talked, Ishi drew a cigarette from a pack in his desk drawer, found a wooden match, and lit up—"we are dedicating this great machine, after more than a year of successful operation. And it is my belief that management is properly a pursuit for the young—and vigorous." He exhaled a cloud of blue smoke.

Tolliver saw the point, at last. Ishi intended to retire,

much earlier than anyone in either Washington or Tokyo had anticipated. The whole delicate political balance was about to be given a good shaking. Did Tokyo know already? The Prime Minister's office? The bureaucracies? Tolliver would have to inform Washington at once.

"I have told no one of my plans, Mr. Tolliver," said Ishi, evidently reading his mind. "Except for my wife and Miss Sugibayashi, you are the first. I cannot insist that you keep the matter secret. But there are some aspects you should be given time to consider."

"Then the press release?" Tolliver indicated his blank tablet.

Ishi dismissed the disingenuous question with a miniature wave of his fingers. "Yamamura has never relinquished his unrealistic desire to have my post. MITI has many sources of information here." Ishi smiled. "And Dr. Yamamura will doubtless create many difficulties when he learns of my plans—unless some fitting compromise has been arranged already, at the highest levels of government."

Tolliver knew that without the cooperation of Yamamura's sponsor, the Ministry of International Trade and Industry, TERAC could never have been built. But the same was true of the U.S. Department of Defense, to which Yamamura was anathema.

As soon as I pass the information to Washington—unless I do it very cleverly—word's sure to get back to MITI, thought Tolliver. He looked past Ishi to the bookshelves behind him, lined from floor to ceiling with books in ten languages. By dint of years of study Tolliver had learned to read six of the same languages himself, including Japanese and two different languages called Chinese. But Ishi's gift for tongues seemed almost casual.

Again, Tolliver rubbed his weary eyes. So you know about me, you old fox. Not surprising, he thought; we all spend half our time peering over each other's shoulders. What is surprising is that you're willing to admit it—which is precisely how you've caught me. I have to help you keep your private little secret, at least until your people can take Yamamura out of the picture.

Tolliver cleared his throat. "I agree that any sort of announcement at this time would be premature, Professor."

Ishi inclined his head. "I am grateful for your understanding. Thank you for your valuable time."

Tolliver rose and attempted another stiff bow. From somewhere Miss Sugibayashi had appeared to open the door. Bemused and frustrated, Tolliver left the office, his heavy shoes scuffling the wool carpet.

Ishi watched as his trusted secretary closed the door. "There is only one thing more you can do for me, Miss Sugibayashi, and then I will not need you anymore today."

"You are well?" Miss Sugibayashi's tone was neutral, but her concern was evident.

"My weariness is not physical," he said, smiling to reassure her. "I am like a little boy who wants to go home from school, so he clings to his winter cold and makes it seem piteous."

"Ahh." She smiled. "Then perhaps I am to telephone your regrets to Professor Edovich and his wife? Perhaps you are too weak to call in person?"

Ishi pursed his lips. "I'm afraid that's the case. My most sincere regrets."

"Yes!" She bowed, grinning, and left the room.

Ishi smiled privately. He opened the current volume of his diary to the first blank page and pressed the paper smooth with the flat of his hand. He plucked a writing brush from its stand, dipped its bristles in prepared black ink, poised the brush over the paper. Then, with rapidity and grace, he drew a series of formal kanji characters down the page:

Know when to stop
And you will meet with no danger.
You can then endure.

He had often pondered these words of Lao Tzu. Unlike his countrymen, Ishi believed there came a time to declare all obligations fulfilled—even those incurred by one's ancestors.

4

On their way to ransom their luggage Hey and
Anne-Marie had to fend off impatient fellow passengers,
official greeters with leis and Polaroid cameras at the
ready, and wild-eyed religious panhandlers. When the belt
finally brought them their bags, Anne-Marie stood guard
over her own leather suitcases and Hey's govern-
ment-surplus garment bag while he went off to arrange
for a discount rental car. All went well until they tried
to get the little red Datsun coupe out of the airport; like
all airports everywhere it seemed to be in the midst of a
vast eternal reconstruction program with eternal metamorphosis as its only goal. Eventually Hey found a busy
highway pointing toward downtown, not before convincing Anne-Marie that she'd trusted her life to a mechanical
incompetent.

"I've got about thirty calls to make when we get to the
hotel," he said importantly, trying to shift gears, racing
the engine. "And we need to get Dan Kono's address"—the car lurched forward—"or even get out to see

him today, if we can. He lives in the opposite direction from TERAC, and it would be good to get him out of the way early."

Anne-Marie tried to ignore the bucking, laboring automobile and meanwhile searched her memory for Dan Kono's role in the cast of characters Hey had earlier listed for her. "He's the land rights leader?"

"He *was* the land rights leader. That's the whole point. Why'd he give up? TERAC's a grand gesture to Japanese and American friendship, a cathedral to science, all that crap, but most of the people on this island wanted nothing to do with it—especially not the native Hawaiians. To them it was just another big land grab."

Anne-Marie sensed Hey warming to his subject and braced herself for a polemic. She did her best to sound interested. "Why didn't they want it? Didn't TERAC mean investment, new jobs?"

Hey turned to sneer at her. "Spoken like a banker's wife." Tires squealed and a horn blared beside them as he almost drove into the side of a speeding taxi.

"Jesus, Gardner!" Anne-Marie grabbed for the dash.

Hey's face turned pink, but he ignored the incident. "This jobs and investment shit . . . "

"Sorry." She grinned at him nervously as she cut him off. "I think maybe I should just keep my mouth shut while you're driving."

Hey was silent, staring straight ahead, chewing his mustache. Anne-Marie looked at him warily. His balding head and his long wispy blond hair pulled back and tied in a ponytail with a rubber band and his little potbelly poking through his cheap shirt were all beginning to assume the proportions of a symbol to her; these were just the sort of eccentricities which characterized the loudmouthed, deliberately rude, self-appointed champions of the downtrodden whom she'd always made it a point to avoid. The losers.

Hey sighed, self-consciously melodramatic. "Okay, I'll do better. Can I make a speech now?"

She forced herself to grin. "If you must. Do watch the road."

"Sure." He drove conscientiously for a few seconds, trying to instill confidence. "Well, the way I see it," he began, "DOE must have conspired with the Defense Department to see that TERAC was built on federal lands that should by rights have reverted to native Hawaiian use. Schofield Barracks, I mean, and Wheeler Field. And somebody must have leaned on the Rook Estate, since they owned the rest. . . ."

Anne-Marie leaned back and listened with half an ear as Hey spun his tale: Rook's directors were not displeased to sell a few hundred acres of pineapple fields to the government at inflated prices, according to Hey, since cheap competition from the Philippines had been turning Hawaiian pineapples into a losing proposition—and legally they could have sold to no one else. As for jobs and investment, it was the Japanese worker who benefited most from TERAC's construction. Even to the hole in the ground, TERAC came marked "made in Japan"—Mitsubishi had supplied the heavy equipment, Sumitomo had constructed the hundreds of superconducting magnets under contract to the TERAC design division, and the office computers were provided by Fujitsu, despite the protests of the hard-pressed American electronics industry. The main computers were American, including a Cray, but these were one-of-a-kind prestige items that did nothing to boost sales back home. But then, had the Japanese government not been paying most of the bills, TERAC never would have been built at all.

For a while it looked as if the Hawaiian people might actually get together and stop the land confiscation. Since almost everyone with a trace of native ancestry was proud to be identified as Hawaiian, part-Hawaiians now constituted the third largest ethnic group in the islands, after the haoles and the Japanese-Americans. Nevertheless, the Hawaiians could not point to a stable, effective political organization; like most minority groups they were most powerful when fired by a specific issue, and when directed by a charismatic leader.

In the fight against TERAC, Dan Kono had seemed to be that leader. The bearded young man was as big and dark and handsome as an ancient alii, though his genes were as much Portuguese and Polish as Hawaiian. But he was all local boy, and when he addressed other locals in eloquent pidgin they grew bold enough to move *da kine* mountains. Kono could switch smoothly to school English when the occasion demanded, a facility that endeared him to haole liberals. He helped form the Oahu Landclaims Alliance—"OLA means *life* in the tongue of our forefathers, and the land is the life of our people," orated Kono—and OLA lobbied, demonstrated, occupied the TERAC construction site, blocked the reelection of one United States senator, and very nearly brought TERAC to a dead halt.

"Then one day Dan Kono just quit," said Hey. "Disappeared. Went fishing. Told his friends to kiss off. By the time they got themselves organized again it was too late. And I'd sure like to know who bought him off."

"You think that would be an important part of your story?" Anne-Marie asked. Her head was spinning with his baroque conspiracies—pineapple barons, unreconstructed Japanese zaibatsu, venal bureaucrats, Polynesian heroes with feet of clay.

"Oh, not really. It's just an interesting piece of color. The real story's inside the Department of Defense." He glanced at Anne-Marie, but remembered his promise and looked quickly back at the highway. "Still, I think Kono was bought off. That's the way these people work; they'll do anything to get their way."

"Well, I'm sure you know what you're talking about. Weren't we supposed to be in the right lane back there?"

"Damn."

After a detour through the industrial wasteland on the shores of Keehi Lagoon, Hey finally found the road to Waikiki. Anne-Marie gaped in dismay at the racing traffic, the tacky shops, the sullen befuddled tourists who crowded the sidewalks of Kalakaua Avenue beneath the grim, monolithic hotels. She'd managed to avoid all this on her honeymoon with Charlie; they'd spent their holiday in isolated Polynesian splendor in an exclusive resort on the Kona Coast.

When the beach unexpectedly reappeared on the right the view improved. For the first time since their arrival Oahu looked somewhat as advertised, complete with brown bodies and swaying palms and rolling waves. They drove past Kuhio Beach Park and Queen's Beach, and beneath dark ironwoods to the foot of Diamond Head. Hey pulled the car to a stop in front of a fire hydrant. At his insistence he and Anne-Marie lugged their bags along the sidewalk to the registration desk, a small office that opened directly onto the lanai of the Crater Hotel, since Hey declined to risk a confrontation with a tip-seeking bellboy, though none was in evidence.

The hotel was simple, and curiously out of date—a pink ten-story apartment-style building with one row of rooms on each floor opening onto an outside passageway, and no view, except of similar buildings on each side. But it was at the quiet end of the beach, the waves crashed not ten feet from the end of the concrete-slab lanai, and it was the very best accommodations *Science Weekly* could afford.

They took the elevator to their rooms on the sixth floor. It took Anne-Marie only a moment to unpack. She cranked open the glass-slat windows on facing sides of the room and let the fragrant breeze move through the darkened room. She sat on the bed and tried to convince herself she didn't really have to go to the bathroom again, not so soon after the airport. She was only a couple of weeks overdue for her period, and really, she'd never been as regular as a clock, and it was too early for this awkward business to start even if she *was* pregnant again. . . .

Damn, she didn't want to think about that. She was here, wasn't she, in Hawaii at last? She tried to clear her mind of everything but the sighing of the wind in the long-needled casuarinas below her window, the crash of the surf, the cooing of the Inca doves. Then she sighed, got up, and went into the bathroom.

When she came out she decided to check and load her cameras. She had two Canons with a full complement of lenses for each; she decided to keep one loaded with black and white and the other with color slide film. She'd keep the Vivitar flash unit on the slide camera. She fished a roll of thirty-five-millimeter Tri-X out of the compartmented canvas bag and threaded it into the older of the two camera bodies. The back felt a little springy against the catch when she closed it. She hadn't used this camera for over a year; she'd probably lost the feel of the older model. She opened it and checked the threading. She could find no problem. She pushed the back down firmly until it clicked shut. The newer model easily accepted a roll of Kodachrome 64.

She wondered what Hey expected her to do while he made his thirty phone calls. She supposed she'd better stick around, in case he wanted to interview somebody like Kono and take her along. She reached for the phone to call Chauncey's office, to let him know they'd arrived, but the phone rang before she touched it.

It was the desk clerk. Anne-Marie had gotten the impression of a dried-up, hennaed creature of indeterminate age and evident inquisitiveness; now she seemed definitely miffed: "I've tried to call your—traveling companion?—but his telephone has been *constantly* busy. Perhaps you would be kind enough to tell him that his car is blocking the fire hydrant."

"Thank you. I'll tell him." Anne-Marie hung up quickly.

She had to wait more than a minute for Hey to answer the door of his room, the next closer to the elevator. "Oh hi," he said, as if he'd forgotten her existence. "Listen, we'll have to put off Kono until tomorrow morning, okay? I might be able to line up an interview with some of the top people in the applications division if I keep on the horn. Can you find something to do this afternoon?"

"Certainly," she said. "The desk clerk wants you to move the car."

"Damn. You do it for me, okay? Here's the keys. I really do appreciate it."

She hesitated before taking the keys. She hoped the look she gave him made it plain she did not intend to be his errand girl, but he only said "thanks" and closed the door.

She parked the car in the underground garage. As she passed the desk on the way back to the elevators the clerk said, "Miss Brand? Excuse me, but are you also known as Mrs. Phelps?"

"Yes," said Anne-Marie.

The clerk's eyes were gleaming. "Well, I didn't *know* that, you see. But I looked at the first name, Anne-Marie—that's a very unusual name, you know, is it foreign?"

"French. Did you have a message?"

The clerk fumbled with a scrap of paper. "A Mr. Tolliver called, and he . . . "

"Please just give it to me," said Anne-Marie tonelessly, holding out her hand. Reluctantly the woman handed her the note.

Anne-Marie read it in the elevator: "Mr. Tolliver for Anne-Marie Phelps. Forgive lack of reception. Things hectic. If you're free please attend buffet supper party at home of Professor and Mrs. Martin Edovich, 4350 Manoa Drive, 7:00 P.M. Bring Hey if you must. Casual for you, formal for him, which amounts to the same thing. Love, Chauncey."

She smiled and refolded the piece of stationery. A moment later she was tapping on Hey's door again. It opened immediately. "I'm on hold," said Hey, cradling the receiver between shoulder and ear, looking at her crookedly, like Quasimodo. He took the car keys and started to close the door.

"We're invited to a party, Gardner," she said. "Do you know a Professor Edovich?"

The phone receiver fell to the floor. "Edovich!" He stared at her. "He's the most important man at TERAC." He stooped to the floor and picked up the receiver. "Say, hon? Never mind, I'll have to call you back later." He hooked his thumb over the button and carried the instrument back to his bedside table. "You know something, Anne-Marie?" he said quietly, looking at her over his shoulder. "I'm glad I brought you along on this trip. In more ways than one, I mean."

"Wonderful, Gardner. Have fun on the phone. I'll be on the beach." She closed his door before he could compliment her again.

5

The Buddha was meditating on the Mount of Snow when he heard sweet music drifting toward him on the chill air. In the notes of the melody the plan of salvation was slowly unfolding. Buddha sought the source of the beautiful song.

At the bottom of an awful chasm sat a hideous demon, singing. Upon catching sight of Buddha he stopped. Buddha entreated him, but the demon demanded to be fed human flesh and blood before he would continue.

Without hesitation Buddha hurled himself from the cliff, offering his own body that the demon might share his knowledge with mankind. The demon disappeared. A giant lotus, suddenly blooming, gently cushioned Buddha's fall.

Peter Slater let a warm eighty-mile-an-hour wind tousle his stiff sandy hair as he headed south on Kamehameha Highway with the top down, listening to the four-banger wrap up a smooth baritone roar under the sucking hiss of its twin carburetors. He kept a practiced eye open for pursuing headlights in the darkness while he exercised the

TR-4 at a speed comfortable to it. Peter had always been
partial to stiff little British sports cars; he was particularly
fond of the twenty-year-old Triumph, with its polished
wooden dash and leather seats (twice replaced) and wire
wheels. He found an atavistic reassurance in finely crafted
material objects, perhaps because the world he believed
was "real" contained nothing of substance whatsoever.
Nevertheless, though he could stand gazing at a landscape
or a blackboard for hours while his mind delighted itself
with abstractions, his (possibly illusory) hunger had finally gotten the best of him.

TERAC ran twenty-four hours a day, and maintained
automated snack bars and lounges for its late-night workers. Peter had become accustomed to blunting his hunger
pangs with packaged noodles or a candy bar on those
nights when he didn't want to leave his computer. On
other days he never came to the office at all, but stayed
at home playing his piano to the ocean. In all cases he
avoided other people. Tonight for the first time a growing
sense of desire for human contact had surfaced in him,
along with the realization that food, real food, was available in quantities at the Edoviches' supper party, to which
he'd been invited weeks ago.

Had he given the matter conscious consideration, he
might have concluded that his willingness to meet people
socially owed something to the feeling that he'd finally
begun to corner the anomalies in his group-theoretical
scheme. He hadn't found that "sour note," as he thought
of it—what a more down-to-earth person would have described straightforwardly as a disagreement of fact with
theory—but though he hadn't identified the particular flat
instrument, at least he'd tracked it as far as a specific section of the orchestra. There had been moments, late this
afternoon, when the music in his head had seemed about
to resolve itself in some profound revelation—if not of salvation, like the song of the demon in that old Japanese
folk tale, then at least of truth. It hadn't happened
yet—the difficulties stubbornly persisted—but at last he

saw the hope of isolating them, perhaps cutting them off from the theme and motive of his work.

He was certainly in no mood to hurl himself from a cliff, though he was always aware that in the end, if deep concentration and repeated calculations couldn't make the music come perfect, he might have to toss the whole lovely scheme out the window. Theories born of a quest for beauty often turn out to be true, to the astonishment of philosophers—but more often they turn out to be false, and eventually, of course, they always prove to be incomplete.

Peter's puzzlement was centered on the behavior of that extraordinary particle which had made TERAC an instant scientific success story, and would in all likelihood make its discoverer, Martin Edovich, a Nobel laureate within the year. If only Peter Slater had dared to predict the character of the particle when its existence first occurred to him—well before the completion of TERAC—he might be on the way to sharing the prize with Edovich. Peter's uncharacteristic shyness in this instance was an indication of just how bizarre this thing called an "I-particle" was.

The I-particle took its name from the inside quark. When quarks had first been postulated in the early sixties there were supposed to be three of them, and even their inventors considered them more mathematical conveniences than real entities. Each quark was assigned a set of numbers, quantum numbers, which governed the ways that that type of quark could combine with others; the idea was that from a few basic quarks many of the different so-called fundamental particles observed in high-energy collisions could be formed.

Three kinds of quark were not enough. Each bigger accelerator seemed to reveal new and unexpected particles. By the late seventies it was thought that six basic quarks were sufficient to form the whole family of particles which included the proton and neutron, while six basic leptons formed the other major particle family, including the electrons and neutrinos. Most theorists hoped that no *more* new quarks would be found, for the most elegant theories of the day explaining the interaction of the subatomic particles had no room for more than six basic types of each.

Alas, in the early eighties the first hint came, by way of astrophysics, that a seventh lepton might exist. If there were seven leptons, then surely there were more than six quarks.

The discovery of the inside quark had to await the building of a machine powerful enough to create, out of pure energy, a particle incorporating one.

Meanwhile Peter Slater and many other theoreticians worked to erect a new form of grand unified theory to explain the relationships of the myriad quarks and leptons and the forces among them. The version eventually accepted by most physicists was that of Patel and Brandenburg (Texas and Utrecht), while a popular but faintly heretical variant bore the name Slater (Berkeley). All versions left open the intriguing possibility that one or more of the higher quarks, and thus the particles that contained them, might be stable.

Slater, in fact, was one of the first to suspect the exact mass-energy where the I-particle was to be sought; had he announced his suspicions, he would have predicted the inside quark before Edovich stumbled over it. And sure enough, there it was, absolutely stable. It had no desire to decay, to change into a more common proton or neutron of much lower energy.

Only Slater couldn't quite believe his own naive calculations. Just how stable were I-particles, really? As stable as protons, as Martin Edovich seemed to believe? As stable as free neutrons? Or somewhat less stable than that?

Slater's refined theory generated precise and unambiguous answers. The trouble was, the data from Edovich's experiments flatly contradicted him. While the contradiction was a small number in a large table of numbers, it was real. It was the loud sour note in Peter's symphony.

To force his conscious mind to let go of the problem

he loudly whistled into the warm night wind and settled deeper into the cozy cockpit of the speeding car. City lights came closer.

Peter Slater differed from the majority of his fellows not so much in his unusual habits of thought—most theoreticians are a little peculiar that way—but rather in his simple affection for the things money could buy. Not research equipment—most physicists appreciated shiny new machines, though theorists like Slater sometimes looked askance at the passionate, grease-smeared experimentalists who actually liked to build the things, and Peter was more fastidious than most. Peter liked what money could buy *him:* good books expensively bound, fine wines, cars that were well made, or at least charming. Not for him the uniform of most working scientists, which if not a crumpled suit was as likely to consist of buffalo-hide sandals or worn-out sneakers, low-slung jeans or baggy corduroys worn through in the seat, topped off with a lumpy cardigan which could have been woven from the coat of a wire-haired terrier. On this fine evening the sleeves of his tailored cotton plaid dress shirt were rolled above his muscular forearms, his khaki twill trousers, straight from the cleaners, were crisply pressed, and his old Bass loafers were polished to a woody shine. He wore no socks, however—an acceptable barbarity in Ivy League circles, and a failing which rendered him at least half human in the eyes of kamaainas.

Luckily for Peter he could buy whatever he liked. The money came not from the practice of science, for even the sort of big science that could build a TERAC could not confer wealth on individuals. Peter's fortune had come down a long way, deriving from rich estates of prime Carolina tobacco land.

Some Slater back along the way had been seduced from Calvinism to Congregationalism, and when it came time for Peter to attend college he was packed off north to Yale, though MIT, Cal Tech, and a dozen other institutions had tried to attract the mathematical whiz kid's attention. His father, class of '50, was fully aware that God had departed and women had arrived since his own and Bill Buckley's undergraduate days, but he trusted the stern religious upbringing he'd inflicted on Peter to keep the young man morally alert. Alas, a mere half semester of anthropology, the most promising of the curriculum's obligatory social sciences, had served to make an agnostic of young Peter, and consequently (though quite indirectly) an ex-virgin.

Content is mutable, but form persists: his head was full of Lie groups and haiku, but Peter passed for an old-fashioned Yalie just the same. His tall bony frame looked fine in Harris tweeds; for a couple of months during his sophomore year he resolutely barbecued his tongue with a pipe; he was invited into all the best societies and joined some of them. He toured the leafy back roads of Connecticut in a restored MG with pretty girls at his side, spunky freckled blond History of Art or Comp Lit majors who invited him to weekends at their parents' places in the city or on the Sound. It was as close to a Fitzgeraldian dream as a man could get in the last quarter of the twentieth century.

At the extremity the universe is a paradoxical and disquieting construct, whether that extremity be the ultimate gravitational collapse of galaxies or the ultimate squirming vacuum of the quantum microworld. Peter's classmates never suspected that he was not really a fun guy and did not think the world was a fun place. In this he kept faith with his dour, God-ridden ancestors.

In some ways he was like those sybaritic young Tibetan lamas who adapt so eagerly to a life of Western luxury, while continuing to preach the dangers of "spiritual materialism." In his search for Truth, Peter had rarely let himself be fooled by Reality.

6

A small crowd milled on the terrace, sipping at their drinks and smiling politely, while Martin Edovich and his musical cronies mangled a Dvorak string quartet. Edovich himself was doing the worst damage, sawing away on his cello with Slavic vigor, while behind him Brownie Lasky winced and screeched along on a borrowed fiddle, and two younger men from theoretical, armed with violin and viola, gamely brought up the rear.

Greta Edovich was prowling the back of the lawn, where shyer guests hid in torch-lit shadows. Greta liked to think she had a sixth sense for spinning just the right line of small talk; coming upon Lasky's wife standing alone, Greta took another sip of her martini, then swiftly opened conversation with a bitter complaint about the impossibility of finding, in all of Honolulu, a really decent bagel. Mrs. Lasky, who was pining for Manhattan, nodded vigorously and prepared to follow up with trenchant observations of her own on the generally wretched quality of life everywhere west of the Hudson.

But before Mrs. Lasky could get in her first word, Greta, who in fact cared nothing for bagels or New York City, broke off in midsentence. "My dear Lisa, excuse me, but would you look at that! The princess and her frog."

Greta was looking toward the long terrace: Gardner Hey had just emerged, blinking, from the back of the house and was tugging uncomfortably at the skinny knit tie he had knotted around the collar of a fresh aloha shirt. Anne-Marie was beside him, slim and cool and self-possessed, her long dark hair framing her face, her gauzy cotton dress swirling in blue arabesques around her knees as she turned to watch the musicians. "What a stunning creature she is!" said Greta. "But *him!* Is he one of Brownie's new little gnomes, Lisa? These days everyone in theoretical looks so terribly . . . *unique.*"

"I'm sure I've never met the young man, Greta," said Mrs. Lasky primly.

"Come with me, then. We must rescue her immediately."

"Oh no, oh no," said Lisa Lasky, alarmed at the thought of putting herself forward so boldly. "You just go on."

"I promise I'll bring her right back here," Greta lied cheerfully. "You don't suppose she's *married* to him. . . . " She arched her eyebrows in mock horror, then set off across the big lawn. She smiled brightly at no one in particular, looking past every face and saying nothing that could entangle her in conversation, meanwhile sipping daintily and a bit precariously at her dwindling martini.

The Edoviches lived in a big stone Gothic house in the lush Manoa Valley above the University of Hawaii, a house much bigger and more flamboyant than Greta would have preferred. But with a crowd like tonight's it didn't seem very big at all. Its slender, many-paned windows glowed yellow above the terrace; in the yard below, a stone-rimmed lotus pool, lit by underwater lamps, glowed a brighter blue. All around the periphery of the grounds stood stately trees and dark masses of carefully tended tropical vegetation, banana plants and hedges of beefsteak and ti, and bushes with pale flowers that gleamed in the darkness.

Students from the university circulated among the guests with trays of drinks and hors d'oeuvres. For people with heartier appetites, long tables had been set up at one end of the terrace, heaped with traditional Anglo-American-style foods—ham and turkey and roast beef, corn and squash and beans, salads and fruits and pies—not the typical potpourri of Polynesian and Oriental foods characteristic of island cuisine. Only a few local people were in evidence at the lawn party, and fewer still Japanese.

Greta climbed the terrace steps, pausing at the top. What an awful noise Martin and his friends were making down at the far end, she thought. If they didn't give up soon she'd have to put a stop to it. She saw the new arrivals, the fat young man and his beautiful companion, beginning to help themselves at the buffet. She pushed her way toward them.

"Why, hell*oo*," she called. "I'm Greta Edovich. Have we met?"

Gardner Hey, caught with a plate of ham in his fist and lacking a proper introduction, peered at her guiltily. Anne-Marie smoothly answered for them both. "I'm Anne-Marie Brand, Mrs. Edovich . . . "

"*Greta,* please! What a lovely name, Anne-Marie—"

"And this is Gardner Hey," said Anne-Marie. "We're here at Chauncey Tolliver's invitation. It's kind of you to have us."

"And very shrewd of Chauncey to ask you to come, my dear." Greta looked dubiously at Hey. "And you as well, Mr., uh—Hyde?"

"Hey," said Hey.

Greta blinked. "I beg your pardon?"

"*Hey,*" Hey repeated. "*Science Weekly.*"

"Gardner is an associate editor of *Science Weekly,*"

Anne-Marie explained. "He's here to do a report on the dedication. And I'll be doing photographs."

"You look absolutely famished, Mr. Hey." Greta spoke cautiously, as if soothing a large animal. "Don't let me interrupt your feeding for a moment."

Hey nodded happily and turned back to the food.

"But you, my dear, you must tell me all about yourself, instantly." Greta took Anne-Marie by the elbow and turned her away from the buffet table; Greta liked to get to potentially interesting guests before they could eat themselves into a stupor or drink themselves into incoherence, as in her experience they so often seemed to do. Bores, however, could stuff themselves; Greta smiled back at Hey as she led Anne-Marie off. "I'll bring her right back, I promise. . . . "

Anne-Marie surrendered to her hostess without protest, but she instinctively kept a firm grip on the plate she held, with its lonely slice of roast beef. She didn't know when she'd have the chance to return to the neighborhood of the buffet, and she was hungry.

"You're a photographer. How exciting!" said Greta. "Would I have seen any of your work?"

"I doubt it," said Anne-Marie. "I've never shown in this country. And most of my magazine work was done in Europe."

"Oh, like *Realités*. What a beautiful magazine."

"Nothing that fancy, I'm afraid. I did news pictures, pictures of people. As a free lance. *Paris-Match, Stern* . . . "

"Oh, Paris. I thought I heard a trace of accent. Are you French, my dear?"

"My mother was French. My father was American. I've lived in many countries. And surely you . . . "

"What will you drink, dear?" Greta said, interrupting her. She snagged a martini for herself off the tray of a passing student waiter; the boy wheeled and held the tray toward Anne-Marie.

"Nothing, really, thanks. It would go straight to my head."

What a dazzling prize for Chauncey, Greta was thinking. How in the world did that shy boy ever manage to arrange this without my finding out about it? She's someone from his past, certainly. And—Greta had noticed the white ring marks on Anne-Marie's tan left hand—she's recently divorced.

"Let's find Chauncey!" Greta cried, holding the full martini glass in front of her like a gleaming lantern. "I'm searching for a crafty man," she announced gleefully, keeping Anne-Marie firmly in tow as she descended the steps to the lawn.

They found Tolliver standing beside the lotus pool, staring into the water and chewing thoughtfully on a bit of lime pulp from his gin and tonic as he listened to one of the junior wives tell about her last golfing weekend on Maui.

"Chauncey, look what I've found for you," Greta called, overwhelming the woman's meandering account. "Miss Anne-Marie Brand!" Tolliver looked toward them, his eyebrows arched in mild surprise. Greta gently but firmly launched Anne-Marie in Chauncey's direction, then stood back to watch the consequences.

Tolliver smiled at Anne-Marie out of a round, freckled face. "I haven't heard that name in a long time," he said. His hair was as blond and pale as Gardner Hey's, but it was cut in a brush, and his watery eyes seemed a little unfocused.

Anne-Marie's color rose, short of a blush. "My own name when I'm working, Chauncey. That's all." She'd known Chauncey Tolliver as long as she'd known Charlie Phelps. A few minutes longer, in fact; they'd all met at a party in Crete the summer Chauncey and Charlie and some of their school friends had been touring the Aegean in a chartered ketch. Then as now Chauncey had seemed a bit out of place, too formal, too restrained. On Crete it had been white ducks and a blue and white long-sleeved

French sailor's pullover, with immaculate white deck shoes—everyone else had been wearing shorts and sandals—and tonight it was a seersucker suit, a white button-down shirt, and a striped tie. Here everyone else was wearing "Aloha Friday" gear—summer dresses, aloha shirts, flower leis. Despite Chauncey's disparaging reference to Gardner Hey in his phone message, Hey was more appropriately dressed than Chauncey himself. Yet Chauncey was a sweet boy at heart, one who'd been secretly in love with Anne-Marie from the beginning.

"I want you to make sure she gets all the pictures she wants, do you hear, Chauncey?" Greta was saying. "Special treatment! I mean it!"

"Just for you, Greta," said Chauncey. He'd already seen to it that Anne-Marie was equipped with press credentials and an introduction to Gardner Hey; he'd acted as soon as she'd called him with the request for help. Chauncey continued to stare at Anne-Marie. "So, Miz Brand . . . "

She took his hand in hers and squeezed it gently. "It's so nice to see you, Chauncey. And I'm grateful."

Greta beamed from the sidelines. Deciding the two of them needed privacy, she impulsively interposed herself between them and the pert, sunburned brunette golfer Chauncey had been talking with. "Bunny, I've been looking for you *all* night," said Greta, just as the woman was about to introduce herself to Anne-Marie. With a tight grip on her elbow Greta led Bunny away, distracting her with an impromptu monologue on great golf courses of the world.

"Why be grateful?" Tolliver asked. "I stuck you with Gardner."

"I didn't really think you'd come up with Time-Life, Inc., Chauncey—despite how spoiled you think I am. And Gardner's a dear, really." She gently removed her right hand from Chauncey's moist grip, to shift the dinner plate she was still holding in her left. She caught Chauncey looking at her bare ring finger; quickly she continued: "I admit Gardner put me off at first, he's so gruff and opinionated. But he's likable underneath it all. You should see him right now—he's having a hard time working up the courage to introduce himself to all these scientists he pretends to dislike. He's going to stuff himself and watch from the sidelines; I think he's really a little awed by them."

"Maybe," said Chauncey, his gaze shifting from her to somewhere on the ground. "I don't know Gardner that well personally. Some of his articles give us a hard time. . . . "

"On the land rights issue? That seems to be one of his pet peeves. He's planning to interview this man Kono tomorrow."

"Oh, really?" Tolliver seemed interested, though he was staring down into the depths of the illuminated pond, watching the moving shadows of the carp as they drifted among the lily stems.

Anne-Marie was used to Chauncey's peculiar mannerisms; though he never talked about it, she suspected he had trouble with his eyes and deliberately avoided staring at people—at precisely those moments when it would have been the most natural thing to do. "Yes, he's hoping he can get Kono to admit he was bribed by someone to sabotage the demonstrations at the accelerator center." Anne-Marie smiled. "His chutzpah is rather impressive, don't you think so? What makes him think Dan Kono or anybody else would admit something like that to a nosy reporter?"

Chauncey smiled. "It does sound absurd. But Gardner's a persistent fellow, no doubt of that. To tell you the truth, Anne-Marie, I had an ulterior motive in fixing you up with Gardner. Him in particular—not that I could have done much better on short notice, I hasten to add . . . "

"It's fine, Chauncey," she reassured him.

" . . . but I was hoping you'd talk a little sense to him,

without seeming obvious about it. Just by being yourself. And he can't help but like you."

It seemed a strange request. Anne-Marie studied Chauncey's averted eyes a moment before replying. "I'll do what I can, Chauncey. But I don't know the first thing about all this business with particles. How could I possibly influence someone like Gardner Hey?"

"That's the point—you're a layperson, a member of the general public. If you don't see anything so convoluted and evil about what we're doing, maybe Gardner will recover a bit of his perspective on the whole thing."

Anne-Marie laughed. "Too late, Chauncey. Gardner's already got me pegged as a member of the sybaritic upper class."

"Well, maybe he'll loosen up," Tolliver said lamely.

"He stared at me like I was a *Playboy* bunny, all the way across the Pacific." She watched him to see if this information would surprise him, but he only continued to look vaguely worried. She looked at the cold limp slice of roast beef on her plate, then bent to deposit the plate on the stone rim of the pool. As she stood up she moved her left hand behind her back.

"Anne-Marie?"

"Yes, Chauncey?"

"I noticed the rings, right away." He seemed apologetic. "How's Charlie? And my little godson?"

"Everything's pretty much what you'd expect," she said. Her anger at his probing never fully formed. Tolliver had no right to impose his notions of morality so blatantly, notions indistinguishable from Charlie's; nevertheless he was effective; her resentment changed quickly to guilt. "About the rings—I'm just living a little fantasy, I guess. Just for the week." She tried to catch his eye, unsuccessfully. "Oh, Chauncey, I was never cut out to be a housewife."

"Bad?"

"It's getting that way."

Tolliver watched a fat carp swim from beneath a lily pad to investigate Anne-Marie's abandoned plate. The food was beyond its reach, in another dimension. "It tears me up to see you hurt yourself." Now he raised his glistening eyes to gaze at the hazy dark sky. "The way you did last time," he added.

"Chauncey, you worry too much. . . ."

"And despite what you think—what the reporters say about public-affairs types like me—I'm not pimping you to Gardner Hey."

"Good Lord, Chauncey." Anne-Marie recoiled half a step. "What have I done to make you say that to me?"

"No, no," he said hastily, "I forgive you. It was stupid of me to say I wanted anything from you, when it's obvious you're so upset. Please forgive me."

In her confusion Anne-Marie realized that Chauncey could not directly voice his anger with her for making Charlie miserable—Charlie, Chauncey's oldest, best friend. But clearly he was trying to hurt her; clearly there were things he was leaving unsaid, things he was unwilling to admit, even to himself. That last "bad time" her frustrated rage against the trap Charlie had crafted for her with her own willing connivance took the form of more than one affair with other men. Chauncey Tolliver had not been one of them. Who did Chauncey really need, Charlie or her? "Sweet Chauncey," she said, her voice thin and reedy, "you'll keep me from going off the deep end. Just to be busy doing something I used to be good at, that'll do the trick. Really. I know it will." She turned away from him, looking toward the buffet tables on the terrace. "I'm starved. I intend to stuff myself, Chauncey. Come on, come with me."

Peter Slater had stalked gruffly past the affable student doorman and made directly for the food on the terrace behind the Edoviches' house. He was wolfing down a heap of delicious German potato salad when the music from the quartet died mercifully—a sudden death, if not a clean one. The audience's applause was exaggerated by relief.

Within moments Peter saw Martin Edovich bearing

down on him, his purple aloha shirt flapping, his red hair shining with perspiration, a huge smile on his big-nosed, square-jawed face. Peter reluctantly put his plate of food to one side.

"Peter, my boy, so glad you came." Edovich grabbed Peter's hand in one of his own stubby paws and pumped it up and down with enthusiasm, pounding Peter's arm with the other hand.

"Martin," said Peter, stoically.

Edovich hit him twice more and then backed off, beaming up at him. "So! You've been working all day again, Peter, it's plain to see. Those crazy ideas of yours." Edovich shook his head with melodramatic grief.

Peter grimaced. "Really, Martin, what a fuss." For some reason Martin had been pestering him about his work—none of Edovich's business, really—ever since Peter had arrived at TERAC. Martin always wanted to know his very latest thoughts, but as often as not he'd scoffed at them when he heard them. Edovich was the only member of the TERAC staff who had loudly ignored Peter's self-imposed ban of silence.

But perhaps Peter should be grateful for Edovich's determination to draw him out. "You won't find a new quark every time you throw a switch, Martin," Peter said stiffly, trying to make a joke of it. "Somebody's got to do the thinking."

"Fair," said Edovich, nodding vigorously. "Fair enough. And that somebody should be you, Peter." Edovich turned to find Brownie Lasky standing over his shoulder, listening solemnly, nodding his long bare head slowly up and down. As chief of the theoretical division, Bronislaw Lasky was on a level with Edovich, who was chief of the experimental division. At least they were equal so far as TERAC's organizational chart was concerned. But Lasky habitually deferred to Edovich.

Edovich looked intently at Peter Slater. "Five years ago we were reading your name, Peter, it seemed like every month. Some good stuff—the Z-zero mass, you should have gotten more credit for that—but you published too much. Too many papers with half-baked ideas in them. We thought you were one of those fellows who'd rather write for the literary magazines than be a scientist—"

"Jesus, Martin," said Slater, offended.

"I'm too blunt, maybe. *I* read you *anyway,* young Peter. You made me think. But now for two years there's hardly a word out of you. . . . "

"No, Martin," Lasky corrected him. "There was that note on contact transformations . . . "

"Yes, yes, Brownie, he still talks to you theoretikers, I guess. But listen, Peter." Edovich poked a square forefinger gently but forcefully into Slater's lean stomach.

Peter knew what was coming, the same old story: Edovich had started looking for the i quark because of something he'd read by Slater. . . .

"Just between you and me and big-ears Lasky here, I think I started looking for that little insider because one of your crazy papers put a bug in my ear," said Edovich. "But you should have told us in plain language! All those crazy matrices—"

"Hell, Martin, the language couldn't be plain, not until after the fact," said Peter coldly. He knew Edovich was not so generous as to announce to the whole world—or to the Nobel committee, for whom he would probably soon be suggesting candidates—the debt he'd repeatedly acknowledged to Slater himself. And why should he? "You didn't really need me anyway—all you had to do was tune through the spectrum once TERAC was up to energy."

"You're a cute boy," said Edovich. "Who needed TERAC? If you'd told me where to look, there are half a dozen machines that could reach TERAC's energy a pop at a time. I could have had one of the fellows at Sandia tune one of their little blitzers. Boom! We could have had the I-particle two years ago. Maybe only a few specimens, but we could have had him."

Peter knew Edovich was talking about experimental

particle-beam weapons; it was no secret that Edovich was mightily interested in the I-particle's potential as a projectile in such devices. Beyond these vague facts Peter knew little about the weapons, and did not really care to know what he was not supposed to know anyway. Except for the maintenance of sports cars he was not interested in engineering.

Moreover, he was beginning to resent constantly being put on the spot. A skeptic might assume that Peter had too quickly grown accustomed to being treated with the awe accorded genius, but a much humbler man would have been equally resentful of the treatment Edovich had been dishing out, as if Peter were little more than a promising but recalcitrant graduate student. As far as Peter could divine it, Edovich's motive was purely and simply to pump him for new ideas. "I wasn't ready to publish anything about the inside quark two years ago, Martin. Even now there's a lot I don't understand."

"He's right, Martin," said Brownie Lasky judiciously. "You're too hard on our young friend."

"No more reticence, my boy," said Edovich, ignoring Lasky. "Forget those resonance worries of yours, we're way past that. Get in touch with the real world. . . . "

"The real world isn't whatever you want it to be, Martin," Peter snapped. "There are clearly theoretical anomalies in your results, as I've told you every time you asked. Your response is to lecture me about—"

"Theory provides explanations. Otherwise . . . " Edovich shrugged. "Worthless philosophy. Don't be another Oppenheimer, Peter, all brains and no . . . *discrimination.*" Edovich's mood, momentarily serious, quickly changed back to jolly good cheer. "You could be the best of us. He could be the best of us, Brownie."

Lasky nodded affably, but he gave Edovich an odd look. It was not in Edovich's character to give credit to anyone besides himself unless he was fundamentally unsure of the other's status. His betters he treated with fawning respect; his peers he habitually tried to bully; his perceived inferiors he ignored. With Peter Slater, Edovich was vacillating between insults and praise, a sign of uncertainty. Hundreds of physicists at TERAC were eager to offer opinions about the precise nature of I-particles, the entities in which Martin Edovich would forever have a proprietary interest. Edovich dismissed them all, certain that he knew better. But Slater's reluctance to endorse Martin Edovich's simple ideas was obviously disturbing to the experimentalist.

. . . and shall I tell you what I really think of your I-particle collector, Professor Edovich? Peter was thinking. If I told you that you should have blown yourself to bits by now, would you have much faith in my powers of prediction?

"Not to change the subject, Martin," said Peter, "but I've always wondered where you got that charming accent." He thought, I think I'll stay reticent . . . until I can figure out why I'm wrong. "Is that really Yugoslavian?"

Edovich chuckled. "You want me to shut up. Okay, I will. But I'll answer your impertinent question." He looked around, saw a college girl passing with a tray, and stabbed his finger at her. She hurried over. "Bring us a martini, dear—two martinis, right, Brownie? And for you, Peter?"

Peter started to shake his head, then changed his mind. "A glass of red wine," he said to the girl.

"Thank you, dear," Edovich said to her. She hurried away. "Now, Peter. In my old neighborhood in Vancouver you can hear girls no older than that young lady speaking perfect Russian. They never came within ten thousand miles of Moscow in their lives. They got the language from their mothers, who got it from their grandmothers, who were saved from the murdering Bolsheviks when they were little children. So it's not such a surprise that a little southern Slav boy raised by his aunt and uncle would keep his accent, is it? I heard English only on the radio, until I was five years old." Edovich smiled frostily. "You're too young to think about the last world war, Peter—besides, you're not the type to care. Do you know the difference between Serbs and Croats? Ever heard of General Mikhailovich and the Chetniks? Don't worry—only fanatics cling to the past, I'm told." He leaned closer, intimately. "But I'll tell you something else, something for the present and the future. There are many people—generals, admirals, members of Congress—who t'ink a t'ick Yooropean akzent means a little zumsing extra upstairs, yah?" Edovich tapped the top of his red head. He turned to Lasky. "You should try it, Brownie."

"Me? I'm from the Bronx," said Lasky, bemused.

"So? I immigrated to this country when I was fourteen, the year I went to MIT," said Edovich. "That makes me from Boston, if you want. I can talk like a New England fisherman if I want, ayah—but I don't have to let the world know it." Edovich saw his wife moving toward them. "Even if Greta would prefer that I did, sometimes. She pictures me as a rare breed of black Boston Irish, I believe."

Greta, the daughter of a Brahmin judge, possessed a keenly developed sense of social hierarchy. When Peter Slater glanced in her direction and saw how determinedly she was bearing down on the three men, no doubt intent on breaking up the shop talk, the look in her eye convinced him that she had pegged him as a young aristocrat and was coming for his scalp.

He quickly looked away. Edovich's good cheer had a sour undertaste to it, and Peter found himself obscurely angered by Edovich's casually manipulative attitude—as if affairs of state, of science, were to be equated to summer theater. "Your powerful friends are probably the same people who think Asians are dumb gooks," he said with prim disdain.

"Yes, my young scholar. You and I know that brains come in only one color. My 'friends' have not had the benefit of our expensive educations, and their lives are filled with the burdens of dealing with others of their sort, every day. Yet they are powerful people, never more so than when they are in the wrong. I use whatever tricks I have to get my way with them."

"Certainly, Martin," said Peter, embarrassed.

Suddenly Greta Edovich was upon him.

"Why, Peter Slater, so nice of you to come!" she said breathlessly, beaming wildly. With her jeweled left hand she nervously patted the fragrant leis of maile and pikake which hung over her ample bosom. "I had begun to suspect you were a rumor, sir—like those bits of things you never really see in your machines. Martin? What do I mean? Those virtuous particles . . . "

"Virtual, Greta," said Edovich. "As you very well know. But Professor Slater is no virtual man; he is quite real, I assure you. As to his virtue, I am not in a position to say."

"It's good of you to have invited me," Peter said dutifully. He cast a longing glance at the buffet tables.

"I only wish you'd been here earlier, Peter," Greta said with instant familiarity. "You know the Japanese so much better than we do, I understand, even though we've been living cheek by jowl with them for years, now."

"Greta . . ." Edovich said, warning her.

"It's a very small island, dear," she retorted. "They paid us a call, Peter, Dr. Yamamura and Martin's little friend Tanawabe . . ."

"Watanabe," Edovich corrected her. "An excellent experimentalist."

"Quite drunk, but *so* courteous. Kissing the ladies' hands. Bowing so low to the gentlemen. Once we almost lost them in the fishpond."

Edovich shook his head, grinning at the recollection despite himself. "Very hard not to laugh, Peter. Lucky for us they stayed only a little while."

"Still, it was nice of Yamamura to put in an appearance," said Lasky, playing the peacemaker. "Even if he did nothing but clown around."

"I wish he'd saved himself the trouble," said Greta

archly. "I'm not at all sure it was an honor. Really, Peter, I have done my very best to understand those people."

"That's true," said Lasky. "Greta has taken courses in Japanese art, cooking, religion—even language, isn't that so?"

"Oh yes, I can *domo* and *dozo* with the best of them," said Greta airily. "I get along quite well with the wives; we have delightful teas together. But Martin, you're always asked to those parties the men are having downtown, with geisha girls and so on . . . "

"Rank debauchery," Edovich observed.

"And I've only been asked *once,* and then they shuffled me off with the rest of the women. And when they come here they only stay long enough to be polite, and they just stand around in clumps looking uncomfortable. And usually they don't come at all, like our honorable director tonight."

"Professor Ishi was not feeling well, Greta, you know that," said Edovich.

"And I've yet to see the inside of *any* of their houses. You see, Peter? Despite all my efforts, I simply can't *relate* to them. What would you do in my place?"

Peter was tempted to tell the woman that she could not expect to impose her own social mores on a millennium of tradition to the contrary, but if she had not already learned that from her extension courses she would not learn it from him. "Actually, I've never even visited Japan," he said noncommittally. "My knowledge is no more practical than yours."

"You're being polite," Greta pouted.

He was saved from contradicting her by the arrival of the young woman with the drink tray. After the men had secured their glasses Greta sent her for another martini. Peter sipped his sour wine and reflected that Greta was probably right about Yamamura—the real Japanese sins were social, not moral, and the worst of these was to behave in an "unexpected" manner. Of course only someone raised in polite Japanese society could have a complete knowledge of what behavior was expected in every circumstance, and from his reading Slater gathered that even the Japanese themselves frequently were trapped in quandaries. Normally they avoided mingling socially with Americans precisely from fear of witnessing or committing some horrid breach of etiquette.

Thus Yamamura's clowning might well have been a calculated insult. Half the joke would have been that Edovich and his wife, and Lasky and the rest, would have had not the slightest clue as to what was really going on.

Then again, drunkenness was an even better excuse for misbehavior in Japan than it was in the West.

The red wine griped his stomach. "I don't want to be rude," he said, "but I've hardly begun to appreciate your marvelous buffet, Mrs. Edovich . . . "

"*Greta,* please!" She was plainly upset that she'd failed to hold his attention. "Stuff yourself, go on, Peter. You tall men are always starved. Where's that girl with my drink?"

Peter nodded to Edovich and Lasky, carefully keeping a straight face. "I look forward to seeing you later, gentlemen." Then he hastily made his escape.

He was only a few steps away from the tables of food when he saw Chauncey Tolliver heading in the same direction. There was hardly a man in the world who professed to like Peter more, or whom Peter liked less. That his once-upon-a-time school chum should be employed at TERAC, an institution which otherwise met every criterion of perfection, struck Peter as nature's way of reminding him of the essentially statistical character of reality, a reality in which absurd coincidences are inevitable.

Peter was on the verge of reversing his steps when he caught sight of the woman at Chauncey's side, locked eyes with her for the merest fraction of a second, and in that instant knew he must endure Chauncey's flatteries for the sake of meeting her.

How precipitately the evening had branched into the unknown, beginning with the rash decision to make himself sociable, now forcing upon him the desire to meet a woman. He would probably mangle the attempt, but he could not mistake the signs which told him he was recovering his natural appetites.

7

The door of the tiny personnel elevator opened onto the main floor of Experimental Hall 30, ten stories below the ground under the gentle lower slopes of the Waianae Mountains, on the northwest sector of TERAC's main ring. Penny Harper's breath clouded in front of her face. It was as cold as a refrigerator down here. She stepped out of the elevator and started across the cluttered floor of the hall toward the control platform of the I-particle collector, her footsteps echoing in the cavernous gloom.

Three stories above her head a big industrial crane lurked in the shadows like a skinny spider, poised to run on steel rails to reach into any corner of the room. To her right a wall of two-ton concrete blocks rose to within several meters of the ceiling, leaving room for the crane to maneuver over it; the exact weight of each block was stenciled on its side, and each was fitted with countersunk eyebolts so the crane could grapple it easily. To the extent practical, all of TERAC was built like this, designed to be erected, torn down, and rearranged like a child's building blocks as changing circumstances demanded.

Bands of bright color relieved the greenish, fluorescent-shadowed drabness of the hall; electrical buses were painted red, structural supports yellow, pipes and conduits blue, and the big steel-shuttered curtain door opening onto the deep shaft which gave access to the surface was painted a rich purple. The vibrant paint did nothing to warm the chill air flowing from the surrounding bedrock.

The ring itself, embraced by its superconducting magnets, was contained in a concrete tunnel, and where it traversed an experimental hall it was isolated behind the concrete-block shield walls. Outside the wall experimenters could come and go freely, protected from the intense radiation of the ring's circulating beams of protons and antiprotons.

Penny mounted the steel steps of the elevated platform. Frank McDonald and Jorgen Stern from the regular evening shift were already hanging their lab coats in their lockers, having seen her approach. Penny was surprised to find Hiro Watanabe buttoning up his own coat. "Hiya, Hiro," she said. "What the hell you doin' here? Didn't I see you makin' an ass of yourself at Edovich's place an hour ago?"

"Oh yes, I'm afraid you did," said the young Japanese, grinning diffidently. "It was necessary."

"Necessary?" Penny wrinkled her snub nose in amusement. "That's a good one, Hiro; I'd sure like to hear how you work that out."

Watanabe smiled disarmingly. "*Hai!* You see, Professor Yamamura, who has done much good for me in the past, was already showing the effects of drink when I arrived at the party . . . "

"Yeah, he was bombed."

"So. Thus it was necessary for me to behave in a similar fashion. Otherwise, upon remembering the night's events, he might have suffered shame."

"Terrific, Hiro. You pretend to be blotto so this old guy who really *is* blotto won't be ashamed of himself." She cocked an eyebrow at Frank McDonald, a thickly mustached Californian in his late thirties. "Hey, Frank, what's cookin'? What's this character Watanabe doin' on my shift, when the man's obviously out of his mind?"

The sober McDonald did not smile. "Cy called in sick, Penny. Hiro's standing in for him."

"Too bad. The expensive air conditioning around here must have given Cy the flu. I guess that means Watanabe and me have to unload the collector, right, Frank?" She displayed her engaging dimples for McDonald, coaxing him. Penny was an ambitious young woman who'd received her Ph.D. from Texas at Austin only the year before; she prided herself on being able to handle every job on the experiment, including the one she'd only been allowed to rehearse—that task, the actual unloading of the collector, was reserved to TERAC's legendary tinkerer, Cyrus Alvin Sherwood, on Martin Edovich's express orders.

"I checked with Martin earlier," said McDonald, who had long been associated with Edovich and often functioned informally as his aide. "He says to let it go tonight. If Cy's still sick tomorrow he'll make other arrangements."

Penny shrugged. "Okay, I can tell when I'm not wanted." She went to the locker and slipped on her own frayed coat, transferring her film badge from the hip pocket of her jeans to the breast pocket of the coat. "Anything I should know before you guys take off?"

Jorgen Stern replied, "Earlier there was some slight increase in noise at the high-energy end of the gamma ray spectrum."

"There should be an increase as summer approaches, perhaps," Watanabe offered. "Because of cosmic rays."

"Even down here?" Penny asked skeptically.

"We were discussing it when you came in," said Stern. "We are not deep enough underground to be significantly shielded, considering there is nothing but a hollow building over our heads."

"Yeah, but you're only talking about an increase from the solar wind. Pretty low energy. Don't forget we're in the tropics."

"Maybe so." Stern dropped the subject. "You were at Martin's house?" he asked wistfully. The gloomy Dane hated to miss a party.

"Oh, yeah, it was a blast," said Penny. "Check it out. They'll be goin' all night."

"Perhaps I will, then. Goodnight to you."

"G'night, Jorgen. Frank." As Stern and McDonald went down the stairs, Penny opened the small brown paper sack she'd brought in, winking at Watanabe as she did so. "Smuggled it from Edovich's," she confided. "Ham. Want some?"

Watanabe smiled politely, and shook his head vigorously—he definitely did not.

The control platform was crowded with racks of electronic monitoring equipment, but there was barely room for a couple of desks, one an old wooden desk someone had probably swiped from condemned Schofield Barracks. Half buried under the piles of computer printout on its top was an old coffee maker. Penny cleared a space, took the ham and some slices of bread from her sack, and proceeded to build herself a sandwich. Then she had second thoughts. She'd been losing the battle of the bathroom scales these past few weeks; better stick to her resolve and save the sandwich for a midmorning snack.

She stepped to the wall of monitors and stared at the counters and dials, wondering about Jorgen's anomalous gamma rays. It was part of her job to program the computers to distinguish beam-collision events from the natural background—indeed, she'd promised herself she'd work through a whole stack of data analyses before morning—and possibly it would be a more interesting task than usual. By themselves the counters could not tell the difference between the energetic muons produced by cosmic-ray hits and the muons that were always emerging from the colliding beams.

She shifted her gaze to the row of big color TV monitors displaying views of the I-particle collector. This was her real love, the powerful and elegant machinery that did the work, without which the eggheads would have nothing to argue about. The collector was a thick, upright, lens-shaped device of bronze and steel some six meters in diameter, supported from the floor by yellow-painted steel bridgework. Through the center of the lens, threading it like a string through a bead, ran the narrow stainless-steel pipe that was the heart of TERAC.

An access port was let into the edge of the collector. A system of steel rods inside a clear plastic cylinder reached from the port, through the shield wall, to the control platform, allowing the contents of the collector to be carried onto the platform.

Penny had often watched the intricate process of removing what Martin Edovich called "holy water," for she normally shared the owl shift with the man who'd designed and built the collector, Cy Sherwood. Sherwood was a Gary Cooperish old guy who'd worked around accelerators for forty years, and Penny liked him most of the time, though she was occasionally exasperated by his corny charm and his insistence on treating her as a token of femininity.

And she'd begun to resent his absolute monopoly on what she regarded as the most interesting work. She was a young experimentalist hungry for hands-on experience with the multimillion-dollar machinery; she thought Sherwood was playing the dog in the manger. But when she'd expressed these feelings to McDonald and others she'd been squelched. Sherwood's wife had died several years ago, she'd been told, and his work was the only thing left that had meaning for him.

Perhaps his loneliness had something to do with his preference for the owl shift. Penny Harper drew the awkward shift because she was the youngest member of the team. Sherwood could have drawn any duty he'd asked for. Maybe he liked being alone with his big steel creation. It was likely to be his last major accomplishment.

The machine he'd built for Edovich was the most ingenious he'd ever made. TERAC produced I-particles from proton-antiproton collisions at the rate of a few hundreds of thousands per day; considering that there are something like forty billion trillion atoms of hydrogen in a cubic centimeter of liquid water, Sherwood took TERAC's parsimony as a personal challenge. He had no intention of allowing a single one of the particles created in Hall 30 to escape his grasp.

Penny, despite her impatience, deeply admired the man for having come as close as humanly possible to achieving his goal. The instruments in front of her indicated the ring's clocklike production of I-particles, a little over sixty per second, and the collector's efficient capture of the strange entities.

She was about to turn away from the monitors and settle down with her stack of printouts when a rush of numbers on a digital display caught her eye. She keyed instructions into the recorder and ordered a graphic copy of the event; within a few seconds the computerized device delivered a sheet of paper covered with spiky lines. Penny studied it a moment.

"Say, Hiro, what do you make of this?" She handed the paper to the Japanese scientist, who looked up from his own batch of printouts and took it from her, smiling politely.

He studied the paper longer than Penny had, to assure her of his serious intent. Then he handed it back. "I don't know what to think. Possibly an instance of cosmic rays, as Jorgen suggested?"

She suppressed a rude reply. "Hey, Hiro," she said, prodding him, "it's the middle of the night."

"Yes," Watanabe responded brightly. "That is true."

"Solar cosmic rays?" A hint of amused contempt crept

into her voice. "The whole earth is between us and the sun, Hiro."

"Ahhh, of course," said the Japanese, brushing limp hair from in front of his eyes. "Please forgive me. I am somewhat confused about the time."

Penny watched him go placidly back to work. With some disgust she prodded him. "Is that all you've got to say, Hiro?"

Endlessly polite, he looked up smiling. "You wish me to say more?"

"I think whatever that was, it came from *inside* the machine," she said.

"That is certainly one possible interpretation," Watanabe said with enthusiasm.

"Oh, go back to work," she said. He did so immediately, and she went to her own desk. She sighed wearily, loudly, asking the spirits of the place for a distraction from the piles of paper confronting her. Nothing happened. She sneaked a glance at the purloined ham sandwich. Conscious of self-betrayal, she reached out for it, brought it to her mouth, and took a healthy bite.

3

"What was that all about?" Anne-Marie asked Chauncey, as she watched Peter Slater disappear inside the house, shouldering other guests aside as he went.

Moments before, the tall scientist had blocked their path and demanded that Chauncey introduce him to Anne-Marie, something Chauncey had been delighted to do. Then Slater had turned on Anne-Marie: "Are you wearing blue contacts?"

Startled, she'd nodded yes, but could think of nothing to say. Chauncey tried to fill the awkward silence, but only the words "Well, Peter" had escaped his lips before Slater had cut him off: "I'm not interested in your gossip."

Another uncomfortable pause. Anne-Marie had murmured, *"Un ange passe,"* and Slater, as if taking it for a cue, had wheeled and stalked off.

Tolliver smiled apologetically at Anne-Marie. "Peter's been through a very great deal lately, and he's a very sensitive boy, I'm afraid. He's just been divorced, for one thing. And that on top of missing out on the Nobel Prize."

61

"The Nobel Prize!"

"Well, nobody knows about these things for sure, of course. But everyone assumes Martin is going to get the prize for finding the I-particle, and most people think that Peter laid a lot of the groundwork, theoretically. He could have predicted it, but for some reason he didn't." Chauncey was chattering nervously.

"You seem to know him well."

"Partly it's my job. But in fact we were classmates at Yale. We were even in the same senior society for a while."

"Chauncey, you amaze me—you seem to be on intimate terms with everybody." She sought to flatter him into relaxation.

"I've never met the President," he said with mock humility. "Although of course I know his daughter."

She laughed. Then, casually, she pressed him for more information. "Were you in one of those secret societies together? Like Skull and Bones?"

"If I'd been in Bones I'd have to walk out on you, you know." Chauncey passed a nervous hand over his blond crew-cut. "Actually Crucible hasn't been around quite as long as Bones."

"Crucible! What a deliciously suggestive name." She smiled wickedly, teasing him to tell her more. "Come on, Chauncey, what really goes on in those places—secret ceremonies? Pornographic movies?"

Tolliver's eyes blinked and looked past her. "Nothing that would interest you. And Pete left us for Cambridge pretty soon after he'd been tapped and accepted. He never let us get to know him very well, really. Some of the fellows never really forgave him, I think." He smiled tightly.

"So you won't tell me," she pouted. "You're still an undergraduate at heart, Chauncey."

His lips twitched into a grin. "We all have our own ways of refusing to grow up."

She looked at him with mild surprise. "Chauncey, I think that's the wisest thing you've said all night."

"I have to talk to some of my people, Anne-Marie," he said distractedly. "Can I leave you a moment?"

"I'll survive."

"I'm sure." He smiled past her, that little tight smile again, then walked down the terrace steps toward the lawn. Anne-Marie noticed that his pink scalp glowed beneath his crew-cut, and his trouser cuffs rode half an inch too high, like a proud badge of conservatism.

Peter Slater sat at the Edoviches' piano, shoving the bench back until his long legs found room. It was a good piano, a Wurlitzer baby grand, and to his surprise it was in tune. He played a few slow chords, then idly picked out sad arpeggios of his own composition, while quietly regretting his stupid behavior. The first-floor living room was dimly lit by a single floor lamp and light that came through the flamboyant windows from the torches on the terrace; the couples who whispered in the shadows paid him no attention.

Her hair was soft ebony, and there was an abundance of it framing her tan oval face. Her lips were full, wide, mobile, and she had the bluest eyes. . . . At first he'd thought they looked so blue because of her blue dress, and because her hair was so dark. Then when he'd looked closer he'd realized that she wore blue contact lenses. The prosaic fact took nothing from the magic, but some positivist quirk had compelled him to confirm his guess, and he'd demanded her secret of her before he'd even memorized her name. After that his embarrassment would not let him stay near her.

Sudden anger was expressed in music: the Shostakovich piece began frantically, but if tolerated would later reward the listener with lyrical melodies. He absorbed himself in the intense, intricate, intelligent score, ignoring the curious faces which peered at him out of the darkness.

"Quite a bash," Gardner Hey said with satisfaction,

waving a whiskey glass. "Met a couple of folks who are gonna be quite a bit of help."

"That's nice, Gardner." Anne-Marie smiled politely, her attention on the music coming from the house. The pianist was an amateur, but remarkably adept.

"Yeah, the big picture's emerging very nicely. This guy Edovich has really got the wool pulled over everybody's eyes. You know he's never stopped working for the Defense Department?"

"Oh?" She looked at him warily. "Is that bad?"

"Well, it isn't *illegal,* if that's what you mean. But TERAC is an international laboratory, it's supposed to be pure science," Hey said indignantly. "Edovich was actually head of Los Alamos for a while, you *do* know that—before he went to NAS, which was supposed to clean up his image, I guess. But I think he never really stopped. . . . "

"*Really,* Gardner," said Anne-Marie restlessly. "You know what puzzles me about you?"

"No." He looked at her suspiciously. "But perhaps I should be flattered that you think of me at all."

"How is it that somebody as cynical as you are about science spends all his time writing about it? Why not write about something you have faith in?"

"That would be nice, Anne-Marie, but I don't know what that would be. That occult stuff of yours, maybe? Like you were reading on the plane?"

"Don't patronize me," she said irritably. "And take off that stupid tie. You and Chauncey are the only people here who are wearing nooses around your necks."

"Gladly." He yanked at the frayed knit tie until it came loose in his hand, then shoved it into his back pocket. "Anyway, I'm not cynical about science, if you care. I *am* cynical about scientists—most of them, anyway. I started out to be one myself. I changed my mind."

"Maybe that's what's really eating you," she said, challenging him.

He glared back at her. "I could have done it. Unlike your husband, I didn't want to play the ass-kissing game."

She looked pointedly at the people on the terrace and the lawn, men and women of many races, young and old, neat and sloppy, sober, drunk, brooding, arguing, laughing, nuzzling in the torchlight. "They all look human to me, Gardner. Maybe you'd rather they spent their time arguing about money and politics instead of playing with their molecules or whatever they do; but that's your hang-up, not theirs."

"Wrong," said Hey, as if grading a quiz. "They get politics and money and science and morality all mixed up. They think you and me owe them a living, even if we're too dumb to know a gluon from a screw-on." He was silent for a moment, peering into his whiskey glass. "You know, when Congress was cool at first about the Japanese offer to finance TERAC, Edovich and Lasky and the big guns from MIT and Cal Tech and Berkeley and Stanford all started screaming—they actually had the gall to bring up Giordano Bruno and Galileo and Darwin and the rest of the persecuted pantheon—just because they couldn't get their *money.*" Hey's face was a mask of disgust. "It's true, Anne-Marie. The big science boys don't give a damn about anything as long as they get the money to build their machines and fly off to their conferences and look down their noses at the rest of us."

"You take it awfully personally," she drawled.

"And you've got a low tolerance for strong feelings, babe." He took a swig of his drink. "I think if you're serious about news photography you'd better grow a thicker skin."

"Thanks for the advice."

"It's free, like the ride."

"Keep your ride, Gardner," she said angrily. "I'll find my way home."

"Sure, it looks like Chauncey'd do anything for you." He leered at her tipsily, then belatedly attempted a smile.

She turned, her skirts swirling about her knees, and walked away.

By the time Peter had concluded the Shostakovich piece he'd succeeded in forgetting where he was. He was startled to hear scattered applause from the small crowd which had gathered around the piano. And in front of him there was a lovely face with impossibly blue eyes.

"Do you know Bach's *Chromatic Fantasy and Fugue*?" she asked.

"I'm terribly sorry for my clumsiness. . . . " he said in a rush, but she had no patience with his apology.

"I just want to hear it, if you do."

Her dissatisfaction washed over Peter like a hot tide, as if he were a minor obstacle, a stone on the beach of stones against which she spent her futile energies. He swallowed his reply, and instead began to play again, the astringent, merciless logic made music.

He soon realized he was playing as well as he possibly could, playing for the face that studied him from beyond the sounding board. The notes rippled and reverberated, and the muscles of his shoulders felt the chords as firmly as his fingertips. Yet after awhile her face receded, the music filled his imagination, and the scenery shifted and dissolved; she had forged a link to his past stronger than she could have imagined, and for the moment he did not wonder what the motive of her request might have been.

He recalled the draped and shadowed Edwardian parlor of his first piano teacher in Durham, stern and gifted old Miss Frankfort, who watched him as intently as this blue-eyed woman, ignoring the pain she knew he felt as he stretched his childish hands for the chords, big as those hands were for a boy of eight.

Now an intricate figure transported him to Saybrook commons, to the piano which stood before a window's Gothic stonework, to the spring sunlight which filtered through a filigree of new dogwood leaves.

That window, a pastiche in stone, dissolved to its original pattern at Caius in Cambridge, dark chords now reflecting the deep polish of black oak centuries old.

Unbidden came the memory of the night in Berkeley when he knew he would leave Kathleen; he had played this same piece endlessly, using it to bar words, bar feelings. He pushed through that memory now, erased the pictures in his head, heard only the music. Yet one picture persisted, the face of the blue-eyed woman in front of him who had called up these woven sinews of sound.

He finished. There was silence for a moment, then—except for a single enthusiast who appreciated Peter's accomplishment and clapped loudly and insistently—a sparse patter of applause rapidly overwhelmed by relieved small talk.

"Not exactly a crowd-pleaser," said Peter.

"You did it well. I remember my father playing that; you play it almost as well."

"Who was your father?" Was she repaying his earlier gaucheries with left-handed compliments of her own?

"Eric Brand. Have you heard of him?"

"Of course, I remember the name." Brand had been a pianist of some reputation; the woman's compliment was real. "I have to admit I haven't followed his career."

"He died, almost ten years ago. Listen," she said quickly, before he could offer insincere commiseration, "I'm starved. Every time I go near the food out there somebody tries to mug me."

He was delighted with her bluntness. "Our host and hostess among them—I've had the same problem. So"—he looked at her steadily, bracing himself for defeat—"would you like to get away from here?"

"Oh yes, I would." Her voice seemed on the edge of trembling.

"Forgive me, but your name . . . "

"Anne-Marie, Peter. Come on, out the front way—before they catch us and make us talk."

* * *

Through the terrace windows Greta Edovich saw them slip away, saw Peter's bony fingers reach out and take Anne-Marie's hand to steer her around a knot of loud talkers, saw their hands still lightly clasped as they disappeared up the steps into the front hall. Greta's emotions were curiously unclear; something in the sight thrilled her, angered her, left her giddy. She turned to Chauncey. "Married, is she? Chauncey, don't tell me your beautiful friend is being a naughty girl." She giggled, a muffled squeak.

Tolliver wasn't amused. He peered grimly down at the tips of his oxfords.

The engine of the little Triumph grumbled as Peter let the car coast in neutral down steep, narrow Manoa Road. Huge black old trees arched over the twisting street; away back at the ends of winding driveways the windows of suburban houses gleamed out of the jungle that threatened to swallow them up.

Inside the car the round dials on the dashboard glowed softly yellow. The car's deep bucket seats and high gearbox formed a barrier between the conspirators.

Anne-Marie was the first to break the silence. "I'm not usually this impetuous." She said it as ritual defense.

"Please don't take it back. After the mess I made of trying to meet you . . . "

"Yes, you did. And you were awfully hard on poor Chauncey."

"It wouldn't do me much good to apologize to you for that. Chauncey and I have known each other a long time. . . . And you?"

"Chauncey? A pretty long time. I like him."

"I don't want to fight over Chauncey."

She eyed him. "Let's talk about food, then." She paused. "You're a prickly case."

"Out of practice. How do you feel about sashimi?"

"Love it. Where did you acquire your taste for raw fish?"

He laughed. "Teenage enthusiasm gone wild. I was in love with everything Japanese when I was a kid. I still am, from afar—that's part of what attracted me to TERAC, I suppose."

"From afar?"

"I've never actually been there. And I don't have any close Japanese friends."

"Pardon me for asking, but how many close friends do you have?"

He tapped the accelerator and slid the car into gear, moving more swiftly through the winding shadows. "It varies," he said after awhile. "Perhaps you and I could be friends."

Her tone was warm, though she did not answer him directly. "Where did you live before you came here, Peter?"

"Berkeley. I taught math at Cal and thought about physics."

"Chauncey told me you were divorced."

"That's right. And you?" He looked at her left hand resting on her thigh. He glanced up at her face and saw her looking back at him with those blue, blue eyes—blue from his memory of them, since he could not really see them in the dark.

She wore them blue in honor of the Mediterranean, the middle of the earth, where her adulthood had been forged. Here, a world away in a baritone darkness which smelled of leather and wood polish and fine-grade motor oil, she reached out her lying hand and touched the prominent knuckles of his long fingers where they rested on the gearshift. He had the answer he wanted.

They were coming down out of the Manoa Valley now; the cheap condominiums and office towers of the city were springing up all around them, and the Friday-night traffic was congealing noisily on every side. He shifted into low, accelerated through a yellow light, then turned left toward the beach. He turned his hand palm up on the gearshift, snared her cool fingers, squeezed them lightly.

When he shifted gears again she moved her hand to her lap.

Peter flattered and bullied the owner of the Yoshino into staying open half an hour longer than usual; the shrewd old woman acquiesced only because she found the image of a six-and-a-half-foot white demon who spoke fluent, if simple, Japanese a source of fascination and amusement. She accepted his check and generous tip politely, but could not resist asking him a question which set him laughing as he left the restaurant.

"What did she say to you?" Anne-Marie asked, piqued.

"She wanted to know why I don't speak Japanese like a woman. She thought all Americans speak Japanese like women."

"Is that really true?"

"It's true that there's a style of speech appropriate to the way women talk in the presence of men—I mean geishas, and others who are acting as hostesses. Including the women who marry servicemen."

"I see." Anne-Marie smiled at the vision of American soldiers speaking in the mincing, giggling tones of geishas. Then she frowned, mock-seriously. "A very primitive culture in some ways, wouldn't you say?"

"Oh, yes. My enthusiasm is by no means unqualified."

They talked about other things on the way back to her hotel. He was conscious of babbling, but it seemed impossible to stop once started: " . . . someday maybe you can show me around. I was on Delos once, some fancy conference, God knows where the grant money came from. But I never got to Crete."

"You live on an island now," she said idly. "From what you've told me I'd have thought you'd be desperate for city life."

"Not me, I'm a country squire. Honolulu suits me fine—it's a cosmopolitan small town, despite its size. If you can picture Dr. Quock's Acupuncture Clinic next door to the Woolworth Five and Dime."

She smiled happily. "That's what I meant by an island culture. My kind of place."

He smiled with her. "It's a very small island. I live all the way at the other end, on the beach at Haleiwa, up on the north shore, away from everybody but the surfers. Still, it's less than an hour's drive." He stopped talking a minute, peering through the windshield at the strolling lovers under the ironwoods and the rolling moonlit surf of Waikiki. "The surf is huge up there; it's like God or the devil beating a drum as big as the world. But it organizes my head for me; it's a place where I can think." He glanced sidelong at her, catching her gaze.

She broke the spell, turning her head away and yawning. "Oohh—I didn't realize." She smiled sleepily, apologetically. "I'd like to see it sometime."

He didn't let his disappointment show. "It must be past four in the morning, your time."

"Peter, let me take you to lunch tomorrow, okay?"

"Well, but—"

"This is the hotel. Don't bother to get out." She had the door open before he'd fully stopped. She swung her legs out.

"Don't run away. I was just going to say I'd like to show you around TERAC tomorrow, if you're interested in a busman's holiday."

"I'd love to, thank you, Peter." She sat half turned toward him, her espadrilled feet set firmly on asphalt. "What time?"

"How much sleep do you need?"

She smiled slowly. Then she said, "I really ought to be available if Gardner has lined anything up in the morning. Can I reach you?"

"No, I don't trust myself to hang around unringing phones. I'll be at the Halekulani Hotel at one, okay? If you can't be there, leave a message at the desk."

"The Halekulani at one." She leaned toward him, twisting her body to reach him. She let her lips linger next to his for half a second. When he moved toward her she retreated. "Thank you, Peter Slater. And goodnight."

He stared after her as she moved her tall body gracefully up and out of the tiny car. She stood and walked quickly away, toward the electric pink glare of the Crater Hotel's neon-lit entrance.

9

Peter Slater's Triumph raced along the high center of Oahu, paced by a small bright moon. Moonlight turned the waving cane on each side of the road to strokes of black and silver. To the east and west the moonlight suffused the cloud-drenched mountains with a soft blue glow, but overhead the stars burned fierce and white in a black sky.

His cheeks burned, and Anne-Marie's perfume lingered faintly. His elation astonished him. He'd been prepared to discount heavily the degree to which she physically attracted him; he found many women attractive. They didn't usually block out every other thought in his head. His first kindergarten puppy-love, his first grade-school sweetheart, his high-school steady, his first grown-up lover, the *au pair* girl he'd met at the home of a randy Cambridge don—and once upon a time, the woman he'd married.... Yesterday, a month ago, a year ago, he would have sworn no woman would ever move him in this way again.

He knew little of Anne-Marie's past, her beliefs, her enthusiasms. She was divorced; she was a news photographer; she was the daughter of an accomplished musician. Bare facts explained nothing. He wanted her to tell him everything about herself. He wanted to explain everything about himself to her. He knew they would mutually understand . . . even when he told her about Kathleen. Kathleen . . .

Peter Slater saw his marriage dissolving and felt powerless to stop it. Kathleen was happy in Berkeley; her career was progressing. His wasn't, and he wanted to be someplace else. They'd slept together three times in the last six months, and each time was less fun than the last. They'd hardly spoken for the past week.

He knew it was his fault. He made an effort. Tuesday night they went to the movies with her friend Joel Weiss from the math department and Joel's wife Susan; it was a benefit screening for a scientists' lobby that Joel belonged to, an award-winning feature-length documentary titled *Horror at Hiroshima.*

Five minutes into the film Peter realized he'd made a terrible mistake. Once again the *Enola Gay* lumbered down that long, long floodlit runway—the image had been reprinted so many times the film grains swam on the screen like black and white amoebas. Once again the music dolorously swelled, and a portentous voice intoned from the soundtrack, *"A new era in human cruelty dawned on August sixth, 1945 . . . "*

Peter hadn't been born when the bombs fell on Japan. He sat through the rest of the film in growing resentment.

The two couples had a drink at Rasputin's after the show. Susan Weiss asked Peter if he didn't think the film was just incredibly powerful. Peter looked at her and saw her wearing the same quilted jacket and kung fu slippers she'd worn for the last five years, and his misery and his arrogance got the better of him. No, he said, he thought the film was distorted and damned near hysterical and showed a perfect lack of understanding of the Japanese people, not to mention of nuclear physics.

Joel wanted to argue with him, and when Peter looked at Joel he realized he'd never liked *him* very much either. How could anybody who called himself a scientist really *do* science when he talked as much as Joel did, mostly about things he really knew nothing about—nuclear waste, recombinant DNA, the fucked-up carbon cycle? Peter looked at Joel and Susan, and then at Kathleen, and he wondered what he was doing there. Unable to answer his own desperate question, he got up and walked out without saying a word.

When Kathleen got home she found him banging on the piano—Bach, of course, never anything but Bach when he was half out of his mind—and first she started to cry, and then she started to pack. He kept playing, even after she drove off in the Volvo.

For the next few days episodes of seething, inexpressible anger would suddenly boil up while he was trying to think about something else. Even his graduate students remarked his distraction. He was losing his concentration, the only tool he really needed, the only one he couldn't do without—the necessary and sufficient equipment of his life's work.

Thursday night he called Kathleen at her sister's house. They talked for an hour and a half and she agreed to come home. When she got home they found they had nothing more to say, and they both tried to pretend that that was all right.

Friday morning he abruptly canceled a seminar and drove his old TR-4 up into the hills. Rain squalls whipped the eucalyptus trees, plastering crescent gray green leaves to the asphalt of the winding road. He parked near the Lawrence Hall of Science, his little green sports car sharing the lot with a fleet of yellow school buses. Sheets of opaque rain obscured what would have been a panoramic view of San Francisco Bay.

He was a little put off by the hall's hunched concrete

shape, which seemed excessively austere for a children's museum. The building had been erected to honor the memory of Ernest Orlando Lawrence, inventor of the cyclotron, but on this dreary day it resembled one of those old gun emplacements which brood over the Golden Gate; it was a fortress, guarding the lofty ideals of Science against the rank Superstition that teemed in the flatlands below.

Peter sat in the Triumph's low driver's seat, unmoving, as ragged dark clouds raced toward him out of the west. He squinted at the city over the car's bulging British Racing Green hood, as if over the cowling of an airplane.

Aim. Push the release. Bomb away. . . . Turn, turn, get away from here.

. . . You should be helping me, Kathleen, you of all people should understand. You should know I can't talk to you, can't lose time talking to you; I hardly have time to record where my thoughts are leading me. I shouldn't be here, in this place; I need to be there, watching the machine run night and day. . . .

For several years Peter Slater had struggled to bring mental order out of a chaos of quarks and leptons and the disparate quanta of interaction, the raw stuff of high-energy physics. His efforts had been bold and open, and more provocative than successful—not quite crazy enough to be true, in the words of Bohr's famous aphorism, yet sufficiently so to gain him a reputation as one of the brightest of the younger theorists. Then news of startling discoveries at the big new TERAC research facilities in Hawaii had suggested that relationships he'd considered too elegant to be credible might actually be true after all. He bitterly regretted the caution that had kept him from publishing; he became close-mouthed and circumspect, and worked on his heretical theories in secret. His friends blamed his irritability, his rudeness in print and in person, on what they perceived as growing domestic troubles, but unknowingly they'd reversed cause and effect. For six months now Slater had been literally lost in thought, impressed by the discoveries at TERAC but irrationally certain that they were being misinterpreted.

A big tour bus pulled up to Slater's left and wheezed to a stop. For a moment the oil-smeared double-decker bus and the tiny sports car sat parallel, neither vehicle betraying a sign of the life within. Then the rain abated. Slater flung open the door of the Triumph, unfolding his long legs, dashing for the museum, while behind him a score of young Japanese tourists scurried laughing from the bus.

They fled to the reservoirs and the rivers by the thousands to escape the flames. They trampled each other and drowned, or died standing up, suffocated, boiled alive. . . .

Inside the hall, noisy excited children from the local schools ran distracted from one display to another. Peter ignored the bright exhibits and the gift shop with its stuffed pterodactyls and made his way to a mahogany-paneled room centered under the museum's dome. It was a quiet room, almost deserted, the only room in the building not designed to attract children. Here were Ernest Lawrence's medals and commendations, preserved under glass. And here were the very first cyclotrons.

One was made of silvered glass like a Tiffany vase; it would have fit easily into the palm of Peter's big hand. Vaguely sexy glass nipples protruded from it, threaded with copper wires and liberally smeared with red sealing wax to keep in vacuum.

A handmade brass pillbox, hardly bigger, was the first real, practical cyclotron, capable of developing energies of several thousand electron volts—not much, even by the standards of 1930, but a hint at the shape of things to come.

The next scale-up was less than a foot in diameter. Its pipes and leads were also smeared with red wax, a Radiation Laboratory tradition for almost a decade—old-timers still remembered the stench of burning wax. When set between the poles of a big telegraph magnet, this little box could crank up a beam of protons with more than a million electron volts of energy, enough energy to turn the air blue—and more than enough to crack atomic nuclei, thus freeing a flood of the then newly discovered particles called neutrons. The atom smasher had been born.

Peter bent over the display cases, peering closely at the handcrafted artifacts. They might have been buried in shattered Knossos four thousand years ago in the Bronze Age, so sophisticated and at once so primitive did they appear. He pictured their workings: inside the disc-shaped box fitted with hollow electrodes, protons—the positively charged particles which were simply the bare nuclei of ordinary hydrogen atoms—spiraled in a strong magnetic field. Alternating voltage nudged the protons to accelerate each time they crossed the gap between the half-circular electrodes; slow protons made tight circuits, fast protons made wide ones, and the time taken to complete each circuit was always the same, precisely matching the AC frequency.

As a mathematically inclined physicist Peter was accustomed to spinning the most subtle and complex symmetries, but he was struck with admiration for the elegant simplicity of Lawrence's cyclotron principle. Impressive beam energies could be built up with only a modest constant input of power. The first cyclotrons had run on house current.

From the prototypes had descended a race of giants with names like UNK and Tevatron and TERAC, with beam energies measured in hundreds of billions or even trillions of electron volts, and diameters measured in kilometers instead of inches. Their power, instead of coming from the wall socket, was supplied by high-tension wires from hydroelectric dams, or by their very own nuclear reactors. They were called synchrotrons and storage rings these days. Gone were the cyclotron's simple symmetries, long since sacrificed to Special Relativity—for the mass of speeding particles multiplied as each single proton acquired the energy of a buzzing wasp, and the crushing strength of hundreds of supercooled magnets was required to keep them from chewing through the walls of their vacuum chambers.

Slater heard a muffled giggle, and circumspectly turned his head to peer at the Japanese tourists who'd filed into the small room behind him. Most of them, though they did their best to appear nonchalant, seemed bewildered; evidently they'd lost their guide.

They wandered silently in the smashed city, naked, stunned, deaf. The retinas of those who had chanced to look up at that particular quadrant of the sky at that particular moment had been burned away. Many walked with a grotesque delicacy, holding their arms stiffly away from their bodies, so as not to touch seared flesh to seared flesh. . . .

The Japanese tourists, all in their late twenties, were dressed as casually and expensively as the window shoppers Peter had seen on Rodeo Drive the last time he'd passed through Beverly Hills. One tall, slender young woman could have been a Paris mannequin. Peter caught her eye as she looked sidelong at him; she was whispering to a friend, rather wickedly and quite audibly: *"Anmari sei ga takai no de koshi wo futatsu ni ot'te kēsu no naka wo mita."* ("He's so tall he has to fold himself in half to see into the case.")

Peter smiled, stood up to his full six and a half feet; he considered speaking to her in Japanese, but he knew he would only make her and all the others in her group intensely uncomfortable. Instead he inclined his head just slightly in her direction, hardly more than coincidence might have allowed. Startled, the woman blushed and hid her face behind manicured fingers. Peter turned away, moving along past the display cases, leaving her to wonder.

Idly he studied the laudatory mementos and tried to put the tourists out of his mind. He was reminded of several facets of Lawrence's career the Hall of Science brushed over lightly, if at all. . . .

In 1935 a rat was placed in a beam of neutrons from a cyclotron. Minutes later it was found dead. For the first time it occurred to scientists that cyclotron radiation could kill. Ernest Lawrence and his associates started hiding behind blocks of concrete while conducting experiments, a wise precaution even though in fact it was established that the rat had perished of mere asphyxiation, the experimenter having neglected to drill air holes in its box.

In 1938 Lawrence cured his mother of an inoperable cancer by irradiating her with a beam of neutrons from his cyclotron.

By 1941 the cyclotron was the *sine qua non* of nuclear research, used to determine the neutron-capture cross section of uranium, to separate uranium isotopes, to create the artificial element plutonium. . . .

Hordes of desperate wounded, fleeing the firestorm, nevertheless halted and stood respectfully aside as the Emperor's picture was carried to safety. Four days later, amid the rubble of ruined Hiroshima itself, its survivors were dismayed to hear the Emperor inform the nation by radio of his decision to concede defeat.

In 1945 Lawrence and other good men met to recommend what use should be made of the thing that had been abuilding on the mesa in New Mexico. Whether their advice was heeded or had been sincerely solicited matters little, for certainly they spent long hours in private soul-searching beforehand. The Nazis were already defeated. Lawrence, Oppenheimer, Fermi, and Compton were asked for their opinions, as scientists, on how the bomb should be used against the Japanese. They needed only a single morning to reach agreement: no warning.

No warning. Fanatic Japanese soldiers, enthralled by warlords and hypnotized by their love of the Emperor, would simply have defied a warning—as indeed they defied the bomb itself—along with the old men, the doctors and nurses and tradespeople and schoolchildren and (to the extent they were capable of defiance) the babies, all the human inhabitants of Hiroshima. Of this the scientists were reluctantly persuaded. In advance.

The bomb exploded two thousand feet in the air, directly above a hospital, driving the pillars of its gate straight into the ground.

Peter left the shrine. He watched the Japanese tourists heading for their bus, dashing through the rain—bright laughing scraps of humanity in the cold wetness. At the last moment before she went out the museum door the pretty Japanese girl turned and glanced at Slater over her shoulder. The sight left him desolate. She was the life he had denied himself; he saw no remedy but further retreat.

He walked out of the museum slowly, into the drenching rain, leaving behind the mementos and the little four-inch silvered glass cyclotron in its display case.

Within two months he had received the appointment he sought and had moved to Hawaii. He got the divorce notice by mail; Kathleen had handled it all herself, with typical efficiency—she was, after all, an excellent applied mathematician. She'd kept the things that meant something to her and let him keep the things he cared about, which for both of them meant pretty much what material possessions they'd brought to the marriage. They'd had no children.

To his left the main gate of TERAC slid by, lit by unearthly pinkish yellow light from sodium-vapor lamps—noon on the planet of a red dwarf star. He slowed for the darkened jumble of shops and houses that was Wahiawa, then accelerated again, down the long northern slope toward the sea.

10

Anne-Marie stared at the ceiling of her hotel room, sleepless, her head buzzing with exhaustion. There was no point in trying to hide the truth from herself. She was pregnant and probably had been for two months. What was she going to do about it?

That, at least, she didn't have to decide until the week was over. She kicked off the sweaty sheets and sat up on the edge of the lumpy bed. A sailing scene, printed on cardboard embossed with phony brushstrokes, hung skewed on the wall behind her head. The curtains of tough polyester mesh moved in the draft; outside, streetlamps gleamed in the darkness. The telephone crouched like a toad on the bedstand.

She could have gone home with him so easily. She'd wanted to. What would the man think when he found out the truth? He was a puritan, by the look of him—somebody who'd want to keep his relationships as neat and abstract as his calculations. She sensed something much less calculating at his core, however, as little

as she knew him—though he would not welcome her
bringing it to the light. She should tell him everything tomorrow, and say goodbye.

Yet why say goodbye? What did she care for his scru-
ples, once she was willing to give up her own? What did
it matter in the long run, a week from now, or a month?
He'd be gone.

She lay down, turning her face to the wall. She let herself imagine his long fingers tangling themselves in her
hair, his lips moving across her cheek. . . . She would tell
him part of the truth. She would not tell him what he
didn't need to know. With images of warm caresses she
tried to lull herself to sleep. . . .

She was seventeen when her father died. He was at the
height of his fame, a pianist of real accomplishment; his
Scandinavian good looks, glacially handsome and moody,
lent a passionately romantic air to his performances. Gid-
dier critics gushed of Liszt and Chopin.

Behind the scenes, Anne-Marie's mother, about as
hardheaded a penny-pinching daughter of the petite bour-
geoisie as ever latched onto a hungry and promising young
performer, managed the Brand family finances with merciless skill. Even when concert managers offered to pay
the bills she would never allow the family to stay in
first-class hotels, for Mme. Brand knew her husband
would not be able to resist room service, or the shops, restaurants, and bars on the ground floor—charges she
would have to meet from his earnings. Wherever Brand
performed on extended tours, his family was to be found
ensconced nearby in a modest pension.

For years after the event Anne-Marie tried to pretend
that her mother's unsmiling grip on her father's money
was the principal cause of his death. The truth was, there
was plenty of blame to go around for that sadly comic
event. The maestro loved womankind. His wife maintained a bitter silence; Brand was an American, after all,
with no proper religion and no *a priori* objection to di-

vorce. But she would not let him spend money on his conquests. When one night he came home late from a performance at the Odéon, drunk, demanding money to pay for a taxi, Mme. Brand, who'd selected their furnished apartment on the Rue St. Placide partly for its excellent Métro connections, refused him. In his rage he struck her. His son, Anne-Marie's older brother by two years, leaped to her defense; then, appalled that he'd raised his hand to his father, the boy panicked and went further, began beating his father savagely, as the tears streamed down his face.

Brand was wholly taken by surprise. Rather than risk his hands by defending himself, he fled. Anne-Marie stood by, peering from her room, too shocked and frightened to interfere. As Brand bolted from the apartment his son followed, far enough to hurl a handful of francs after him. Brand stopped to pick the coins off the sidewalk before the taxi driver could get to them; then he disappeared down the block, loping wildly in the direction of the Métro.

Later that night he was shot dead. The husband of the woman with whom he'd sought solace had returned unexpectedly from a business trip to Switzerland.

Anne-Marie got control of her trust fund on her twenty-first birthday. She vanished from the apartment, and from her classes at the Sorbonne, leaving only a forwarding address with the bank.

Her twin passports served her well; those countries unfriendly to the U.S. were usually tolerant of the French. And she had a better passport than any document, her youth.

She traveled the rim of the Mediterranean. Once she risked life imprisonment, smuggling enough hashish to buy cameras; the experience was terrifying, and she never repeated it. For three months she was the lover of an English classicist at the university in Alexandria, tolerating his condescension to learn what he knew of the occult, of Hermes Trismegistus, of the cabala, of alchemy.

Eventually Crete drew her, and there she took up a restless residence, and there, eventually, she met Charlie. . . .

The surf that boomed outside the veiled window was the surf of a different shore, but her heart's nervous beating was the same. She'd tasted the Fruit of the Tree, and though the taste was sour, it had made her hungry.

But perhaps Peter Slater would not need to hear about all that—for the use she would make of him, in the time she would know him. His remembered features were becoming vague now, as she conjured a dark solid form, possibly his, to lie down beside her. Slowly her busy brain relinquished its grip on consciousness, and she drifted into the warmth of her shadow lover's embrace.

11

For half an hour Hey and Anne-Marie drove through Saturday morning's getaway traffic, until at last the suburbs dropped behind, the traffic thinned, and the scenery grew wild. Black lava cliffs, strangely eroded and dry as any desert, fell off swiftly into the surging ocean. They passed the spouting Blowhole, a geyser of channeled surf set into a miniature moonscape at water's edge, and drove on toward land's end at Makapuu Point. For the first time since leaving San Diego Anne-Marie began to feel she was a long way from home; the feeling wasn't altogether a good one.

Hey and Anne-Marie had exchanged few words but many yawns. She was sleepy but otherwise content, while he was blatantly suffering from an overdose of good whiskey. To her surprise, he'd mumbled the briefest of apologies for "anything I might have said" when she'd answered his knock on her door. She thought that covered a lot of territory, but she hadn't needled him; she'd nodded and smiled and allowed him to treat her to Egg McMuffins at the McDonald's in the Kahala Mall.

At last they rounded the point and came upon the village of Waimanalo from the south. On their left was a thin straggle of bungalows on stilts, fronting the highway; on their right, behind the steel guard rail, heavy surf rolled in from the Kaiwi Channel. Molokai was a blue silhouette on the horizon. They drove to the single stoplight, past a curious agglomeration of suburban ranch houses, rusting Quonset huts, and wooden shacks with horses tied outside. Behind the town rose the sheer gray wall of the Makapuu Pali, a cliff as sere and imposing as the brow of a war god's idol.

They had to turn back and retrace their route, but Hey finally found the faded, hand-lettered numbers on a roadside mailbox. He parked the Datsun on the highway's sandy shoulder to avoid blocking the drive, two ruts across a patch of lawn leading to an empty shed of corrugated iron. Anne-Marie waited beside the car, her cameras slung over her shoulder, while Hey got out and crossed the lawn to the house.

Hey mounted the wooden steps and banged on the door. A scrawny little dog of indescribably mixed breed suddenly darted from under the raised house and bounded up the steps toward Hey; he flinched away from the beast, but it merely sniffed at the cuff of his chinos, yawned, and rolled over on its back, inviting a tummy scratch.

Anne-Marie looked around for a picture. The sun was midway up the sky, strongly cross-lighting the pitted cliffs, glaring from the narrow beach, the weathered houses. The surf groaned against the shore. Intermittent cars whined by on the highway. The fronds of stunted coconut palms rattled fitfully in the breeze.

Anne-Marie found an abandoned pickup truck, splayed on rusted wheelless axles, staring blindly at her from under a tattered banana plant beside the shed; the inner surfaces of its headlights were coated over with cataracts of bright-green algae. Very arty. She snapped a few frames of Kodachrome. Then she became aware of that damned insistent urge to pee.

The door of the house had opened and someone inside was talking to Hey. Anne-Marie walked quickly to the porch. The mongrel dog writhed invitingly, and she stooped to scratch its pink stretched abdomen; the dog's rows of nipples were prominent. Anne-Marie looked up at the woman inside the house. "Please," she said, "could I use your bathroom? I know it's an imposition, but I really need to."

The woman was young, a dark solid beauty quite the opposite of slender Anne-Marie, the kind of lush beauty celebrated in paintings on black velvet. She looked Anne-Marie over with a quick, perceptive glance, then said cheerfully, "Sure, you come in. You too, mister." She held the door open. The dog tried to squeeze in behind Hey, but she stopped it with a foot. "Not you."

Anne-Marie got a hasty impression of the interior: cool, dark, and empty. "Down the hall," the woman said.

The bathroom smelled of strongly perfumed soap. There was no tub. The shower stall was hung with wet cutoffs, enormous in girth, and the floor was gritty with sand. Through the closed door Anne-Marie could hear the woman's voice: "You stay if you want to. Dan won't talk to newspapers, though. So you probably wasting your time."

When Anne-Marie emerged a minute later she found the young woman standing with her back to her, blocking the hall, her arms crossed under her heavy breasts. Hey sat facing her on the worn plastic couch in the living room. Dusty surfing and football trophies stood on top of the television set. On the wall was a color photograph of a group of musicians and dancers in traditional Hawaiian costume.

The woman moved aside as Anne-Marie came up beside her. "You okay?" she asked, with what sounded like real concern.

"I'm very sorry to push in on you like that."

"You don't have to be sorry." The woman's dark eyes swept knowingly over Anne-Marie's midsection, then returned to her face. "I'll get you some hot tea."

"Really, there's no need . . ."

"You sit down with your husband."

"We're not married," Anne-Marie said quickly.

The woman laughed. "Me and Dan aren't married either. Makes my parents real unhappy, but I tell them, if God is love, He'll understand." She went down the hall to the kitchen.

Anne-Marie glanced at Hey, who was grinning at her foolishly. She followed the woman into the kitchen and found her putting a stainless-steel kettle on the gas stove. "I mean, my husband is in California," she explained. "I'm working as a photographer for Mr. Hey's paper."

The woman turned to her. "I didn't mean to embarrass you. My name is Ana."

"Mine's Anne-Marie. You're very kind."

"I don't see very many people these days. Dan stays away from people."

"Who are the dancers in the photograph?" Anne-Marie asked, not wishing to pursue the question of Dan Kono—that was Hey's business.

Ana smiled. "I'm one of them. I look different in a ti-leaf skirt, huh?" She cast a brief deprecating glance down at her faded muumuu. "My parents have a dance troupe, they dance at the big hotels. I used to be in it."

"Why did you give up dancing?"

"I didn't give it up, I just don't dance for haoles anymore." She looked up at Anne-Marie. "Except my friends." She changed the subject. "You really a photographer? Not like the ones who used to come around after Dan, for sure."

"I'm just getting started again. I used to take pictures before I was married, when I lived in Europe."

"A real world traveler, huh?" Ana smiled. "Maybe you better slow down now, Ana-Melia."

Anne-Marie said nothing. The water was boiling. Ana poured it over tea in a round pink unglazed pot. After a few moments Ana poured the tea into a chipped china cup and handed it to Anne-Marie. "Healthy," she said, smiling. "Full of secret Hawaiian herbs. Don't you laugh."

Anne-Marie took the cup from Ana's strong, gracefully upturned hand. She felt a rush of gratitude for the young woman's kindness, so immediately and unconditionally offered. For the moment it didn't matter if the offer arose from the woman's loneliness, or because Ana imagined that she had perceived some kinship between them; for the moment the whole relationship was contained in the warm, complicated flavor of the tea.

Anne-Marie heard the front door open. Alarm flickered across Ana's face; she put her teacup down and hurried toward the front of the house.

Anne-Marie followed. From the living-room window they could see Gardner Hey on the lawn, watching a Toyota Land Cruiser back into the driveway, pushing behind it a high-prowed fishing boat on a two-wheeled trailer. The boat was made of plywood, painted bright blue and white, the colors of the sea; the Land Cruiser was a sun-dulled beige, streaked with rust the exact hue of volcanic dirt.

Two men were in front; the driver glanced at Hey, then ignored him as he steered the boat and trailer into the corrugated-iron shed. When the car stopped Hey stepped forward. "Mr. Kono, I'm Gardner Hey, with *Science Weekly.* I'm here to cover . . . "

The driver opened the door in Hey's face. He was a tall thin man; his naturally dark complexion appeared unhealthily sallow, as if he'd been spending too much time indoors. His black hair was curly, and he had a sparse beard, a would-be Vandyke.

Inside the house, Anne-Marie raised one of her cameras in her right hand and reached to move the curtains aside with her left.

"That one, you don't take his picture," Ana said sharply, reaching in front of Anne-Marie to catch her hand.

"That's not Dan Kono?"

"Luki, his brother." Ana was gently urging Anne-Marie away from the window, still holding her hand. "Dan's with him. Better you put the camera away now. Maybe Dan will let you take his picture another time."

Anne-Marie supposed a hard-boiled press photographer would have ignored Ana and started clicking away, but she did not protest.

The real Dan Kono got out the other side of the vehicle and joined his brother in unhitching the trailer. He was taller, heavier, and much darker than Luki. His beard covered his jaws and chin, and he wore dark glasses and a ragged straw hat that covered most of the rest of his face. The dog, which had emerged from under the house upon the arrival of the Land Cruiser, now joyfully pawed and slobbered over Kono's bare brown legs and tough bare feet; Kono ignored the dog. He and Luki lifted the trailer from the hitch and rolled the boat to the back of the shed.

Hey watched impatiently as they hung up the oars and fishing tackle. "Look here, Kono, maybe you never heard of my paper, but we're legitimate. Do you want to see some ID?" He was still addressing Luki. "TERAC is celebrating its birthday Monday, did you know that? That's why I'm here. You had a lot to say about TERAC once."

Dan Kono did not even glance up as he finished securing the boat's little outboard motor. The saturnine Luki looked at Hey without apparent malice, but with no more interest than he might have shown a lizard.

Gardner Hey's blond pigtail quivered indignantly. "You can't stonewall me, Kono," he said to Luki. He moved to block the men's exit from the shed. "You let a lot of people down. I think you owe them an explanation."

Luki lifted a burlap sack out of the bottom of the boat.

Something in it flopped and struggled. "You in my way," Luki said reasonably, gently but irresistibly pushing the smelly sack into Hey's chest until Hey stood aside. Luki and Kono walked past Hey toward the front steps. The dog tangled itself in Kono's feet and was bumped aside roughly; it barked reproof.

Hey's pale face suffused with blood. "I know you were bought, Kono," he said loudly. "I guess I'll be able to figure out who did the buying without too much trouble. . . . "

Dan Kono stopped, one foot on the lowest step; he half turned toward Hey, but did not look directly at him. "All this time you been talking to the wrong man, reporter. Looks like you can't figure out much of anything." He turned to his brother. "Go inside, Luki. I be a minute."

Luki did not move. He continued to watch Hey with apparent detachment.

"Luki!" Kono said sharply.

Luki spread his arms and shrugged. The burlap sack thrashed. Luki grinned, and still did not move. Goaded by his brother's intransigence, Dan Kono lost control of his temper, slowly at first, then with heavy acceleration, like a stream bank crumbling in the rain. "Get off my land, reporter." He moved toward Hey. "Or maybe I throw you off right now."

"You can't threaten . . . "

"Damn snoop!" Kono charged him, and Hey tripped over his own feet trying to back up. He sat down hard. Kono was on him; Kono reached down and took a twist of Hey's shirt collar in one enormous brown hand, the back of Hey's waistband in the other.

Hey's feet pedaled air as Kono marched him across the lawn to the Datsun and threw him against the door. "Get out!" Kono slammed his huge hand down on the fender of the little car, his fingers spread wide, leaving a five-fingered dent in the thin sheet steel. Hey, now pale with terror, scrambled into the passenger side of the car and jerked the door closed behind him, rolling up the window as quickly as he could.

The little dog was standing in the middle of the yard, barking frantically in the general direction of the commotion, but afraid to look anyone in the eye. A flock of mynah birds flew down to join the chorus, yawking and strutting.

Ana charged across the yard; the dog yipped and scurried out of the way. "*Uoki,* Dan! You end up in jail again."

Anne-Marie stepped tentatively onto the porch behind Luki. Startled, he flinched away from her and dropped his sack. A dozen silvery little akule flopped out onto the porch.

Meanwhile Hey had squirmed into the driver's seat and started the car; he forced it into gear with a clang and popped the clutch, spinning the wheels on the sandy shoulder. The car lurched onto the highway, weaving erratically.

Anne-Marie ran to the edge of the road in front of Kono and watched the little red car dwindle in the distance. "I don't believe it! He forgot me."

"Who the hell is this?" Kono demanded of Ana, glowering at Anne-Marie.

"You leave her alone, she's okay," said Ana, stepping protectively in front of Anne-Marie.

Kono opened his palms and shrugged. "Sure she's okay, Ana. I just want to know who she is. And what's she doing with those cameras?"

"Nothing, she don't want to leave them in the car, that's all, Dan," Ana said quickly.

"Good idea. Some local boy might steal 'em," said Kono sarcastically.

"I can't believe he forgot me, that—pig," said Anne-Marie.

"You don't worry, Dan will take you home," said Ana. Kono looked at her incredulously, but she ignored him. Then, half a mile away, the red car skidded to a stop and began backing up along the narrow shoulder, trailing white coral dust. Anne-Marie sighed with relief. The car bounced to a stop a dozen yards away, keeping its distance from Kono.

Anne-Marie turned to Ana. "Thanks for everything."

"Maybe we see you again, huh?" Ana looked hopeful.

"I hope so." Anne-Marie marched determinedly toward the Datsun, clutching her cameras in both hands.

"Hehena!" Kono snorted. "Crazy haoles."

Anne-Marie tugged twice at the locked door before Hey remembered to unlock it from inside. As she slid into the seat she heard Luki shouting after them: "And don't come back, reporter, or my big bruddah ram an oar up you haole ass." He giggled gleefully.

Anne-Marie peeked at Hey as he busily accelerated away from the disastrous attempted interview. He refused to look at her. She looked away at the dry cool landscape of dead rock, holding her hands to her burning cheeks and trying not to laugh out loud.

12

Peter threaded the narrow back streets of Waikiki and turned into the narrow drive of the Halekulani Hotel. The old hotel's quiet gardens and bungalows had succumbed to the wrecker's shovel, victims of inflation and the state tax collector's distorted notion of "best use" of the land, but the rambling colonial main building remained. Peter left his car with the valet and went inside.

Visiting scientists and a few of the better-living reporters mingled with the other guests in the open lobby, with its floors of polished ohia and its pillars of dark lava. After the lavish Kahala Hilton, the Halekulani was the hotel of choice for island visitors with taste and means. Peter made a quick scout around and did not see Anne-Marie. He went to the desk. "Pardon me, is there a message for Peter Slater?"

"Are you a guest, sir?"

"No, I'm meeting someone for lunch here. Miss Anne-Marie Brand."

"Oh yes, I know the lady you mean," said the trim, middle-aged clerk. "She's with *Science Weekly,* isn't she? She and her friend over there?" He nodded in the direction of a small library off the main lobby, where Peter could see a short man with a blond ponytail hunched over a telephone, shielding its mouthpiece with his hand.

"I wouldn't know about him," said Peter. "But if she inquires, would you tell her I'm on the lanai?"

"Certainly, sir."

Peter walked to the terrace, doing his best to be casual while avoiding the people he recognized. There went the man from the *Times,* the affable gray eminence of science reporters, one of the few writers Peter could remember by sight. But he also recognized two or three of his colleagues from Europe and the east coast, and he was not here to talk physics. The sight of them reminded him that he had agreed to deliver a background talk on grand unified theories to interested science writers, sometime during the coming week. He hated these affairs, but public-relations efforts were essential to the survival of an institution like TERAC, and all staff members were expected to pitch in. He successfully eluded his acquaintances and reached the terrace bar.

The view from the Halekulani's Diamond Head Terrace was precisely that view which had become Waikiki's trademark, the silhouette of the volcano's eroded cone thrusting out into the blue Pacific, past a curve of yellow sand fringed by arching palms. Peter sat in the shade of a gnarled hau tree and sipped a gin and tonic, trying to imagine what it would have been like to have been here in the 1930s, Waikiki's heyday. He failed in the effort—all he could see over the edge of the terrace was bodies lying scattered on the beach, pale lumps of seared flesh, seeming victims of some unnatural disaster. In the thirties there had been only a handful of hotels near the beach; those packed bodies on the sand were both cause and effect of a grim metamorphosis. By shifting his gaze just a little to the left Peter could see, flatly lit by the midday sun, the ugly towers which daily sucked the tourists in and spewed them out again.

A man loomed over him. "Peter Slater? I'm Gardner Hey, *Science Weekly.*"

Peter squinted up at the reporter, who'd ambushed him out of the sun. Hey was already pulling out a chair, seating himself without invitation.

"Heard you were looking for Anne-Marie. Anything I can help you with? I think she's out there soaking up rays with the rest of the bodies." Hey leaned across the table and offered his hand.

Peter took it with the limpest possible enthusiasm. "Hello," he forced himself to say. For Anne-Marie's sake he avoided the brutal curtness he would normally have employed against such presumption.

"I guess you don't remember me," Hey said with sour satisfaction.

"Uh, didn't I see you at Martin's house last night?"

"Not what I meant. I interviewed you about intermediate vector bosons—because you predicted the precise mass of the Z-zero. But that was after they finally found it at CERN."

Peter was one of several theorists who'd suggested the mass of the Z-zero. He'd been interviewed by several reporters after the particle had been found, reporters who cared little for the scientific implications of a theory which allowed such precision; instead they'd wanted to know why the Europeans had beaten the Americans to a significant discovery yet again. "No, I don't remember you," said Slater bluntly.

"That's okay, I understand." Hey beamed. "Well, Slater, this is a real break for me."

"Oh?" Peter looked away and raised his gin and tonic to his lips; he took a sip and then became conscious of Hey staring thirstily at his glass. He lowered it and signaled the waitress.

"Yes, sir?"

"This gentleman will have . . . ?"

"Make it a Mai Tai, hon."

"My tab," said Peter. She nodded and left.

"Thanks, you can write that off, right?" Hey settled into his chair. "I've been looking for people who can help me get a really good deep background on the inside story at TERAC. Who could be better than you?"

Peter was silent a moment. Then he said, "What do you want to know? I'm giving a talk to a group of you people Monday night. Or Tuesday night, I forget which."

"Yeah, I know all about that. I've done my homework, Slater. In fact, I have a degree in physics myself, did you know that? NYU."

Peter murmured something wordless, meant to be polite. Degrees were less important than apprenticeships, affiliations. If Hey held a dozen advanced degrees he'd still be a reporter to Peter.

Hey leaned closer across the table. "I didn't see many Japanese at Edovich's place last night. How's he getting along with them? With Yamamura, especially. You've got the world's biggest proton linac out there—isn't it true Yamamura wants to use it to produce antiprotons and nothing else?"

"What do you mean?" Peter asked.

"Pure antiprotons, you know. For rocket fuel, or explosives, something like that."

"Sensei Yamamura heads the applications divison," Slater said stiffly. "I suppose he'd like to see more time devoted to his own projects. But he's only one vote on the planning board."

Hey produced a portable cassette recorder from his hip pocket and set it on the table between them. "You don't mind? So I get the facts straight. No quotes unless you say so."

Peter didn't know on what grounds to object, other than those of simple courtesy, which he doubted Hey understood. He shrugged at Hey. "I don't believe in secrets."

Hey grinned wolfishly. "Neither do I. So what would

Yamamura do with this stuff if he got his way? Build a Jap bomb?"

"The Japanese won't touch weapons technology, Mr. Hey. Don't tell me you're not aware of that."

"Oh, I know the party line. But they don't look like such moral types close up."

"Their reasons aren't moral, I'm sure. Why should they give their Asian markets a scare? Or give the Russians an excuse to get tough? What's in it for them, Hey? We're the ones who're pushing them to spend more on defense—after we dictated their constitution, which forbids it. It's a question that's brought down more than one government in the past twenty years."

Hey grunted. "All right. It was just a flyer. What about space?"

Peter said, "That's plausible, if you're writing fiction. Yamamura's allegiance is to MITI, the big bureaucracy that coordinates industrial effort and marketing. Energy is one of their main concerns. Space could help them there. And a Japanese space program could produce unique industrial products." Peter grinned coldly. "Sure, there's a plot for your next novel. But it's worse than science fiction, Hey; it's fantasy—there's no way a plasma of antiprotons can be stored, except in a ring like TERAC's. Hardly portable."

"Magnetic bottles . . . "

"In theory, but no one's ever demonstrated a magnetic bottle that doesn't leak. With antimatter a leak would be catastrophic."

"You can say that again!" said Hey with enthusiasm. "You'd need just about *that* much antimatter"—he held his thumb and index finger a couple of millimeters apart—"to blow up Honolulu!"

Peter looked at the chubby pink reporter with undisguised distaste. "I didn't mean that kind of catastrophe, Mr. Hey."

"Huh?" Hey shoved the tape recorder an inch closer to Peter. "What did you mean, exactly?"

"I meant that any small leak would violate the integrity of the container, short it out, render it useless. No disaster, just a harmless, expensive fizzle."

"Oh. Okay." Hey seemed disappointed to learn that Honolulu was safe after all. He tried another tack. "What about Edovich? What's he really doing with that I-particle stuff of his, that 'holy water'? I mean, just between you and me, Slater, I know the answers to these questions already. But I always like to confirm my facts with more than one source."

If Hey hoped Peter would be impressed by his inside knowledge—the nickname 'holy water' was never mentioned outside TERAC—he was disappointed; Peter was no longer listening to him.

"Whatever you say, certainly," Peter said absently. "Perhaps we should pick this up at another time—I'm not really the guy you want to talk to anyway, you know."

Hey turned to see what Slater was looking at, and saw Anne-Marie coming toward the terrace across the beach, long and brown and bare in a scrap of bikini. Among the parboiled tourists she was a creature of fire and gold, a salamander at home in the heart of the flame.

"I'm a theorist," Peter was saying, unaware that Hey had followed his glance. "I don't really have much to do with Edovich and the other experimenters. I've only been here a few weeks anyway." Abruptly Peter turned his gaze full on Gardner Hey. "I despise the term 'holy water,' Hey," he said vehemently. As suddenly as it had come, the passionate moment passed. The ocean behind Hey was dazzling with hot reflected light; Hey seemed an insubstantial shadow. Peter laughed then, forgetting to whom he was talking perhaps, or simply laughing at his own intensity, incomprehensible to the world at large. "Hell, in my theoretical opinion Edovich's collector should have blown itself to pieces months ago. Obviously it hasn't; obviously my theoretical opinion isn't worth a damn."

"Did I hear you right, Slater?" Hey was gaping at him. But Peter had risen from his chair. Anne-Marie caught sight of him and smiled, and came smiling to take his hand.

A curious thing happened then.

She merely leaned forward to give him a friendly kiss. Their lips touched; for an instant the universe was contained in their mingling breath. A charge, a shock of recognition, ran through them both, from brain to breast, to groin, to ground; for an instant, personal space and time were annihilated. They forgot who they were. They were lost without reference or definition on a strange beach, surrounded by strangers, and in that forgetful instant the nature of their relationship was transformed forever. Or at least for the moment.

They stepped apart quickly, awkwardly. Anne-Marie was now acutely conscious of her near nakedness in the string bikini she'd bought a half-hour earlier in one of the hotel boutiques; it had seemed playful at the time, now it seemed vulgar. Peter, afraid to look at her, started to blush.

"I'll be right back," she said. "Meet you . . . ?"

"Uh, front door?"

"Okay, five minutes." She walked quickly into the hotel, swinging her canvas tote off her shoulder as she went, eager to get back into her street clothes. She stared past Gardner Hey, acknowledging his presence only with heightened color in her cheeks.

"Beautiful woman," said Hey, when Peter returned to the table.

"Yeah," said Peter. "Well . . . it was"—he cleared his throat—"talking to you." He slipped his wallet from his trouser pocket and placed a five-dollar bill on the table, then walked away.

Hey sat alone for a moment, then tossed off the rest of his Mai Tai and got to his feet. He sauntered into the sprawling old hotel, swinging the cassette recorder idly from its wrist strap. He decided to reject the cassette, although it was only partially used; the interview with Slater had been brief and largely uninformative, but there was that one provocative remark. . . .

He went to the public telephones near the main door, took a pen from his pocket, and labeled the cassette with Slater's name and the date. He heard a squeak of tires outside and looked up to see the eager valet leap out of Slater's Triumph. Slater tipped him and sank into the driver's seat as Anne-Marie ran to meet the car and, with practiced agility, folded her long legs into the low seat. Slater put the car in gear and smoothly drove away.

Hey tapped his front teeth with the end of the ballpoint, wondering what use he could make of his part-time photographer and her penchant for finding new friends.

They ate lunch in Chinatown, fleeing Waikiki by mutual, unspoken agreement. Later they drove toward TERAC. So elated was Peter Slater that it seemed to him the little car drove itself, or flew itself, floating above the road, steering a sure daring path among tossing leaves of cane.

Peter slowed at the main gate's guardhouse, long enough for the young woman in guard's uniform to note the sticker on his bumper and wave him through with a smile.

"Is this some kind of restricted area?" Anne-Marie asked.

"Only because there are some potentially dangerous places, like any factory or power plant. Anyone can come in if there's someone to meet them. They give public tours, through Chauncey's office, in fact." Peter steered the car to a stop in the lot adjacent to Tomonaga Hall; the parking spot had his name painted neatly in black on a concrete billet.

"You're hot stuff around here, Professor Slater," Anne-Marie remarked.

"They flatter us," he said, but he was pleased that she'd noticed. "In lots of ways. Makes us feel pompous, talkative. They get more ideas out of us that way, and we get to make fools of ourselves a lot."

She laughed. He came around to her side of the car as she got out, and they linked arms. "Funny," she said, "you don't strike me as the type that needs coaxing. Hardly shy."

"You don't know what it's like from inside," he said, glancing at her. "Maybe shy's not the word. Cautious."

He walked her through the grounds, lushly planted with tropical and semitropical shrubs and trees from every major continent. Sunlight glittered from myriad rippling leaves in innumerable delicate shades of green; the black monoliths of the administration and office buildings rose up out of the tame jungle around them, a university in the middle of a botanical garden. "I didn't know anyone still built public places this beautiful," she said.

"We're lucky to work here," he said; it was a ritual response.

He took her to the low building that housed the auditorium and facilities for visitors and the press, named Dirac Hall in honor of the British mathematician whose theories had first suggested the existence of antimatter, in the 1930s. From the lobby windows they could see a panoramic view of the immense main ring, and the broad green lawns which sloped away from the south side of Tomonaga Hall, where Peter's office was located. Workmen were still putting the finishing touches on the facilities for Monday's ceremonies.

At the opposite end of the marble-floored lobby an elaborate visitors' display had been erected, a reconstruction of a section of the interior of the main ring. Big red and blue magnets were strung together end to end, actual prototypes of the magnets installed in the tunnel, and at each end of the display area photomurals had been erected to simulate the view below—a long succession of magnets stretching away in front and behind, eventually curving out of sight in the circular tunnel. A sign noted that the tunnel contained over a thousand such magnets in its nineteen-kilometer circumference.

Anne-Marie was disappointed. Meticulous as the display was, it managed only to suggest how much more impressive the real thing must be. "Why can't we go into the tunnel?" she asked.

"Nobody can when the ring's operating. See this pipe in here?" Peter pointed to a section of stainless-steel tubing visible in the gap between two of the huge magnets; the pipe was oval in cross section, about a dozen centimeters wide, and ran lengthwise through the magnets—one could imagine it circling back on itself only after having traversed the entire circuit of the ring. "This is the vacuum chamber that contains the circulating bunches of protons and antiprotons. It's really the heart of the whole machine. The purpose of these big red magnets is to keep the particles focused, tightly bunched together—the blue magnets steer them in a curve, keep them inside the pipe. The point is, when you force a charged particle to go around a corner in a magnetic field it shoots out radiation sideways—like the headlight on a toy locomotive when it's running around under a Christmas tree. Synchrotron radiation can run the gamut from gamma rays to visible light, depending on the machine and the kind of particles and their energy. And in this machine they're energetic! So you wouldn't want to be in the tunnel when the ring's operating. Plus beam collisions also produce radiation, of course—that's what they're for. And whatever the beam hits gets hot fast."

"I know it's stupid, a naive thing to say"—Anne-Marie hugged her bare arms—"but all this talk of radiation kind of gives me the creeps."

"Lots of people have that reaction. Just keep in mind that an accelerator is nothing like a nuclear reactor. No fission, no waste to speak of. They have to pour energy *into* this ring to keep it operating. If it ever gets into trouble, it switches itself off. The operators don't have to try to stop a chain reaction."

"Gardner said there's a nuclear reactor on the site," said Anne-Marie.

"True." Peter hesitated, frustrated by the difficulty of communicating concepts that were basically different, not fine distinctions at all, but which had become inextricably confused in the public mind by the ubiquitous word "radiation." "For the amount of grief it's caused the TERAC people I'm sure they're eager for the day when they can get rid of the thing and get their electricity from space satellites or ocean thermal stations or volcanoes or any other damn thing. I guess what I'm saying is that the reactor isn't really part of TERAC—it just happens to be at the other end of our power line. It's a good little reactor, one of a kind, safe, clean, all that—but I'm not going to defend it. I happen to think the whole nuclear power business is an unfortunate and inelegant application of technology, but I also think . . . Well, hell, it's not my business; that's what I think."

Anne-Marie looked at him speculatively; was he saving his opinions because he thought she wouldn't approve of them, or because he wasn't sure what they were? "Still, accelerators are dangerous too," she said, prodding him.

"Not to the public. And accelerators are a lot less dangerous than playing around on mountaintops in thunderstorms, the way they did in the twenties and thirties. Men have been killed by lightning doing high-energy physics."

"You sound as if you admire that."

"Knowledge is what makes us human. Knowledge and freedom."

Very Protestant, she thought—for he'd revealed that much of his history to her—very New Testament: Ye shall know the truth, and the truth shall make you free. An impossible idealist, that's who she'd snagged here. "I'll stop being superstitious," she said, smiling. "So what's the purpose of all this hardware, Professor? Is there more to this tour?"

"Feel like a long walk? A couple of miles?"

"It's a beautiful day for it."

"Then let's walk around to the hall where they've got the I-particle collector set up. That's the star experiment these days."

Thirty spokes
Share one hub.

Adapt the nothing therein to the purpose in hand, and you will have the use of the cart. Knead clay in order to make a vessel. Adapt the nothing therein to the purpose in hand, and you will have the use of the vessel. . . .
    Thus what we gain is something, yet it is by virtue of Nothing that this can be put to use.

—Lao Tzu

An access road meandered around the grassy perimeter of the TERAC ring, sometimes running inside the berm, sometimes outside it, sometimes along its crest. Though easily navigable by trucks and heavy equipment, the road, like all other features of the research facility, was carefully designed to offset the usual institutional monotony typical in big government projects. Each of TERAC's outlying buildings was of a different height and mass, made of clustered pentagonal columns of dark rock and smoked glass. The ring itself was uneven in height, and had the natural geometry of the eroded craters that everywhere pock the Hawaiian Islands. Red mud kicked up by frequent rains blended and obscured the boundary between walls and natural earth, so that the buildings had the appearance of giant boulders washed out of the ground. Inside the ring stood lakes edged with papyrus and bamboo—cooling ponds for the helium refrigerators and electricity-generating reactor.

Anne-Marie tossed her hair and let the warm afternoon sunshine fall on her upturned face. She felt as if she were alone with Peter in the midst of an Oriental pleasure park;

she would not have been surprised to see peacocks and tame deer wandering in the compound.

"I remember Gardner calling TERAC an 'overgrown peashooter,' " said Anne-Marie. "He was so wrong. This place is a work of art."

"Maybe he meant protons and antiprotons—that's usually written 'p' and 'bar-p' "—Peter drew a $\bar{p}$ in the air with his finger "—if he has a sense of humor."

"Not Gardner. Contempt seems to be a reflex with him. Though he does try to be nice, in his way."

"Known him long?"

"Chauncey introduced us a week ago. But tell me about TERAC."

Peter was pleased. "Well, 'peashooter' wouldn't be a bad analogy for certain modes of operation," he said. "For example, when we shoot a beam of particles at a fixed target, like a scrap of dense metal or a tank of liquid hydrogen. The linear accelerator that feeds into the main ring works that way all the time, but for now the main ring is set up differently. It shoots protons and antiprotons at each other. Three bunches of each are stored in the vacuum chamber, circulating in opposite directions at regular intervals and at precisely the same rate. So there are six evenly spaced locations around the ring where collisions occur, and that's where the six experimental halls are placed." Peter pointed to the tops of the various halls, some nearby, some in the distance. "Now whenever subatomic particles collide, something interesting flies out of the wreck," he continued. "Experimenters who want a great many particle interactions, lots of debris—mesons, hyperons, antiparticles—tend to favor fixed-target configurations, Gardner's 'peashooters.' It's hard to miss something when the target atoms are just sitting there, packed close together. But a lot of the collision energy is wasted pushing the pieces around—like a cue ball, all its energy goes into breaking the rack."

Peter's enthusiasm grew as he became more specific. "When a proton meets an antiproton, though—whenever any particle of ordinary matter meets its own antiparticle—something interesting happens. They cease to exist! They annihilate each other utterly. All the mass of both particles goes into creating a blob of hot dense nothing that just sits there for the tiniest slice of no time, having no inclination to go off in any particular direction or to turn into any particular thing." He paused. "Well, that's hardly accurate, there are some interesting constraints . . . "

"Never mind," she said. "I think I get the picture."

"It's like a miniature version of the universe at the moment of creation," he said. "Anything can happen—given enough energy." Peter smiled. "I. I. Rabi once said that nothing in quantum theory would prevent a grand piano from flying out of such a collision. He wasn't too happy about the lack of precision."

"And the particles in TERAC have lots of energy?"

"A very great deal. They're headed right for each other at close to the speed of light; by Special Relativity that makes them enormously massive. They've got lots of plain old Newtonian momentum. All that mass and energy is available for the creation of new particles, like the I-particle."

"No pianos yet?"

"Not yet," he laughed. "But who knows?" They had arrived at Hall 30, west of Tomonaga Hall and higher up the slope of the Waianaes. A branch of the access road ran down behind the dark building, which rose only slightly above the berm. "Most of this hall is deep underground, because the ground is higher," said Peter. "We have to take an elevator to get to the control room." He looked at her bare arms. "It's going to be cold down there. I should have remembered to warn you."

She shrugged. "I'll call help if I have to."

Buried deep underground, the steel and cement and plastic and copper guts of the monster obeyed an aesthetic of their own. They stepped out of the elevator into the garish refrigerated pit. Anne-Marie stared around her. "I take back what I said about a work of art. This is one of the ugliest places I've been in recent years." She squeezed her goose-pimpled arms to her waist.

"Don't tell that to the troglodytes," he replied. "They've been known to turn savage."

He led her to the control platform. They were greeted at the top of the steps by Frank McDonald. "What can I do for you people?" he asked cautiously; he'd never seen either of them.

But McDonald recognized Slater's name immediately when Peter introduced Anne-Marie and himself; McDonald in turn introduced his colleague Jorgen Stern, who shook hands with Peter with vigorous enthusiasm.

McDonald said, "Sometimes it seems we're running the dullest experiment in the place. Nothing to analyze, like the other detectors—we just get to count what we collect. Cy Sherwood is the only guy who has any fun—at least he gets to unload the collector. But he built it, so I guess that's fair."

"And that's it?" Slater asked, indicating the image in one of the big TV monitors mounted high on the racks against the shield wall.

"You bet. Looks like a big lens, doesn't it? The doughnut goes right through the middle of it. Here, take a look." McDonald stepped to the wall of instruments and switched on another video screen, one that displayed a computer-generated schematic of the collector's interior.

Sherwood's I-particle trap was designed to guide a newly created particle out of the vacuum chamber and gently to rest; to provide each positively charged I-particle with a single orbiting electron, so that it formed the nucleus of an atom; and finally to lock this bizarre atom (as massive as an atom of uranium) into a chemical bond: joined with ordinary atoms of hydrogen and oxygen, the "superhydrogen" atom formed a lopsided water molecule.

This cuckoo molecule, this ugly duckling of molecules, was left to jostle among billions of its mundane fellows until the day came when enough princely I-particles had been gathered to warrant boiling off the dross and releasing them from their molecular bonds.

"That's the proton-antiproton collision point, right there in the middle," said McDonald, tapping the glass screen to indicate the center of the collector. The computer-generated diagram showed that inside the lenticular chamber twelve silicon crystals radiated away from the vacuum chamber like spokes from a wheel. "The crystals act as wave guides to channel the I-particles into little magnetic bottles at the perimeter of the collector. Strong fields sweep out all the other junk in there, and incidentally give us the data we need to figure out what's going on inside the machine."

"Very neat," said Peter, admiring the simplicity of the experimental design. "Change in net charge distribution tells you when you've caught one?"

"Yep. We get about five per second in each bottle, something under four thousand a minute for the whole machine. The bottles are automatically flushed with ionized water vapor, then neutralized with monatomic hydrogen. The vapor condenses on these crystal plates. Cy comes in on the night shift and blows the condensate into these little pressurized vials, then draws the whole thing off with this rig here." McDonald patted the long bench-mounted rod assembly that faced the collector's access port, resembling the breech of a cannon. "And there's your holy water."

"*Holy* water?" asked Anne-Marie, for the first time interrupting the arcane dialogue. She cocked her head at McDonald.

He looked flustered. "That's what Martin—Dr. Edovich—calls the water that contains superhydrogen atoms—atoms with I-particles in their nuclei. But probably we shouldn't use that expression. . . . "

"Because the public might find it offensive," said Jorgen Stern, amused at his colleague's discomfiture. "As I do."

"Dr. Edovich has a Catholic sense of humor," Anne-Marie remarked. "But don't worry, your secrets are safe with me. I'm a photographer, not a reporter." She slipped the older Canon out of her string-bag purse and held it up for McDonald to see. "Okay with you?"

"I guess." He grinned awkwardly at the camera. She raised it to her eye, aimed, and snapped three frames in rapid succession.

"Mind if I take some other pictures?" she asked, looking around the immense interior of the hall.

"Stay on this side of the shield wall," McDonald said. "If you tried to get into the ring you'd dump the beams and get us all in real trouble."

"I'll be good." Anne-Marie set off to wander around the room, peering and crouching in search of dramatic compositions, while Peter and McDonald continued to chat. Finally she returned to the platform. "A strange labyrinth," she said. "And I'm freezing, Peter, just as you promised."

"Okay, we'll get out of here," Peter said. "Thanks for letting us take up your time, Frank. Jorgen."

"Our pleasure. Come back soon," said McDonald.

"It would be delightful to talk to you at length some day," Stern said solemnly.

The experimenters turned back to their monitors.

Peter and Anne-Marie were already well on their way to the surface when Frank McDonald noted the peculiar gamma-ray burst the detectors had recorded while they'd been talking with the visitors. "Cosmic rays again, Jorgen?" he asked idly, making a pencil notation on the printout so that the event could be easily located in the record.

"What else?" asked the Dane. "But not earthshaking, would you say?"

"No, hardly that," McDonald agreed.

The afternoon stretched toward evening, and Peter and Anne-Marie found themselves having dinner at a north-shore restaurant without having bothered to discuss the options together. The ono was grilled perfectly, the

California Chardonnay was better than passable, the sunset was spectacular. On the way to the car, he asked her straight out: "Will you come home with me now?"

Her answer was equally straightforward. "I won't be a guest in your house yet, Peter. Not yet. I want to be with you in no man's land. Not your place. Not mine. We'll pretend the room is Crete, or Avalon, or the Misty Isles—or nowhere but where it is, a funny little hotel."

He said nothing, but shifted down, accelerated smoothly into the gathering dusk, then reached over and tentatively squeezed her hand.

13

Cy Sherwood ran his knobby fingers along the edge of the kitchen table, feeling the ridges of thread that emerged from the worn plasticized cloth. The setting sun's last warm rays penetrated the screen door and reflected from the tabletop into his watery eyes. The odor of plumeria was heavy in the air.

The sweet smell reminded Sherwood of his wife's perfume; she'd died only two months after they'd moved to the island, when the little house in Mililani Town was still only half furnished. That was four years ago. He'd left the rest of the household goods in storage when they did finally arrive; he was accustomed to bare houses.

Sherwood's head was bowed. His thoughts were of little besides the ache in his chest. Last night the pain had gotten so bad he'd stayed home from the job for the first time he could remember. He'd awakened from a feverish sleep with a creeping fear: he must work or die. He spent the day in bed, resting as much as he could, afraid to drink too much of the cough medicine he'd been treating himself with—"GI gin," alcohol laced with codeine. Finally as evening approached he got out of bed, shaved his sparse gray whiskers, and combed his short gray-blond hair. He put on khaki trousers, a plaid shirt, and old work shoes. Then he forced himself to eat a TV dinner, a Salisbury steak that tasted like warm damp cardboard. He left the smeared aluminum tray on the kitchen table—and now he sat still, resting again, giving thought to each breath. It would not do to arrive early. All must appear as usual. Everything was normal—it had to be.

Masses of dark, long-needled ironwoods bent and sighed in the breeze, black against the white sand which glowed with phosphorescent brightness under the newly risen full moon. The beach curved for miles to the north and west, past the antenna farm and the military's resort cottages at Bellows Air Force Station. Big waves, midnight blue and silver in the moonlight, rolled in from the channel.

Clearly visible each time it crested the waves was a twenty-foot rubber Zodiac moving slowly toward the beach, with three men aboard. Its twin fifty-horsepower Mercury outboards gurgled and grumbled in low gear. Dan Kono, keeping to the shadows of the ironwoods, took a big swallow from a can of Primo beer as he watched the boat slide in over the surf.

The driver killed the power as the boat grounded in a surge of foam, and the other two men leaped from the prow, pulling the lightweight craft farther up on the sand. The driver stayed with the boat as the others trudged through the fine deep sand, up a steep, vine-covered dune, and into the black shadows of the trees. They spoke briefly; something changed hands. Then one man ran quickly back to the Zodiac while the other stayed behind and watched.

The driver jumped from the boat; together the two men shoved the stiff rubber craft back into the water, got it turned around, rammed it over the breakers. They clambered aboard, slick as frogs. The driver pulled himself to his feet behind the midships control housing, and the twin Mercs fired instantly. With a contemptuously loud roar the boat leaped forward, racing back out to sea, slapping into the incoming waves with reports like pistol shots.

Kono squeezed the empty beer can flat with the fingers of his right hand and let it drop noiselessly onto the thick carpet of feathery needles. He leaned against the tree's rough bark and waited quietly. After a moment he heard the slap, slap of rubber go-aheads.

The man passed, and Kono stepped out of the shadows behind him. "Say, brah—"

The man turned instantly, his bearded face pale in the moonlight, a blade glittering in his hand. But the edge of Kono's open hand slammed into the man's wrist and the knife flew spinning into the darkness of the trees. The man cried out in pain and bent over, hugging his arm to his waist.

Kono looked at him silently. "Chry not make ass, Luki," he said with disgust. "Maybe next time I break you arm."

"What da fuck, Dan!" Luki gasped. "What you—"

"Lucky fo' you I'm not da police," said Kono, cutting him off. "I could see you comin' all the way from da reef. Beautiful night you picked, nice full moon."

The shiny black boat was still clearly visible against the starry eastern sky, the snarl of its outboards still plainly audible above the surf.

Luki bared his teeth. "So wha?" he said defiantly. "Job's all done." He straightened, still rubbing his wrist.

"Yeah, and here's da evidence that *you* did it." Kono stooped and picked up a small plastic-wrapped bundle from the ground at Luki's feet, where it had fallen when he turned. Inside the misty plastic film was a wad of bills. Kono stuck the package of money into the waistband of his cutoffs, letting his ample belly settle over it, hiding it from view. "Dumb ass."

"What you gonna do wi' that, Dan?" Luki asked nervously.

"Make sure you don't spend it anytime soon, little brah. Da kine *friends* of yours . . . Could be marked. All we need." Kono grabbed Luki's shoulders and shook him hard, looking at him sternly. "Shit, dumb ass."

Luki looked at his big brother meekly. Then a hint of a grin crept onto his face.

Kono turned Luki around roughly, but without anger. He settled his huge arm over Luki's shoulders. "Let's go hide this up in the brush and get us some beers, little brah."

Penny Harper parked in a pool of light from a streetlamp, outside Hall 30. She saw Cy Sherwood just entering the building ahead of her. He held the elevator door open until she caught up. "How are you feelin', Cy?" she asked, joining him in the narrow elevator cab. She hoped he didn't detect the disappointment in her greeting; though he must already know what a hurry she was in to get somewhere in her career, he didn't need to know that she thought he was in her way.

"I'm fit as a fiddle, Miss Penny, thank you much. 'Course my ears are still ringin', so don't take this dive bomber down too fast, okay?"

She grinned tightly and stabbed the down button. "You had us worried when you skipped out last night. You're not going to give us all the flu, are you?"

"Mighty sweet of you to be concerned, hon, but it's just a little cold, that's all." Sherwood smiled slyly at the chunky young woman. "Frank stood in for me, didn't he? He must have kept you pretty good company."

"It was Hiro, not Frank," Penny said grumpily. "The trap wasn't unloaded last night. Martin said it could wait a night. If you hadn't shown up tonight, I'd have done it myself."

"Sorry to disappoint you," he said dryly. He visibly stifled a deep cough. Penny looked at him sidelong, but said nothing. They rode the elevator in silence, a strangely matched pair, the I-particle team's oldest and youngest members. Though Penny Harper's Ph.D. was only a year old, she knew that Cy Sherwood had no degree at all, not even a high school diploma. He even enjoyed correcting people who called him Doctor—"It's just plain Mister," he'd say with a grin, watching them squirm as they wrestled with their prejudices—for he'd never bother to correct them until he'd sufficiently impressed them with his quirky genius.

As Penny had heard the story, Sherwood had never collected a diploma because he was congenitally unable to pass a written test. It was said to be a miracle that he possessed a driver's license. Yet he supposedly shared the kind of mechanical genius Eskimos were said to have, the kind of intelligence that, presented with a pocket watch or a transistor radio for the very first time and knowing nothing of its purpose, could nevertheless strip it to its individual parts and quickly reassemble it in working order.

Scuttlebutt was that only chance and the United States Army had brought the reticent lad—son of an Oklahoma water-well driller and part-time preacher—to the attention of the men who made a physicist of him. Sherwood was a very young private in the Army Corps of Engineers when he was sent to Eniwetok, and once he'd grasped what everybody was doing out there on the flat yellow atoll he'd entered right into the spirit of things. Immediately after each test shot he'd lay bets with his buddies on the weapon's measured yield in equivalent tons of TNT. To his fellow GIs this game was like a baseball pool, only less scientific: there were no slugging averages and no inside dope to go on, only the ambiguous evidence of their own seared eyeballs, so to them the results of the pool had little more significance than a number drawn from a hat. The yield figures were supposed to be top secret, of course, but the younger scientists were mostly contemptuous of military secrecy and would pass the figures on to any enlisted man whose interest seemed sincere.

After half a dozen shots it became apparent that Cy Sherwood was going to win every time. His buddies refused his bets, so he told them his secret: he'd found out how much pressure it took to crush an empty beer can (using a medical scale and a "prepared sample" can), and during the set-up for each shot he'd staked out half a dozen beer cans at known distances from ground zero. Then, after each test, he'd volunteer to drive the instrument recovery teams in, and as his jeep jounced along through the coral dust of some devastated islet he'd observe what the blast had done to his beer cans. The degree of tin-can-crushing as a function of distance allowed him to calculate the overpressure, the force of the shock wave. That and a few other factors gleaned from books and conversations with the scientists allowed him to reckon the yield. When the unofficial figures became available, they always came close to confirming his guesses.

Word of Sherwood's ingenuity and accuracy got back to the senior scientists. Word also got to the provost marshal, a man with no sense of humor, who was obsessed with security and who wanted to "make an example" of Sherwood. But the scientists made another kind of example of him, arranging to have him sent to Cal Berkeley at government expense; there he flunked every exam but nevertheless amazed his professors with his extraordinary, stubbornly plainspoken mental gifts.

After five years he'd earned no degree, but he was in on the ground floor at the nearby Lawrence Livermore Laboratory, which was just starting up. There, some years later, he met and befriended a pugnacious, brilliant, and secretly bewildered youth named Martin Edovich.

Penny knew that at least one Nobel Prize before the one Martin Edovich was expected to collect had been earned with a Sherwood-built experiment.

The elevator door opened onto the cold concrete cavern.

On the work platform Stern and McDonald rose quickly, eager to leave. "Nice to see you back, Cy," McDonald called as Sherwood and Harper climbed the stairs. "We were afraid you'd caught pneumonia."

"Feelin' strong as a horse, Frank," said Sherwood.

Penny saw him avoid the younger man's eyes, looking past him to the bank of monitors. "Anything worth mentioning?" Sherwood asked.

McDonald glanced at Penny.

She wrinkled her nose. "More of your cosmic rays?"

"We've had some anomalous gamma ray bursts," McDonald told Sherwood. "Very brief. Nothing we can pin down. They're tagged in the log." He gestured to the pile of printouts on Penny's desk. "They don't seem to be related to the operation of the collector in any way we can determine."

"I've been thinking about that very point, Frank, and I'm not so sure—" Penny began, but she was interrupted by Sherwood.

"Unless you have somethin' solid, let's leave it to the theoretikers," he said impatiently. "Long as the machine's workin', our job's done." Sherwood was notoriously prejudiced against speculation in the absence of cold facts; he considered data collection the only legitimate occupation of an experimental team.

Penny said nothing, but went to the lockers and began pulling her lab coat on over her thick wool sweater. McDonald and Stern hung up their coats and said their goodbyes. Penny slipped her film badge into her breast pocket; she went to her wooden desk and laid out tonight's snack, a couple of pieces of soggy pepperoni-and-mushroom pizza left over from her hasty dinner at the Pizza Hut in Wahiawa.

Sherwood too bundled himself against the cold, in his old olive brown cardigan and starched, fraying lab coat. His chest cough seized him again. He repressed it, and the effort must have cost him something; he laid a big wrinkled hand on the breech of the collecting rig and leaned wearily against it, letting his eyes close for a moment.

Penny watched him, concerned and resentful—he was

determined to do everything himself, even if it killed him. She knew he loved the thing he'd built—maybe it was all he had left to love, that machine poised in stasis behind the radiation-shield wall, subtly colored, its yellow bronze and white stainless steel blending in concentric circles, smoothly textured, cold, untouchable.

Sherwood stood stiffly erect. He walked to the instruments and switched on the monitor that showed the interior of the collector; on the screen, magnified a thousand times, condensation crystals shimmered in blue light. Sherwood began running his checklist, testing the teleoperator controls one at a time, confirming that the rods and grapples which were to reach into the heart of the collector were functioning perfectly.

A single slip or falter and the fragile condensation plates could shatter, leaving the precious droplets of holy water to disperse and evaporate in the cold, dry air.

14

The curtains billowed hugely into the room. The breeze that passed through the glass slats cooled their hot skin, and for a moment Anne-Marie considered getting up and cranking the shutters closed. Instead, she pushed closer into Slater's side, as if impelled by the fitful gusts.

He moved his hand, lightly ruffling the hairs on her arm, the fine hairs that glowed softly in the dark, by the backlight of distant windows seen through the curtains' rough weave. The hairs stood erect from her chilled and goose-pimpled skin. Neither of them spoke.

She watched him like a cat from ten centimeters away, saw the surface of his eye glistening with reflected light, but could not see into it, because he would not look at her. His face was a perfect sculpture, but there were tiny, tiny lines around the corners of his eye, fine cracks where acid rain had etched the marble.

And yet—and yet. The words of Rilke's "Elegy" came to her in the tropical night: *Jeder Engel ist schrecklich,* "Every angel is terrible." He had appeared when she least expected to encounter him, was least prepared to resist him. The backs of her long thighs ached with his perfection, the twin ridges of muscle which ascended her abdomen to her rib cage ached with the perfection of him.

> *If the archangel came now, the perilous one,*
> *from the back of the stars, but one step lower and to-*
> *ward us,*
> *our own high-beating heart would slay us. Who are*
> *you?*

An hour ago she knew him—by his life story and by her willingness to make a myth of him. In the erupting crucible of their desire all such knowledge had been annihilated. They were creatures of polar flesh and bone, fitting perfectly, perfectly fitting, not fit to exist outside this midnight room. How could they reconstruct their lives when the sun rose?

Is that why he would say nothing, would not look at her? Perhaps she had frightened him, for it was plain that this time was not real and must vanish in the blink of an eye. If reality were made of such stuff, men and women, lacking eternal life, must go mad of despair. Memories, luckily, are short, and even fear is on our side, for the fear of imminent loss drips acid on perfection.

She moved a little away from him, rolling onto her back, arching her feet with a little delicious secret stretch of sore muscles. There are other islands where the goddamned rosy-fingered dawns are not so inevitable. She remembered the gray winters on Crete, the bright fragrant springs, the hot dull summers, those autumn days when the skies are drained of color but gleam like polished carbon steel. . . .

The stones of the ruins crumbled away like yellow cheddar.

There were times when she'd been tempted to taste the rock. What was the flavor of a roasted paving stone from the great court at Phaistos, say a bit of limestone from the very crust where the southeast corner had fallen away down the steep hillside in some earthquake? Would that stone have the flavor of bulls' blood? Of spilled oil and ruby Cretan wine? Of fire and slaughter? Would the cheese be a bit past its prime, or were thirty-four centuries about right to cure it to its peak?

She'd always liked to let herself go a little mad at Phaistos, it was so clearly the best, cool and aloof on top of its hill. It was a high city, an acropolis, and one felt a heady freedom there, with the cool breeze sighing in the dark pines north of the central court. (Just here they'd found the Disk, the never-deciphered, clearly meaningful wafer pressed with strange symbols, looking good enough to bite—a giant chocolate-chip cookie, an awesome hieroglyphic eucharist.) Phaistos got a good bit of tourist business, but thankfully nothing like the twittering rush at Knossos, and whenever her head was really big, whenever coming down off a champagne high required getting even higher, up where she could see the peaceful farms and villages of her Middle Earth, she took the bus to Phaistos. The plain of Mesara stretched away beneath the jagged spine of the island; across it to the north rose Ida with its cuneiform black stain, Mavros Spilios, the cave where Zeus was born.

But in fact Anne-Marie spent most of her time among the fashionable villages of the north coast, Ayios Nikolaos and its sainted fellows, where the discotheques ground on until daybreak and the tourist shops beseeched one to "Rend a Car, Scooter, Bicycle, and Donkeys too!" with the hearty reminder that "In Addition you may shop all sorts of Drinks."

Which is what she'd spent much of her time doing, or rather allowing others to do for her, meanwhile pursuing a haphazard career in photography. What she occasionally got *Stern* to pay her for, or *Paris-Match,* or any of a dozen lesser sensation-mongering rags, was not news, but gossip. Anne-Marie was a part-time paparazza, one of those who make a living selling pictures of the rich and famous—preferably scandalous pictures, but anything vaguely insinuating would do in a pinch.

What she didn't earn from photography came in the monthly check from Paris. To stretch her budget further she sometimes found it convenient to rely upon the kindness of strangers.

It was fun for a while, even honest in its way. She peddled snaps of Liza and Calvin and Roy and Rudi and Katja (once of shriveled Jackie), and occasionally some aging roué would see himself pictured in the international gossip pages, caught with his pants down, so to speak, and he would chide Anne-Marie for her lack of discretion. But few of her victims ever got really angry. To begin with, she never deceived them as to her purpose. And her company itself was compensation. Sighing, her hapless subjects reflected upon her wit, her beauty, her education (few jet-set photographers were versed in the comparative history of modern European languages), and their own desires to possess her.

Her life seemed nothing but one long cocktail party of shifting venue—here on some sun-drenched, whitewashed terrace overlooking the sea, there on the bright blue sea itself, aboard a wide-beamed sailing yacht—always with a drink in one hand and a Canon in the other. She went through three cameras in two years, losing them to salt corrosion. The last one she managed to buy with her own honest gains in the photography business. Her photos were often remarkably well focused, considering.

She tried to despise herself; the situation seemed to require it. But she succeeded only part of the time. She was young, and full of recuperative vigor. She was free of the Sorbonne and of her mother; life held no essential restraints. Her activities hurt no one, so far as she knew.

This phase of her life was ended by trivia, by an accretion of minute but telling observations. When she'd arrived on Crete her skin had been as smooth as a ten-year-old's, with the dry delicate texture—the smooth nontexture, really—of a pre-adolescent girl who happened to have spent a summer in the sunshine. But after two years in the Aegean her salt-cured fingers could feel the pebbly surface when they brushed her cheeks. At the age of twenty-three and a half she sniffed the first cool whiff of mortality, her own.

And within a very short time her endless party had begun to look very much like a *Totentanz,* a dance of death. Previously Anne-Marie's self-disgust had been assumed, a mere patina of pretended decadence laid over healthy basic appetites—but her new fears were real. Her father visited her often in her nightmares.

She met Charlie Phelps at a party at the Minos Hotel in Ayios Nikolaos, where his yachting party had tied up for the week. Charlie had family money, an assured future, a modicum of charm. And of course he fell for her instantly (he was the type), and he was noisy and insistent about it, pursuing her from the hotel to the shadows of the grape arbor outside the taverna up the beach. He caught up with her only because she let him; half a year earlier she would have brushed him off with a laugh. Now, capitulating to her fears, stifling the screams of her daemon, she agreed, before the moon had risen, to marry him.

Outside the Crater Hotel the full moon was high, its light filling the room, filtering through the mesh curtains. Anne-Marie moved off the bed and went into the bathroom. When she came back Peter was looking at her. She sat on the bed, curled her long legs under her, and reached out a slender finger to touch him in the hollow of his throat, as if to tickle him into speech.

He studied her. "I was afraid," he said after a moment. "Afraid it would be a masque. Everything was too perfect." He was silent a moment. "But—it's still perfect. And now I'm afraid that . . . "

"Hush. I know." She rested her palm on his chest. "I knew what you were thinking."

"I forgot." He smiled. "You told me all about your psychic powers."

"Of course," she said lightly. "And I don't mind if you're a skeptic, either. After all, you *are* a Pisces with Libra rising. If you weren't half a dreamer, half a judge, I'd have to be skeptical of myself."

"How do you know I'm a whatsis with the other thing rising?"

"My reasoning is perfectly circular," she confidently replied. "From the way you behave."

He chuckled. He took her hand and carried it to his lips.

"Oh, no," she said archly. "Let's put it to an empirical test. Was your birthday between February twenty-first and March twentieth?"

"March eleventh. Good guess—one out of twelve," he said, belittling her.

"Would *you* bet on those odds?"

He smiled. "Good guess. Like I said."

"You behave exactly as theory predicts—the super-skeptic, but oh, so charming. If you didn't, I'd have to doubt the theory, of course."

"Hmph. You're stealing my lines. 'Theory' indeed."

"Ancient hermetic wisdom, if you prefer. But I see by your increasingly scarlet aura that all this superstitious talk is making you angry." She leaned toward him until her lips were a few centimeters from his. The wings of her hair shadowed his face. "Did anyone ever tell you you're beautiful when you're angry?"

He burst out laughing. She kissed his open mouth hungrily, muffling him. In self-defense he took handfuls of her hair and pulled her face away, gasping for breath. She smirked at him, her lips wet and gleaming.

"I wanted to talk," he protested. Outside, the trade winds sighed.

"Make a choice," she whispered, still smirking, her voice husky. "Are you for life, Professor Slater?" She rolled a knee over his stomach. Her body said, Talk to me this way.

15

If, just as the metalworker was about to cast something, the metal leapt up and said, "I am determined to become the finest sword ever made," the smith would certainly consider he had got hold of some sinister material. . . .

—KWANG TZU

Small motors whirred as the long rods slowly withdrew from the access port. Expressionless, unblinking, Cy Sherwood stared at the television monitors, his fingers delicately nudging and tweaking the rheostats of his control panel. Steel forceps, wreathed in tendrils of milky vapor which flowed from the collector's cold innards, appeared in the opening, gripping a tiny crystalline vial with dumb, gentle pressure.

Penny Harper looked on, bored, more interested in—tempted by—her salvaged pizza. She made an effort to contemplate the stacks of computer data she'd plowed through the night before, and the newly accumulated figures, and she wondered what she was going to do to keep herself awake all night.

The interesting anomalies had proved too parsimonious in detail to allow any intelligent guesses: here and there an elevated reading at extremely high frequencies, but no correlating readings in particle counts, and thus not a clue as to what, if anything, was going on. Noise, just noise, that's what it would turn out to be. Unexplained, unexplainable, and unimportant.

The stainless-steel plug swung into the access port, and the bronze cover of the I-particle collector fell into place with a solid clunk, sealing itself with hydraulic clamps. The forceps, confined inside their clear plastic tube, were carried back through the shield wall. Sherwood's eyes flickered away from the monitor screen to the glittering object itself, the precious vial. Travelers hit their stops, and the rig quivered to a halt.

Inside the box, remote sensors—counters, a snorkel lens—reached out to within a few millimeters of the crystal vial and sniffed it cautiously; coached by Sherwood's moving fingers on the control knobs, the steel forceps slowly rotated the vial for inspection. Its image filled the big TV screen. The apparent viscosity of the fluid inside it was an effect of magnification; its bright blue color was similarly an artifact of the television circuitry—to touch, taste, sight, or smell, the substance in the vial was indistinguishable from ordinary water.

Sherwood was satisfied with his inspection; he allowed the sensors to retract. He shoved his left hand into one of the thick black plastic gloves fitted through the workbox's glass wall. He pulled a steel container into position under the forceps; it was the size of an ordinary Thermos bottle, but it had a double outer wall of stainless steel, an inner sheath of inch-thick lead, and a padded core of Styrofoam. With the fingers of his right hand Sherwood manipulated the forceps controls, guiding them to insert the crystal vial firmly into a crevice in the padded interior of the container: once in place the vial was held immobile.

"That's got her," he said with satisfaction. They were the first words he'd spoken in over an hour.

His face contorted in a grimace, and his right hand trembled on the controls, but his fingers did not slip. For a moment he was rigid, his eyes closed, his face drained of color.

"Cy?" Penny watched him for a second, then started to rise.

Sherwood blinked and let his breath out in a long sigh. Quickly he steered the open forceps away from the vial, ignoring Penny. She sat down again.

He pushed his right hand into the other glove in the box wall, picked up the steel lid of the container, and screwed it firmly into place. Pulling his hands out of the gloves, he unsealed the glass box and reached in for the steel bottle. He hefted it in his big right hand, grinning at Penny as he did so. "You could throw this up against the wall and she'd be safe now, Miss Penny. Maybe *now* I could let you carry it."

Experimental protocols required that the extracted I-particle fluid be immediately delivered to a shielded holding tank in a vault at the far end of the proton linear accelerator, deep under the Waianae Mountains—a trip of some five kilometers, all of it underground. "What would you say if I took you up on that, Cy?" Penny asked, concerned.

"Oh, I'd panic, and take it all back," he admitted cheerfully. "You might get lost between here and the vault, after all." His smile suddenly disappeared. He was seized with a spasm of coughing, but this time he made no effort to suppress the lung-wracking coughs. He kept a tight grip on the steel bottle.

Penny watched, almost feeling his pain. "Maybe you *should* let me deliver it, Cy—"

But Sherwood recovered, pulling in a big breath. "No, no, an itchy throat, that's all. I'll run right out there. Back soon." To avoid further discussion he shoved the bottle into the side pocket of his lab coat and turned to the steel stairs. He took the steps lightly, skipping over the bottom ones as if to prove his youthful vigor.

Penny watched him stride to the purple-painted steel curtain door on the far wall. He threw the heavy circuit breaker that set its motors to whining. The door clattered open, rolling upward toward the ceiling. The light from the control platform spilled out under the opening door, onto the floor beneath the wide circular shaft which served as access for the heavy equipment which had to be lowered from ground level, thirty meters above. Beyond the reach of the work lights, blue moonlight fell in tesselated shadow on the concrete floor under the shaft. The moon was directly overhead; its light was filtered through the grate at the top of the shaft.

When the door had opened high enough, Sherwood stepped through. Beside the door switch on the other side of the wall sat a stubby electric utility cart, a tractor, parked alongside a couple of bicycles. The staff members used various means of transportation to get around inside TERAC's extensive tunnels; Sherwood's favorite was this little tractor, a massive battery-powered vehicle with hard rubber tires, painted in broad black and yellow chevrons. He reached over and switched it on, then walked to the outer circuit breaker.

Penny sighed and turned away, exasperated with the old coot; it would serve him right if he caught a good case of pneumonia, the way he was hogging all the fun. Her last view of him was of his tall frame striding with determined good health toward the switch on the wall, his white lab coat gleaming in the spilled light from the interior of the hall, stark against the blue shadows.

She heard the curtain door rattling down as it started to close, and the clicking of the electrical relays on the little cart as Cy put it in gear and drove it away. Willing enough to let frustration excuse self-indulgence, she reached for the leftover pizza, only half looking at it.

As her fingers nudged the aluminum wrap, the whole wide concrete room filled with light, and all its bright painted colors bleached to a bone whiteness that the wondering Penny found lovely to contemplate. But quickly the room became painfully transparent, as if she were looking through the walls into the interior of the earth, which was not Earth at all, but rather open, endless space. The effect was sublime.

Her analytical mind did not wholly cease to function in those microseconds. From the corner of her eye she saw the LED counters windowed for hard gamma radiation blaze with a spurt of numbers, all of them at once, just before their plastic faces melted.

The heat was reflected from her white coat, but her dark hair began to singe. She was tossed against the nearest equipment rack. She was knocked unconscious so quickly that she neither heard the explosion nor felt its shock.

16

Peter awoke from a confused dream—a forge, hammer blows, lurid flames in the darkness—to see that the moon had moved far enough west to be visible through the rippling curtains.

He heard a phone ringing, a muffled thudding through the cinder-block walls of the funny old hotel—doubtless the source of his spectral hammer. The phone seemed to be in the next room, the room that belonged to Gardner Hey. And Hey must have answered it, for it stopped in mid-ring.

What time was it? It was quiet outside, and black, except for the moon—and the streetlights, which showed as bright blobs in the curtains' reticulation. Past midnight, then, certainly. Who would be calling Gardner Hey at this hour?

Anne-Marie was sleeping soundly, one long brown leg thrown over his, her head pillowed on his outstretched arm, her face nuzzling his side. When the night air had grown chill they'd retreated under the sheets and thin blanket; beneath the covers all was warmth and comfort.

So what did he care who was calling Gardner Hey? But he was reminded that he'd have to be careful, *discreet* that is, about leaving in the morning—unless he wanted to be pestered by the man's insinuations.

Fondly he pressed his lips to Anne-Marie's hair, filled his nostrils with her sweet smoky aroma. She was a marvel, so quick to guess his secrets. Ancient hermetic knowledge, indeed! She was a sensitive, intelligent woman, adept at reading the myriad nonverbal cues people constantly broadcast about themselves; perhaps that's what had drawn her to photography, that sixth sense for the decisive moment. Surely she'd seen through him when he was overloaded with sensations, virtually radiating desire—seen through him, but matched his feelings with her own. . . .

He secretly smiled to himself in the darkness. Best to steer away from particular memories, perhaps, before he tempted himself to wake her from a sound sleep. He wriggled the numb fingers of his left hand, but did not move his arm from beneath her sleeping head.

He pondered the source of her fascination with the occult, which sooner or later seemed to entangle a lot of thoughtful people who were not already mired in establishmentarian science or religion. It *was* the religious impulse, at base. Even reason itself could function as a religion, he supposed—but only for those of severely limited imagination.

He'd toyed with "psi" himself, written a couple of papers now much quoted by crackpots, to his chagrin. The reason he and so many other theoretical physicists were suckers for the stuff was easy to understand—for two-thirds of a century an enigma had rested at the heart of theoretical physics, a contradiction, a hard kernel of paradox. Quantum theory was inextricable from the uncertainty relations.

The classical fox knows many things, but the quantum-mechanical hedgehog knows only one big thing—at a time. "Complementarity," Bohr had called it, a rubbery notion the great professor had stretched to include numerous pairs of opposites. Peter Slater was willing to call it absurdity, and unlike some of his older colleagues who, following in Einstein's footsteps, demanded causal explanations for everything (at least in principle), Peter had never thirsted after "hidden variables" to explain what could not be pictured. Mathematical relationships were enough to satisfy him, mere formal relationships which existed at all times, everywhere, at once. It was a thin nectar, but he was convinced it was the nectar of the gods.

The psychic investigators, on the other hand, demanded to know *how* the mind and the psychical world were related. Through ectoplasm, perhaps? Some fifth force of nature? Extra dimensions of spacetime? All these naive explanations were on a par with the assumption that psi is propagated by a species of nonlocal hidden variables, the favored explanation of sophisticates; *ignotum per ignotius.*

"In this connection one should particularly remember that the human language permits the construction of sentences which do not involve any consequences and which therefore have no content at all. . . . " The words were Heisenberg's, lecturing in 1929 on the irreducible ambiguity of the uncertainty relations. They reminded Peter of Evan Harris Walker's ingenious theory of the psi force, a theory that assigned psi both positive and negative values in such a way that the mere presence of a skeptic in the near vicinity of a sensitive psychic investigation could force null results. Neat, Dr. Walker, thought Peter Slater—neat, and totally without content.

One had to be willing to tolerate ambiguity; one had to be willing to be crazy. Heisenberg himself was only human—he'd persuasively woven ambiguity into the fabric of the universe itself, but in that same set of 1929 lectures he'd rejected Dirac's then-new wave equations with the remark, "Here spontaneous transitions may occur to the states of negative energy; as these have never been observed, the theory is certainly wrong." It was a reasonable conclusion, and that was its fault, for Dirac's equations suggested the existence of antimatter: the first antiparticles, whose existence might never have been suspected without Dirac's crazy results, were found less than three years later.

Those so-called crazy psychics were too sane, that was their problem—they were too stubborn to admit that the universe was already more bizarre than anything they could imagine in their wildest dreams of wizardry.

Anne-Marie's eyes flew open. "What are you thinking?"

He laughed. "You're supposed to tell me." He raised himself on one elbow and looked at her, smiling.

"Unfair," she said. She yawned enormously, teeth gleaming in the darkness, then turned her face away from him. She stared out the window. "What time is it?"

"I don't know. One or two, I guess."

She looked back at him. "I've been wasting time. Sleeping."

"The world will still be here in the morning."

"That's what I don't want," she said. "Can't you stop the sun from rising?" She scraped her nails lightly over his belly.

"I haven't worked out the details yet," he said. "Give me time." He lowered his mouth to kiss her. His shoulder overshadowed her face.

Somewhere nearby a door opened and closed, and footsteps hurried away in the night, but they paid no attention.

17

Assistant Fire Chief Ferdinand Kawaiola was a big sil-ver-haired Hawaiian who'd put in twenty-five years with the Honolulu Fire Department before taking a much-better-paying job with TERAC's emergency ser-vices division. His friends had criticized him for it, but he had grandchildren who needed his help to get a good edu-cation. When the alarm came in from Hall 30, Kawaiola responded like a veteran, reflexively. He and his men were already roaring along in their yellow trucks, sirens screaming and lights blazing, following the access road to the hall, when it occurred to Kawaiola that something was wrong. Unusually wrong, that is.

An operating accelerator is dangerous. Inside the ring there's enough radiation to make people very sick indeed, and in the unlikely event that the main beams ever got loose—although they'd dissipate in an instant—it would be as if a couple of bombs had been set off in the tunnel. The beams were regular death rays that could slice through sheet metal and people alike, rupturing helium lines, shorting out megagauss electromagnets, causing them to disintegrate in a spray of shrapnel. Nobody went inside the ring when the beams were up. Any attempt to enter without a key and without the authorization and co-ordinated assistance of an operator in the main control room instantly dumped the beams, squirting energetic protons and antiprotons straight into the roots of the mountain, where they could drill holes in the basalt without doing harm.

Kawaiola had memorized all this during hours of orientation lectures and drills. He'd mentally filed radiation along with all the other things he'd learned to watch out for, in order to stay alive inside burning tenements, exploding chemical warehouses, blazing tank farms, and now, berserk accelerators.

But TERAC, far from going berserk, seemed to be operating as usual. The beams had not dumped, at least not according to the lights on the situation board back in the fire station. Kawaiola had been in such a rush to get to the scene of the problem that it had taken him half a minute to realize the significance of those unblinking lights.

With his big brown left hand Kawaiola easily steered the chief's car, a bright yellow Land Cruiser, while he wrapped his right hand around the radio microphone. "Control room? What kind of situation do you think we've got over here, huh? Is this a fire, or what?"

The radio speaker crackled. "Can't tell you for sure, Chief. We got a box alarm. We can't rouse anybody in the hall by phone. Health physics is on the way." Health physics officers were casual folks, by and large, but in a situation like this they put on their lead suits and yellow booties and carried Geiger counters. Sometimes they also carried .38-caliber Police Special revolvers, to indicate their sincerity.

"So the beams're still up, right?" Kawaiola asked.

"That's right. Don't let anybody attempt to enter the ring. Health physics will order a controlled dump if necessary, once they've had a look."

"Okay. Roger, Control. Talk to you guys later." Kawaiola hung up the microphone. He steered off the access road, sailed over the berm in his Land Cruiser, and skidded down the short drive to the entrance of Hall 30. The big tanker and the ambulance followed close behind him. Sirens died; red and white lights continued to flash and revolve. The firemen dismounted and stood by their trucks.

Kawaiola ran to the edge of the wide round shaft and peered down into blackness. Steel stairs, starting from the near section of the wall, ran down into the murk, out of sight; work lights should have been burning to light the steps, but the nine-story descent was blind. The air in the shaft was thick—cement dust rather than smoke, or so Kawaiola judged by its astringent odor. Kawaiola knew he should wait for the health physics officers to set up their line, the hotline across which all exchanges of people and material were monitored, but they were late, and years of experience urged him to hurry. In a fire, and in most other emergencies, time was never on the side of the rescuer.

Kawaiola knew that a wall of concrete blocks shielded the Hall 30 control platform from the inner ring. The access shaft was even farther from the ring, outside the control room and normally separated from it by a steel shutter, so as long as he stayed in the control area or the shaft he and his men should have nothing to fear from the ordinary operations of TERAC. Besides, they all wore chirpers, which would warn them audibly if things got hot.

"Luther, Marcos, let's check this out. Button up good," he called. "Marcos, you take the elevator inside the building. The rest of you guys stand by."

Kawaiola and the two men he'd designated sealed their faceplates and opened their respirator valves. Marcos headed for the elevator in the building. Kawaiola unlocked the steel gate to the stairs with his master key, and he and Luther started down, directing powerful torch beams into the gloom below. Within three stories they noticed that the bulbs of the lights along the stairs had been shattered in their sockets. Another three stories and they reached the ceiling level of the underground hall; they could see that the foot of the staircase had been twisted and loosened where it was stapled to the concrete wall. Wiring conduits had been ripped loose. Across the hall the steel curtain door had jammed open a couple of feet above the floor, punched in as if by a big fist. In the concrete floor there was an incipient crater, a spiderweb of cracks a yard wide.

They descended the loose stairs cautiously, their flashlight beams probing through the fine dust that hung suspended in the air. On the far side of the shaft the beams picked out the heavy utility tractor, flipped upside down, its little hard rubber tires in the air. A man's foot protruded from beneath the tractor, missing its shoe. A pool of blood was still spreading.

"Hank, we need your team down here on the double, with everything you got. We got one badly injured. And at least one more around here someplace." Kawaiola heard the acknowledgment in his helmet radio as he hurried down the last few steps of the twisted stairs. Reaching the floor safely, he signaled his partner to come after him and to check the control room on the far side of the mangled door. As he moved across the floor, Kawaiola heard his chirper's oscillator burp halfheartedly—low-level gammas, barely significant. "Keep an eye open for ruptured shielding," he warned Luther.

Kawaiola hurried to the wrecked tractor. He saw that the man under it had no use for an ambulance. He played his flashlight beam over the scene. A bright metal object reflected the light. He bent to inspect it: a large stainless-steel cylinder, the size of a Thermos bottle, apparently intact. Had the dead man been carrying it?

"We've found a woman," said Luther's voice on the radio. "Alive, unconscious, flash burns, maybe worse."

"Marcos with you?"

"Here, Chief. The elevator's working fine," said Marcos.

"What's the damage?" Kawaiola demanded.

"Not much," Marcos replied. "Some stuff knocked over. Papers burned, but no fire now. Looks like that steel door caught hell, though."

"Sure did," Kawaiola muttered. He heard feet clanging on the stairs above, and helmet lights stabbing through the darkness.

"That you down there, Chief?" said a voice in his helmet.

"Yeah. This man's dead. There's a woman hurt in the control room. Go on in there and take her out by the elevator. Be careful of the steps at the bottom."

"Okay."

"Health physics here?"

"Right behind us. Are we gonna be hot?"

"My chirper can't make up its mind. Some stuff, not much."

"My wife'll be glad to hear it," said a fireman.

Kawaiola took a last look at the dead man. He bent and picked up the steel cylinder, hefted it; it was surprisingly heavy.

"Give us a hand over this railing, Chief."

Kawaiola moved quickly to help the arriving firemen maneuver their equipment past the damaged section of stairs; absently, he shoved the steel cylinder into his overalls pocket as he went.

18

Smoky orange flames flickered outside the bedroom window. Greta Edovich regarded them dreamily in her vanity mirror as she brushed out her long blond hair in swift, strong strokes, working with the deft efficiency of years of practice. She'd heard you weren't supposed to do your hair like this anymore, but it had worked fine for her, and she wasn't the type to try to improve success. Crystal lamps shaped like miniature kerosene lanterns were ensconced on either side of Greta's mirror, and the Chinese porcelain lamp on the bedside table had a tall shade of lemon-yellow silk; the light in the room was diffuse, warm, flattering to Greta's fair skin. And outside the window, orange flames . . . but they were only the massed scarlet flowers of a tall poinciana, a flame tree, mellowed by the room's soft light.

Martin was already in bed, sitting up in his peppermint-striped pajamas, propped up by pillows against the headboard. He was reading, something he did in every spare moment. He wasted no time as he flipped through

142

a pile of reports and preprints, slowing only occasionally to grunt with interest, putting most of the papers aside without a second glance.

Greta eyed him surreptitiously, allowing herself a fond smile. She loved him, and she knew he loved her. It was a relaxing, gratifying sensation, like the glass of B&B she'd warmed in the candle flame after their dinner this evening. The night had been easy, pleasurable, a leisurely dinner out with Chauncey and the Laskys at a new French place he'd found in Kahala—a welcome escape from the drudgery of cleaning up after Friday's crowd. The conversation had gone on much later than anyone had expected.

Complacently, Greta reflected that she and Martin had had many such good times in their lives, made many interesting friends, visited many fascinating places—Europe, India, China, Japan—almost always on Martin's business, of course—the international science business. She supposed it was remarkable that she and her husband of a quarter century still found it easy and pleasurable to be with each other—to talk about nothing much and even still, every once in a while, to work up a satisfying fit of passion. She eyed him in the mirror; her cheeks grew warm. But she still had thirty-five strokes of the brush to go.

The only person who obviously hadn't enjoyed the evening was poor Chauncey. That woman was on his mind, that Anne-Marie Brand or whatever her name was. If Greta had known she was married to Chauncey's best friend (and, she admitted to herself, if she hadn't been a little tipsy) she wouldn't have teased him so unmercifully about Anne-Marie's running off with Peter Slater Friday night. Like a couple of teenagers, the two of them, grinning and giggling. And the woman with a young child at home! But Chauncey had defended her, poor boy; obviously he was in love with her himself. And he'd defended Peter just as strenuously.

For a moment Greta speeded up the pace, pulling the brush through her hair with extra vigor. She shifted uneasily on the stool, then relaxed, stealing another glance at Martin. He was tugging hard at his sparse red forelock—he'd found something fascinating in his papers, no doubt, some new discovery in particle physics or, just as likely, some exploitable development in one of his pet government agencies.

Greta kept on brushing. Maybe it wasn't the Brand girl's fault, altogether. Peter Slater was no innocent, that was plain enough. He was newly divorced, no doubt starved for sex, though beautiful as an angel, and arrogant—because all he had to do was crook his finger; in Greta's experience men who knew they were irresistible often managed to be so. And Greta was not exactly naive on the subject. Since she'd married Martin . . . well, nothing serious—that one time, when she'd been stuck on the spouse's tour in Hamburg for a week, with Martin too busy to talk and her with nothing to do. It hardly counted, all heavy breathing and blind fumbling and clumsy dry rubbing and poking in the dark. But before Martin . . . well, that was a long time ago. Greta knew what the Brand girl must be feeling, though: like all women, she was getting older all the time.

Greta's hand went to her face, and for a moment the busy brush paused. One had to see things in context. Fifty wasn't thirty-five. Or twenty-five, or however old the girl was. . . .

Greta surrendered to the vivid image that had been pressing against the edge of her consciousness, of Peter and Anne-Marie tangled in each other's arms, long smooth-muscled limbs interwoven, torsos surging, mouths open, hair streaked with sweat, clenching, clenching . . .

"What?" Edovich asked, looking up from his papers.

"Pardon, dear?" She looked at him in the glass.

"I thought you said something," he said. Then he yawned.

"Just a tangle," she said, and blushed.

"A tangle? Woman, I am astonished you have any hair left." He laid the stack of papers aside. "What are you trying to brush out of your life, my lovely?"

Quickly she set down the brush and reached up to turn off the lamps on the wall. "I was stalling, I suppose, darling," she said. "Until you'd finished your terribly important paperwork." She rose and turned gracefully. Her peignoir lifted and rippled about her legs, which were dark shadows beneath the rose silk of her nightgown. They were long legs, smooth enough and slender still, in the dark.

Edovich smiled at her a bit groggily and reached for the lamp switch.

Downstairs the telephone rang.

"*Ne*, I don't believe it," he said angrily.

"It must be a wrong number," she said. She sat at the foot of the bed and turned toward the door. The phone kept ringing.

"I've said we must have a phone in the bedroom," he said irritably.

"Martin, I'm sorry."

Immediately he was remorseful. "Forgive me, Greta." The phone kept ringing. "Perhaps in the spare bedroom, then," he said, rolling his eyes comically. "Do you think if I get out of bed it will stop? If I place the soles of my bare feet on the rug, will it stop?"

She smiled. "You might have to place them on the cold bare boards in the hall first. So don't." She turned. "Let me answer it."

But he'd jumped out of the bed, whipping the covers aside, and was trundling toward the bedroom door, saying gruffly, "It's not for you." He tried to make a joke of it. "It had better not be for you."

She followed him as far as the bedroom door and stood there, listening to his footsteps traveling down the stairs and across the big living room. Despite his hopes, the phone monotonously rang for the whole distance.

She heard him answer it, monosyllabically, gruffly. There was silence, followed by short questioning sounds from him, muffled sounds, apprehensive.

Then a cry of surprise. Of sorrow?

19

Matsuo Ishi watched Edovich with quiet sympathy. "The woman was painfully grieved, was she not?"

Edovich had just hung up the phone in Ishi's office. His normally ruddy face was ashen—he had broken the news of Sherwood's death to the man's only surviving relative, a younger sister living in Stillwater, Oklahoma. In Oklahoma the sun was high in the morning sky. On Oahu it was still the dead of night.

Edovich nodded, not looking at Ishi. "Poor old lady." He rubbed his thick hands over his red eyes, then stared at the ceiling of Ishi's office. "She gave me the name and number of a friend. Better that we make the arrangements through her."

"Mr. Hein will do so. He is most efficient." Ishi drew on his stubby yellow cigarette, then exhaled slowly, watching Edovich, who made no move to get up from his chair. "The hospital informs me that Dr. Harper is in stable condition," Ishi remarked, almost casually. "Perhaps her injuries will prove to be less severe than we had feared.

Colonel and Mrs. Harper received the news with commendable courage, both of them." Harper's parents lived in San Antonio; her father was a retired Air Force officer. "An example to us all, don't you agree?" Ishi added. He stubbed out his cigarette.

Perhaps Edovich took the hint, for he got to his feet stiffly, making a desultory attempt to tuck the tail of his white shirt back into his trousers.

Ishi stood and moved slowly from his desk to the door of the adjoining conference room. He beckoned Edovich through with a bow.

Square lamps of paper and lacquered wood threw intricate shadows on the polished paneled walls of the long room. Miss Sugibayashi had wheeled in a cart with coffee, tea, and a selection of little cakes and cookies. TERAC's senior staff quietly pursued separate conversations in English and Japanese, Shigeki Yamamura and Umetaro Narita, a radiation-effects specialist, standing near the cherrywood conference table close to Ishi's office door, while Lasky, Tolliver, and Ilse Friedman were gathered in front of the floor-to-ceiling windows at the far end of the room. The window curtains were open, and everyone could see the distant glare of floodlights playing on Hall 30, an incongruous blaze of light in the darkness.

Conversation stopped when Edovich and Ishi entered the room.

"Sir, excuse me—"

"Mr. Tolliver?"

"We already have a roomful of reporters over in Dirac," said Tolliver apologetically.

"Reporters so quickly?" asked Ishi, annoyed.

"Yes, sir. Not our doing." Tolliver picked nervously at the cuticle of his thumb, avoiding Ishi's gaze. "The newsrooms monitor our emergency communications through Honolulu Police and Fire. I've got to have something for those people soon, before they start running around loose."

"A nuisance," said Ishi unhappily. "It is essential to

draft a statement that will not excite the curiosity of irresponsible persons."

"Certainly, I agree, sir."

"However, I'm afraid you will have to bear with us a moment longer, Mr. Tolliver. Our future course is to be decided."

Ishi sat at the conference table, arranging his notepad and smoking paraphernalia carefully in front of him. Sam Hein from the personnel office was hovering near the door, waiting to get back to his paperwork; Edovich handed him the slip of paper on which he'd written the name and number of Sherwood's sister's friend.

"Mr. Hein," said Ishi. "Please inform Miss Sugibayashi immediately when you have made travel arrangements for Dr. Harper's parents, and for Miss Sherwood. I shall want to meet them when they arrive, if possible."

"Certainly, sir."

"And be aware that plans for Mr. Sherwood's funeral will have to be coordinated with the pathology laboratory at the hospital." Ishi's expression showed his extreme distaste. "There will be an autopsy."

Hein nodded and left. Ishi peered around the room. "Please, everyone be comfortable." He paused while people found seats. Edovich joined the group of Americans near the window, where he remained standing. "Due to your commendable efforts," Ishi continued, "the crisis is fully under control. We have now to consider the matter of resuming normal operations." He looked hopefully at the other staff members. "But possibly we are all in agreement?"

No one spoke. Imperceptibly, Shigeki Yamamura began to sway from side to side in his chair. Soon his movements were so noticeable that he had attracted the anticipatory gaze of everyone in the room. The other staff members had long ago concluded that Yamamura's manners were as unpleasant as his dwarfish person. Yamamura had risen rapidly in the postwar economy of Japan, through native intelligence and ruthlessness. He was a man without family or social connections; that proved an advantage, with the nation in ruins. He was a clever scientist with an eye for exploitable techniques, mostly borrowed. By the time Japan's traditional societal structure of interlocking loyalty groups had rebuilt itself, Yamamura was firmly entrenched in the industrial-bureaucratic hierarchy. And by then, though he sensed that his eager venality did him no credit, that his career was on the point of stagnating because of it, his behavior patterns had become fixed.

Now his face was twisted into a scowl, and it was plain to all that he was wrestling with how to make the most of Edovich's misfortune without unseemly gloating.

At last he broke the suspense. "There is no problem to start the ring," he said gruffly, essaying a strained smile.

"Good to hear you think so," Lasky said immediately. There were simultaneous expressions of relief from the others.

Yamamura interrupted them. "It is necessary, however, first to disconnect the I-particle experimental collector, because of radiation difficulties." He continued to smile.

The room fell silent. Edovich stood with his back to Yamamura, his attention taken by the crowd of people and vehicles, made miniature by distance, gathered around floodlit Hall 30.

"Dr. Yamamura—" Bronislaw Lasky spoke up for his friend Edovich, addressing Yamamura in soothing tones. "Dr. Yamamura, the radiation signature is hardly characteristic of *any* of the experiments in the ring. For one thing, there aren't many 'neuts,' isn't that right, Ume?" He smiled at Narita, who shrugged and grinned.

"Yes, as you say," Yamamura replied impatiently. "The evidence cannot be explained by reference to what is known. A mystery! Therefore the collector must be dismantled."

"Did any of you go there?" Edovich demanded. He turned slowly to face the room, speaking thickly. "*I* went there. I found a hole in the floor—*outside* the control room. A steel door pushed in from the *outside*. A tractor tossed like a toy." Edovich glared at Yamamura. "Cyrus Sherwood was my good friend for many years. He was murdered."

Yamamura's eyes glittered. "With great respect, Professor Edovich, if a bomb is what you suggest . . . "

"It was a bomb," said Edovich. "It was sabotage. Nothing could be more plain."

"What evidence for this?" Yamamura asked, grinning around the room, as if to display his good-natured reasonableness.

Lasky brushed the question aside. "Everyone who has visited the site confirms that the ring was completely untouched, Dr. Yamamura," he said. "So how could the collector, an integral part of the ring, be implicated in any way?"

"The unfortunate Mr. Sherwood was handling a container of the I-particle fluid, was he not? What you have called 'holy water'?"

"We don't know that," Edovich said sharply.

Yamamura sneered at him. "Your own protocols require . . . "

"My experimental protocols are none of your business, Dr. Yamamura," said Edovich hotly. "I suggest that you are out of your depth, sir. Even if Sherwood did have the fluid in his possession—and if he did I have no doubt it will be found, once there has been time for a thorough investigation—still there is no path known to theory by which I-particles could even remotely be involved in such an explosion. Brownie?"

"Certainly, Martin, within accepted . . . "

Edovich didn't wait to hear the rest of Lasky's explanation. "The inside quark is absolutely stable, Dr. Yamamura. Professor Lasky will give you references to numerous papers which, if you will take the time to read and understand them, will prove this elementary fact to you beyond doubt. I-particle fluid is inert."

Yamamura stared at Edovich, speechless, infuriated. Such insulting bluntness was unheard of in Japanese conversation, even the least polite. Rude as Yamamura was by the standards of his own society, he would never have deliberately impugned another man's intelligence in front of his peers. Yamamura's wrinkled face appeared on the point of tears.

Ilse Friedman broke the awkward silence. "Suppose for a moment there was a bomb, Dr. Yamamura. The bomb itself could have been the source of the radioactivity." She looked inquiringly at Narita; again, the muscular young man simply smiled and shrugged.

Yamamura squinted suspiciously at Friedman. He'd never gotten used to women who behaved as if they were the equal of men. Friedman was a tall stern woman who favored peasant skirts and wore her gray hair in a page-boy; she cared nothing for Yamamura's prejudices or anyone else's. Yamamura replied shortly, "A fission bomb would have been much more powerful." He looked away from her.

Friedman persisted. "A subcritical mass . . . "

"With a fizzle much evidence of debris would be found," said Yamamura.

"A fizzle would have been very dirty, very hot," said Narita. He smiled at Lasky. "Lots of neuts."

"Of course, of course," said Edovich impatiently. "The bomb was probably as simple as a chunk of brass pipe stuffed with guncotton. The whole purpose of these people is to discredit us. They salted the thing with something radioactive, medical waste for all we know, just to make it look like an accident that was our responsibility, and they tossed it down the access shaft. Proper security could have prevented this."

"Ingenious. Now we are creating evil personages who are throwing salty bombs." Yamamura was exerting himself to be insulting. "What of Occam's Razor, Professor Edovich? I am assured this is a principle of Western science, not to make unnecessary difficulties of explanation."

"Dr. Yamamura, you have never accepted the basic research purposes of this institution," said Edovich. His voice was low, deceptively steady, but his complexion was brick-red. "You—you and your bosses at MITI—believe the I-particle collector is an obstacle to the pursuit of your silly ideas about antimatter fuels, or whatever science fiction you have been reading lately. You are well informed about my experimental protocols, that is clear. You have easy access to every part of this facility . . . "

Yamamura had half risen from his chair. Umetaro Narita got up and began speaking rapidly to him in Japanese. Lasky jumped to his feet and took Edovich by the shoulder, forcing him to turn away. Chauncey Tolliver hurried to Edovich's side.

Matsuo Ishi gaped at Edovich, shocked by his display of temper. Miss Sugibayashi turned visibly pink around the ears and busied herself aimlessly rearranging the items on the tea cart.

"Martin, this can't possibly help Cy Sherwood," Lasky said in a low, urgent voice, "and it won't do any good for Penelope Harper. Don't say things you'll regret tomorrow."

"I know what you're going through, Martin, my God, it's terrible," Tolliver was saying in his other ear. "But this could be very bad for the program, very bad."

The two men continued to argue and cajole Edovich, while at the other end of the room Narita and Yamamura hissed and shouted at each other, Narita simultaneously doing much head bobbing, inserting little placatory bows into the midst of his strenuous criticisms of Yamamura's unseemly emotionalism. Yamamura snarled something and turned away, stalking to the tea cart. Miss Sugibayashi stumbled away in terrified retreat. He ignored her, taking a handful of cookies and cramming them into his mouth one after the other.

The phone rang. Miss Sugibayashi, grateful for the distraction, hurried into Ishi's office to answer it. Ishi had pulled off his spectacles and was polishing them ferociously. Miss Sugibayashi returned and spoke to him in rapid Japanese. He got up abruptly and limped into his office, clearly relieved at the opportunity to leave the disgraceful scene.

Ilse Friedman restlessly got up and stalked over to the conference table, where Narita was busy doodling on a notepad with intense concentration. "What's up, Ume?" she asked. "Did I hear Miss Sugi mention Gambito's name?"

Narita looked up at her and nodded. "Something about the firemen," he said. His handsome, self-assured face was expressionless. He was a muscular young man who'd studied physics at Kyoto and Cal Tech, and who spoke English flawlessly. "Gambito is the health physics officer in charge over there."

"He's the one who hit the dump button?"

"On my advice," said Narita. "I'll take responsibility for that decision, as I said earlier."

"Well, you didn't really have a choice, did you?" Friedman said. "It was Class A—dead and injured, radiation leak . . ."

"Yes, and I'm sorry, Ilse. I know it's a pain in the neck for you."

"Nothing that twelve hours of diddling and fiddling won't fix. We'll have beams again in practically no time."

"I said I'm sorry, Ilse," Narita repeated. "It's true the gamma irradiation these two bulls are snorting about is barely enough to give us a reading. Nevertheless, it's a mystery. I don't make policy. I follow the book."

"Then tell me what you *do* think, Ume," she demanded. "Is it an operational hitch or not? When we start up the beams again I'm going to be the one in central control giving the orders. I'd better be sure of what I'm doing."

Narita leaned closer, almost whispering. "Martin's on the right track, that's what I think. But don't ask me to take sides publicly. That's not how we get things done in Japan, and all this shouting is just going to make for more problems."

Friedman looked at Yamamura, who was still angrily devouring one almond cookie after another, spilling crumbs down the front of his dark suit coat. She smiled coldly. "Accusing Yamamura is an absurdity."

"Of course," said Narita. "But there are plenty of kooks and malcontents on this island who'd love to embarrass us. And especially us Japanese. Just look at the timing of this whole thing—"

"Um, yes—right in the middle of the dedication ceremonies." Friedman looked toward the door of Ishi's office. "Puts him on the spot, doesn't it?"

"I'm glad I've got a book to go by," said Narita fervently. "He doesn't. No matter what he does, it's wrong."

Ishi's door opened and he entered the room. He sat down and arranged his papers as before. He lit a fresh cigarette and inhaled slowly, giving the people in the room time to find their places. Miss Sugibayashi entered quietly and sat beside him, armed with a stenographic pad.

Ishi began. "A stainless-steel cylinder approximately thirty centimeters in length and ten centimeters in diameter was found near Mr. Sherwood's body by the assistant fire chief, Kawaiola. That would certainly be the container of I-particle fluid, would it not, Professor Edovich?" When Edovich nodded, Ishi said shortly, "It then appears that the possibility of the I-particle collection experiment's direct involvement with the explosion has been eliminated."

"Why didn't the fireman report this fact before?" demanded Yamamura, stricken.

Ishi did not answer him directly, but instead referred to his notes. "Mr. Gambito found the cylinder in the pocket of Mr. Kawaiola's protective coveralls, which Mr. Kawaiola had removed along with the rest of his equipment when crossing the hotline. Upon questioning by Mr. Gambito, Mr. Kawaiola recalled that he had been inspecting the bottle when called to assist other firemen, and must have put it in his pocket at that time." Ishi took another slow drag on his cigarette, perhaps waiting for another outburst from Yamamura or Edovich. When none came, he continued: "Mr. Gambito has examined the cylinder.

It is undamaged. The vial of fluid inside it is still intact. There are no signs of radioactive contaminants." Ishi looked up at Edovich. "The cylinder is being delivered here, Professor Edovich, so that you can confirm its proper identity."

Chauncey Tolliver smiled hopefully. "In that case, sir—"

"Yes, Mr. Tolliver, I have not forgotten you." Ishi stared at his notepad again, collecting his thoughts. Then he looked up, his smooth, aged features set in determination. "This is my assessment. The explosion occurred well away from the ring. The operation of the ring was not affected, except by such deliberate safety measures as were taken by Mr. Gambito upon the advice of Dr. Narita, all of which occurred well after the fact of the explosion. The container of I-particle fluid which had been removed from the collector by Mr. Sherwood has now been found intact." Ishi turned his gaze on Yamamura, who was staring with almost comic disappointment at the half-eaten remains of an almond cookie. "Dr. Yamamura, you are quite right to stress the presence of radiation, the source of which remains a mystery. I have sent cables to the Department of Energy and to the Science and Technology Agency requesting help in our investigation, as I have already explained. However, it appears that neither the I-particle collection experiment nor the operation of the ring can be linked with the incident through any simple chain of reasoning." Yamamura bowed curtly toward Ishi and was silent.

Ishi turned his attention back to Tolliver. "If you will pardon me for saying so, Mr. Tolliver, the subject of radiation, in whatever context, seems to excite the American press most unreasonably. In your briefing I advise you to avoid this unfortunate topic." Ishi drew another lungful of smoke, exhaling it slowly as he watched Edovich, who was beginning to pace restlessly in front of the picture window. Ishi's gaze flicked back to Tolliver. "Furthermore, Mr. Tolliver, you must make no reference whatever to any hypothetical *causes* of the incident. If you are asked about the operation of the ring, you may reply that we hope to have it working by this afternoon. That is all."

Tolliver nodded and, after a glance at Edovich, quickly left the room.

After carefully stubbing out his half-smoked cigarette, Ishi rose from his chair. "Again, I thank you all for giving of your time at this very early hour." He started to turn.

"A moment, sir." Edovich had stopped pacing. "Simply to be sure—I understand Ilse will fire up the beams as soon as I can persuade Dr. Narita's colleagues to clear out of my hall, correct?" He smiled. "I'm sure the other experimenters will be as glad as I am to hear it."

Ishi blinked in surprise. "Excuse me, Professor, but no such decision has been reached."

Edovich reddened. "Professor Ishi, a moment ago you told Mr. Tolliver we would be resuming operations this afternoon."

"Forgive me if I was unclear. I said this was our hope."

"Hope!" Edovich puffed out his cheeks. Then, with a visible effort, he forced himself to relax. "Then how soon can we expect a decision, Professor? It's not for myself alone I ask. All the other teams are losing irreplaceable time."

"Professor Edovich, there is still disagreement as to the best course," Ishi explained, with the merest hint of exasperation. At moments like these he was tempted to believe that the Western mind, Edovich's in particular, was exceedingly obtuse.

"Of course there is disagreement, sir!" Edovich said hotly. "When has it ever been otherwise in complex matters? But the majority opinion is plain." Edovich glowered at Yamamura. "Some persons will have to learn that they simply can't have things their own way in the face of superior will."

Ishi said calmly, "In that unhappy event, Professor, I will personally inform the disappointed party, whoever he may be. Good morning to all of you." Ishi limped toward his office, with Miss Sugibayashi close behind. The staff members nodded politely or bowed as he left. Edovich stared belligerently, then stalked into the hall.

Inside his office Ishi sighed deeply, letting the air hiss out between his teeth. He turned to Miss Sugibayashi. "You received a thorough education as a child, Miss Sugibayashi. Were you exposed to the teachings of Lao Tzu?"

"Oh no, Ishi-sama. Of the Chinese classics I recall only some bits of Confucius." She lowered her eyes. "Not with much pleasure, I confess."

Ishi nodded. "In my humble opinion, Lao Tzu is a much wiser man. When I am surrounded by abrupt characters like Yamamura-san and this startling fellow Edovich, I am reminded that Lao Tzu said, 'Governing a large state is like boiling a small fish.'" Ishi limped to his desk and sat down tiredly. He looked up and saw Miss Sugibayashi standing and smiling uncertainly. Noting her confusion, he elaborated: "One must take care that the delicate morsel is not jostled to pieces—"

"Aah," said Miss Sugibayashi, nodding vigorously. "I understand, Ishi-sama." Then she blushed fiercely. "Ishi-sama, I believe the Americans have a similar saying—"

"Oh?" Ishi was surprised.

"Yes, the Americans say, 'Porcupines copulate *very* carefully.'"

Ishi solemnly regarded Miss Sugibayashi; it was indeed a wise observation.

20

Gardner Hey's early-morning phone call had certainly proved to be right on the button—his informant's tipoff had been fast and accurate. So fast that Hey had given himself a good scare when he got to the TERAC gate—he was only the second reporter on the scene. But he was in luck; the *Advertiser* man had gotten there a minute before him, and he'd already told the guards the word was out over the police radio. And even as Hey was flashing his credentials at the flustered guards, who'd heard nothing from their own people except that there was some problem in Hall 30, the TV people came screaming in with their remote vans. The reporters were directed to the auditorium in Dirac Hall, where a sleepy young man from the PIO tried to keep them happy with coffee and doughnuts while an equally sleepy guard made sure they didn't leave the premises.

By the time Chauncey Tolliver appeared, over an hour later, the score of reporters in the room were seething with anger and boredom. Tolliver, who was neatly dressed in a tan summer-weight suit, white shirt, and black knit tie, looked tired but composed. He faced the reporters with little sympathy, wordlessly conveying the message that his problems were much worse than theirs; he read only a brief statement: "This morning at approximately one oh seven A.M. an explosion of unknown origin occurred just outside the main work area of Experimental Hall 30. We have been able to determine that this explosion had no connection with the operation of the main proton-antiproton storage ring, or with the conduct of the experiment to collect I-particles which is located in that hall. Two scientists were at work in the area. Cyrus Alvin Sherwood, age sixty, died almost instantly, before assistance could arrive, from injuries suffered when he was crushed under an overturned utility tractor. Penelope Louise Harper, age twenty-six, is currently in serious but stable condition at Tripler Army Hospital, suffering from extensive burns. The families of both victims have been notified and are presently en route to Honolulu." Tolliver said, "That's all I can give you right now, except for these standard biographies on Mr. Sherwood and Dr. Harper." He gestured to a stack of Xeroxed documents on the table near the podium. "I can also let you have copies of sketch maps showing the location of Hall 30 with respect to the rest of the ring, and a very general plan of Hall 30 showing the area where the explosion occurred. Here, David, would you flick on that overhead?" Tolliver pointed out the site of the explosion on the projected line maps, which filled the huge screen at the front of the auditorium. "And now I'll take Q and A."

During the question period which followed, Tolliver remained polite but distant. No, he said, there would positively be no scientists available to answer questions at this session—come back at the briefing scheduled for 11:00 A.M. No, there was no damage to the ring; in fact, the staff hoped to resume operations later that day. No, there was no possible connection between the explosion and the operation of the ring, or the experiment—because the explosion had occurred on the other side of a steel door, in a ventilation shaft. Outside access to the shaft? Well, he couldn't answer that for sure—he hadn't been to the accident site personally—but he was inclined to doubt it. Good question, though; he'd make it a point to find out. The map said *access* shaft? Oh, so it did.

As soon as the questions became repetitive, Tolliver ended the conference. The reporters headed for their cars and mobile electronics vans, or for the phones in the lobby. Gardner Hey followed slowly behind the locals. *Science Weekly* was just that, a weekly, so there was no point in his worrying about getting scooped. Nevertheless, in the ongoing tournament between the shining knights of the investigative press and the dark lords of bureaucratic news management, Hey was certain that another round had gone to the bad guys. Tolliver was surely hiding something, if only Hey could figure out how to get at it.

He chewed the ends of his mustache and dragged his ragged sneakers along the shining black marble of the lobby floor. He glanced idly at the display set up at the end of the lobby, the display that showed what the inside of the tunnel looked like, the place that was too dangerous to enter. . . .

Out in the parking lot the press got an unexpected break: Martin Edovich was fumbling for the keys to his Mercedes Benz. They cornered him against the door of his car. His fringe of red hair was in disarray, he was tieless, and his shirttail was hanging over one side of his trousers. He looked suspiciously as if he'd been crying. Once the print people had him immobilized the TV people rushed him, shoving microphones and minicam lenses into his face. "Were you there?" they shouted at him. "Was it really an accident?" Somebody turned on a Sun-Gun, and Edovich winced away from the painful light. The lush trees of the TERAC grounds showed as ghostly, staring shapes in the humid darkness beyond the livid splotch in the parking lot.

"One of my oldest, dearest friends is dead," Edovich

pleaded. "Another colleague lies gravely injured. Now please excuse me." He tried to get his key into the door lock.

"But what did it *look* like? Come *on,* Doc, give us *something.*"

Edovich's grief and fatigue rendered him incautious. "I was on the scene, yes. It was no accident."

They pressed him eagerly. "Sabotage? A bomb?"

"I wouldn't—I won't rule that out," he said.

Then he seemed to lose control for a moment, fulminating about "unscrupulous attempts to discredit our research," with the spit flying from the corners of his mouth, and—unhappy phrase—"foreign interests." And the TV camera operators with their portable Japanese cameras, and the print reporters with their Japanese cassette recorders, got it all down on various gauges of Japanese magnetic tape.

Soon Chauncey Tolliver ran up and forced his way through the ring of reporters. Edovich shook his big head at their questions and pushed them away with his thick peasant's hands and, shielded by Tolliver, struggled into his car. Tolliver summoned a guard, and informed the reporters they would have to leave, or wait in the auditorium. For their own safety, of course. Most chose to leave.

Hey drove his rented car toward the city. Already the sky beyond the Koolau Range was pale with the sun's approach; to the west the moon was finally down, leaving a paler glow of its own beyond the watery horizon off Barber's Point.

Hey's bosom swelled with anxiety and frustrated ambition. Surely he was in a better position than these local yokels to figure out what was really going on at TERAC; if he could do so, it could be the making of his career, his ticket out of what he had come to think of as the ghetto of science reporting, a field so specialized that most editors could not understand what he was writing about, much less the majority of the reading public.

But there were so many possibilities here, almost too many. Internal jealousies at TERAC, radical opposition from outside—he could document both these alternatives in depth. And he had not forgotten that startling remark of Peter Slater's: "In my theoretical opinion, Edovich's I-particle collector should have blown itself to pieces months ago," or words to that effect.

But the explosion had been nowhere near the collector! That's what they claimed, anyway. . . .

Somehow he had to find out if that was the truth. And quickly, before they could hide or destroy the evidence. He gripped the wheel of the little car and drove on faster toward the sleeping city.

21

Hey stepped off the hotel elevator and walked along the open-air hallway to his room. He glanced at Anne-Marie's door, next to his, and wondered where she'd spent the night. He hadn't seen so much as a wisp of her lovely dark hair since he'd said goodbye to her and Slater yesterday afternoon.

As he unlocked his door and started to step inside he heard her door open. Surprised, then intrigued, he pulled his own door to within a fraction of an inch of closing behind him, and stood listening in the dark.

"Downstairs in ten minutes?" he heard a male voice whisper. The reply was inaudible, but he heard her latch close, and the man's footsteps moving away down the balcony toward the elevator. Cautiously he stuck his head out. Beyond the balcony the sky was turning from gray to blue, and the fronds of the tall coconut palms were clacking garrulously in the first fragrant breath of the morning's onshore breeze.

Slater's tall frame was unmistakable, even in silhouette:

he was wearing the same knit sports shirt and tan slacks as he'd been wearing the day before.

Hey had an idea. He waited until Slater had stepped onto the elevator, then he went to Anne-Marie's door and knocked quietly. The look on her face when she opened it changed quickly from warmth to shock. "Gardner! Oh—I . . . "

"Say, I'm sorry to bother you, honey." He sounded as sincere as he could manage. "It's about those pictures we talked about getting this morning, remember?"

Her face fell. "Oh, yes. I'd sort of . . . "

"Well, I was just going to say you can forget about it if you want. I mean really, what's the chance they're going to run pictures of a bunch of distinguished old farts, really? It's a waste of your time and talent. And frankly, I thought you might appreciate at least one whole day of a real vacation—"

She hesitated, and he thought he might have blown it with the "waste of your talent" bit. She was sharp, damned sharp, he had to keep that in mind.

"That's nice of you, Gardner," she said. "I don't want you to think I'm not here to work."

"Not for a minute. Anyway, it's completely up to you." He stood there waiting.

She delayed only a moment more. "Okay, Gardner, I'll take off. In case I don't see you tonight, where do you want to meet tomorrow morning?"

"Like we arranged for today, same time, same place—Halekulani at seven-thirty?"

"Fine. See you then. And I do appreciate it."

She started to close the door. His timing was impeccable—he was already turning away, allowing the door to close behind him, when suddenly this little thought just happened to occur to him: "Oh, say. Would it be all right if I borrowed one of your cameras? Just to take some souvenir shots?"

She paused, reluctant—but she'd never been a fanatic about her personal gear, and it was late to start getting finicky now—and, as of two seconds ago, she owed him a favor. "You know how to use thirty-fives?"

"Oh sure, I used to have a Nikon." He grinned, trying to make a joke: "Until I dropped it out of a helicopter over Mount St. Helens."

She smiled wanly. "I'll get one for you."

She closed the door gently; she had no intention of letting him see the inside of her room. He snickered. He'd bet they'd torn hell out of that bed.

The door opened and she held out an old Canon, fitted with a normal 50mm lens. "It's loaded with Tri-X, okay? I took some indoor shots yesterday, nothing very exciting. You may as well use up the roll."

"Great, thanks." He reached for the camera, but she held onto it.

"Twist this ring for manual, otherwise it's set on automatic exposure. The meter shows in the viewfinder. To advance, you . . . "

"Say, I know all that stuff. Don't bother, really." He lifted the camera out of her hands. "And thanks a lot, I really mean it."

"Well—" She looked at him, a little confused. "Thanks yourself, Gardner. Oh, here's an extra roll of film—"

"In case I get carried away?" He took the film. "Thanks again. Have fun," he said lightly, and walked quickly away. As he entered his room he heard her door close behind him, and he allowed himself a broad smile.

Now to make the phone call he'd planned.

Anne-Marie and Peter Slater drove to the Halekulani for breakfast on the lanai—he assured her it was the best to be had on the island. Her early-morning queasiness had passed, and she was ravenous. They ate popovers, torn open and smeared with guava jelly, and split papayas with sweet pink interiors, and strips of thick salty bacon, and eggs scrambled *aux fines herbes,* and piles of crisp fried potatoes. Finally they relaxed with cups of rich black

Kona coffee. All the while bold sparrows hopped among the tables, panhandling for crumbs.

A surprising number of people shared the lanai at this early hour. At the adjacent table Anne-Marie was amused to recognize an English racing driver and his dark Caribbean mistress conducting a lovers' spat over their orange juice. During pauses in the quarrel the man's eyes kept shifting away from his girlfriend to Anne-Marie.

Way out beyond the breakers dedicated surfers bobbed on their boards, lit by the flat yellow light of the newly risen sun. A morning squall swept up suddenly behind the hotel; fat raindrops drummed exuberantly on the awning overhead, and on the wide leaves of the enormous hau vines that encircled the lanai.

Anne-Marie leaned back in her chair and took a deep breath of the ozone-fresh air. She was relaxed, even a little sleepy, and she felt a simple contentment that would have surprised her if she'd been aware of it.

The unhappy lovers got up to leave, their breakfasts half finished. The Englishman gave Anne-Marie a last suggestive stare as he passed. She ignored him. The sky turned black as the squall swept on out over the surf and the surfers.

Without getting out of his chair, Peter stretched and gathered up the fat Sunday paper the Englishman had left at his table. Only after he had it neatly stacked beside his plate did he look at the headlines. "Jesus!"

"What's the matter, Peter?"

"In a minute," he muttered, and continued reading.

The direct rays of the sun came out behind the rain squall, turning the sea from jade green back to turquoise again, simultaneously painting an enormous triple rainbow on the back of the retreating squall; the primary bow glared with the violence of a neon sign. The birds sang to burst their throats in the sweet air.

When Peter reached the bottom of the column on the first page and turned the front section of the paper around Anne-Marie could see the headline:

Explosion Jolts Terac, Kills One

Honolulu, exclusive to the Advertiser: A man was killed and a woman severely injured when an explosion ripped Experimental Hall 30 at the Teravolt Accelerator Center (TERAC), the controversial Japanese-U.S. research facility located in central Oahu, at approximately 1:07 A.M. HST today. . . .

"Gardner, you pig!" said Anne-Marie under her breath. "You knew it all along."

Abruptly Peter excused himself and went in search of a telephone. Anne-Marie sat rigid, wishing she had someone to call. Her gaze followed his lanky figure as he moved swiftly away through the hotel's open, high-ceilinged dining room, which was beginning to fill rapidly with eager tourists.

She'd betrayed herself, eagerly helped Gardner Hey betray her. Not Peter's fault, far from it; nevertheless, he'd been the formal and material cause—she'd been drunk on the sensation of him while Hey was sticking to his job. And stealing hers.

The little red Datsun hissed through a wet patch on the highway; the wipers cleared muddy pink film from the windshield. Along the highway the tall green cane slid by in a blur, gleaming wetly in the morning light. Instead of turning north on Kam Highway, Hey stayed on H-1 until he reached Kunia Road, a two-lane blacktop that ran north through lush cane fields and pineapple plantations in the foothills of the Waianae Range. He followed the road north for four miles, then pulled into the parking lot of the Hawaii Country Club. From the hillside the handsome new clubhouse commanded a wide view of central Oahu, Pearl Harbor, and Honolulu, all the way to distant Diamond Head. The club, once a modest working-class establishment, had profited from an influx of golf-playing Japanese; already out on the fairway were a few fanatics for whom an early Sunday morning was an excellent time to avoid the crush.

Hey stepped out of his car and walked slowly along the edge of the lot, reconnoitering. The course was laid out along the bank of a stream which ran down out of the mountains toward Pearl Harbor. On the far side of the steep ravine the cane grew thick and tall, and a few hundred yards away the grassy berm of TERAC rose up out of the cane like the overgrown wall of an abandoned fort.

Suddenly Hey began waving jauntily in the direction of one of the distant foursomes. No one gave any sign that he'd seen or recognized Hey, but he set off across the fairway at a brisk clip; he hoped anyone watching from the clubhouse would assume he had business to conduct.

The group he'd chosen to aim for was a quarter of a mile from the parking lot, and by the time he'd reached the spot they'd disappeared from view around a bend in the stream, just as he'd hoped. As soon as he was hidden from the clubhouse Hey turned and hopped awkwardly through the stream, splashing bright-red mud up his legs to his Bermuda shorts. He plunged into the cane field. The tall cane was as thick and stiff as cables, the long wet leaves as sharp-edged as paper. Gooey mud sucked at his sneakers. He could hear rattlings and scurryings among the stalks—rats, probably, or the big ugly toads that came out after a soaking rain. He dodged to avoid an enormous iridescent spider, black splashed with gold, hanging in a web stretched between rows of cane. Then, abruptly, he emerged into the open.

Across a narrow rutted track stood a chain-link fence, and beyond it another muddy road—then a strip of rank grass, and TERAC's high berm, blazing electric green in the hot morning sun. Steam rose from its sides. The fence was eight feet high and sturdy, but there was no barbed wire on top. With much gasping and cursing Hey was able to clamber over it. He dropped to his knees on the far side.

Thirty yards to his right a concrete bay projected from the berm. Cautiously Hey approached, and found a steel door bearing the universal radiation warning symbol, black dot and triangles on a field of yellow, with the legend Danger, Keep Out. Hey tested the door: it was open. He slipped inside.

A forty-watt bulb illuminated the bare concrete cell. A telephone call box and a fire alarm were set into the wall, along with a bank of circuit breakers. In the middle of the floor was an iron hatch. Hey lifted it as quietly as he could; the air that flowed out was as cold as the breath of a glacier. He peered down into a seemingly bottomless shaft. A button-sized circle of light gleamed a hundred feet below.

Hey was in an emergency exit from the tunnel. Normally this hatch was locked fast from the outside, though it opened readily enough from below; had the ring been operating, the open hatch would have set off bells and flashing lights, and the broken circuit would have dumped TERAC's beams. Now all was quiet. Hey took a deep breath and lowered himself into the shaft. Iron staples fixed into the wall made a ladder; he went down hand over hand.

Before he reached the bottom of the shaft he paused, hiding in the darkness. He could hear the hum of high voltage, the rattle of exhaust fans, the gurgle of pumps, but no human sound. He was still soaking wet from his adventures in the cane field, and the cold was penetrating; he began to shiver convulsively. The chill was so pervasive that he seriously considered delaying his attempt until he'd gone back for proper clothing—but he had no way of ensuring that everything would go as smoothly, later in the day. Clenching his jaw, he forced himself to climb down the remaining rungs to the floor of the tunnel.

Turning away from the wall, he saw in front of him a train of enormous magnets, big as freight cars, strung in a line that dwindled almost to nothing in both directions before disappearing around the gentle curve of the tunnel. For a moment he was made dizzy by the ring's immensity, and he lost his bearings—should he move left, or right?

Then he remembered that he need only go clockwise to find his destination in the circular labyrinth: he'd entered the ring between Hall 24 and Hall 30, that is, between 240 and 300 degrees of rotation from north.

To keep the camera from dangling in front of him and bouncing against his ribs he'd buttoned his shirt over it. He freed it now, slipping the lens cap into his pocket. Teeth chattering, he started to walk, remembering to stop after a few steps and look back for landmarks. A big number "27" was painted in yellow numerals two meters high on the wall beside the ladder, along with a sign that read Emergency Exit Only and an arrow that pointed straight up. He needn't worry about finding the right exit.

He walked on, his tennis shoes squishing on the flat concrete floor, echoing dully in the tunnel. After several minutes he came to a yellow nylon rope strung across the width of the tunnel. Cardboard radiation symbols were hung on the rope, and a sawhorse carried a larger sign: "Entry Forbidden. Area Closed by Order of Health Physics Department." This was the so-called hotline, the perimeter inside which protective measures must be taken against contamination by radioactive substances, and outside of which no possibly contaminated articles, including protective clothing itself, was to be carried except in sealed containers. Hey ducked under the rope and kept walking.

He decided to move more cautiously, even though no guards were visible. He ducked into the open space under the magnet supports and began to crawl on hands and knees directly beneath the vacuum chamber. He had to lift himself over a cross-brace every couple of yards. Although the magnets were really no colder on the outside than the ambient air, the joints of the liquid-helium pipes which cooled them to within four degrees of absolute zero on the inside were rimed with frost, and condensed vapor continually cascaded toward the floor; he might have been crawling on the floor of an icehouse.

At last he reached the edge of the tunnel. The walls opened out, the floor dropped away, and the stainless-steel pipe of the vacuum chamber was carried on steel trestles across the hall, through the heart of the disclike, luminescent I-particle collector, to the tunnel mouth opposite. Hey crouched beneath the last big quadrupole magnet and stared, shivering, at the fabled device.

He'd seen photographs of it, of course, and he understood its operating principle, but the real thing had a noumenal quality that struck through his cynicism, stirring the ancient hopes that had animated his childhood longing to be a scientist. In those halcyon pre-adolescent days he'd conceived of scientists as handsome fellows who spent their nights gazing through telescopes and their days mixing chemicals in test tubes, and who took occasional vacations to dig up a Mayan pyramid or two in the jungles of Central America. The I-particle collector hadn't been built by men like that, TERAC couldn't have been built by men like that, and the grown-up Gardner Hey resented it. In fact, these men (hell, some of them were even women) were no better than he was, proud, spiteful, ambitious, often wrong but never willing to acknowledge error, perhaps not even to themselves. Hey could not forgive them for their imperfections, which made him uneasily aware that he might have given up his own dreams too cheaply.

The I-particle collector was apparently undamaged. Hey was disappointed; it looked as if Tolliver had been telling the truth after all. Two people in white coveralls and yellow booties and gloves were poking about the hall, sniffing at odd nooks and crannies with hand-held counters, but that was probably only a routine activity after an accident. They weren't even wearing respirators, which indicated that there had been no escape of gases or volatile substances, no radioactive dust in the air. Hey snapped a picture of the two investigators. The "click" sounded frighteningly loud to his ears, but the two people on the floor apparently heard nothing. He snapped a couple more frames. Then he sat there, feeling foolish and frustrated.

The access shaft where the explosion had supposedly

occurred was to his left, beyond the wall of movable concrete blocks—the sketch maps handed out earlier by Tolliver's office told him that much. The wall of blocks did
not reach all the way to the ceiling. Perhaps there was an
opportunity for him there. . . . Hey poked his head out,
beyond the lip of the tunnel, and peered at the wall. Only
a few feet from where he crouched in hiding, a steel staircase ran from the floor of the hall up to the boarding platform of the overhead industrial crane. From the crane
platform Hey would be able to see over the shield wall.

He had nothing to lose by making the attempt. Hey
waited until the two investigators were occupied at the far
end of the hall, then crept along the steel balcony from
the tunnel mouth to the stairs. He moved up them as
swiftly and silently as he could, congratulating himself
now for having worn his usual sneakers. He reached the
platform unobserved and peered over the wall.

He could see the hall's control platform below, raised
to the level of the ring—the access tube from the I-particle
collector reached it through the shield wall. Racks of electronic equipment, though unmoved, appeared scorched,
and shards of glass, plastic, and scraps of singed paper lay
strewn on the deck. An old wooden desk was charred
black on one side, the side facing away from the shield
wall. Two people in white suits and yellow booties were
collecting the debris in clear plastic bags and cataloguing
it on notepads.

Opposite the hall from the ring was a big purple-painted
steel-curtain door, bulging like the bottom of a fat man's
hammock. Hey was impressed—it had taken some little
explosion to do that! He lifted his camera and snapped
shots of the control platform and the steel door. He paused
to look more carefully; through the gap under the door
he could see half a dozen more people in white coveralls,
and he barely made out what looked almost like a crater,
a fracture pattern in the concrete floor. Shivering with
cold and excitement, he snapped half a dozen frames.

Tolliver had not volunteered the word "radioactivity"

in his description of the incident, and in response to questions had repeatedly denied any release of radioactive substances from the ring or the experiment. Now Hey could see and appreciate how cleverly Tolliver had weasel-worded his replies. The investigators in the access shaft were all carrying counters, and using them. There was radioactivity associated with the blast, all right, if not with the ring itself. Suddenly, it seemed, Hey had a story—or at least an angle—worth pursuing.

"You up there! What the hell do you think you're doing?"

The man's angry voice came from right below him on the control platform. Hey jerked away from the edge of his steel balcony in involuntary fright.

"You can't be in here without a badge, man! Without something on!" The men on the platform exchanged words hurriedly, then both began moving for the stairs on the other side of the shield wall, which also connected with the crane platform.

Hey now badly wanted to escape with his photographs intact. It was quite possible that the health physics people wouldn't give a damn about his pictures, but it was equally possible that they'd confiscate his film, even destroy it if—as Hey thought entirely possible—they had something to hide. He scuttled frantically for the steps; he went down them three at a time and fled into the tunnel.

His slapping footsteps echoed loudly as he ran. He had a good start, and the bad guys were wearing funny little plastic shoes, but he was in lousy shape; he considered it prudent to allow for the possibility of capture. As he ran, he twisted the rewind lever on top of the Canon, awkwardly trying to spool the film back into its canister. How could he save his pictures?

At last he saw the big 27 painted on the wall. He skittered to a stop and fumbled with the camera, meanwhile casting desperate glances down the tunnel. At last he was able to pluck the film canister out of the camera and shove it into his shirt pocket. Then he scrambled up the ladder into the escape tube.

There he paused. He hooked an arm through an iron rung and hung suspended in the dark shaft long enough to insert the fresh roll of film Anne-Marie had given him into the camera, then thread it into position. Once it was well in place he started climbing again, trembling and sobbing with exertion, afraid his moist palms would slip on the steel bars and send him tumbling awkwardly down the tube.

He heard them: they were at the bottom of the shaft; they were coming up. They weren't wearing their silly booties now.

At the top of the shaft he rolled out onto the floor. His breath came in tearful gasps. Years of desk work, long airplane trips, barroom nights had conspired to leave him helpless in the pinch. He staggered to his feet and pushed the door open.

The bright morning sunlight blinded him. The day's moist heat was enervating. He wobbled almost drunkenly toward the eight-foot chain-link fence.

He heard sirens to his left, behind him. A yellow Land Cruiser crested the top of the berm a hundred yards away and lurched down the steep slope toward him, skidding in the thick grass.

His hand went to the film canister in his shirt pocket. Now he knew that he would not be leaving TERAC before he'd done an awful lot of talking.

22

"I'm sorry, Peter, I'm ruining what was supposed to be a lovely day."

The newspaper story had sidetracked Peter's plan of persuading Anne-Marie to check out of her hotel and spend her remaining nights in Oahu at his house. After reading about the night's events she was distressed and distracted.

"I don't blame you for being upset," he said, but in truth he didn't understand why missing a press conference, or whatever it was she thought she'd missed, was so important to her. The duty officer had told Peter there was nothing he needed to do or could do; he was prepared to put the incident aside. He was determined to cheer her up. "I know a special place for a picnic. Up north. I go there when I'm feeling cooped up, harassed."

She agreed, without much enthusiasm. In Waikiki they bought bread and cheese and thinly sliced prosciutto, and in an all-night liquor store they found a cold bottle of Clos des Mouches. They packed their booty in a little Styrofoam cooler in the tiny trunk of Peter's Triumph and headed for the north shore. Peter went over the Koolaus and up the windward coast, avoiding the more direct route through the center of the island, which would have taken them past TERAC.

At Pupukea Beach they turned into the hills. Peter nursed the Triumph along in low gear, steering it around potholes and round lava rocks as big and porous as Mediterranean sponges. They parked at the top of the ridge and walked to the ruins of Pu'u o Mahuka. Low walls of rough black rock enclosed grassy earthen terraces bigger than football fields. High on the ridge stood an immense pile of stones shaped like an altar. Little round rocks wrapped in leathery ti leaves, still green, had been left on the heiau's altar within the past day or two, like candles lit to the saints of the place. Evidently someone still believed the temple retained a degree of its former power.

Peter and Anne-Marie were alone, except for a middle-aged couple with a guidebook who were already on their way out. On a wall which clung to precipitous cliffs overhanging Waimea Bay, Peter and Anne-Marie laid out their picnic. They ate slowly, talking little.

Palms and guavas hung limp under an oppressive sun. To the north and west the Pacific Ocean spread glittering to meet the vaporous sky at a horizon half a hundred miles away. The stones were hot, the white burgundy deliciously cool. Peter poured another glassful for Anne-Marie.

"You know, an industrial accident doesn't seem like the kind of news that's worth chasing, to me. Is that what's really got you down?"

"An industrial accident? You make it sound so trivial," she said.

"An accelerator's about as safe as an oil refinery, or a steel mill, maybe a little safer. But I'll bet the cause of the explosion turns out to be a cracked gas bottle, a liquid hydrogen leak, something mundane."

She sipped the wine. "What about the sabotage hints

the paper was full of? That's the kind of story Gardner loves."

"That doesn't say much for Gardner, in my book."

"Did you know the man who was killed?"

"Not personally. He was a kind of character around the place. An untutored mechanical genius. Hated theory, they say, and would only listen to enough of it to get a grasp of what he was supposed to build."

Anne-Marie looked at Peter oddly. "Forgive me, Peter, but all this doesn't seem to upset you as much as I'd have expected. I can understand why you wouldn't want to get in the way out there, but you're not even curious."

"What you really want to know is, why isn't my heart on my sleeve?" He smiled ruefully. "That's it, isn't it? People have been after me about that all my life."

"And I'm as bad as the rest of them." She looked away from him.

"I'm not hiding anything, Anne-Marie. It's a habit." He saw that she was offended; he sighed. "Okay, just what are you supposed to do about death? I feel sorry for the old guy, sure. But we're all going to die. I feel sorrier for the woman—for her pain." Peter knew he must sound cheaply cynical, yet he plowed on, trying to express his sincere conviction. "We're smart monkeys, that's what I think, and our individual lives are insignificant—when they aren't downright ludicrous. What saves us is, we've got brains, and if we use them we can discover things that make us forget just how ludicrous our own existence is."

"What kind of discoveries could make us forget something so hilarious?"

"The elegance and symmetry of the universe, that's what. Have you ever thought we may be the only creatures within ten-to-the-fortieth stellar systems, within the entire cosmos, who have even the dimmest glimmer of what the hell's going on? Do you realize that even we, as emotionally and intellectually crippled as we are, could not have existed if the universe had not conformed to the most exquisitely balanced initial conditions? And that we—some of us—can begin to appreciate in fine detail the exact nature of those initial conditions? This knowledge is precious, Anne-Marie, precious and beautiful. It's worth having been alive for, for a little while, just to contemplate it."

His fervor made her angry. "For a while? You accept death so complacently?" She glared at him.

" 'The more the universe seems comprehensible, the more it also seems pointless.' Steven Weinberg said that a couple of decades ago. It's irrefutable."

"That's what you believe? Oh, Peter, that's so bleak—"

"Still, trying to comprehend this pointless universe can be—amusing." He half smiled at her.

She shivered in the heat. "And here I am, feeling sorry for myself."

He regretted that this sunny day had, under what baleful influence he knew not, illuminated the stoic despair that lurked so near beneath the surface of his thoughtful calm. "Dammit, why don't you do the talking?" He took a mouthful of wine.

At first she did not respond to his ill-tempered invitation, but after awhile she said, "It's not just that Gardner lied to me, it's that he did it so easily. He read me so right: I'm not *really* a photographer, and he knows it. Because if I were, I'd be out there right this minute fighting with the rest of them to get pictures of the dead bodies and the property damage. I would be using whatever leverage I had. You, for instance—I'd do whatever I had to to get you to sneak me where nobody else can go." She took a sharp breath, then let it out in a rush, a wordless curse. "I don't care. I literally don't give a fuck. And if you want to be good at something you have to *care*—poetry, music, those damn weird quarks of yours—even stocks and bonds, for God's sake." She laughed bitterly; then, suddenly agitated, she stood up and walked away from Peter.

"Take Charlie, for example. Charlie just loves his work, and he's good at it, too. His daddy made him rich, and by God he's gonna make his kids five times as rich. And maybe he's a better person than I am, after all. At least he knows what he is."

"Charlie?" He looked at her, apprehension rising in him.

"I wasn't going to tell you, but it seems stupid to hide it." She wheeled on him, staring at him so coldly he thought there was hatred in her too-blue eyes. "I'm married, Peter. I have a little boy, too. I just let you think I was divorced because I was . . . I wanted you." She grimaced, and tossed her long hair. "For a couple of days."

His face was blank.

She laughed at him, bitterly. "You don't think it's a compliment? You should. All the men who give me the rush tell me I should take it as a compliment. Getting laid. What a favor." She walked away from him another few steps, then stood with her back to him, looking down at her sandaled feet which crushed the rank grass, her toes rouged by lava dust.

Peter sat on the wall, studying her bare brown shoulders, her slender torso silhouetted in her translucent cotton top, the faded denim skirt wrapping her smooth legs. "I'll play the game any way you want to, Anne-Marie. You're in charge. That's fine with me." He slid off his perch on the lava wall and walked to her, forcing himself to smile. "So! Why don't we eat, drink, and be merry, while your vacation lasts—Mrs. . . . . it isn't Brand, is it?"

"The real name is Phelps." She stepped farther away. "And I've got a headache."

"I want you to leave the S.O.B. with his stocks and bonds," he said angrily, impetuously. "I love you."

"You're a great big handsome male with his head full of abstractions, Peter." She turned on him. "That gush of hormones you think is love gives you no property rights. Peter, listen to me! I've run away from every honest thing I could have done with my life, usually in favor of letting some guy take care of me. Not this time, thanks."

His head was reeling, but he sensed he should keep things casual. "You're pretty honest, aren't you? You're being more honest than you really have to be." He smiled, a big smile this time, nothing held back; it stretched his jaw muscles. "I think I resent it."

She was unamused. "Yeah. Do I get a choice? Or am I supposed to behave like a female monkey, full of love and care, functioning with nothing *but* hormones?"

He was honestly apologetic: "Despite what I said, you don't look much like a monkey to me."

Though she would not concede him an answering smile, her reply was gentle: "You're capable of love and care yourself, Peter—I didn't intend to mock you. But is that enough to make your life worthwhile? Or even to keep you amused? You're good at what you do, dammit, and that's what really counts for you. I want to be good at something too. I just wish I knew what the hell it was—"

"Anne-Marie, I'm sorry." He suspected that in some way obscure to him he'd been presumptuous. "What can I do to help you?"

"I don't need help," she said, so quickly she contradicted herself. "I wouldn't know what to do with help," she added a moment later, more persuasively. Then she was silent. "This place makes me cold," she said irritably. "It's creepy."

He followed her as she climbed toward the high altar. "It's an old temple, that's all," he explained. "It hasn't been used in a couple hundred years."

"Oh?" She paused to look at the offerings of stones wrapped in leaves. "Did they kill people here?"

He came up beside her. "The old Hawaiians killed a lot of people." Uncertainly—prepared to be disappointed, equally prepared to forgive her any amount of superstitious nonsense—he asked, "You don't believe in ghosts, do you?"

She laughed. "Don't be silly, Peter." A puff of breeze set the palms to clacking and snickering.

"The place does have an interesting history," he said, relieved. "In the eighteenth century the old Hawaiians sacrificed the crew of an English ship here, the *Dedalus*—

caught them down there at the river, way below, getting fresh water."

"*Dedalus?* The original labyrinth builder. Maybe Hawaiians just don't get along with you scientific types."

"That's a strange connection to make," he said.

"I'm just making small talk." She reached for his hand, pulled it toward her, spent some seconds inspecting it. There were no ring shadows on his long fingers. "Peter," she said softly, looking up at him, "it's not going to be fun anymore. I think we'd better say goodbye."

She brushed his lips with her own, and her fragrance filled his nostrils. He tried to bring her close, but she gripped his hands tightly between their bodies.

He said, "I think you wouldn't be here, with me—with me or anybody else—if you weren't going to leave him."

"But *I* don't know that. I do know I'm not leaving my little boy—and I don't know why I'm here, except that you're a very attractive man, and if I had to throw myself at somebody I made a good choice in you." She released his fingers and pushed him firmly away, both her hands on his breast. "Peter—what a stupid cliché—there's no future for us." She smiled and nodded ironically. "So thank you, sir, for a memorable weekend—and for this lovely picnic—and now please take me back."

He stepped away, speechless. Rarely in his life had he been denied anything he'd asked for. Yet somehow he'd known all along the things he really wanted would be forever beyond his reach.

23

Chauncey Tolliver walked into the little windowless room where Gardner Hey sat fidgeting in a gray-painted steel armchair. Aside from another chair and a table of similar construction, the room was bare. "Sorry about all this, Gardner," said Tolliver, brisk and guardedly sympathetic. "Not a good time for journalistic initiative. Man killed, very expensive equipment, possible danger, all that . . ."

"What better time for journalistic initiative, Chauncey? Anyway, can I get out of here now?"

Tolliver looked at the bruised and muddy reporter, then glanced away at the blank wall behind him. "Gardner, we need to reach some sort of an understanding."

"Hold on, Chauncey," said Hey warily. "No deals."

Tolliver sat in the other chair. For a moment he said nothing, absorbed in studying the tip of his polished oxford. "I'd like you to listen to me, that's all," he said without looking up. "You saw what it was like in there. Whoever bombed us could try it again. A place this big, understaffed on security—"

"I haven't necessarily bought the sabotage angle you're peddling, Chauncey," said Hey. "You're real good at what you do, I've got to give you that—you've got everybody believing you *were* bombed. Because you've played it so coy."

"Come on, Gardner, you give me way too much credit," Tolliver said sharply. "I haven't been coy. I was ordered not to say anything about possible causes of the explosion by Professor Ishi himself. And I had nothing to do with Martin's little impromptu press conference. I would have prevented it, you know that—you don't send a man whose best friend has just been crushed to death out to talk to reporters."

"Was that guy really Edovich's best friend?"

"Best professional friend, anyway. They knew each other thirty years, met when Martin was still a student. Martin never knew his own father, you know. Maybe Cy wasn't exactly a father figure to him, but he was a dependable older guy who really liked Martin, showed him lots of tricks, took a personal interest in him—he was family."

"Okay, Chauncey, I'm touched." Hey was not displeased that he'd gotten a rise out of Tolliver—the smooth IO wasn't so unflappable after all. "What do you want to say to me?"

"First, here's your camera." Tolliver took the Canon from his jacket pocket. "And I need your signature on this release." He took a folded form and a ballpoint pen from his inside jacket pocket and held them out, along with the camera.

Hey took the camera but ignored the form. He thumbed the camera's film-advance lever; it moved easily. He looked up at Tolliver with a questioning smirk.

Tolliver's freckled face turned rosy beneath the brown spots. "Yes, we developed it. You won't want it back; it was blank, just as you told Gambito."

"Chauncey, poor fellow, you're handing me your balls in a sack. Unreasonable search and seizure, due process, assistance of counsel—you've violated half the Bill of Rights—"

"Dammit, Gardner, argue law with Gambito if you want. He's a hardnosed ex–warrant officer who'd just love to charge you with trespass, breaking and entering, resisting arrest—not to mention U.S. Code Title Nineteen, which we don't talk about too much around here because we don't want to rudely remind the Japanese that they're our guests here, even though they paid for the place."

"Come off it, Chauncey, this is an open facility."

"So next time you'll know, Gardner, parts of it are labeled 'secret.' Which parts you don't need to know. No big deal—some contract work, like every lab in the country." Tolliver settled his distracted gaze on Hey, staring at him blurrily. "But," he said, pronouncing it distinctly.

Hey was silent. Chauncey was being unfair, it would never hold up, there was no question of Hey's actually spending time—Title Nineteen was worth five years, just for peeking—but even due process would be a hassle. Hey chewed the ends of his mustache absently; that unconscious habit undermined his efforts to stare Tolliver down, and finally those watery, unfocused, not unfriendly eyes defeated him. He reached for the release and the ballpoint, and without reading the form, scrawled his signature.

"Thanks, Gardner. I know it's your business to be inquisitive. And it's mine to maintain good relations with the press. This helps us both."

"I've heard enough speeches," said Hey, standing up slowly, stretching his sore muscles. "Just open the door."

Tolliver stood and opened the door, but casually blocked the opening. He was an impressively large man, seen close up. "Is that your own camera, Gardner?"

"No, Anne-Marie loaned it to me."

"I appreciate the fact that you're keeping her out of your extralegal adventures." Tolliver sounded sincere. "She means a lot to me."

Hey hardly hesitated to plant the vengeful little barb:

"She's so busy chasing that guy Slater she hasn't had time to take pictures for me." He laughed.

Tolliver looked as if he'd been poked with a cattle prod; the big muscles in his jaw tightened spasmodically. "Is Slater the one who let you in?" he said, forcing the words.

The non sequitur caught Hey by surprise, but he recovered quickly and laughed again. "I can't answer questions like that, Chauncey." Smugly he added, "Find out on your own."

Tolliver's gaze slid away from Hey to the blank wall behind him. Suddenly he smiled, the picture of joviality. "Okay, Gardner, it's a deal. I'll find out on my own." He stepped aside and held the door open for Hey. "The men's is down the hall to the right, if you want to freshen up. Your car's out front in the red zone. We brought it around—thought it might be more convenient."

Hey said, "Shit," under his breath—he'd claimed he'd taken a bus, when they'd asked him. "I suppose you searched the car too?"

Tolliver smiled. "Thanks for the release, Gardner. Goodbye."

Hey walked quickly out the door and down the hall.

Tolliver could not resist a huge, weary yawn. Slowly he made his way back to his office, rubbing his watery eyes.

24

Dan Kono was watching from the living-room window when the passing police cruiser pulled a fast U-turn across the highway and skidded to a stop in the powdered coral of the highway shoulder, blocking his drive. Kono ran for the back of the house, but he was too late. Ana met him in the kitchen, slamming the screen door behind her. "Dan, a man came in the yard! Don't go out there!"

"Nothing for you to worry about, Ana." He sighed, defeated. "Only police."

"Police! What the hell they want again?" Ana's fear turned to anger. "That goddamn Luki. You were up all night, Dan—trying to keep him outa trouble, weren't you?"

"*No,* Ana—I was right here all night with you. Make sure you remember." Kono put his enormous brown hands on Ana's shoulders and looked into her eyes, which suddenly brimmed with frustrated tears. He spoke to her slowly, softly: "Maybe they take me away, huh? Only for a little while. They got nothing. I done nothing. So the law says they have to let me go. You want me to recite the Bill of Rights to you? I know it by heart." He smiled at her, patted her arm. She looked up at him out of welling eyes, hurt and distrustful.

Outside in the front yard the dog began barking frantically.

"Here they are, Ana. Now promise you won't say anything about Luki."

"Oh Dan, why won't you let your friends help you? Your friends, your family, they could make these damn cops get off your back—"

There was a loud knock on the front door. Kono ignored it, still holding Ana. "I got no friends since I quit on them. My family is you, lei-Ana, just you and Luki—"

"Let them take *him* away. Then you could hold up your head again."

"Promise me, Ana!" he ordered.

She twisted until he loosened his grasp. "Okay, no family, no friends, no lawyers," she said angrily. "Do it the way you want, all by yourself. And leave *me* all by *my*-self."

He released her. The knocking was louder this time. He turned away from Ana and walked into the living room. Through the curtained window he could see the uniformed police still sitting in their cruiser; the yellow caution light on their roof rack blinked monotonously. Parked on the shoulder behind the police car was an unmarked gray AMC sedan.

Kono yanked open the front door. A haole with short-clipped brown hair, wearing a light gray summer suit, stood on the porch. Kono spoke first. "What da hell you want, cop?"

The man held out his leather badge case. "George Linka, Mr. Kono. Federal Bureau of Investigation. May I come in?"

"Up you ass."

The FBI agent colored slightly under his tan, but otherwise maintained a neutral expression. He slipped the badge case into his jacket pocket. "Mr. Kono, last night the TERAC research facility was heavily damaged by an explosion. Will you please tell me your whereabouts between ten P.M. last night and four o'clock this morning?"

"I was here all night. Ask my lady, if you want."

Linka ignored the suggestion. He took a leather-bound notebook from his shirt pocket. "Mr. Kono," he said, glancing at his notes, "according to the proprietor of the Thrifty-Quik store on Paolima Street in Waimanalo, you bought a case of Primo beer from him at approximately nine forty-five P.M. last night, and during the course of conversation with him you divulged your intention to meet some friends of yours in the Beach Park."

"You believe dat snitch Wong? He tells da fuzz whatever he tinks you want to hear, man. Den you don't bust up his Mah-Jongg parlor out behind."

"Who did you meet on the beach last night, Mr. Kono?" Linka persisted.

"I was home," said Kono stubbornly.

The agent looked at his notes again. "Your neighbor Mrs. Halemanu reports that she was roused by the barking of your dog at about four o'clock this morning and from her bathroom window saw you entering the front door of your house."

Kono sneered. "Someday dat ole lady gonna see flyin' saucers come in her own front door, way she hits dat booze."

Linka sighed. "Mr. Kono, in the past you made frequent threats to do to TERAC exactly what was done to it last night. Despite your apparent inactivity with respect to the facility for the past several years, your statements were taken seriously at the time and are still taken sufficiently seriously that, on the strength of them, I obtained a warrant for your arrest from Federal District Court Judge Baldesaro Lum this morning." Linka took a document covered in blue paper from the inner pocket of his jacket. "Do I have to serve you?"

Kono said nothing, did not even glance at the document.

"Okay, Kono, I'm arresting you as a potential material witness. I'm taking you to the Federal Building. You have . . . "

"I got da right to remain silent, for starters. I got da right to legal counsel. An' I know fer sure anyt'ing I say you gonna use against me. Let's go."

"I see you're well acquainted with the procedure," said the FBI man dryly. "Would you like to bring a change of clothes? Say goodbye to anyone?"

"Let's go." Kono stepped onto the porch, forcing the agent to move aside. He slammed the door behind him.

Ana came from the shadowed hallway into the living room and peered through the window, watching Kono, massive and defiant, march across the lawn ahead of the FBI man toward the waiting cars. The agent who'd been lurking in the backyard appeared at the side of the house and hurried across the lawn to catch up with the others. Ana kept watching until all the cars—there were three of them, one of which had remained out of sight up the road—had turned across the highway and disappeared toward Kaneohe and the Pali Highway to Honolulu. Then she sat down on the couch and burst into tears. Living with that no-good son of a bitch Kono had cost her the respect of everyone she loved. Was it worth it? Because she loved him more than all the rest of them, was it worth it?

Not for that, no. It was also because she respected him, even when she couldn't understand why he was doing what he did, even when he was willing to give up everything for the sake of his crazy, evil brother. She knew—they both knew—there were ways to get rid of Luki, to make sure he could never hurt Dan again. But Dan wouldn't think of that.

She stared at the telephone. A few words to Dan's father . . . She shied away from the thought almost as soon as it formed. If only there were *something* she could do.

An idea occurred to her, an idea born of desperation—a silly wish more than a real hope: there was someone she could call who didn't fit the category of Dan's family or friends, someone who might be able to help.

She leafed through the tattered telephone directory until she found the number. After two rings a woman answered the phone: "Diamond Head Crater Hotel. How may I help you?"

"I want to speak to Anne-Marie. She's a photographer. I don't know her last name, she works for a newspaper. I got a story for her."

"You don't need a last name, dearie, she's got several—and *everybody* wants to talk to Anne-Marie. Let's see if she's in her room."

Ana clutched the telephone, hoping Anne-Marie was there, willing herself not to cry. The phone buzzed unanswered.

25

Gardner Hey was turning the red Datsun onto the ramp down to the hotel's parking garage when he saw Slater's Triumph pull up to the curb behind him. Hey slammed on the brakes, killing the engine. He abandoned his car on the ramp, and ran to the Triumph before Anne-Marie could get out. "I need your help," he said. "Both of you." He leaned on the door, trapping Anne-Marie inside.

"What the hell do you want, Gardner?" she asked angrily.

"I can guess you're probably pissed," he said, "but I had to risk getting thrown in jail, and I didn't think you'd be interested."

"You didn't ask. You lied instead."

"Okay, okay, but I need you now." He crouched down and looked at Slater, whose fingers were drumming on the wheel. "Slater, did you mean what you said yesterday? About not believing in secrets?"

"Yes, I did," said Peter coldly. "So what?"

"I took some damn good pictures of the explosion site.

They caught me, but I switched the film first. I tossed the good roll over the fence. You've got developing stuff, right, Anne-Marie? And I need a different car. Mine's too obvious—they're probably watching for it."

"You don't need us, Gardner, you need a chauffeur and a Fotomat." She looked across at Slater. "It's up to you, Peter."

"How'd you get in there, Hey?" he asked suspiciously.

Hey replied with instant enthusiasm. "I took a hell of a chance, but it was kind of exciting—I just walked in behind some investigators and grabbed a bunch of coveralls and plastic booties and shit like that, and they didn't even notice me for about ten minutes, and then I had to run for it. I got out through an emergency exit. But they caught me anyway."

Peter thought about that for a moment. It sounded like the sort of thing the brash reporter might attempt, the sort of thing most people on the staff would never dream of watching out for. He glanced at Anne-Marie. "Do you want to go?"

"Sure," she said airily. "For the ride."

Peter got out and started unfolding the convertible top from its recess behind the seats. "When I get this up you can squeeze in behind," he said to Hey.

"Great! I really appreciate this," Hey replied.

"Go park your car before somebody hits it," Peter said sourly. Hey nodded and ran off. Peter said, "He's a ghoul."

"No," Anne-Marie said, "he's a good reporter, damn him."

An hour later Peter sat in the Triumph with Anne-Marie, facing a wall of green cane. The car was splashed up to its windows with red mud; he'd parked it on a cane road north of the Hawaii Country Club, well hidden from Kunia Road. Gardner Hey was off somewhere in the wet, tangled mass of vegetation crawling around on his hands and knees, searching for a tiny tin cylinder of film.

They were silent. Peter had gone along on this dubious adventure for the chance to pursue any one of myriad unspoken and unexplored topics with Anne-Marie. Now he could find no nubbin of a grip on any of them. He found himself brooding about her child—a messy complication, to be sure. He remembered the dismaying discovery he'd made early in his marriage to Kathleen, that two people didn't marry each other, rather two families married each other. Oh, he'd gotten along fine with Jack and Helen, he'd never blamed them a moment for any of his troubles with their daughter, but they were always *there*, a presence to contend with. If he persuaded Anne-Marie to stay with him, would this creep Charlie become a member of Peter's family too? And what about the kid? What if he and Peter didn't like each other? What if the kid had no enthusiasm for spaceships and dinosaurs?

Anne-Marie was brooding about Peter's money. Charlie's money could take Carlos away from her, but Peter's money could help her keep him. That meant more than just a casual relationship with Peter. It meant subordinating herself again; it meant what the extreme feminists did not hesitate to label whoring. There seemed no room in male-female encounters for the idea of help, simple no-strings-attached help.

Here was the focus of the dilemma which drove so many women into barren, resentful mutual-commiseration societies—the same situation that threw such a golden glow on rare, direct female friendships. To assert her individuality a woman practically had to cut herself off from the network of social reciprocity on which civilized existence depends. It was hardly a modern problem. During those intense adolescent days when she was intellectually disentangling her soul from the convoluted guilt systems of the Roman Catholic Church she'd come to the conclusion that the concept of "original sin" was merely an expression of the human predicament: a human being had individual wants and needs doomed to be at odds with the best interests of the group, whether that group be family, tribe, city, or nation. Merely to exist was to exist in conflict, in sin. Kant had formulated the Protestant version of this impossible morality, but his reason-riddled *Gedankenexperiment* ("What if everybody behaved this way?") was an absurd prescription for getting on with life, a fundamental irrelevancy.

Before either Peter or Anne-Marie could find words to express their worries, Gardner reappeared, smiling, covered with mud, slick as a greased piglet. Peter winced at the sight. Anne-Marie got out of the car and tilted the immaculate leather seat forward, allowing Hey to squeeze muddily into the cramped rear compartment. Anne-Marie slipped into the bucket seat again, and Peter set off slowly for the highway, his overloaded car dragging its muffler along the muddy ridge between the cane road's ruts.

Anne-Marie locked herself in the bathroom with her Nikor tank and reels and the packages of powdered developer and fixer she'd brought with her in her luggage. She told Peter to close the drapes and turn off the lights.

Peter waited in Hey's room. Hey, doing his best to be nice, gave Peter a glass of Jack Daniel's over little cylinders of ice from the machine in the hall. They sat in rattan chairs that were too hard, too low, and squeaky, sipping their drinks and staring morosely out the window.

Hey broke the silence. "After we talked yesterday I went over to the university and read up a little," he said tentatively. "On antimatter? Like you said, storing up a bunch of antiprotons does seem pretty impractical. Given current technologies."

"Yes," said Peter.

"Yes, but—there are other theories. One in particular from ten or twelve years back. I did an article on it when I was still freelancing. Freund and Hill?"

Peter showed interest. "Peter Freund and Chris Hill?"

"You know them?"

"Sure, we all know each other in this business, Hey. But there are hundreds of theories—"

"This was a letter to *Nature,* must have been 'seventy-eight. According to them, if you have a massive stable quark—which they originally thought might be the bottom quark, before that was found, and now turns out to be the inside quark instead—you could combine it with ordinary up quarks to get a stable baryon. Which is . . ."

"The I-particle, yes, yes."

"Yes, and the *anti*quark . . ."

"We thought of that," Peter said impatiently. "The anti-inside should form a stable meson, right?"

"Yes," said Hey eagerly, encouraged by Peter's responsiveness. "So you have this stable baryon, the I-particle, and you have a stable meson, and they both become the nuclei of ordinary atoms, and you have two ordinary gases, and you store them in ordinary bottles, and so forth—but if they ever mix together, so the quarks and the antiquarks come in contact—*wham!*" Hey looked at Peter happily.

"Very elegant, Hey," Peter said dryly. "And very clever of you to have tracked the idea to Freund and Hill—I hadn't realized it was original with them."

Hey beamed with pride. "So that's what Edovich is really up to," he said confidently. "He's bottling the stuff, both kinds. There must have been a contaminated bottle, and that's what blew up." He took a deep swallow of his bourbon.

"Nice scheme, but the inside quark isn't the one you need to make it work," said Peter.

Hey looked at him. "I haven't forgotten how to use a programmable, Slater. I did a lot of calculations—"

"I'm sure," said Peter, cutting him off. "But the meson you want doesn't exist. We looked for it. You said the key word yourself: mass. The meson would be lighter, and we would have found it even before we found the I-particle. The I-particle has two up quarks, the meson version would have only one, so it should be roughly three hundred MeV lighter. There's nothing at that energy, not even a resonance."

"How do I know that?" Hey demanded.

Peter smirked.

"Oh, hell," said Hey, crestfallen. He realized that he could not seriously entertain the idea that six experimental teams made up of scientists from all around the world, all of whom had access to the same beam interactions, would have any motive for entering into the kind of conspiracy he'd reflexively suggested. "What did you mean then, yesterday?" he asked, almost meekly. "I was sure you were talking about antimatter, when you said the I-particle collector should have annihilated itself already."

Peter sat quietly, chewing his tongue, then took a sip of the watery bourbon and grimaced. At last he said, "I'm not going to tell you, Hey. Your imagination is too good. I would not have used the word 'annihilation,' by the way, and I did say that I was referring to a hypothesis contradicted by the data. By the rules of the game I should have forgotten it already. But you don't play by the rules, do you?"

Hey was sullenly quiet.

Peter continued, "I didn't used to play by the rules either, I used to talk about whatever came into my head, and cling to crazy notions long after everybody had proved them wrong. But I'm learning, slowly. Especially I'm learning to keep my mouth shut around people like you."

Anne-Marie pushed into the room, shouldering the door open, holding a long wet strip of negative in both hands.

The men got to their feet. "What do you think?" asked Hey.

"The whole thing is light-streaked," she replied, disgusted. "There's an image, but nothing worth printing. Even the pictures I took yesterday are fogged."

Hey avoided the gaze of the others, turning away. "All those people were wearing suits," he said portentously.

"Suits? What kind?" Peter asked.

"Radiation suits, you know—"

"Hoods? Respirators?" Peter persisted.

"That film was fogged by radiation," said Hey.

Peter was genuinely surprised. "I hope not, for your sake. Protective clothing is simply routine after an accident, you know—"

"Damn it, Slater, I'm not that stupid! There were a dozen people crawling all over that control room, wearing coveralls—"

"Coveralls!"

"—and a big hole in the floor. Don't insult my intelligence by telling me fairy tales about—radium watch dials, or something."

"No," said Peter sarcastically, "the simple explanation is that you fogged the film trying to unload it and run at the same time."

"To hell with you," said Hey.

Anne-Marie stood holding the wet strip of film, which dripped chemicals smelling faintly of vinegar onto the synthetic-fabric rug. "I wish you *had* taken this to the nearest Fotomat, Gardner. What do you want me to do about it?"

"Leave it here," he said. "It confirms what I suspected."

"Hey, really—" Peter searched for words to calm the man, who was evidently humiliated by his failures but could not bring himself to concede this second, more basic blunder. Hey's only defense seemed to assert some Byzantine plot against the world.

"Edovich wants everybody to believe he was bombed," said Hey, pacing and tearing at his mustaches. "And the sabotage angle is plausible, very plausible. So plausible it stinks. I think Edovich is trying to divert attention from what he's doing." Hey stared belligerently at Slater. "You've got the clue. I think you'd better tell me."

Peter sighed and closed his eyes, rubbing the bridge of

his nose as if bored. "Martin Edovich is a very emotional man. He'll cool off."

Hey stopped pacing. "I'm going to print what you said. It's on tape, you know."

Peter opened his eyes. "That's right, you do have a recording. And I know how easy it is for you people to make us look like fools." In the afternoon light from the window Peter's irises were golden, and his pupils were black pinpoints; he looked about as friendly as a hawk. "Most scientists don't have the resources to defend themselves against libel. Be warned that I do."

Hey tried to laugh; it came out as an uneasy squeak. "The TERAC people threatened to throw me in jail, and now you're threatening to sue me—I've got to figure I'm onto something."

Peter took a deep breath. "I'm going to try to explain myself one last time, Hey. Based on theoretical considerations of my own, symmetry principles of the most general sort—but not generally shared, I must re-emphasize—I would have expected the inside quark to be less than perfectly stable. Nothing dramatic, although maybe I made it sound that way, and believe me I now deeply regret it. The point is, all the data we have so far tell us the inside quark *is* stable. I've examined that data over and over again, Hey. It's unequivocal. The problem is with my hypothesis—not with nature."

Hey's wrath was not deflected by Peter's attempt at sweet reason. "I don't know whether you're defending Edovich out of a feeling of solidarity with all the rest of the arrogant S.O.B.s, or because you're in on the scam. Either way, it won't work."

"Have it your way." Peter set the glass of bourbon and melted ice on the dresser.

"You still have my camera, Gardner," said Anne-Marie.

"Just leave the film, okay?"

"Sure." She tossed it on the bed. "A little lint can't make it any worse than it already is." She took the camera from the dresser, where Hey had left it. "See you at the conference tomorrow?"

"I'll be there."

"Do you care if I am?"

"Chauncey Tolliver hired you, sweetheart. Suit yourself."

She walked out of the room. Peter followed her, closing the door firmly. Hey stood stiffly, tugging and worrying the ends of his mustache.

Outside the door of her room Anne-Marie turned to face Peter. "Peter, I'm sorry to have to say it, but nothing's happened to change my mind. The longer we stay together, the more it's going to hurt us both."

Peter stepped toward her, his jaw muscles knotting. He spoke with an effort. "Anne-Marie, I just—can't accept that."

She backed away from him, frightened. "Don't pull that masculine stuff on me, Peter. Trying hard doesn't make things right."

He stopped and stared at her bitterly. Then he turned and walked rapidly, stiffly away.

She stepped into her room and closed the door behind her, leaning against it wearily, her hands squeezing the doorknob as if she were trying to strangle it. She felt vertiginous, disembodied. She groaned aloud, fending off the wet, black, questing mouth of her despair.

"Ahh, shit," she said aloud. Then she giggled at the ludicrous sound of her feeble, obscene voice.

She turned away from the door. The red message light on her bedside telephone was glowing.

26

Ishi hung up the phone. The news was good, but curiously unwelcome: Umetaro Narita, on behalf of the Health Physics Department, could find no reason why Ishi should not order the restarting of the ring. All signs pointed to an explosion deliberately set by saboteurs or malicious vandals; the incident of the trespassing reporter proved that it was a simple matter to penetrate TERAC's outer perimeter.

There was no positive evidence of sabotage. Nevertheless, Narita had been unequivocal: whatever had caused the explosion, the explosion itself was an external event.

Ishi sat in his study at home, pondering his course. He had hoped that the results would be at least a *little* more equivocal. Certainly he wanted TERAC to be perfect, but a tiny worm of suspicion that it was not made him flinch at Narita's good news.

Investigative teams were on their way from Tokyo and Washington. Could he use the ongoing investigation as a plausible excuse to delay the restarting of the beams? He could conceive of no legitimate way to do so. Delay in restarting would have only detrimental effects on many expensive experiments, reflecting on his abilities as an administrator, and thereby reflecting on the Prime Minister's wisdom in having chosen him for the director's job. After only a few minutes he reached the necessary conclusion: he would order that the ring be restarted as soon as possible.

Now, by his own word (and nothing had arisen to alter the circumstances of his promise), he was obliged to inform Yamamura personally that the decision had gone contrary to his advice, his wishes.

How best could he break the news? That evening the full moon would rise to the south of east, in the direction of Diamond Head. There was still time to prepare an impromptu tea, to create a proper frame for viewing that spectacle. And Ishi would like to make tea for Yamamura-san, even if for no better reason than to show his gratitude for the magnificent banquet Yamamura had arranged on his behalf. After the ceremony he and Yamamura could share a light supper and discuss whatever matters needed discussing.

Ishi reached for the telephone. First he would call Yamamura, then Friedman. After that, the others.

Ilse Friedman hung up briefly, then picked up the phone and began to make calls of her own, to the control room operators of the linac control center, the pre-injector rings, the cooling rings, to her main deputy in central control. They in turn would notify their deputies and assistants, and the personnel responsible for operation of the sources and pre-accelerators, for monitoring power sources, rectifiers, coolant flow, and all the other myriad intricate processes essential to the huge machine's proper functions. With luck, the restarting process would consume a few hours, not the half day or more Friedman had pessimistically predicted early that morning.

*   *   *

Yamamura's gray Datsun sedan wound jerkily through the deep shadows of the Nuuanu Valley toward Ishi's home. Yamamura steered the little car stiffly around tight corners and along the unfamiliar narrow streets. He was almost trembling with gratitude for the unexpected honor Ishi was about to bestow. Ishi was said to be an expert amateur of cha-no-yu; on these grounds alone Yamamura would have been delighted to accept the invitation to tea. Moreover, the circumstances of the invitation foreshadowed a change, a decision, perhaps an announcement of some importance.

Through sources of his own, Yamamura knew that Ishi would soon leave his post as director of TERAC—a suspicion that he'd shared, in utmost confidence, with his superiors in Tokyo—and he hoped that Ishi perhaps appreciated the excellent advice Yamamura had given him concerning the proper administration of the facility. Could it be that Ishi would put in a special word for Yamamura with his own people back home? Could it be that he had already done so, and now had good news to share?

Yamamura swerved into the steep drive that led to Ishi's house and parked in the cul-de-sac under the ancient koa trees. High up on the hillside the roof of the teahouse was visible, above and behind the low eaves of the brooding colonial estate. The house and gardens were already in shadow, but the last rays of the setting sun illuminated the mists that gathered higher up the valley.

Etsu Ishi, wearing a kimono of finely patterned blue cotton, cheerfully greeted Yamamura at the door. In the hall he exchanged his shoes for tabi and his Western suit coat for a short-sleeved kimono jacket. Mrs. Ishi led him through the house and up steep stone steps to a little arbor of pine and bamboo beside the gate to the inner garden. There they lingered awhile, while Mrs. Ishi engaged Yamamura in polite chit-chat about his two sons, who lived in Japan. She excused the unfinished landscaping, which Ishi had been rearranging ever since his arrival on the island many years ago. After a few minutes Mrs. Ishi left, with apologies, going to prepare their supper.

Yamamura sat quietly for a moment, sensing the cool evening air that flowed down from the ridges. Bamboo sighed and rustled. The scent of ginger floated delicately in the shadowy garden; he saw a white ginger flower, luminescent in the green darkness.

He heard a sharp splash of water as it was poured into the stone basin in the inner garden, then Ishi's footsteps on the path. Ishi appeared at the wooden gate; in his simple tan kimono with its short coat of charcoal gray he emerged out of the shadows like a creature of the forest taking shape before Yamamura's eyes. Ishi bowed.

Yamamura suppressed the urge to greet him aloud. Talk was not necessary. A hint of worry creased Yamamura's brow. In the presence of men skilled in the old ways he sometimes felt inept—or, alternately, belligerent. But Ishi was smiling calmly. After all, this tea was quite impromptu, not a solemn occasion, not *ichi go ichi e,* "one chance in one lifetime." Yamamura was reassured.

He followed Ishi into the inner garden, along a path of steppingstones. He noted the fresh green moss at his feet, sparkling with the artificial dew Ishi had sprinkled there. He was aware of Ishi's footsteps ahead of him; how graceful the lame man seemed, here in his little garden, with his robes flowing so softly around his twisted legs. What a contrast to the hard corridors of TERAC! There poor Ishi stumped along, tiny and deformed in his dark Western suit, a wizened goblin overshadowed by loud towering foreigners.

The teahouse made no pretense to age, though it had been constructed in the traditional sōan manner, with much rough-planed pine, and walls of thin adobe plaster. Ishi disappeared behind the little hut, and Yamamura continued walking to the guests' entrance. There a stone lantern glowed softly beside a washbasin, also carved from stone; Yamamura stooped to splash water over his hands with a bamboo dipper.

The gentle shock of the cool water refreshed his senses. He saw the play of yellow candlelight on the water in the granite bowl, and felt himself coaxed by the flickering fairy light to enter a tranquil world of natural simplicity—a world out of time, yet still a part of the olden Japanese times—separated by an unimaginable gulf from the harsh modern jumble of the Hawaiian Islands. In such a place even he, tense and temperamental as he ordinarily was, could forget his ambitions and dissatisfactions for some little while.

The guests' entrance was tiny, and Yamamura bent low to crawl through. Thus everyone entering the teahouse was made equal; thus all were born equally into this world apart.

Somewhere a last steel door clanged shut and a massive key was twisted, sealing the ring. The persistent soft chime in the central control room fell silent.

Ilse Friedman sipped thin, sour coffee and paced the length of the long room, watching the operators at their consoles. Intercoms hissed and mumbled, screens glowed, a man yawned and stretched. The air conditioner rattled; Friedman made a mental note to have Maintenance tighten the loose grate. It was probably the only system in TERAC not functioning perfectly.

Computer-graphic displays of the ring and its subsystems indicated the staged withdrawal of beam stops and focusing quartzes downstream from the proton source. Energetic protons entered the antiproton assembler, where they smashed into a tungsten target. A spray of antiprotons and other debris resulted, from which all particles except antiprotons were stripped away. In repeated circuits of the assembler the intensity and luminosity of the antiproton beam was raised to the stupendous value that made TERAC the world's most efficient collider as well as its most powerful.

"There's nothing wrong with this machine," muttered

one veteran controller, a gray-haired man in his fifties. "You been makin' false log entries again, Ilse?"

Friedman did not bother to answer the rhetorical question. She glanced at Martin Edovich, who stood by himself in a dark corner of the metal cave, scowling silently. He had nothing to do until the Hall 30 controls were repaired, but his impatience would not let him rest.

A speaker hissed abruptly: "Rated antiproton intensity at our end."

A young woman with long blond hair depressed the microphone button on her console, leaning forward impatiently. "If you're at rating, AA, when can I have you?"

The reply came back as a drawl: "Anytime you want, gorgeous. I'm your slave."

A row of yellow buttons on the woman's console turned green. She tapped rapidly on her keyboard. Obstinately she kept silent.

The speaker hissed plaintively: "You guys ain't got no sense of humor."

The older man lolled in his chair. Casually he pressed the intercom button. "The humor comes when the experimenter asks for a beam." He was rewarded with laughs from half a dozen remote operators, all patched into the system.

Even Ilse Friedman grinned. She sipped her coffee, barely noticing it was no longer warm. She resumed her pacing, letting her gaze rove over banks of blinking lights and digital displays and screens showing bright schematics or dull gray TV images from remote cameras trained on TERAC's vital interior parts. One by one the great machine's components were brought on line and tuned, the pre-accelerator, linac, cooling ring and accumulators, main ring injectors, the main ring itself—helium refrigerators and pumps, transformers, steering magnets, focusing magnets, rectifiers, pulse cavities . . .

In the darkened room of plastic and steel the world closed in, buzzing and clanging and whirring, all its unearthly sights and sounds passing unsensed by its controllers, who watched only for the minute signs of error, of deviance, of incongruity.

Yamamura heard a sound, a soft rustle of cloth on wood. Ishi bowed from the doorway of the preparation room, then brought in the tea utensils and deftly arranged them near the brazier. Without the least hint of hurry, he began to make tea.

Yamamura was seduced, almost entranced, by the delicate strength and bold precision of Ishi's actions.

. . . the folding and unfolding of the cloth . . . the warming of the whisk . . . the measuring of the green powder . . . the precise and graceful manipulation of the water scoop . . . the merry bubbling of the water in the jar, the comforting aroma of brewing tea . . .

The ritual words came naturally to Yamamura, of themselves, almost as if he had thought of them for the first time: *"O temae o chōdai itashimasu"*—"I'll partake of your tea."

The tea was good.

Yamamura returned the empty bowl to the mat, and for a moment gazed at its pitted surface, its irregular glaze, turning it in his hands. It was a simple bowl, not of great age, nor of surpassing artistry. It had no reputation, no name. Still, the hands of its maker were figured in its rude shape; it was a product of human sensitivity.

Current surges through the windings of the iron magnets; liquid helium flows through their cold metal hearts. Each magnet grips the steel vacuum chamber between its shaped poles in fields of crushing strength; so powerful are the magnetic fields that the windings of nitinol-tin which create them, bracketed by steel collars, strain to blow themselves apart.

Soon each single speeding particle inside the vacuum chamber possesses the energy of an angry wasp. The particle beams will chew through the walls of the chamber in an

*instant, destroying the magnets, if ever the powerful fields
lose their grip.*

*Faster and faster the pulsed beams circle—meeting, an-
nihilating, meeting again, recreating the primeval void six
times over, a billion times a second.*

Out of the void, new forms appear.

Ishi had withdrawn, removing the tea implements. Yamamura sat quietly for a moment, appreciating the clean,
cozy room.

There were no flowers in the alcove. The traditional
cherry blossoms of spring would have struck an odd note
in the country of eternal summer. Nevertheless, the bare
room was gently scented by the garden's distant ginger.
And without an arrangement of flowers beside it, the
scroll with its sternly drawn kanji characters was even
more boldly highlighted. Yamamura did not recognize the
words—they were not one of the Buddhist homilies—but
he recognized the masculine hand as Ishi's own, and Ishi's
taste for the philosophical Tao was well known.

"Let everything do what it naturally does," said the
scroll.

Yamamura's mind wandered. By now the full moon
must have risen almost high enough to clear the ridge of
the Koolaus. So skillfully had Ishi managed the evening
that the moon seemed to be arriving just as the world of
the teahouse was ready to open out to receive it. With regret, Yamamura slowly left the house.

As he walked along the path, the meaning of the scroll
struck him. He so forgot himself that he staggered. With
great effort he recovered, resolving to behave normally
throughout the evening. Yet his resentment had been kin-
dled.

Friedman made a note in the log: "6:42 P.M. Both
beams at full power and intensity. TERAC operational."

27

Hiro Watanabe lay face down on the futon in the bedroom of his small house in Halawa Heights and tried to forget about everything except the delicious sensation of his wife's fists pounding his aching back. His eye half lidded, his cheek pushed into the crisp fresh fabric, he looked through the open sliding-glass door of the balcony and watched the moon rise above Pearl Harbor, beyond the lights of Pearl City spread out below.

After a few minutes Mariko's strong hands moved up to take hold of his shoulders. She began kneading them vigorously; at last the ropy muscles began to unknot. Despite the warm sensuality of her attentions, he could not totally rid his mind of worry. Hiro Watanabe was in a bind.

The trouble had come to a head at the Edoviches' party Friday night. Yamamura had drunkenly complained of Martin Edovich's arrogance in loud Japanese, and Watanabe had known it would not be long before he started expressing his sentiments in serviceable English. In Japan drunken insults are readily forgiven the next day; in America this courtesy could not be depended upon. Watanabe, who had a bit of a comic flair, had successfully distracted his beloved oya with a mock-drunken display of his own. But just as he'd managed to hustle Yamamura offstage and into a waiting taxi, Watanabe had encountered a face from his past—the reporter, Gardner Hey.

Watanabe owed Hey a favor, a fact the reporter was not shy about exploiting; he was most interested in the dispute between Martin Edovich and Shigeki Yamamura, and it was clear that Watanabe was in a peculiarly good position to help him. . . .

Watanabe turned on his elbow and reached up to take his wife's soft, strong hand. "You are very good to me, Mariko."

She looked at him with gentle concern. "I know you have been worried, Hiro. Do you want to tell me?"

He made no reply, but only looked into her dark sympathetic eyes. After a moment she disengaged her hand, closed her loose kimono, and got up to fix his dinner.

After dinner Mariko brought an extra jar of warm sake to the low Japanese-style table in the dining room. Watanabe sipped it with pleasure; his tongue was loosened, and he began to tell his wife the story of Gardner Hey.

After working on superconductivity research at the TRISTAN ring in Tsukuba, the young Watanabe had received a postdoctoral fellowship to Cornell University to help with the clever modifications of the small, versatile CESR ring there. Yamamura had helped him get the post, believing that exposure to foreigners would be of use to his protégé in the rapidly changing world of international big science. But Watanabe was desperately lonely in upstate New York. When Gardner Hey came up to do a story on the ring for *Science Weekly,* Watanabe found in him a sympathetic listener, not to mention a persistent one. Hey had insisted on buying Watanabe one drink after another at a local Ithaca hangout, and the following day Watanabe could only vaguely remember the wild, loud stories he'd pressed on the reporter.

For three weeks he lived in terror of what would be written about him. When the issue of *Science Weekly* with the CESR story in it finally arrived, Watanabe was relieved and grateful to see a brief but friendly sidebar on the trials of young Japanese researchers in the United States. His name was mentioned only once, in a thoroughly respectable context.

Thus Watanabe was put in Gardner Hey's debt. Moreover, he conceived the notion that Hey could be trusted. . . .

The 10:00 P.M. television news carried a one-minute item on the restarting of TERAC and a thirty-second tie-in on the arrest of Dan Kono.

Gardner Hey sat in his hotel room, rubbing his hands over his eyes. He had a terrific headache. He knew he shouldn't keep drinking, but somehow he had to dull the pain. He took another deep swallow of the bourbon, then set the glass down shakily. After a second he got up, walked to the TV set, and punched it off.

It seemed to him that he must be all alone in his suspicions about TERAC. Despite the way Dan Kono had treated him the day before, or perhaps because of that treatment, Hey was unwilling to believe the big Hawaiian had been involved in any bombing. A genuine protester would have bombed something with symbolic value, like Tomonaga Hall—not an obscure experiment the public couldn't understand. No, the Hawaiians were tools, at worst—or mere scapegoats.

Two options remained. Somebody inside TERAC was out to get Martin Edovich. Or something was wrong with his experiment.

Hey thought of Watanabe, a real ace-in-the-hole informant. But who was he really working for?

Hey peered at the creased strip of negatives lying on the bedspread. The photographs themselves weren't worth much, though Hey could tell even in negative that Anne-Marie had taken good pictures, and that his own showed a good many details of the accident scene. Despite the fogging, they could be printed for an interesting "before and after" of the scene.

The fogging itself was the key, however. Some thought had persuaded Hey that the film had not been fogged by high-level radiation, as he'd first suspected. They weren't crazy out there; they never would have restarted the ring. But a burst of X-rays or gamma rays, something intermittent—the possibilities were intriguing. A pattern began to form in Hey's pattern-susceptible mind as he stared at the blank gray glass of the television screen.

There must be something unusual about "holy water," something Watanabe knew about, perhaps, and had passed on to Yamamura. Something that could be used to embarrass Edovich? Something Peter Slater suspected?

Slater's ill-considered remark had now become vital to Hey's case against TERAC. Hey picked up the phone.

"You knew about it, my friend, fifteen minutes after the fact . . . "

"I explained, Mr. Hey, the central control room called me to make sure I was not in the hall . . ."

". . . and *you* opened the hatch for me. What I'm asking you to do now is simple."

Watanabe looked up at his wife's worried face. She watched him quietly from the shadows of the bedroom door. He took a breath. "It is not simple, Mr. Hey," he said sternly. "Security has become very stringent since you allowed yourself to be caught. Moreover, I don't see how this information could possibly be of use to you."

"Peter Slater told me it was important."

"You have been talking to Professor Slater?" Watanabe's surprised tone held a hint of deference.

"Yes, yes, I have," said Hey, seizing his advantage. "Slater implied he has severe doubts about the stability of the inside quark; that's why I have to have the data from the stability experiment."

"But the results are widely known, Mr. Hey," said Watanabe, genuinely puzzled.

"Watanabe, I must see the current data. Right away. The raw data."

The threat in Hey's voice was plain. Hey knew a great deal about Watanabe that would shame him irretrievably. With an anguished glance at his wife, Watanabe whispered, "All right, Mr. Hey. But I have no plausible excuse to be in the area of the vault. Certainly not on a Sunday night. I will think of some tale and go there in the morning."

"That late? The speeches will already be started."

"I can do no better."

"How soon can you get it to me?"

"I refuse to be seen with you at TERAC," said Watanabe sharply, his fear evident. Mariko started toward him, but he turned away from her abruptly, hiding his face.

"During lunch, then? Most people will eat at the cafeteria, except maybe the fat cats with expense accounts."

"As far from TERAC as possible," said Watanabe.

"This end of the island, then. Make it the Blowhole. You can get there and back in an hour; we'll mingle with the tourists."

"One P.M. then. At the Blowhole. I can think of nothing better."

Hey hung up the phone. He went into the bathroom and swallowed six aspirins, trying to ward off the hangover he knew would be upon him in the morning. As he forced them down, one after the other, he stared at his puffy, bristling face in the mirror. He looked positively demonic.

Terror, that's what he needed to break this story open.

He had to shake things up, make somebody mad, scare somebody badly. How else could he get past the bland smiling face of the TERAC hierarchy with its double-talk of sabotage and symmetry principles, its calm assurances that Hey hadn't really seen what he thought he'd seen?

Hey went into the bedroom, stripped off his shirt and shorts, and threw back the bed coverings. The fogged negatives fell to the carpet as he burrowed between the sheets. A ghost of a frown flitted across his brows: what if Slater were right? What if he'd merely fogged the film accidentally as he was reloading?

An absurd suggestion. Within moments Hey was unconscious.

28

Peter played the piano with barely restrained violence, lunging at the keyboard in isometric slow motion, flinging a torrent of notes out to challenge the boom of the surf, which hurled itself against the pale sand a hundred yards from his house like mountains of molten lead, gleaming in the moonlight.

Across the darkened living room a hanging Japanese lantern, a rectilinear thing of pine strips and translucent paper, frail as a kite, threw a soft white glow on the dining table. Spread with a heavy linen cloth and set with blue-figured stoneware, the table was wholly undisturbed. Peter had plotted a culinary coup, but he'd never even had the chance to do the shopping. There were no lamb chops to be grilled, no mushrooms to be stuffed and baked, no Brussels sprouts to be steamed, no crisp lettuce to be tossed with dill dressing. The young Burgundy rested in the rack, but it would be drunk alone, if at all. Anne-Marie had not come home with him, and would not. Bach assuaged him.

The small, modernistic house Slater was leasing near
Haleiwa, all raw planks and angles, had been built by a
young man from San Diego who'd made a killing in real
estate, and who fancied himself a surfer. While Oahu's
north shore is not a particularly fashionable neighborhood, it is sometimes literally underneath the best surf.
The builder's ardor for the sea had cooled rapidly the previous March, when a late-winter storm had sent fifty-foot
waves onto the beach, washing away the carefully landscaped yard to within a foot of the lanai, leaving behind
the wreckage of boats and houses and the bodies of two
of his neighbors.

Peter had never met the man, who'd turned the house
over to an agency a week after the storm. For almost a
year it had gone unrented. Under the terms of his lease
Peter could do what he wanted with the place; so far that
hadn't involved much beyond chucking out the fishnets
and the glass floats over the bar and ripping out the royal
blue wall-to-wall shag carpet, which had acquired the
odor and texture of a wet sheep dog. Peter had moved in
a decent secondhand Baldwin, hung some fashionably
narrow blinds over the huge plate-glass windows that
faced the sea, and replaced the surfing, sailing, and skiing
posters with a couple of big Japanese scrolls, nothing valuable enough to worry about risking in the damp salt air.

Despite its simplicity, he'd looked forward to showing
the place off to Anne-Marie. Apparently that would never
happen.

He fairly leaped for the telephone when its ringing interrupted his playing. "Hello?"

"Peter, it's me."

"I tried to reach you."

"I'm not at the hotel. I'm with a woman named Ana
Apana—I met her yesterday. She lives with Dan Kono.
Do you know who he is? He used to lead a protest group
against the construction of TERAC. This afternoon the
police took him away."

"They arrested him for the bombing?"

"I'm not sure, exactly. It doesn't sound like there's any evidence against him. But Ana's worried. She called me at the hotel and asked me if I could help her."

Peter was silent a moment. "And you thought of me," he said, keeping his voice carefully neutral. He'd been Gardner Hey's chauffeur only because he hoped it would give him an opportunity to change Anne-Marie's mind. Things had not turned out as he'd hoped.

"I don't know if I can help her or not," said Anne-Marie slowly. "But Peter, I've been thinking about things and I—I have this very strong feeling about Gardner."

"What's he got to do with this?"

"Well, first of all, you were right about the film. I'm sure he did fog it when he reloaded, or maybe before. The back of my camera is a little bent—I noticed it yesterday when I first loaded it, but I'd forgotten when I loaned the camera to Gardner. He probably popped it open without realizing it. Most likely when he was rewinding the exposed film back into the cartridge."

"Okay, Anne-Marie, but I still don't see what this is all about."

"Look, I know he makes mistakes. But I want you to help him, because I think he's right. Even though he's wrong, he's right, do you know what I mean? I'm certain Dan Kono had nothing to do with the explosion. And what you were saying this morning, about an industrial accident—if that were true, they wouldn't be arresting people, would they? I just have this very strong feeling, Peter, and I know it probably makes you angry for me to say it, but Gardner is right that something strange is going on out there. The place gave me the creeps when you showed it to me, if you want to know the truth."

"Have you been talking to Gardner?" Peter asked calmly.

"No. Dammit, don't be that way."

Peter thought a moment. What she said made sense only if the premises were true, that Dan Kono had nothing to do with the sabotage (and, by extension, that there was no sabotage), and if it wasn't an accident then it had to be an inherent problem of the experiment or the ring. How could such a string of contingencies be assessed? He did not know. "Anne-Marie, I want to help you. Even more desperately, I want to see you. You know that I would get involved with almost anything for that. . . ."

"That's not why I'm calling you, Peter." Her voice was flat. It left no doubt she meant what she said.

"I think Gardner Hey is a creep, to tell you the truth." He said it with vehemence. "I don't think his schemes are worth a damn. Where's the evidence? Nowhere. I just don't believe Martin Edovich is some kind of a mad scientist, cooking up a witch's brew beneath the noses of his unsuspecting colleagues. That's the way I feel. What can I do?"

"You could trust me, Peter. I'm not stupid."

Peter stared at the relentless surf outside the windows. He spoke only after a long pause. "I can love you, Anne-Marie. I do love you. If things were different between us . . . but as it is, I can't act on the basis of your . . . I mean, on no other basis than your intuitions."

For a moment the line was silent. Then he heard her hang up. In the seconds it took him to return the telephone to its hook images of dire revenge flamed across his vision. He despised unreason in every form, and Hey embodied it—a man who by every objective criterion should know better. Belief systems must be supported by evidence, else the most elegant structures were empty of meaning. Peter had forced himself to renounce what was contradicted, but Hey would not. And in his arrogant fanaticism, Hey had corrupted Anne-Marie.

His resentment over Anne-Marie's resolve became inextricably entwined with his defense of rationalism against the likes of Gardner Hey. Peter was no fool; he knew human beings were all a little nuts, that he owed much of his own success to the appreciation of the absurd. But there are moments when the coolest Stoic surrenders to miserable passions.

29

Anne-Marie was disappointed in herself. She had asked Peter to do something she could not have done, to help a person who'd already rejected him, in a way that violated his own feelings. "He won't help either," she said to Ana. "I'm not much use to you."

Ana sat quietly on the couch, resting her cheek against her fist, staring out the window at the deserted highway and the rolling surf beyond. The shadows clustered thickly in the bare room. She turned to Anne-Marie. "You wanna go for a walk on the beach? That phone ain't gonna ring anytime soon."

"Whatever you say."

They walked along the shoulder of the highway for a quarter of a mile, until the beach on the other side of the guardrail widened and curved away to the east, and they could walk on the sand. At first they walked quietly, hearing only the susurrus of the surf on the sand. But as they approached a distant bright flicker of orange firelight beneath the ironwoods, they heard the cheerful ring of slack-key guitar, and laughing voices in chorus:

> *"Liliuokalani, farewell to you,*
> *And Princess Kaiulani too—*
> *Don't have time to fret the past;*
> *Got to find another brew . . ."*

Ana shied away from the singers, walking as close to the water's edge as she could and keeping her eyes on her bare feet. But as they passed the firelight, one of the men around the mesquite fire called out to her. "Ana! You can't go by. Come talk a little."

Ana turned and, to Anne-Marie's mild surprise, smiled happily. "Come, I'll have you meet my friends," Ana said, and took Anne-Marie's hand, leading her toward the group under the trees.

There were a dozen men and women, and half a dozen fat children. Some of the men were as big as any humans Anne-Marie had ever seen, with seallike pendulous bellies hanging down between their thighs. Some were compact and muscular, darkly handsome, not at all shy about staring suggestively at the beautiful haole across the ruddy flames; she looked coolly away, but not without appreciation of their own self-possessed masculine beauty. Someone put a can of Primo in her hand, and she sipped the watery beer. Someone else handed her a plastic plate heaped with spicy barbecued chicken and unidentifiable crisp vegetable slices. She kept silent and watched, nibbling, as the men sang and the women got up to dance—solid women, with the singular grace of controlled weight in motion—and finally Ana, after much teasing and prodding, got up to join them.

She was an extraordinary dancer; Anne-Marie realized that within moments. Her hands and hips and face and body blended dance and drama in fluid mime. The song was in Hawaiian, and Anne-Marie understood not a word, but its moods were evident in its liquid sounds—humor, struggle, pain, hope—and some of its content was vividly apparent from Ana's dance: the love of a man for a woman, the birth of a beloved child, a death—the child's?—the continuing round of daily existence, farming, fishing . . .

The dance ended abruptly, as if there were more to the story Ana had not chosen to tell. But the people around the fire praised her enthusiastically, stood to hug and pat her, took her to sit by them and continually reassured her with caresses and little squeezes of her hands in theirs. Watching the ambiguous scene, Anne-Marie felt tears pressing against her eyes.

There was an old man who had kept silent, grinning and laughing and hugging his knees, while the others sang and danced. Now he began to tell a story, an incomprehensible tale told in rapid, passionate Hawaiian. The others around the campfire fell silent within moments after he started. His bright wet eyes stared into the flames and he gestured vigorously, and Ana got up from her place and moved to Anne-Marie's side, and she whispered the words of the story into Anne-Marie's ears.

Maui's father dared him to challenge Hina, goddess of the night, first woman—if he won, all humans could live forever. But it was a big chance. Maui was half a god, but he was mortal like any man.

Hina's hair was like tangles of seaweed, her eyes were like this red fire, her teeth were like a shark's—and she was a giant, big as that island Molokai there. But Maui was not afraid of her. He went with his friends the little birds of the forest, and he traveled to her home in the moon, you see? There, where the horizon is light against the sky.

Hina was asleep when they came there, which made the job seem easier. Maui told the birds he would enter Hina between her legs, crawl up through her, and come out from her mouth. Then she would be defeated! She would know he had beat her! But the bold plan can only succeed if no one laughs!

The old man fell silent a moment, glaring around the

circle at the campfire, daring his listeners to mock him. And none did, though their cheeks trembled with mirth.

With dignity, the old man resumed his tale.

If anyone laughs or makes another sound, I will be killed, Maui tells the birds. All the little birds promise to be quiet.

Maui takes all his clothes off, even his underpants. He dives into the soft wet opening between Hina's legs . . . the old man's eyes roll as if with inexpressible pleasure . . . *and he struggles and wiggles this way and that, and slowly he gets up inside her, until only his legs can be seen, kicking up and down like a man swimming as hard as he can. Oh, those little birds, they try so hard to keep from laughing . . .*

A child shrieked with laughter, then ran off into the night, embarrassed, to roll gleefully in the sand until the hot ticklish urge had passed.

. . . and Maui still kicked and jerked like a man doing his best. But it is such a funny sight, really so funny. Now the little honeycreeper can't hold himself, he has to let go, it is too funny. Pee-pee-pee-peep, he goes, so happily . . .

Several children dissolved in paroxysms of giggles, and a couple of adults snorted and coughed. The old man leaned his skinny frame closer to the fire, as if to tell them that the weakness of the character in the story was no excuse for their own, and his leathery brown face grew frighteningly solemn.

The goddess wakes up. Fire shoots from her mouth—she is a sister of Pele, you know that—and she feels the stranger inside her private place, pushing at her womb. She is angry. She crushes her legs together. She twists this way and that way, grinding her thighs. Maui is helpless. He dies. Now he is dead.

The old man leaned back away from the flames. His listeners were as solemn as he. He spoke sadly.

And since then all humans have had to die. No hope of salvation, no matter what they tell you.

There was silence for a moment. Then one of the

women said softly, cheerfully, "But if you gotta go, that's the way, eh?" And everyone laughed and applauded the old man, who was grinning now, displaying his toothless mouth, and someone passed him a beer.

But Anne-Marie saw that Ana was not smiling, that instead bright tears had sprung to her eyes. Within moments Ana was on her feet, speaking rapidly, a speech which included the words *aloha, mahalo,* and then she was tugging at Anne-Marie's hand, and they were walking back along the moonlit beach.

Later they sat together on the couch in the dark living room. "At least Chauncey said they'd have to let Dan go soon," Anne-Marie said, resolutely cheerful. She didn't tell Ana the rest of what Chauncey'd said: *unless we get some hard evidence against him.* Chauncey hadn't been friendly on the phone; he'd made it plain he thought Kono had had something to do with the explosion.

Ana smiled sadly at Anne-Marie. "It's just nice for you to be here."

Anne-Marie took the girl's brown hand between her own. "Ana, why am I the only one? You have friends who love you, I saw that. Why isn't anyone here to help you?"

"Because . . ." Ana stopped. Then, quietly at first, she began to cry. Anne-Marie moved to her and cradled her against her shoulder, smoothing Ana's long sleek hair with her cool fingers; she stared past the unhappy girl's head to the moon-silvered surf. The low palms in the yard stood black and stiff in the cool, still air. A pickup truck grumbled past on the highway, its radio turned up so loud a few distorted notes of a pop Hawaiian tune were left twanging in its wake.

Ana shuddered and pulled away, staring at the floor. Wiping the tears from her cheeks, she began to speak, quietly. "Dan's old friends won't talk to him, his mother and father won't let anybody speak his name around them, his cousins come here and try to pick fights. All because he quit OLA when everybody thought OLA was going to win. They thought Dan was going to get their land for them, and he let them down. And because I stay by him, they give me the same treatment." She paused.

"Your own parents?" Anne-Marie asked.

"Oh, they're nice to me when I go to their house, as long as I'm by myself. Like tonight—long as I don't remind anybody I live with Dan." She looked up bitterly. "But they don't forget. Listen, Anne-Marie, I want to tell you something. . . . " Suddenly Ana was whispering hoarsely to Anne-Marie. "But you have to promise not to tell anybody else, ever. It could—get me killed."

From Ana's voice and posture Anne-Marie knew her friend was not dramatizing. "Certainly I promise."

Ana abruptly rose from the couch. "I could use a beer. You want one?"

"Why don't you tell me about it first?" Anne-Marie suggested gently. "Then, maybe."

"Yeah." Ana nervously twisted her hands in front of her. "Luki's in pakalolo in a big way—that's marijuana, you know?"

Anne-Marie nodded.

"But that's not so bad over here, lots of people do it. But you can never tell about them. . . . And Luki's kind of crazy. He pushes people until they do stupid things. He always knows how to make people go—out of their heads, I guess. Even if he just stands there watching them with a funny look on his face."

"Does he know what he's doing?" Anne-Marie asked. She remembered Luki vividly, his odd disjointed mannerisms. The man had terrified her, partly because she suspected he was not completely in control of himself.

"Oh, he knows." Ana smiled crookedly at Anne-Marie. "People think he's stupid, retarded, because that's the way he acts sometimes. He's not."

"He's frightening," said Anne-Marie.

Ana shivered. "Yes. If he ever comes around when Dan isn't here, I hide until he goes away. It's because of him—because of what he did, and because Dan covers for him—that Dan has to take on everybody's hate." Ana's words, heavy and insistent, flowed into the moon-shadowed room. . . .

Anne-Marie learned of Luki's partners, the growers with their secret patches of pakalolo scattered among the dense, wet, inaccessible jungle valleys of Molokai's east end, and of his other partners, the grinning sunburned haoles who controlled the mainland markets from their Kahala beach houses. She learned of the time a nervous rich kid from Omaha, a fat little guy with red hair whose father owned a string of movie theaters in the Midwest, had tried to score a lid from Luki in a Waikiki bar. . . .

Luki brought a package to Ala Wai harbor the next day.

The kid's boat was big, a ketch with a fiberglass hull and a hardwood deck, titanium masts, its own radar. Luki checked out the kid, who was being cool, and his girlfriend and the other couple; they were all scattered around the boat, sipping their chi-chis and improving their tans. The other boy was tall and serious-looking, with dark hair; the girl with him was a large blonde, round-faced and crafty. But it was the kid's girlfriend who flipped Luki's switches.

She wasn't exactly pretty, and she wasn't very tall, but she had the look about her, the superior haole look that drove Hawaiian boys up the wall—the little frown, with brows straight across and wide thin mouth pursed tightly. And she wore her dark gold hair down to where her bra strings tied behind her. And the little triangles of rough cotton barely draped over the nipples of her small ovoid breasts in front, and the other triangle of her string bikini only loosely covered her sweet mound. Her skin was all red-brown and freckled, and she raised up on her elbows and looked down between her toes, humming, and ran her green-eyed gaze over Luki, then looked away with a tiny yawn. And she turned over on her towel on top of the

Luki started baiting the kid in his subtle fashion, under-cutting the kid's every attempt to be smooth, but never coming right out and challenging him. The kid had to test the hemp before he paid—"Hemp?" said Luki, but it was okay by him, if the kid couldn't tell the real thing by look-ing at it. The kid clumsily rolled a fat reefer, and Luki just smiled lazily, as if haoles always made that much of a mess. The kid lit up and toked deeply, closed his eyes, held his breath, exhaled with a big sigh—did the whole num-ber, and turned purple trying not to choke—and finally pronounced himself satisfied.

Dan was there, watching the whole performance. Luki had talked him into coming along, said he was going to introduce him to some big-spending liberals. Dan knew his brother; he should have known him better. Dan almost walked when he saw what Luki had rolled up inside that yacht-club ensign, but he didn't want to panic the people on the boat. Now he was caught.

He never knew how Luki did it. But somehow, without a word, with a look or a shrug or a sneer, Luki suddenly convinced the kid he'd been had—that the perfectly good dope he'd just tasted for himself was inferior, perhaps not even the real thing. And Luki fed the kid's conviction all the while he was taking his money, so by the time Dan finally grew wary and started hustling Luki off the boat, the kid was already heading below decks. He came back up with an enormous pistol and pointed it at Luki and Dan and demanded his money back.

It was what Luki had been waiting for, an excuse. He whipped out his knife and dived for the kid, and the kid shot at him, the shot going wild, and Luki was almost on him when Luki slipped in something, the girl's suntan lo-tion maybe, and went down and bounced his face off the deck—and the panicked kid had the gun aimed right at his head, squeezing the trigger, but Dan was already there and hit the kid in the side of the head so hard it threw him up against the rail, and he yelled and fell over, but before all that a bullet had ripped a hole as big as a quarter through the teak plank beside Luki's ear. Luki was out cold. Dan picked him up in his arms and ran with him along the dock, past the people who were already coming to see what the noise was all about.

Next day they learned the kid had drowned, sunk like a stone to the bottom of the harbor. The three other people on the yacht told the cops a story about three big black GIs who'd tried to hold them up, which nobody believed. They said not a word about dope. The whole lid must have gone into the Ala Wai Canal. Some witnesses remembered two "beach boys" running away from the scene, but the descriptions weren't too good.

Around the beach the word was out—night before last, Luki had been seen with the drowning victim, and today Luki's face was a mess. So the smart money said Luki did it. That crazy Luki. The cops didn't bother him; Luki's Kahala friends had connections. A little while later the friends reminded Luki that he had to be more careful, by busting two of his ribs.

"All that happened maybe six or eight months before the OLA campaign really started getting big," said Ana. "The local people were winning! We don't win that many, Anne-Marie, it was kind of a strange feeling. Everybody knew it was because of Dan. He was like a god, he couldn't do anything wrong. Then he came home one night"—Ana paused. When she resumed, it was with a little groan. "Eh, what a night. Somebody from out at the construction site, he wouldn't say who, had come to him. This guy claimed to know the truth, that Luki murdered the haole kid over a bad dope deal. This guy claimed they'd tracked down the other people on the yacht and made them confess; he said they'd serve them papers and make them fly back to testify. Dan had one choice, the guy said. If he didn't want to see his little brother in jail for life, he had to lay off TERAC."

The night had grown cold. Ana crossed her arms under her breasts and hugged herself. "If they'd threatened Dan he would have told them to go to hell. And I think if Luki really did it with his own hands . . . well, even then Dan might have told them to go to hell. But Dan said he couldn't let his little brother go to jail for what he didn't do."

"But Luki did do it," said Anne-Marie. "He was responsible."

"Yeah. That's not the way Dan sees it." Ana looked at Anne-Marie sternly. "Dan killed the kid. Luki could tell the cops the truth, the witnesses could tell the truth, Dan could tell the truth himself. Still, Luki would get nailed. Nobody would ever believe good Dan Kono could kill. He was OLA. He was life."

"So he quit. He let himself be coerced."

"Now he spends his time fishing and trying to protect Luki from his friends. And I keep praying that somebody gets Luki soon, so Dan can go free." Ana glanced at the photograph of her family's dance troupe on the living-room wall. "God forgive me." She restlessly got up from the couch. "I guess I don't want that beer anymore. How about you?"

"That tea you made yesterday was awfully good."

"Okay, let's make some. Then I'll take you back to your hotel, if you want."

"I'm staying with you, Ana." She rose from the couch and followed Ana into the kitchen.

Ana turned on the kitchen light. A gecko, splayed on the far side of the window screen, chirped in surprise; the sound made Anne-Marie laugh. Ana put the kettle on and scooped tea into the round pink pot. While they waited for the water to boil Ana impulsively stretched on her tiptoes and kissed Anne-Marie's cheek. "You're my best friend in the world, and I've only known you since yesterday. I want you to tell me all about yourself, Ana-Melia, world traveler. I want to know just exactly how and when you got the baby you're carrying, and what you're going to name it, and what kind of house you live in with your husband, and . . . and I want you to tell me how you're going to live happily ever after."

30

The myriad creatures in the world are born from Some-thing, and Something from Nothing.

—LAO TZU

It was a perfect April morning, gentle and bright, but Gardner Hey was having a hard time appreciating it. At ten o'clock it was coffee and doughnuts, followed by speeches; at eleven o'clock it was California champagne, green tea, and cookies, followed by speeches. The corks shot off the champagne bottles by the dozens, like the rat-tle of small-arms fire. Hey's stomach was aslosh with cof-fee and aspirin, and he felt as if all the plastic corks had hit him in the head. He'd read somewhere that the most energetic cosmic ray particles are kinetically equivalent to well-hit tennis balls; he supposed the run-of-the-mill cos-mic ray particle would thus be equivalent to a well-popped champagne cork. The thought that millions of the things were continually perforating his body made him queasy.

Between speeches the talk among the writers was all

about the accident, and Hey, although he did not participate, noted that the sabotage rumor had firmly entrenched itself. The incident had served to ensure a full turn-out for the ceremonies. He filled his third plastic cupful to the brim with the cheap champagne—it tasted like weak lemonade with bubbles—and gingerly steered his way back to his bleacher seat past reporters from the *New York, London,* and *Los Angeles Times*es, Tokyo's *Asahi Shimbun,* and that gray-haired fellow from *Science News* who wrote about high-energy physics as if it were a form of Gnostic mysteries. Hey ignored his peers; he was waiting for the right moment.

Professor Ishi had the last speech before lunch, and he'd chosen to speak on the history of nonlocal field theories. Hey suspected he'd deliberately chosen the least sensational, least topical subject he could think of, though it was clearly of sincere interest to the distinguished physicist. The quiet voice, the warm sun, and the bubbles did their work; happily the loud snores of the old gentleman in the row above him in the hillside bleachers helped to keep Hey from nodding off himself. Soon raw nerves restored his alertness.

Nevertheless, he almost lost his chance. Ishi's talk was suddenly over, and Ishi was bowing to polite applause. The applause continued as Ishi limped toward his seat on the wooden platform. Hey stood up and began stepping over his neighbors' toes to reach the grassy aisle. Edovich, Lasky, Yamamura, and Friedman had risen from their seats on the platform and gathered around Ishi, offering their murmured appreciation. Chauncey Tolliver had taken the podium microphone and quickly began to speak.

"Thank you all for joining us here this morning," said Tolliver. His smooth voice echoed from the windows of Tomonaga Hall behind the bleachers. "Lunch is on the house, remember—we'll be serving in about forty-five minutes. The young people with the bright orange badges are here to give you any assistance you need—raise your hands, will you, gang? So ask them if you can't find the cafeteria. Our next program starts back here at two, when Professor Lasky will address himself to, uh—" Tolliver fumbled with his notes while Ishi and the others started to move slowly toward the wooden steps at the end of the platform. Most of the audience members were similarly ignoring Tolliver's announcements, and were milling about in the bleachers. "Oh, here it is, 'current issues in theories of weak interaction decay modes.' And of course tours will continue to leave every . . ."

Tolliver broke off, startled. Gardner Hey was clambering onto the wooden platform from the front; gaining the boards, he stood up and raised something over his head, a long dark strip, a roll of film. Tolliver heard him shouting, "I have evidence of a cover-up! Proof! Proof of a cover-up!"

Uniformed security guards were fumbling with their holsters, but a plainclothes guard standing near the stairs toward which Ishi and the others were moving had already drawn an automatic pistol from his shoulder holster, an action so frightening in its own right that Ishi froze when he saw it, and turned back to see what was happening.

"These are photographs of the actual explosion scene," Hey shouted, his voice carrying easily across the grassy slope now that everyone had fallen silent, and was staring at him with curiosity and apprehension. Hey noted uneasily that several pistols were aimed at his face. He could not have asked for better help in getting the attention of the crowd. Cameras appeared, and the sound of clicking shutters punctuated the still morning. With his arms in the air, holding the film aloft, Hey looked like a politician riding in a parade, but his bare pink tummy protruding over the waistband of his chinos robbed the image of dignity. He cleared his throat and continued. "I believe Martin Edovich is manufacturing a secret substance, a weapon of some kind—a dangerous substance which caused the accident early yesterday morning. I believe Professor Ishi knows the truth but has deliberately concealed it from the public, and from his own colleagues. . . ."

Tolliver spoke into the microphone, his voice booming in the silence. "Gardner, my friend, what has . . . ?"

"Let him talk!" someone in the crowd shouted, and others joined in. "Let's hear him out."

Tolliver shrugged and stepped away from the podium, shaking his head curtly at the guards. Reluctantly they holstered their weapons. Tolliver sighed and stared at the tips of his shoes.

Encouraged by the audience's support, Hey continued breathlessly: "Yesterday I got into the hall where the explosion occurred and took pictures of the scene. One thing I learned is that the site is contaminated with radiation." Hey glanced at Ishi; the little man stood confounded at the head of the stairs. "And Professor Ishi knew that and directed Tolliver to conceal it from the press."

"Tell us about your so-called secret substance, Gardner," the red-haired woman from *Time-Life* demanded. She had a reputation as one of the brightest of the science-writing corps, someone who forced scientists to dispense with homilies and defend their statements at the most basic level.

"I don't know the details," said Hey. He lowered his arms, sheepishly. "It has to do with antimatter, though—an antimatter reaction initiated by the inside quark. But Peter Slater can give us the details. Two days ago, before the accident, he told me he was surprised the I-particle collector hadn't annihilated itself. And I have that statement on tape."

"What's your comment on this, Professor Ishi?" a man with an Australian accent shouted. The cry for a statement from Ishi was taken up by other members of the Western press, though the Japanese journalists kept a worried silence.

Grimly, Ishi started toward the microphone, but Tolliver stepped to it first and said in a low, disgusted voice,

"Peter, you were good enough to warn me this might happen. Will you see it through?"

Necks craned, and after a pause of a few seconds Peter Slater reluctantly rose from his position in the very highest row of the bleachers. He made his way down the hillside to the speakers' platform, while the writers and other guests muttered and clucked. Peter was impeccably dressed, as if for an examination, in linen slacks and jacket, with blue broadcloth button-down shirt and a blue flower-print tie; he and Chauncey looked like male models from the pages of a Sunday supplement. He took the steps on the far side of the platform from Ishi two at a time and walked toward the podium. Before acknowledging Tolliver, he looked toward Ishi and abruptly bowed to him, bending from the hips. He straightened up and spoke rapidly in Japanese, then bowed again. Ishi bowed also, and some of the reporters tittered at the sight of the tall Westerner trying to get his head lower than the little Japanese.

Tolliver looked coldly at Hey. "You wanted to ask Dr. Slater some questions?"

Hey was stymied; his assumption and hope had been that Slater would shun the press. Hey was saved from his indecision by another shout from the audience.

"Who are you?" asked the Australian. "Are you the antimatter expert?"

Peter's face flickered with contempt, but quickly settled itself in a broad, almost friendly smile. "I understand your need to identify the people you quote, sir, but let me assure you I have hardly more interest in antimatter *per se* than I do in what you ate for breakfast this morning. My name is Peter Slater, and I'm a theoretical physicist with a big mouth." The self-deprecatory approach earned Peter a few friendly chuckles. "I'll get right to the point," said Peter, adjusting the microphone to point up at his lips. "Gardner Hey says there was—is—some sort of very mysterious radiation at the site of the explosion in Hall Thirty. His evidence for this is that his film is fogged. My contention is that he did indeed expose that film to intense electromagnetic radiation—at the frequency of visible light. I think he exposed the film by improperly unloading it." He smiled, all charm.

"What about the pictures? Can we see prints?" a woman called.

Peter turned to Tolliver, who shrugged. Peter said, "It seems to be okay with TERAC." He turned to Hey. "It's up to you, I'd say."

"Sure," said Hey, trapped. "But tests—I'll have to have tests, first, and . . ."

"Of course," said Peter smoothly. "By the way, did you know Anne-Marie told me the back of the camera was bent?" He looked at the audience. "Mr. Hey failed to inform his photographer on this job that he was going to try to break into TERAC yesterday. Instead he tricked her into lending him one of her spare cameras. Had she been operating it, I doubt the film would be fogged."

Mutters from the audience indicated that Hey had just lost the sympathy of the photographers among them. But the reporters had not all been distracted. "Hey claimed *you* predicted the explosion," said the woman from *Time-Life*. "Is that true, Dr. Slater?"

Peter looked at her. She was young, stylishly dressed, with a square freckled face and a midwestern show-me attitude. "How much detail do you want?" he asked.

"Yes or no will do," she shot back.

"I'm afraid it won't. What I said to this man was that if the theories I held when I arrived at TERAC had been accurate, it would be surprising that the I-particle collector was still functioning. But it *is* still functioning—eventhough this explosion happened some distance away from it. I'll remind you of that, if I may."

"What theory *did* you hold when you arrived?" the woman persisted.

Peter took a breath and forced himself to relax. He went so far as to lean against the podium with his weight resting on one foot, assuming a coolly aristocratic pose of hip-shot nonchalance. But his words were precise and technical.

"If you've read the literature, you can guess I expected to find evidence of the instability of the inside quark. There would be a specific half-life for the I-particle. I-particle fluid, in other words, would be radioactive. But it isn't. The data show that the I-particle is stable, the inside quark is stable, nothing is going to blow up, and nothing *has* blown up—at least, not for that reason."

"You subscribe to the sabotage theory of the explosion, then?" the woman asked him.

"Certainly not," he replied sternly. "I have no theories at all, if that's really the word you want. Any number of things could have caused that explosion. All I know is, the properties of the inside quark are not among them."

"Thank you, Dr. Slater," said the woman, signifying that he had satisfied her for the moment.

Peter took her acknowledgment as a signal and ignored the other reporters who began shouting his name. He turned to Ishi, who stood quietly a few feet away, and spoke a few words to him in Japanese. Ishi shook his head. Peter turned back to the microphone. "We could go on like this forever. Personally I'm looking forward to Brownie Lasky's talk this afternoon, and I wouldn't mind getting a bite to eat first. Professor Ishi has nothing to add, either. So why don't we all just sort of ramble in the direction of the cafeteria and I'll field whatever questions you have. Chauncey?"

"Fine with me, Peter," said Tolliver.

There was a general movement in the direction of the cafeteria on the ground floor of Feynman Hall, some two hundred meters away through the shrubbery. Reporters and other guests clustered around Peter, slowing his progress to a crawl, but only a very few writers approached Gardner Hey, who stood sulking and abandoned with his strip of film.

Chauncey Tolliver pressed close to Peter as he made his way across the lawn. "Thank you, Peter," he said eagerly. "Good show. A little of the old forensic ultraviolence, eh?"

"I didn't do it to save *your* ass, Chauncey," said Peter sourly.

Suddenly Peter found himself face to face with Miss Sugibayashi, Ishi's secretary. "Dr. Slater," she said breathlessly, trying to bow while reporters jostled and shouted around her. "Professor Ishi would be very much obliged if you would be able to visit him in his office today, should you have the opportunity."

"Certainly, Miss—" He was unable to remember her name. "Please tell Professor Ishi that I was planning to go up to my own office in about an hour. That would be about one o'clock. Would that be a convenient time to visit him?"

"Oh, certainly. I will tell him. *Domo arigato gozaimashita.*" With another rudely interrupted bow she departed.

Peter grinned and mumbled at his questioners, and meanwhile craned his neck for a glimpse of Gardner Hey. The reporter had vanished. Chauncey Tolliver had also disappeared, leaving Peter to carry the information-management ball on his own. And Anne-Marie had never put in an appearance. Peter had never felt lonelier, nor had he ever been the object of so much unwelcome attention.

31

Flogged by humiliation, Gardner Hey drove with more urgency and less skill than usual. He was determined not to be late for his appointment with Hiro Watanabe. Traffic was heavy on H-1, and somehow he got in the wrong lane at Aloha Stadium and found himself heading past the airport on Kamehameha Highway; recovering the freeway cost him twenty minutes in the streets of downtown Honolulu.

But he'd started early, and when he pulled into the Blowhole parking lot forty-five minutes later he was no more than five minutes behind schedule. He left the car in the trash-littered lot and walked quickly to the crumbling cement railing. The cliffs and ledges of the twisted landscape were distorted like a pool of congealed black molasses; here rivers of the viscous, runny lava known as pahoehoe had run flaming into the sea, and bubbles of gas and tubes of liquid rock had made a petrified sponge of the stony mass, where the cold sea could still penetrate and intermingle with the land. The air was warm, sour, clammy. The surf was calm, and the Blowhole expelled only an occasional vaporous breath.

Hey saw no one around; the quiescent Blowhole had not attracted many tourists. With a heavy onshore surge the hole would have been erupting great gouts of water, and the lot would have been full of cars; today there was only one other, a maroon Mercedes coupe. Presumably it was Watanabe's.

Below the parking lot and twenty feet closer to the Blowhole was a second gallery walled with cinder blocks; most of the lower gallery was invisible from above, snugged into the lava cliff. It was an excellent location for the exchange of data, hidden from the highway and from casual tourists in the lot. No doubt Watanabe was waiting there. Hey walked quickly to the stairs and jogged down them, under the overhang. The cliff wall was covered with spray-painted graffiti. Twenty yards away the Blowhole sighed like a dreaming sea creature. No one was in sight.

Hey tried to convince himself not to worry. It was still early. But if Watanabe didn't show up, he had little hope of proving his case. Had Watanabe succeeded in getting the stability data? Would Hey's grasp of physics be sufficient to interpret it?

He heard footsteps descending the stairs: Watanabe! Hey moved to greet him. But the man who came around the shoulder of black rock was not Watanabe. "Chauncey! What are you doing here?"

"You didn't take me seriously, did you, Gardner?"

Hey looked at him belligerently. "I took you very seriously. You made it clear there's something to hide."

"Hm." Tolliver looked around the lonely site. "Well, it will be interesting to see who shows up here to feed your fantasies."

"If they were fantasies, you wouldn't be here, Chauncey," said Hey. "Why don't you tell me about it, while you're here? It'll come out, you know. What is it that your friend Edovich is making?" Hey projected all the confidence he could muster.

"That was a pathetic performance you put on, Gardner," said Tolliver.

"It wasn't so bad. It got a rise out of you." Hey laughed nervously. "How did you know where to find me? Not a bug, or else you'd know who was meeting me. Something in my car?"

Tolliver said nothing, but merely cocked his head as if listening, his eyes as watery and unfocused as ever.

Hey stopped grinning. "I think I'll just go have a look." He started to move toward the steps, but Tolliver put out a hand and poked him hard, just under the wishbone. Hey yelped in pain and surprise.

"Stay here," Tolliver said harshly.

Hey stared at Tolliver, shocked and a little frightened. He began tugging at his mustaches, his racing thoughts mirrored in his involuntary grooming motions. When cornered, his instinct was toward bravado. "You're letting your past catch up with you," Hey blurted.

"What does that mean?" Tolliver asked irritably.

"I was saving it for my book, but somebody needs to teach you that you can't hide the truth indefinitely. It's all there in the record for anybody who knows how to dig."

"You're babbling."

"How you were in Air Force Intelligence, and met Martin Edovich when he was coming back from South Korea? How a year later he made you his chief of staff in the Foreign Office of the National Academy of Sciences, because you were so 'useful'—'It is useful for the National Academy of Sciences to maintain liaison with the intelligence community.' He wrote that in a letter to the chairman of the NAS Ethics Committee. Your name's deleted in the copy I got under Freedom of Information, Chauncey, but I knew who you were before I asked."

Tolliver laughed. "Who cares about that stuff these days, Gardner? Maybe you still dress like a hippy, but the sixties are long gone."

"You've showed up everywhere Martin Edovich has worked," Hey insisted. "That's no coincidence."

"He's been a good friend to me," said Tolliver. "That's something the Japanese could understand, even if you can't. Martin Edovich is a great man." Tolliver studied the horizon.

"Oh, Chauncey, you stand there so naked. The mask slips a little, and you're so naked." Hey trembled with alternating apprehension and glee; he was subject to a terrible temptation, for nothing gave him more pleasure than to let one of these manipulative S.O.B.s know he'd gotten the goods on them. "A great man. A good friend. You do have a hard time making friends, don't you, poor Chauncey? Nobody really likes you very much, especially the ones you really *want* to like you—like Peter Slater."

Tolliver's pale skin was flushed, and his scalp glowed pink under his crew-cut. His astigmatic gaze was fixed on Hey's pop-eyed face. He stepped closer. "Try closing your mouth, Gardner." Tolliver's hand went to the knot of his tie.

Hey felt the cinder-block wall against his back, heard the surf washing the lava below. Chauncey wasn't going to push him over, that was absurd—a guy could break a leg like that. On the other hand, if he could get Chauncey to take one more step, maybe Hey could get past him and get out of here. He continued the verbal enfilade: "Maybe it's the way you treat your friends, Chauncey. Not to mention their wives. That Charlie Phelps, now—he must be an awfully good friend of yours, the way you do favors for *his* wife. Too bad Slater got to her first, though. On the other hand, think of it as doing favors for two of your good friends at once—"

Tolliver's big hands with their white knuckles had moved from the knot of his tie to caress his own throat. He issued a gagging whisper, incomprehensible. He leaned closer.

"Remember that tour you and the Edoviches took to Hamburg back in '81 or '82?" Hey grinned wildly. "That little *ménage à trois?* Martin's been a father to you, hasn't he, Chauncey? But Greta's been rather more than a mother. Unless you were a very precocious little boy—"

Tolliver's splotched and livid face filled Hey's field of view; the man's watery eyes seemed to be pouring tears.

Hey bolted for freedom. Instantly his fat stomach lodged against Chauncey's muscular, seemingly iron-plated abdomen. Pinned against the wall, Hey was defenseless against Chauncey's slashing attack, the elbows like picks and the flat stiff hands like adzes that opened bloody bruises on his cheeks, that left his ears ringing, his earlobes feeling as if they were half torn from his head. With utter horror Hey realized that Tolliver was trying to hold himself back, that he wasn't using half his strength. In panic Hey shrieked and squirmed, pushing away from Tolliver with all his might.

Suddenly he found himself toppling over the balcony, bouncing from the jagged cliff, slamming into the lava shelf below. As he struck he rolled and cried pitifully, "You've hurt me!" He sounded bewildered, almost disappointed.

"Gardner! My God, I'm so sorry—" Tolliver clambered down the sharp irregular face of the rock, calling, but Hey would not wait to be helped. He lurched to his feet and then, squalling for someone to save him, he hopped and limped on a wounded leg away from Tolliver, across the surf-drenched lava shelf.

Hey looked back in terror as Tolliver, loudly protesting his good intentions, easily caught up to him. Hey swung desperately, striking out to save his life.

32

On the wall of Ishi's outer office hung a magnificent sumi painting depicting a gnarled old pine clinging to a granite crag, its trunk drawn with a few vigorous twisting strokes of a thick brush, its windswept needles added with swift splashes of ink. Absorbed in studying the painting, Peter did not hear Ishi's approach across the soft wool carpet.

"Dr. Slater, I'm so delighted you could spare a few moments," said Ishi, speaking English.

Peter got quickly to his feet and took Ishi's extended hand, bowing as he did so. "My pleasure, sir."

"Please sit down." Ishi sat primly in a spoke-backed wooden armchair, facing Peter on the overstuffed couch. "Miss Sugibayashi will bring us tea. Have you eaten?"

Peter said, "I had thought about skipping lunch today, in fact."

"I will ask her to bring us a light meal, if you wish to nibble. Forgive me that there is no time to entertain you out." Ishi raised his brows inquisitively. "You are looking forward to Professor Lasky's talk this afternoon?"

Peter smiled. "He is always informative. Perhaps I have already heard his views on this topic."

"Quite." Ishi leaned back. "Then we can chat without hurry."

"I would enjoy that," said Peter.

Miss Sugibayashi entered with a tray of tea articles, which she set on the low maple table between the two men. Swiftly she made cups of thick green tea; Peter admired her efficient skill. He supposed he should be feeling some disapproval of her subservient role, but the Japanese did not pretend to espouse equal rights for women, and did not practice them. Miss Sugibayashi bowed and went to prepare lunch.

Peter sipped his tea. "I have been admiring the scroll on the wall," he said, to make conversation. "I am reminded of the haiku of Shiki: *Shima areba matsu ari kaze-no oto suzushi.*"

Ishi looked at Peter speculatively. "Your knowledge of our culture is quite remarkable, Dr. Slater. Elder brother mentioned a similar poem to me when he gave me the scroll."

"I'm no scholar, sir. The poem is in a popular English translation."

"I suspect that now you are trying to imitate us Japanese with a show of modesty." Ishi smiled, and turned to glance at the scroll. "In what period would you place the work?"

"Ashikagan, perhaps," said Peter slowly. "The style resembles that of Sesshū. Or Sesson."

"Remarkable, indeed. It is said to be by Sesson himself—a youthful effort, and not very successful, I fear."

"Nevertheless, it is most affecting." Peter did not care to underscore the elaborate compliment he had paid Ishi, for he assumed the old man had understood him. The haiku could be translated, "Islands all around, each with its pine tree; and the wind—how cool its sound." Ishi's first name, Matsuo, meant "pine tree," a symbol of strength in adversity.

Ishi smiled at him and took a long sip of tea. He sighed faintly. "Forgive me, Dr. Slater, but I am at odds to know how to communicate with you. Since you have been so good as to join our staff, I had been looking forward to seeing you now and then. But you have acquired a reputation for preferring solitude. Then this morning, you came boldly to my defense. You behave as loyally to me as if I were your own sensei. What am I to make of all this?"

"I assure you I'm thoroughly American, Professor. I was defending myself, too. And I was hardly bold."

"Hmm. Well, I will not contradict you." Ishi studied his round, rough cup. "You are familiar with the concept of giri?"

"I think one would have to be raised in your culture to understand its force."

"How would you translate the word?"

Peter thought a moment. "As 'reciprocal obligation,' I suppose." He smiled. "In the United States repayment is usually treated as something to be delayed as long as possible."

"Ah. Well—" Ishi looked up with some relief as Miss Sugibayashi emerged from the pantry with a tray. "Here is our luncheon."

Miss Sugibayashi quietly served the wooden bowls and small lacquered plates—soup, fish, vegetables—and Peter and Ishi ate at their leisure, talking of inconsequential matters. When they set down their chopsticks Miss Sugibayashi reappeared to whisk away the dishes, leaving behind small porcelain cups and a warm bottle of sake.

Ishi leaned back in his chair. "Does tobacco offend you, Dr. Slater?"

"Certainly not."

Ishi lit one of his strong yellow cigarettes and exhaled a cloud of smoke. Thoughtfully he said, "Today, Dr. Slater, my awareness of giri is heightened. If perhaps Dr. Yamamura had come to my defense this morning, and performed as ably as you did, that would have imposed an almost unbearable obligation."

Peter was disturbed. "Sir, let me assure you that I acted completely selfishly."

"I speak more bluntly than I am accustomed; please forgive me." Ishi regarded Peter with eyes that were half shut against the cloud of cigarette smoke.

Peter shrugged uncomfortably.

"It would be a relief to me if you would accept this poor effort by the boy Sesson." Ishi gestured at the hanging scroll.

Peter's tan skin grew pale. He had behaved as any unpredictable barbarian, been too lavish in his flattery, and Ishi must have interpreted his remarks as crude bargaining, asking payment for services rendered.

Ishi suddenly smiled. "I have terrified you, Dr. Slater. Perhaps you think I am an Arab who is forced to give you anything in his tent that you admire—and tonight I will send my cousin to slip a knife in your ribs. I wish to give you this solely because of my admiration. Because 'it is better to give than to receive,' as they say in your country."

Peter had no choice. He smiled and shrugged his bony shoulders eloquently. "My most sincere thanks. I will treasure the work."

"You honor me by accepting it." Ishi's smile faded. "There are some matters on which I would like to hear your opinion, if you can stay a few minutes longer."

Peter listened quietly, now that Ishi was finally willing to broach his business.

"You were right to mock that pathetic newspaper person," Ishi said sharply. "His charges were without merit. Nevertheless—" Ishi paused to draw on his cigarette. "It is true that there was a mild residue of radioactivity at the site of the explosion."

"Really?" Peter shifted uneasily. "I hadn't heard that."

"It has not been publicized. It was not the kind of thing the reporter was talking about—it was confined to a small area, which had already been decontaminated by the time of his trespass. Nevertheless—"

Peter said nothing, waiting for Ishi to continue.

Ishi stubbed out his cigarette, then poured himself another thimbleful of sake. "If you will permit a shallow analogy: some questions are mutually exclusive. I may ask where the electron is, or I may ask what its momentum is, but I may not simultaneously ask both questions about the same electron." He sipped the warm sake. "From my isolated position, I can ask only one question about yesterday's tragic event: was it caused by a malfunction of our operation here? Dr. Yamamura suggested that it was; Professor Edovich implied some other cause. Dr. Yamamura was wrong. Was Professor Edovich right? I cannot tell. I can answer only one question at a time."

Peter said, "In the case of the electron, uncertainty is a matter of fundamental principle. But surely the cause of the explosion is not, in principle, hidden forever?"

"Analogies should not be overextended; they are useful only to stimulate the creative process. I wish to emphasize my personal limitations as an investigator in this matter. Other investigators—"

Ishi let the sentence dangle, but the request was blunt enough. What could Peter learn that the investigation teams from Washington and Tokyo could not, however? He was a theorist. After a moment's thought, Peter said, "As a theorist, I have naturally found the results of Professor Edovich's experiments of great interest."

Ishi's response was almost eager—apparently Peter had given him just the response he was hoping for. "They are puzzling in some aspects, are they not? Certainly they fully confirm the Patel-Brandenburg version of the hyperweak interaction."

"Which allows the absolute stability of the inside quark—"

"You were among the last to be persuaded of the Patel-Brandenburg scheme's correctness, if I recall?"

"That's right," said Peter. "Even if it's correct, it doesn't *require* the stability of the i quark, it only allows it." Peter was silent a moment. Then he said, "But the i quark certainly appears to be stable, experimentally."

Ishi toyed with his sake cup. "Well, you have been converted to the path of 'true religion.' " He looked at Peter. "In my country, of course, it is not required to give up one religion in order to believe simultaneously in another."

Peter laughed at Ishi's transparent shrewdness. "Forgive me, Professor, but you are a regular Mephistopheles. Would you tempt me to give up my soul in pursuit of knowledge?"

"My goodness, I hope I am not behaving in such an evil manner," said Ishi, the picture of wizened innocence. He drained the last drops of his sake and regarded the cup with satisfaction.

Peter watched until Ishi once again caught his eye. "I'll need to know everything you know," he said.

Ishi put down the cup and sat back, clasping his hands. "The most recent news is rather unpleasant. Mr. Sherwood, the gentleman killed in the explosion, appears to have been suffering from an advanced case of lung cancer."

"Cancer! Did he know it?"

"If so, we have not found any doctors who shared his knowledge. I mention this first only because it is an example of the many suggestive circumstances which stand between us and the truth of this complicated matter."

Peter nodded, silently studying the frail sake cup he had forgotten he was holding.

Half an hour later he stood at the entry level of Hall 30, feeling ridiculous. The health physics officer beside the elevator door, a middle-aged woman, had issued him white coveralls, a paper cap, and plastic gloves and booties in vibrant yellow. Only after she'd approved his couture did she issue him a big yellow temporary I.D. badge and allow him to descend.

When the elevator doors opened on the main level Umetaro Narita was waiting to meet him. "Dr. Slater. Good to see you looking well." Vapor puffed from his lips.

"Thanks. Dr. Narita? We've met, haven't we?"

The young Japanese smiled thinly. "Indeed. We got into quite a discussion during the symposium you conducted at Cal Tech, autumn before last."

"Oh, yes—very stimulating." Narita had ripped apart some of his theoretical assumptions; Peter had profited from the corrections, at the cost of a bruised ego. "Good to see you again. Tell me, is this rig-out really essential? I notice you've managed to avoid the cap and gloves."

"We're trying to remind people down here to be aware of discipline. The funny suit helps." Narita did not offer to make an exception for Peter. "I'll show you around."

They walked across the cluttered floor of the hall toward the control platform. "Anything new?" asked Peter.

"New complications, that's all."

Folding tables had been set up at the foot of the platform, where three people in coveralls were examining disassembled electronic units from the equipment racks. Narita identified them as accident investigators from the Office of Science and Technology in Tokyo, specialists in electronics. On top of the platform, Frank McDonald and Jorgen Stern had their heads together over the breech of the collection assembly; as Narita and Slater reached the top of the steps they straightened to greet the arrivals.

"Dr. McDonald, Dr. Stern, this is Dr. Slater."

"Nice to see you guys again," said Peter, shaking hands.

"You know each other?" asked Narita. "I heard you kept yourself locked up in the big black tower, Dr. Slater."

"Peter paid us a visit on Saturday," McDonald said. "How is your beautiful photographer doing?"

"Oh, you know how it goes sometimes," Peter said, shrugging.

McDonald's bristly eyebrows lifted. "Sorry to hear that. Some of us were wondering—was she the one who loaned that guy the camera?"

"Yes, and he ruined all her pictures."

"He showed you these pictures?" Narita asked. "Could they be of use in the investigation?"

"I doubt it. I suppose you could subpoena them."

"I probably broke the camera when she took my picture," said McDonald; he was plainly disappointed to hear that his portrait had been lost.

Peter looked around the control platform; the loose debris had been collected, the area cleaned up, but the effects of the blast were apparent. The rows of television and computer screens were all shattered. Soft plastic dial faces on some of the equipment had partially melted, or bubbled into frothy translucence. Surfaces of the one wooden desk were thinly layered with char, like a coat of black paint sprayed from a single direction, its unburned areas as sharply defined as shadows.

"Hot," said Peter.

"Yes, that appears to be the single most distinctive characteristic of the explosive, with one exception," Narita said. "Have a look at this." He indicated a desktop minicomputer, shielded behind a heavy cabinet; it appeared to have survived undamaged. Narita switched it on. "Two times two is four," he said, tapping the keys. The screen displayed a random cascade of meaningless numerals, letters, and symbols until Narita switched it off.

"Fried," said Peter. "Don't these things have buffers?"

"From what they're finding out, we suspect it wasn't a normal power surge," said Narita. "It may have been induced inside the circuitry by electromagnetic pulse."

"There's evidence of pulse damage in a number of devices," said Jorgen Stern. The Dane's fair skin was flushed, and his eyes were bright; he was eager to have a hand in solving the mystery. "The fire alarm box went off without anybody touching it; it was the first signal of the explosion."

"Anything else significant?" asked Peter.

"Tell him about your cosmic rays," McDonald prompted Stern.

"Hiro's cosmic rays, really. We noticed random spikes

of gamma-ray noise late Friday and on Saturday. Nothing to get excited about. Hiro suggested they were probably cosmic rays hitting the detectors; it sounded reasonable to me—so, as his popularizer, I have now inherited his cosmic rays."

"Could I have a copy of the detector records?" Peter asked.

McDonald gave Narita an inquiring glance. "You've got the printout."

Narita nodded impatiently. "You can look at them in my office."

Peter said, "I'm a little out of my depth with this electromagnetic pulse business. I've only heard the term in connection with nuclear explosions."

"Yes, that's certainly how EMP became notorious," Narita replied. He rested the palms of his hands on the edge of the undamaged metal desk and leaned back. "In 1962, a bomb test two hundred and fifty miles up in space and eight hundred miles to the south over Johnson Island managed to turn out hundreds of streetlights in the middle of the night here on Oahu. It set off burglar alarms, and knocked out power to some neighborhoods. Nuclear bombs produce copious amounts of gamma rays, which knock off Compton electrons in the upper atmosphere, and they in turn produce the pulse."

"But that's not the only source," said Stern eagerly. "Any powerful explosion, say of TNT, will blow positive and negative ions apart at a differential rate."

"I see; and that would briefly create a strong electric field," said Peter.

"Which generates the pulse," said Narita. "It's broad-spectrum, peaks in less than a microsecond, and it's completely harmless to people, in itself. But it's hell on microcircuitry." He patted the minicomputer.

"Normally you wouldn't notice," said the Dane. "The explosion would destroy the machinery anyway."

"That would rather tend to obscure the evidence,

wouldn't it?" Peter remarked wryly. He looked at Narita. "What does all this say about the nature of the explosive?"

Narita shrugged. "I don't know. It was hot; it produced EMP, which implies it was rich in ions." He straightened. "Want to see ground zero?"

Peter nodded. He turned to McDonald and Stern. "Thank you, Jorgen. Frank." He started to follow Narita to the edge of the platform, then turned back. "How soon do you expect to be back in business? What's the status of the experiment?"

"We can't unload the collector until we get this teleoperator's controls debugged," McDonald said. "But the collector just keeps on collecting."

"Don't you have to empty it periodically?"

"Oh, no—it can store I-particles indefinitely. It's got more capacity than we could ever possibly use. We don't like to unload too much at once, but that's only a precaution—you know, against spilling a couple million dollars' worth on the floor."

Peter grunted. "Well, best of luck."

He went down the steel steps carefully, trying not to trip over his plastic booties. Narita led him to the purple curtain door. They ducked under the twisted steel and walked to a discolored area in the floor of the access shaft, surrounded by chalked circles and arrows. High above them the midafternoon sky was obscured by sheets of protective polyethylene which had been drawn across the grating at the top of the shaft. The light in the room had a diffuse and milky quality; the white uniforms of the half-dozen workers in the shaft seemed to glow softly. Peter looked at the indentation in the floor, cracked and powdery. "Not much of a crater."

"Almost none. The concrete was baked, not shattered. The damage to the door and the other hardware was done by shock from expanding hot air." He gestured at the chalk lines. "From the nature of the hole, and the sight lines to localizable effects in here and on the platform, we're pretty sure the gadget was right on the ground, and very small. I can give you figures for force, pressure, temperature, and so on—if you're that curious." Narita looked at Slater oddly. "Professor Ishi said you would be."

Peter let the implied question slide by. "I'm not that kind of physicist," he said. "Without your analysis the raw data wouldn't help me."

"Professor Ishi apparently thinks it's going to take a theoretician to solve the mystery." Narita's tone was challenging.

"I hear Martin Edovich thinks it was a length of plumbing—stuffed with guncotton and salted with nuclear waste." Peter smiled mischievously.

Narita relented and grinned. "Well, you don't have to understand theory to win a Nobel Prize."

"You had to remind me," said Peter. He looked around the hall. The investigators shuffled about in the half-light, stretching measuring tapes, pointing transits, their murmured conversations echoing incomprehensibly. "Is that the cart that killed Sherwood?" Peter asked, indicating the now upright vehicle.

"Yes. It was on its side when they found it." The two men walked to the cart. Sherwood's body was outlined in chalk on the floor, with the outline of the cart superimposed.

Peter crouched to check the angle from the point of the fatality to the blast center, and thence to the control platform in the next room, which was visible beneath the damaged steel door.

Narita watched him. "We wondered about that, too," he said. "The best answer we've come up with is that he was standing on this side of the cart when whatever it was went off. Maybe he heard something, saw something. Maybe he stopped to investigate. Incidentally, if he hadn't been crushed he would have died of burns. His eyes were gone."

"I heard." Peter turned to look at the tunnel mouth in

the right wall of the shaft. "Can I get to the vault through there, or is it closed off?"

"I have a man stationed at the cooling ring, at our hotline. He'll let you borrow a golf cart or a bicycle."

"You want me to ride a bicycle in *this?*" Peter spread his hands.

Narita laughed. "Leave the funny suit at the hotline. Keep the badge, though, if you plan to come back this way."

"I will."

When Peter got to the mouth of the tunnel he turned to look back. Narita had already turned away. He and the other investigators moved gleaming in the pearly light of the shaft like Jules Verne submariners in a mythical sea, their muffled shapeless feet hardly seeming to touch bottom.

The utility tunnel was clean enough, but ugly, filled with pipes and buses and racks of cable. After walking almost two-thirds of a kilometer Peter arrived at the hotline in the curved, shielded tunnel of the small antiproton cooling ring. There a black-bearded officer, with the bulge of a pistol showing under his cardigan, took Peter's protective clothing and loaned him a bicycle. Peter wobbled off in the direction of the linac.

Soon he'd remembered the hang of it and was whizzing along with his flowered tie flying over his shoulder. He hadn't ridden a bicycle since his days at Cambridge. It was actually easier to navigate here, underground, than through the narrow stone alleys and dark gateways of the ancient university, for here the road ran straight as a laser beam into the basalt heart of the Waianaes. The tunnel had been poured as a continuous concrete tube from the inside of the mountain out; if the earth moved, the linac would not. On its integrity depended TERAC's uniquely intense feeder beams of protons and derived antiprotons. The steel sections of the linac grew perceptibly shorter as Peter neared the end of the tunnel, forcing the perspective and making the four-kilometer-long piece of pipe appear even longer than it was.

The tunnel end was a five-story chamber of raw dark rock, sweating and clammy. Peter squeaked to a stop and leaned his bike against a steel railing; a ramp descended to the floor of the gallery, past stair-stepped openwork spires of black ceramic insulators and bulbous shiny silver capacitors, tall spindly devices which fed on current from the nuclear plant and shot million-volt pulses of electrical energy through the linac's ionizer hundreds of times each second.

A single guard sat at the base of the humming injectors, reading a thick, battered paperback. She was local, a thin dark girl with glistening black hair cut short and straight, and she was bundled into a shiny blue jacket lined with fake fur, a garment so generously cut it threatened to swallow her. She looked up at the sound of Peter's footsteps, saw his yellow badge, and got to her feet, half politely, half curiously.

"Hello," said Peter. "My name is Slater."

"Hello, Doctor. This place is popular today."

"It is?" he asked curiously.

The dark young woman smiled prettily. "Two strangers in one day is two more than usual. Normally I only see the people who work on the generator or change the ion sources."

"Who was the other stranger, if you don't mind?"

"Dr. Watan—" She paused.

"Watanabe? With Edovich's group?"

"That's him. He was in about ten o'clock. I guess it's because of the explosion, huh?"

"Uh—that's a reasonable inference. Perhaps you should . . . " He stopped himself; he'd been about to tell her to consider the matter confidential. How easy it was to fall into the trap of secrecy, of need-to-know, of privileged information. "Well, anyway, is it okay with you if I look in on the stability experiment?"

"Oh, sure. That's what Dr. Watanabe wanted to see, too."

"Is that right?" Peter looked at her a moment, puzzled. But then, what else would the man want to see? He turned. "That's it over there?" He indicated a steel door in the raw stone wall.

"Yes. No secret password necessary. Just push."

He went to the door and shoved; it swung open easily. He entered a long, narrow chamber cut from living rock. The steel door slammed shut behind him; only a bare forty-watt bulb in the ceiling lit the cold passage. In front of him was another steel door.

Suddenly he stopped in his tracks. What was he doing here? He'd wondered about Watanabe, and too easily brushed the question aside. What was Watanabe doing here this morning? What was Peter Slater doing here now? It had seemed self-evident that when one was asked to investigate the theoretical aspects of the explosion, one should look in on the stability experiment—the end of the line for the material Cy Sherwood had been carrying the night he was killed. But that was not self-evident at all. Absolutely nothing connected the explosion to this room five kilometers away, buried under a thousand meters of solid rock.

Apparently in his subconscious he thought otherwise. Some thread of causation wound through the convolutions of his brain, never emerging into the light of logic. Anne-Marie had given him the thread, perhaps, when she spoke of Gardner Hey as being right, "even though he's wrong."

Gardner's theme was conspiracy, secret substances, antimatter, the stuff of fantasy. Peter's theme was the incommensurability of data and his own stubborn beliefs—science, perhaps, but not logic. Could the double-stranded thread lead him out again, to the truth?

Perfectly logical systems are barren, incapable of discovery. He opened the door to the innermost chamber of TERAC.

The crude rock closet contained a six-foot sphere of welded steel rods, studded with tubes that, from behind, looked much like automobile headlights; they were photomultipliers, all aimed at the invisible center of the hollow sphere. Peter knew that the focus of their attention was a clear plastic bottle, hardly bigger than a milk bottle, perched on a stand as if it were a flower vase. To get at the bottle one had to roll back half of the hinged rig, like splitting a giant grapefruit. Peter was content to peer inside with the aid of an eyepiece set between the clustered photomultipliers: the little bottle could not have appeared more mundane. Nothing was out of place.

Thin cables, bunched and neatly taped together, ran from the set of photomultipliers to a steel cabinet in one corner of the small cold room. The cabinet contained a computer and a printer. There was nothing else in the gloomy vault. The whole space was lit with a single dim bulb.

Peter stood quietly, watching, listening, as the machines hummed and spasmodically clicked.

The design of the experiment was simple, derived from that of the much larger proton-decay experiments of previous years. The plastic bottle contained water, some molecules of which held I-particles. If I-particles were not perfectly stable they would eventually decay into less massive particles, which would depart the scene of the dissolution at a considerable speed—faster, in fact, than the speed of light in water. They would thus emit flashes of the blue light known as Cerenkov radiation. The photomultipliers, of which there were some two hundred, would detect these flashes.

The photomultipliers would also detect other, similar flashes, such as the products of cosmic-ray collisions with atomic nuclei in the water. But each type of event had a characteristic pattern, or "signature," marked by the number and angle of flashes. Thus the computer could distinguish between the decay of an I-particle and some other, less interesting event.

The stability of the I-particle would be determined by how often the computer detected one's decay. The plastic bottle inside the iron sphere inside the rock cube contained somewhat over two billion I-particles, scattered among a vastly larger number of ordinary protons and neutrons. If the lifetime of the I-particle were less than two billion years, chances were even that at least *one* would have disintegrated by now.

There were numerous complicating considerations, but in general the longer the stability experiment ran uneventfully, the more stable the I-particle was proved to be.

The photomultipliers had recorded numerous Cerenkov events since they'd been installed a year ago, but not one was even suggestive of an I-particle decay. Virtually every such event could be attributed to cosmic rays penetrating the mountain of rock above the little plastic tub of water. This incontrovertible absence of confirming data had led Peter Slater, with much reluctance, to abandon his elaborate notions of the I-particle's nature.

Even as Peter stood in a state equivalent to meditation the computer's paper carriage jumped, and the printer typed out a graphic representation of another interaction in the tank. Peter looked at the entry: like those he'd pored over for weeks, the pattern of flashes inside the tub of water was characteristic of those to be expected when an energetic cosmic-ray particle struck a molecule of ordinary water. On an impulse he tore off the paper, and fished the folded sheets out of the catch bin. There were only a couple of pages—Watanabe, of course: he'd taken the accumulated data away that morning. Peter tapped some interrogatories on the computer's keys and, satisfied that it would do as he instructed, told it to give him the data for the last three days. The machine complied instantly, generating a manifold of green-striped paper. Peter tore off the bundle and rolled it into a tight cylinder.

With a glance around the freezing vault he left, closing the steel door tightly behind him.

He emerged from the outer door to find the guard read-

ing her paperback. He felt a moment's compassion for her
loneliness; she'd been abandoned in a troll's hole, set to
guard a little tub of stubbornly unremarkable water. As
he approached she looked at him with a ready smile.

"That's exactly what Dr. Watanabe wanted, a computer printout," she said cheerfully, grateful for the opportunity to exchange a few words.

He paused beside her. "He didn't happen to say what
he was after, did he?"

"Oh, he started to give me all kinds of reasons. I said
it didn't matter to me. He had the badge."

"Can you remember anything he said?" Peter was surprised at the urgency in his own voice; why not ask Watanabe in person?

The woman looked at him ruefully. "Doctor, I couldn't
follow him at all. Something about—'decay'?" Her expression changed to one of alarm. "There's nothing dead in
there, I hope."

She was pulling his leg; he laughed. "Might as well be,
for all the action we're seeing." He studied the small dark
woman in her big thick jacket, wondering if she had a big
thick gun tucked out of sight inside it. Her smooth
heart-shaped face, elflike and foreign, a whimsical dark
miniature of the faces he'd grown up with, seemed to prof-
fer secret knowledge—if only he knew what questions to
ask of it. "Did you ever meet a man named Sherwood?"
he asked suddenly.

"Cy was my friend," she said. "Poor old guy. I was on
owl shift up until the end of December, and he used to
come in here every morning about two o'clock, with that
holy-water stuff. When he came out of the cave we'd talk
awhile." Her expression warmed. "He'd talk about his
wife a lot. She died a few years ago. He was really a nice
old guy."

"Did he ever mention he was sick himself?"

"No, what did he have?"

"Chest trouble," said Peter, and left it at that—perhaps
there were good reasons for discretion, occasionally. "He

didn't express any dissatisfaction with TERAC or any of the people here?"

She smiled at him, gently mocking. "No, he didn't 'express any dissatisfaction.' He was in love with this place. He talked about his machines like they were pets, like they were little kids."

"Okay. Thank you"—he peered at her stitched name tag—"Officer Medeiros. You've been a lot of help."

"See you around next year, Doc," she said.

Peter climbed the ramp to his bicycle. He clipped the roll of papers to the rack behind the seat, then wheeled away. As he pedaled along beside the seemingly infinite steel vacuum chamber he thought about Sherwood. Revenge was out of the question, it seemed. As for suicide, there was no one close to the man who could profit from his insurance. He was no villain in this matter, then, but its principal victim.

The tunnel ran on, as straight a line as any pictured by Euclid, and from it tangent rings circled back on themselves.

Something else the knowing little guard had said—that silly play on physics jargon, about something "dead" inside the vault. The casual half-jest stuck in his mind, lodged fast in the craw of reason. It irritated him. Somewhere in the black chaos of his unconscious, it prodded something awake.

33

Twenty-four hours after they'd picked up Dan Kono the Feds released him. There were no charges, no apologies, no explanations. He had only the memory of a long series of interrogations by a variety of bland-faced agents.

Half an hour after he called Ana she drove the rust-streaked Land Cruiser to a screeching stop in front of the Federal Building on Ala Moana. She abandoned the driver's seat and ran around the front of the vehicle to throw herself on him, trying to surround his thick body with her arms. She kissed his bearded cheek passionately, saying, "Dan, don't you go away again ever," and in almost the same breath, "Anne-Marie stayed with me, she's my friend, you be nice to her."

Kono was surprised to see the strange haole woman in the passenger seat. "Photographer—what the hell she want?"

"Dan, I said be nice," Ana demanded.

He looked at her sourly. "Who's gonna ride in the back?"

"I will," said Ana, breaking away from him, but Anne-Marie had already swung her long brown denim-skirted legs over the back of the seat, to settle among the fishnets, spare tires, and greasy coils of rope in the back of the vehicle. She waved happily at Ana through the rear window.

Kono drove silently, glowering, answering Ana's nervous questions with monosyllabic grunts. Without consulting anyone he steered the Land Cruiser toward Waikiki, over the canal bridge and past the yacht harbor, turning onto Kalakaua Avenue in the heart of Waikiki. "Where you want to be let off, photographer?" he asked.

"She's staying with us, Dan," said Ana. "I asked her to, when I didn't know how long they were gonna keep you. And she checked out of her hotel."

"She can check back in again," he said.

"Ana, it's all right—" said Anne-Marie from the back, leaning her face close to Ana's.

"Hell, no," Ana snapped angrily at Kono. "No family, no friends, you said. Okay, Dan, I found somebody to take our side, you only met her once in your life. She did a lot for me. You're not kicking her out. Not unless I go, too." As a tearful afterthought, she added, "For good, dammit."

"Okay, Ana, keep it down, okay? I didn't know." Then he was quiet again, still scowling. He didn't like it, but he also heard the sincere determination in Ana's voice. He eyed Anne-Marie in the rear-view mirror. "You doing this for a story, photographer?"

"I'm retired," said Anne-Marie dryly. "I don't give a damn about news."

"Okay," said Kono, and added, "Then you welcome to stay."

"Many thanks," said Anne-Marie. "But Ana—now that you've got this irritable hunk of yours back home, I'm thinking of going back home myself. Maybe I could hitch a ride to the airport when I pick up my stuff?"

"Tonight? You bet not," Ana said heatedly. "We gotta

celebrate a little, make some chang-alang-lang out back, maybe I dance for you two. For the three of us." For a moment no one spoke, while the Land Cruiser whined along in high gear. Ana said stubbornly, "You go home tomorrow, not tonight."

Kono took a left past the last concrete monuments on hotel row and followed Kapahulu to the freeway. It was early yet, before the rush hour, but H-1 was busy as far as the outlying suburb of Hawaii Kai, which nestled in the lee of brooding Koko Head. Once over that hill the Land Cruiser was abruptly alone on the road.

The twisting highway descended the slope of the dead volcano toward the Blowhole. Anne-Marie sat on the hard folding bench in the back of the Land Cruiser, uncomfortably twisted, made nauseous by the swaying of the high-sprung vehicle. She peered morosely out the back window. She remembered those few minutes on the beach at the Halekulani, before she'd become deeply involved with Peter Slater, before the accident at TERAC, before she'd gotten into this collection of sticky messes with Gardner, and Ana, and Dan Kono—for those few minutes, she'd had nothing to do but lie on a warm beach and let the sun deepen her tan. She was envious of her own recent past.

She'd come to Hawaii to resurrect her *amour propre;* what a shambles she'd made of that project. And at no time during her adventures had she acknowledged the inconvenient, demanding fact that cells were multiplying and organizing themselves in her uterus. "I'm not a monkey," she'd told Peter indignantly. What then 'is a human—a large primate given to articulating its own irrationality?

Through the Land Cruiser's salt-streaked window the Hawaiian landscape looked as bleak and dreary as her life's prospects.

They passed the Blowhole parking lot; it was crowded with cars. One was a little red Datsun like the one Gardner drove so badly. Another was a police car.

Gardner, I did what I could, she said to herself, but you rub people the wrong way, you really do.

The highway ran on down to the beach, and looking back the way they'd come Anne-Marie could see the Blowhole and its overlooking galleries as if in cross section. A knot of people stood on the flat lava shelves beneath the jagged ledges. A spurt of foam erupted from the hole in front of them.

"Ana, isn't it strange for people to be standing around the Blowhole?" asked Anne-Marie.

"Oh, there's always tourists around there. And kids at night, watching the submarine races."

"No, I mean right by the hole. They're practically looking into it."

Dan Kono grunted and swung his head around to look back. He steered the Land Cruiser onto the shoulder, killed the engine, and swung himself easily out of the vehicle to the ground. He walked to the guardrail, cupping his hand over his eyes to shield them from the bright western sun, and stood unmoving for several seconds. Then he got back in and restarted the Land Cruiser, wheeling it across the highway in a quick U-turn.

"What is it, Dan?" Ana asked him.

"How do I know?" he grumbled. "Something funny, like the photographer says."

All the stalls in the big lot were filled. He left the Land Cruiser standing on open pavement, jumped out, and headed for the stairs, not waiting for the women. Ana helped Anne-Marie over the front seat. Together, they followed Kono.

Anne-Marie paused by the red Datsun, parked near the head of the stairs. Ana giggled. "Look, there's Dan's hand." Sure enough, the five-fingered print of Kono's hand in the car's fender was thrown clearly into relief by the low afternoon sunlight.

"Gardner's always right there where the news is happening," Anne-Marie said cheerfully.

The women went down the cement steps. They had to

duck under the pipe railing and clamber down rugged out-croppings to reach the horizontal strata below. The swell had risen and the Blowhole groaned and shot gouts of froth with each onshore wave, then hungrily sucked air as the seas receded. They tiptoed across the wet lava bench toward the group near the water's edge; there Dan Kono was talking to an Oahu sheriff's deputy.

The deputy was saying, "Old man Tabilang over there was fishing on the point when he looked back and saw these two guys fighting. He decided to get a closer look, he says, but by the time he got around the rocks he saw only one guy, running back up to the parking lot. So he looked around for the other guy awhile. When he couldn't find him he came up to the highway. He flagged me down about five minutes ago."

"Looks like he flagged down half the island before you come along, Jimmy," Kono said.

The Hawaiian deputy looked very young behind his sil-vered aviator glasses. "You could be a big help if you'd help me get these people out of here, Dan."

"You think I want to help you, little Jimmy Wikiwiki?" Kono sneered. "You one respectable fella, now, eh?"

"Have it your way, Dan," the deputy said coldly. "When the fire department gets here you'll all clear out or get cited."

Kono smiled and turned away. The Blowhole sighed wearily. Kono waved "mabuhay" to Tabilang, a wizened little brown Filipino who wore a tattered white T-shirt, purple shorts, and rubber boots. The Blowhole shot a stream of white saltwater twenty feet into the air; it fell like warm rain over the group of men and boys gathered nearby.

"I don't see Gardner anywhere," Anne-Marie said to Ana. With the exception of a well-dressed young Japanese tourist who was posing his wife against the spectacular background of the nearby Blowhole and frantically snap-ping pictures of her every time it erupted, the only people near the hole were locals. "Who's the man Dan's talking to?"

"He's a good fisherman," said Ana. "He lives over in Waimanalo, near us."

Anne-Marie watched the young deputy speak angrily to the Japanese tourist, telling him to get back behind the wall; the man grinned and waved, backing off, snapping pictures, and finally retreated, laughing. His wife ran giggling after him.

Anne-Marie approached the deputy, but before she could speak he turned on her. "You too. Get out of here. Can't you read signs?"

"I'll go right away, officer," she said soothingly. "But can you tell me where to find Mr. Hey? He's a reporter."

"How would I know? I ain't seen no reporters yet."

"His car's up in the lot. He's a short man, fat, with long blond hair—"

The deputy stared at her silently. Anne-Marie saw her own anxious face doubly reflected in his mirror shades, and behind her face, tiny in the forced perspective of the lenses, the Blowhole shooting another column of white foam into the air. The deputy reached for his notebook. "What's the guy's name?"

"Hey. H-E-Y. Gardner Hey."

The deputy scribbled laboriously in the book with a blunt stub of pencil. "And you say his car's in the lot?"

"Yes. It's a rented car, from Richard's Rents. A red Datsun two-door. So you have seen him, then?"

"No. But you're describing the guy Tabilang says is missing. Come with me, will you please, Miss?"

He led her to the group near the hole. Tabilang was gesturing at Kono, and the two were trading questions and answers in rapid pidgin. Kono turned to the deputy as he and Anne-Marie approached.

"Tabbi says he thinks the guy's in the hole, Jimmy. He tell you that?" Kono looked triumphant; he'd learned facts the deputy hadn't.

Anne-Marie's hand flew to her mouth. She gasped, and

the sound turned to a whimpering cry as it left her suddenly pale lips. She turned away, and for a moment wished she could throw up. But nothing came.

Ana ran to her. The Blowhole boomed and gushed, and no one moved under the descending torrent of surf; everyone was watching Anne-Marie. "It's Gardner," she whispered to Ana.

Ana stared at her a moment, uncomprehending. Then she turned and looked at the Blowhole with horror, at its jagged maw, its lava teeth sharp as glass knives.

"What's the matter with you two?" Kono demanded.

"It's the reporter, Dan," said Ana. "The one who was with Anne-Marie."

Kono grunted, surprised. He studied Anne-Marie, then turned back to the fisherman. "Tabbi, dis fella, him big, fat, eh? Gottim long hair, lika hippie?"

"Das him, brah."

Kono glanced sidelong at the hole. The hole drew in an agonizingly congested breath and then, with a preliminary belch, threw another spurt of water into the air. The wind carried the salt water sleeting into the faces of the onlookers, stinging them with astringent warmth.

Ana wiped the back of her hand across her mouth and stepped away. The fishermen and teenagers too suddenly decided to back away from the hole.

Sirens sounded on the bluff; the fire department was arriving, along with reinforcements from the sheriff's department. Anne-Marie glanced up, distraught, and for the first time noticed the crowd of curious onlookers who jostled each other at the railings, snapping the scene with their Polaroids and Instamatics. She turned away. She walked to the edge of the sea, where the clean surf smashed against the dark rocks. Rising up into the air, the white surf drenched her to the skin.

She stood there in turmoil while behind her men in wetsuits descended the stairs and clambered out onto the rocks. They carried air tanks and regulators over their shoulders, and surfboards under their arms, and coils of rope with triply barbed grappling hooks affixed.

She forced herself to watch. The next half hour was Dantesque, a vision of hell populated by slick black demons delving busily in the wet petrified ash. The small group of locals who had been first to arrive on the scene were allowed to stay nearby, on the presumption that they might be able to provide useful information.

The fire department's rescue team had been well prepared to go into the mauling surf, as they routinely did in cases of drowning or shark attack. But the suggestion that there was a body in the Blowhole left them nonplussed. After much frenzied discussion they did the only thing they could do: they began tossing their grapples into the hole, then dragging them out again, with much cursing, much snagging and tangling of coils of rope.

Meanwhile the inspector from the sheriff's department interviewed witnesses. He came at last to Anne-Marie. He seemed unnecessarily interested in her relationship with Gardner Hey, whose identity as the renter of the red Datsun had been confirmed by radio, but she was patient with the man and answered his impertinent questions fully. As he was about to leave he casually asked her if Tabilang's description of the other man rang any bells. "Supposedly he was tall, short haircut—also blond—wearing a tan suit and a tie."

Anne-Marie stared mutely at the man and shook her head. But when he left Ana came instantly to her side. "You know who it was, don't you?" Ana pressed her, her instinct for truth as alert as ever.

"No, no. It reminded me—"

"Reminded you of who?" Ana insisted.

"A friend of mine. Chauncey. Chauncey Tolliver. But that's stupid. He's an old friend of—my husband's."

"Who you talking about?" Kono demanded, breaking a long silence. He'd been absorbed in the efforts to recover the body; now he glared at Anne-Marie. "You say somethin' about a guy named Tolliver?"

To Anne-Marie he looked as menacing as the day she'd first met him. She nodded dumbly.

"He's the guy who killed Mr. Hey, Dan," said Ana with assurance. Then she glanced at Anne-Marie. "Maybe," she added.

"Maybe!" Kono turned away, brooding. Abruptly he turned back, scowling at Ana. "He could do it okay, you bet. He's *that* man." He hid his face from her. His enormous body was wracked with emotions he could not express. Without warning he raised his great head and shouted across the black rock at the rescue team. "You bums never gonna accomplish *anything* like dat." He strode toward the Blowhole.

"What does he mean, '*that* man'?" Anne-Marie asked Ana.

"The guy you said? He musta been the one who threatened to turn in Luki." Ana was off, running after Kono.

Anne-Marie followed her, confused, her head pounding. Kono stood beside the Blowhole, staring into it; it erupted almost in his face, sending a solid wall of water only inches in front of him. He seemed unaware of danger. When Ana approached him he snarled at her, sent her away, and turned back to the hissing, vomiting hole. He studied it as if it were a live thing, as if his life depended on understanding it.

Ana turned to Anne-Marie, stricken with terror. "He's going down in there."

The local fishermen watched Kono, awed. They turned away slowly, whispering to one another, looking back at him over their shoulders. The teenagers made faces and shrugged, but looked wide-eyed at Kono between posturings. Anne-Marie heard the boys and men talking low in Hawaiian; she heard only one word she understood, "Maui."

"Goddamn old storytellers, they should keep their mouths shut," Ana said angrily.

Kono stood quietly, studying the Blowhole, the timing of its inhalations and exhalations, the rhythm of the surf.

He knew now when to expect the waters to retreat—at those moments he moved confidently to the edge of the hole and peered down into its twisted black interior, watching as long as he could to see what ledges and pockets were laid bare by the falling waters, where a man might find holes for fingers and toes to prevent being cast out by the convulsions of the returning swell.

Kono turned to a fire department rescuer, a sun-blackened blond haole youth, and asked for a rope. The fireman stared dumbly at him a moment, then thrust the rope to him with its grapple still attached. Kono tore at the knot and tossed the steel-barbed trident hook aside, knotting the supple line through his belt loops. He turned back to the hole. A surge of surf: he began counting. Again the water boiled up at his feet and soared howling into the afternoon sky. It began to suck away into the earth.

Kono scrambled after the receding waters, his rubber-sandaled feet and his callused hands finding holds willy-nilly; he ignored the inevitable cuts and scrapes his descent exacted. No one dared watch him. No one heard his rapid shouted counting, or saw the desperation with which he threw himself down the jagged stair, or felt the terrified grip as his fingers fastened on a ragged ledge of stone, the frantic intake of air—

The sea tore at him, surrounded him, pressed relentlessly, screamed in his ears, filled his nose and ears and mouth. . . .

—and then relief: the sea was gone, grumbling. He took a deep breath, ignoring the salt water that flowed from his nostrils and eyes. He'd spent many hours beneath the blue black reefs, without thought of mask or tanks. Water alone did not frighten him.

He scrambled lower into the hole. Those who might have been brave enough to watch, and there were none, would have lost sight of him now, for he had crawled under the tube's lateral angling roof, toward the sea—

The sea came back, stronger this time, eager to tear him from his perch. The light was extinguished, all but for a dim blue glow. The water boiled indecisively a moment, then pulled back as hard as it had pushed, sucking him toward blackness. . . .

—and left him again. The light from above was dim. He had only seconds to act. The water pooled and swelled beneath him, black, resentful, popping his ears with booming compressions of air. The lava tube continued beneath the water's lowest surface. Taking an enormous lungful of air, Kono dropped into the seething blackness.

The water was warm, deceptively gentle, its flavor almost sweet; he could see nothing, but he feared no monsters. Even tough moray eels would seek out quieter caverns. He had no time to enjoy the calm, though—it would last only seconds, and his need was to find refuge.

He kicked hard, sensed the loss of a sandal, mourned it. His hands encountered eroded rock; he held tight, brought his knees up to his chest, felt for rock. One foot was shod, one was bare. The sea came back—

And pushed past him with strength that made him despair, endlessly. Then sucked out again, endlessly. . . .

—but this time no relief, no chance for air. He must end his mission now, or quickly retreat in failure. With the last of the sucking seaward surge he allowed himself to drift free. Almost immediately he came upon the dead man's hand. It was a hand as warm and soft as the sea, grown gentle in death, acquiescent and pliable, cooperatively articulate.

Kono yanked the slipknot of the rope free and whipped the cord around the corpse's weightless chest, dancing with the dead man where he floated freely within the narrow arch of a lava bubble. His own lungs now bursting, Kono swam for the surface. The sea came back—

It ground his head and shoulder against the lava walls. Black shapes swam in front of his eyes, urging him to relax, to let go, to inhale. . . . By experience, he knew them for the paltry demons of hypoxia. He had plenty of oxygen left, stored in his bloodstream. He gagged and resisted, husbanded his strength, and when the currents were once more neutral, he let himself be carried toward clear air. . . .

—and the skylight above him. He forced himself to keep counting. He would not allow himself to be dragged back into the hole after this, by misgauging the thrust and rush of the channeled surf. He climbed, limbs trembling, to the dazzle.

He fell out upon the wet black bench, the white foam swirling about him, mingling with blood from his head and hands and lacerated shoulder. Ana was beside him, wiping the snot and spume from his nose and mouth, helping him crawl away from the angry bellowing Blowhole.

The firemen brought him bottled oxygen, but he refused it. He breathed the pure air of daylight deeply, his huge sleek chest and belly rising like a beached sea lion's, then falling again, mocking the rhythm of the sea. Presently he sat up, supported beneath his massive shoulders by Ana's small hands.

Anne-Marie stood apart, watching in silence. The firemen were bringing the drowned corpse to the surface, patiently guiding the tangled rope through swirling knots of current. At last the drained, bruised head emerged, blossoming like a time-lapse flower amid fronds of white water. Gardner Hey, heavy-lidded, sleepily amused, looked without feeling upon the speechless crowd.

34

Earlier that April Monday an old man named William Barosz had stood in unfastened galoshes at the edge of a helipad shaded by tall ponderosa pines. Once upon a time the skies of northern New Mexico had been the bluest in the world. The big coal-burning power plants up north had put an end to that, but on days like this one, 7,200 feet up in the Jemez Mountains, with the air washed clean and two feet of wet new spring snow rapidly melting under the close hot sun, it seemed as if the clock had turned back.

From Honolulu to Los Alamos is over three thousand miles on a great circle; an Air Force spy plane could have covered the distance in an hour and a half, but if the pilot had wanted to talk to anybody when he arrived he'd still have had to land sixty air miles away, in Albuquerque, and hitch a ride like any other ground-pounder. Barosz had no idea where, besides Albuquerque, the courier he was waiting for had come from. It was not his business to know, and he had learned decades ago not to press for information that they—the Defense Department, the AEC, or the Department of Energy, or whatever they called themselves these days—didn't want to give him. Sooner or later he'd get the true poop. For the moment the old man was content to open his sheepskin jacket to the sun, close his eyes, and turn his tanned face to the sun, letting its warmth rouse memories behind his eyelids.

He thought about the old days a lot, lately—must have something to do with his long overdue retirement. Back then, the work had been hard, sometimes fun, and when you got right down to it, ethically pretty simple. Beat the Nazis. Or the Japs. Whoever.

They'd all had a purpose then, and they'd reveled in each other's company, told stories on each other, played practical jokes—Fermi's dry wit, Feynman sneaking around opening people's safes—and in general they had *not* been a whole lot like these humorless button-pushers he'd been working with lately, the damned efficiency experts who were his bosses, some of them forty years his junior.

Well, in a year or so he could put them out of his mind: it would be just him and Madge in their cabin up in the Red River Valley, with a little time left for some trout fishing, gardening, pinyon fires in the stone fireplace. Before death came, or the nursing home.

Hell with it; first he had to get the bugs out of the popgun project.

At last he heard the whistle and thrum of the approaching helicopter. He opened his eyes. The little red and black Jet Ranger came straight in and settled to the wet concrete, its rotor blades slicing flat cones out of the thin air as its engines idled down. The passenger who got out on the far side and came around the nose of the machine was a woman—each time it was somebody different. She wore a brown wool pantsuit and clumpy high-heeled shoes, but he easily recognized her as regular military clad in mufti. She marched defiantly erect as the chopper's drooping blades snickered a few inches over her head. She carried a clipboard in her right hand and kept her left thrust firmly into the pocket of her jacket.

She stopped three feet short of the old man—just far enough to be out of his reach, he noted—and paused to glance at the photograph attached to the clipboard. She looked up and stared at his face. "You are Dr. Barrus?" she asked, mispronouncing his name in the usual fashion.

"Don't I look like him?" His voice was a rasping whisper.

"Yes, you do." She paused. "I'll note you said yes." If the stocky young woman were making a joke she gave no hint of it by her sober expression. "Please sign this," she said, holding out the clipboard. "Press hard. You're making multiple copies."

He did as he was told and handed the clipboard back to her. Swallowing, she pretended to inspect the signature. Plainly she was frightened. His face had that effect on people sometimes.

Abruptly she removed her hand from her pocket and held the thing out to him: it was a blue steel cylinder the size of a Coke bottle. A short length of tough steel chain was welded to the cylinder, its other end welded to a handcuff around the woman's wrist.

He peered at the handcuff a moment, seeing the fine blond hairs on the woman's pallid skin, the scrawny wrist and forearm thrust out of a blouse sleeve that was touchingly too short and too roomy. She'd borrowed the civilian clothes, perhaps, or more likely bought them on orders, with no self-confidence, no sense of fashion, only a sense of duty. Barosz fished in the pocket of his threadbare corduroys for the key he'd received in the mail two days earlier. Like the courier, the key was a new one every month. He unlocked the handcuff, but was careful not to grasp the cylinder until the woman pressed it into his hand, as a final secret signal that he was indeed the intended recipient. This was standard procedure; Barosz no longer registered its absurdity. "Thanks," he said.

She said nothing. After a moment's hesitation she

turned on her heel and marched stiffly back to the helicopter. Seconds after she climbed in, the aircraft lifted away, shrieking, into the dark blue sky.

The driver supplied by security waited at the edge of the helipad. He opened the rear door of the gray sedan from the motor pool, helped the old man in, then drove off slowly through pools of melting slush toward the maximum-security section of the technical area.

The old man idly hefted the massive steel cylinder in his right hand. Beam weaponry was his field these days, a specialty he no longer had to disguise as research on inertial fusion; recent administrations had made his kind of defense work fiscally respectable again, and Barosz's project had profited greatly from the Air Force's fear of Soviet killer satellites and antimissile defense plans.

The work had gone well. A number of once seemingly insurmountable barriers to space-stationed death rays had yielded to intensified R&D: automatic aiming and tracking systems, for example, or the trick of pulsing small nuclear explosions to produce bursts of electromagnetic energy without destroying the beam projector at the same time (although Barosz had to admit they owed a lot to the X-ray-laser boys at Livermore in learning to lick that one). Yet some of the underlying difficulties with particle beams still resisted solution. Charged particles were easily deflected by magnetic fields, including Earth's own, and neutral hydrogen beams, despite early promise, lacked punch. What was wanted was a particle that could be given a charge, like the H-minus hydrogen ion—readily accelerated and just as readily neutralized after acceleration—but a particle sufficiently massive to resist deflection and deliver the goods when it struck the target. The team had tried a number of approaches, some of them real messy. Beams of uranium, ugh.

The stuff in the little steel bottle showed definite promise, however. Inside the bottle was a tiny glass vial which contained a feeble solution of very peculiar particles, singly charged but with hundreds of times the mass of ordinary protons. An energetic beam of things like that would have real stopping power.

The car slowed, and Barosz showed his badge to a guard whose face was as familiar to him as his was to the guard. The man waved him through casually. Three fences later the car stopped in front of a drab, flat-roofed concrete and steel building, Building W, indistinguishable from its neighbors except by the adjacent electrical substation, which was crowded with rows of transformers and capacitors. The driver escorted Barosz to the outer door of Building W, and from there another guard walked with him into the drab interior, along a linoleum-tiled corridor smelling of wax and ammonia, through double steel doors rigged with alarms, on into the inner sanctum: a drafty hall, lit by fluorescent tubes overhead and cluttered with concrete blocks, steel beams, bunched electrical cables, tubes, pipes, tanks of gas—a miscellany of ugly machinery with no obvious purpose.

In the midst of the clutter gleamed a thick-walled stainless-steel vacuum chamber, twenty meters long and ten across, portholed with thick glass. Inside the chamber was a partial prototype of the beam weapon. His popgun, Barosz thought of it, smiling to himself.

He was greeted by the mildly curious stares of his research associates, a score of men and a handful of women, all of whom seemed very young to him. They were all competent, of course, some of them even brilliant, but to his eye they were a colorless lot. Not like the old days.

Barosz remembered that afternoon in 1943 when Oppenheimer had rushed through the halls of their wooden office building waving a tiny glass vial (not much bigger than the vial inside the steel bottle Barosz now held), pausing for excited conferences at every office door—showing off the diminutive flake of silvery, cyclotron-created plutonium inside it. That was the first time any of them on the Hill had seen a tangible amount of the legendary substance.

The matter contained in Barosz's steel bottle was stranger stuff by far, but from all the excitement on his coworkers' faces he might have been holding a can of air freshener.

He handed the bottle over and let the young scientists go about their business. He retreated to the glassed-in control room that overlooked the laboratory from the second story and there busied himself with calculations, keeping himself out of their way. They would not be long at their job; the test had been scheduled days before, awaiting only the arrival of the peculiar fluid.

He didn't know why it took so long to get hold of a batch of the stuff, but he could guess. For this test he'd insisted on a minimum of four times the usual quantity. That surely had something to do with the extra delay. And he supposed the supply was limited; who knew how many other users he had to compete with?

He rubbed his scars and waited for the loading to be done with. It occurred to him that he felt better looking down on the tricky procedure from high above, from behind the control room's shatterproof leaded glass. It wasn't like him to be nervous—simply a false association, that's all, which he blamed on the transient memory of Oppenheimer's speck of plutonium. The watery substance in the steel bottle was nothing like plutonium. It wasn't even radioactive, much less fissionable. His fear was an involuntary response to a false stimulus whose prototype was buried deep in his past.

Plutonium had given him the scars on his face, made his left eye milky and dead, robbed him of most of his voice. One of these days, he knew, it would finish the job of killing him.

He'd been washing out the sink. For several weeks he and the others in the shed (that old wooden one, long gone by now) had been using the sink to rinse out laboratory vessels, many of them unknowingly contaminated with plutonium. As a rule they'd all been very cautious around the stuff, made nervous by its toxicity. They hadn't realized it was collecting, grain by heavy grain, in the sink's trap. He'd bent over to lift the sieve; there'd been a flash of blue light; the eager metal had dissolved itself. It took only a moment for him and his friends to deduce the truth. By then the world was swimming, and the stabbing pains had begun. . . .

Several hours passed before the beam weapon was ready. Meanwhile the sun had set beyond the Valle Grande, though no one inside the laboratory had marked its setting. A delivery boy (who surely has a Top Secret clearance, Barosz thought with amusement) brought a cart of sandwiches and hot coffee to the control room.

Finally all the circuits had been checked for the last time. Sirens and lights warned off casual visitors; the cold steel of the oval vacuum chamber rippled with the darting red reflections of revolving lamps. Scientists and technicians left the floor and took shelter.

Barosz nodded to the man at the control panel, who tapped a code to initiate the computer-controlled firing sequence. Video recorders rolled. A dozen monitors displayed the beam projector, inside and out. Barosz watched the seconds flicker out of existence on the digital display. Thirty seconds . . .

The prototype accelerator drew power from the banks of capacitors outside the building at voltages sufficient to send a spark leaping thirty feet to ground through the atmosphere. In space a nuclear-powered beam projector would be a potential bomb, but this earthbound test device had no need of nuclear fuel. Twenty seconds . . .

One shot at the target of laminated steel and Lucite, that's all they'd get: a microsecond pulse. Just one in ten million ions in the pulse would be a weird new particle, barely enough of them, all together, to determine if deflection and deposited energy matched the calculated values. Ten seconds . . .

And assuming it all did work the way it was supposed to, they'd still face the problem of securing a steady supply. But Barosz happily looked forward to that problem, for it would be somebody else's.

Four seconds. Three. Two—

High-speed recording disks in the control room, triggered prematurely by remote sensors inside the prototype, preserved extraordinary images transmitted through the magneto-optic shutters of armored cameras: a fireball was seen to be growing like a monstrous egg inside the beam projector's steel casing, that casing itself suddenly become eerily transparent.

The prototype disintegrated and vanished in a white mist of vaporized steel and glass. Electromagnetic radiation reached the control room at the speed of light, quickly enough to sear Barosz's remaining eye before the blast wave, traveling at the leisurely speed of sound, blew out the building's walls and sent the pulverized remains of the roof into the starry night sky in a towering cloud of debris.

Later that night the electronic disks and certain other partial records were recovered. Some evidence had been destroyed or distorted by electromagnetic pulse, but other recordings had been well preserved. To the testimony of these unbiased mechanical witnesses were added the impressions of seven human beings who had survived the destruction of Building W. The old man was not among them; he and seventeen others had died.

The evidence confirmed that the countdown had never been completed. The explosion had apparently occurred inside the beam projector's ion source. In time the investigators began to ask just what the ion source had contained, and where the stuff, whatever it was, had come from.

35

Peter dropped the heavy stack of inert paper on his desk, frustrated by its mundane diagrams. The computer printout only confirmed the guard's feeble joke: the stuff in the cave was dead. The latest records contained no hint of unusual activity.

The late-afternoon sun swarmed in through his office windows, washed out the green symbols on the screen of his little desk computer, set the chalked figures on the blackboard ablaze. He'd gone through all the motions again, arrayed all the appropriate sets of wave equations, thought it all through once more—and still he had nothing to tell Matsuo Ishi.

He tugged the curtains closed and switched off the computer. He was pushing too hard, trying to force an answer; Peter knew too well the signs of an incipient block. Time to go home, play some music, walk on the beach. . . .

He left the Triumph in the carport, banged into the dark empty house, jerked open the blinds, and peered through salt-streaked windows at the deserted ocean. The swells were running crossways along the empty horizon, toward the low sun; the surfers were all gone down to Makapuu, he guessed.

He tugged open the knot of his necktie, fetched the neglected Burgundy from the rack, pulled its cork, and drank off a glass. He refilled the wineglass and set it and the bottle on top of the piano, lifted the lid from the keys.

What sort of mood was he in, underneath all the irritation? Not baroque—nothing so formal, so purely, showily mathematical. No, the feeling was classical, certainly—constrained but not enslaved by form, able to express a little passion, a little individuality, a little—inwardness . . . ?

Peter grinned. Could one really trick the subconscious in such an obvious manner? He doubted it. But why not play a little Beethoven anyway—beautiful music, and a hell of a workout.

A couple of sonatinas written when the genius was eight or nine, just to limber the fingers: *Für Elise,* that was pretty. Peter's long hands drooped over the keys, simultaneously working them with the forceful precision of metal cams and the relaxed delicacy of opening flowers, rippling the arpeggios up and down, spinning out the pleasant melody.

Then on into the sonatas, to the *Tempest,* descending figures of the right hand and ascending figures of the left creating musical collision—flirting at first, then opposing openly, finally combining in resolution.

Peter had stopped trying to pin down the particular within the universal, but still a theme would catch at his imagination now and then, snag a vaguely conceived mathematical entity and drag it along into interesting conceptual juxtapositions, which had nothing really to do with the rather simple harmonies he was producing by a sort of remote-controlled hammering on piano wires.

He came to the late sonatas, those written when the irascible genius was stone deaf. The easily impressed thought it a miracle that Beethoven could write such music and not hear a note of it. Yet the man had been a pianist since childhood. The *Ninth Symphony* came even later than these piano pieces—he'd conducted its premier, hearing it only in his imagination.

Beethoven had allowed his imagination to mislead him on occasion, no doubt of that. Peter's musical Cambridge friend had once led him to a trove of pre-1840 printed scores which reproduced the master's erratic notation even when it ran wildly counter to common sense. Peter remembered picking through the originals and encountering those held notes boldly marked *crescendo,* those long deltas drawn backward. One doesn't hold down a piano key and somehow make the note grow louder.

But perhaps it was no mistake. It was music a deaf man could hear.

Peter played and the sonata resounded, spilling in swirling waterfalls of sound, thundering in articulate pronouncements of feeling and thought.

And here, as he recalled, came one of those imaginary crescendos. Peter smiled as he leaned, swaying, on the note. He tried to feel it throbbing, growing ever louder and more powerful—

Arrested, seized with sudden knowledge, Peter jerked his hands from the keyboard as if his fingers had been burned.

The note faded. And only then did the greater chord come pure.

The inside quark—represent its quantum properties by this written musical note, this imaginary note—this creation of will.

Peter almost laughed with delight at the obviousness of it all. All along he'd only had to turn the problem around and look at it from the other side. Instead of trying to find out *why* the I-particle looked stable, Peter should have been asking himself how it would behave if it really *were* stable.

It would not behave like the stuff in the cave. Whatever

was inside the little bottle the photomultipliers were monitoring, it did not contain I-particles.

Peter took the glass of Burgundy, got up from the piano, circled the room glass in hand, grinning at his own cleverness. He stared out the glass walls at the contrary surf, its sidelong edges glittering in the low sun.

After a moment his jubilance suddenly faded. He began to do simple arithmetic, adding up the hours, the minutes—

He crossed the room swiftly, reached for his phone. "This is Peter Slater, Miss, uh—" Damn, he couldn't remember the woman's name. "I must speak to Professor Ishi immediately. . . . Yes, it's extremely urgent."

Ishi was on the phone a moment later. "You have learned something, Dr. Slater?"

"Something very disturbing, sir. I'm afraid the chain of reasoning is rather involved, but I believe TERAC is in great danger unless the I-particle collector can be made inoperative. Immediately."

"Professor Edovich's experiment? You wish to have it discontinued?"

"Yes, sir. If this is not done, Professor, I very much fear there will be another explosion comparable to the one that occurred Sunday morning. But this time it will be *inside* the collector."

Ishi was silent. Then he said, "I will convene the planning board."

"Sir, forgive me, but . . . "

"I understand your sense of urgency, Dr. Slater. But if your 'chain of reasoning' is as subtle as I fear, I simply cannot justify taking a drastic unilateral action."

"May I come to your office and prepare a presentation, then?"

"Of course. Right away."

Martin Edovich was late joining the group; the stress of the past two days showed plainly in the pouches under his eyes, the splotched skin of his face. He sank into a chair with little more than a weary nod to the others. Lasky, Yamamura, and Friedman were already present; Narita had been asked to come and, because he had to travel from Hall 30, arrived last.

While the staff members assembled, Peter stood at the window distractedly watching workmen ten stories below dismantle the bleachers and speakers' platform. He worried that he was supposed to attend a banquet tonight, and give a talk—or was that tomorrow night? The banquet was tonight, the talk was tomorrow night, that was it. . . .

"Please, Dr. Slater, whenever you are ready?" Ishi's voice was calm. Miss Sugibayashi sat by him, taking notes.

Peter turned and half smiled, half grimaced at his disgruntled audience. Abruptly he pulled back the mounted screen paintings which concealed the blackboard, revealing with awkward drama a dense agglomeration of equations and curious X- and H-shaped diagrams he'd drawn there: Feynman diagrams, with converging lines and loops and wiggles jumping between them, and differently labeled diverging lines springing from these symbolic quivering interactions.

Martin Edovich groaned aloud. "*Ne,* Peter, we're all happy you've decided to start talking to us, I'm sure—but this is not the time to show off."

"Martin, I believe the I-particle collector could suffer a catastrophic rupture at any moment—virtually at any second." Peter's voice was strained. "I need to . . . "

"You want to persuade me to turn it off, yes, yes," said Edovich tiredly.

"Or if that can't be done in the right way, to shut down TERAC. Dump the beams," said Peter.

Ilse Friedman moved tiredly to a more comfortable position on the couch. "Really, Dr. Slater, we went through this all very thoroughly thirty-six hours ago."

From his place at the head of the conference table Ishi said quietly, "I myself asked Dr. Slater to look into the circumstances of the explosion. His ideas are provocative.

I might even say"— Ishi paused to light the cigarette he'd removed from his case, and puffed out a cloud of blue smoke—"in the absence of arguments to the contrary, that his conclusions are somewhat persuasive."

Bronislaw Lasky leaned forward. "Let's hear them then," he said genially. "At the very least we'll have some fun, eh, Martin?"

Edovich regarded Lasky sourly, but said nothing; he acquiesced with an airy wave of the hand.

Peter turned to the board and studied it, at the same time giving some attention to his political problem—his uncongenial reception had reminded him that he would have to persuade emotionally as well as logically. Lasky was the only real theorist in the group, though Edovich and Narita were sharply aware of theoretical issues. Friedman was an accelerator builder. Yamamura's vote was to be discounted, since it was so predictably against Edovich to begin with. And Ishi had put himself above the battle.

Peter decided Lasky was the key. Though Lasky's personality was weaker than Edovich's—he habitually deferred to the man on any issue on which he had not formed an opinion—nevertheless he was an independent thinker. With Lasky on his side—and Friedman, too, if he could convince her that her machine was in danger—Peter could override any reluctance Martin might have. "The point is, a concentration of I-particles will explode," he began forcefully. "I assert that roughly two or at most four days' accumulation will explode violently—that's what happened yesterday morning. Mr. Sherwood had not unloaded the collector the previous night, as you'll recall. And that's what could happen now, because the collector has been operating almost a whole day. The probability that it will go off increases every moment, as more I-particles are brought into close proximity with each other."

"But the stability experiment?" Lasky asked, almost gently. "Certainly that very large accumulation of I-particles argues against you?"

Edovich growled at him, "Let him hang himself in his own good time, Brownie."

"The fluid in the stability experiment contains no I-particles at all," said Peter. "It is not 'holy water,' as Martin has sometimes called it. In fact it's ordinary distilled water, or so I'd guess." Peter paused. "And I want to emphasize that this conclusion holds no matter what assumptions one makes about the I-particle's stability." His glance, subtly questioning, flickered toward Lasky, and from the expression on Lasky's face Peter knew he had stifled a nascent objection. "And of course I also believe the steel bottle found near Mr. Sherwood's body contains ordinary water."

Yamamura, who until now had been silent and watchful—sulking, perhaps—suddenly issued a strangled, inarticulate exclamation and leaned forward impulsively, slamming his fist into his hand.

"That steel bottle is now in your possession, Martin, isn't it?" Peter asked.

Edovich's tired eyes opened a little wider, but he did not move. "That's right. I will happily surrender it to you for any test you care to make," he said with heavy sarcasm.

"I can't think of a chemical test that would be worth the trouble, can you?" Peter said reasonably. "You could centrifuge it and subject it to mass spectrometry or field ionization, perhaps some other technique—it's easy to tell an I-particle from a proton once you've got hold of one—but the ratio is so low to begin with you could spend years searching."

"Precisely. Your ridiculous assertion amounts to a perfect tautology," Edovich said angrily.

"No, Martin, there are other options." Peter's patience was beginning to fray. Martin seemed to receive his ideas as if they were personal attacks instead of considered differences of opinion. "With a little thought it becomes obvious that any fluid containing I-particles can be distinguished from plain water, simply by observing the nature and frequency of particle decays in the fluid over time. In other words, the stability experiment has *already* proved it contains no I-particles."

His audience regarded him quizzically. Lasky leaned forward, his expression changing to one of genuine interest. "That's certainly a provocative suggestion, Peter," he said. "What exactly do you have in mind?"

"I mean that the fundamental properties of the I-particle are its charge and mass and spin. It is two hundred times as massive, has the same charge, same spin, and occupies essentially the same spatial dimension as a proton. If we consider the internal mass distribution—almost all the mass is concentrated in the inside quark—we can see what peculiar effects should show up in its magnetic moment. . . . "

"That's been measured in the French experiment in 18," said Lasky quickly.

"And it's *at least* ten percent off the computed value," Peter said, completing Lasky's thought. "But what shows up directly in the stability experiment is the interaction of the magnetic dipole moment with the I-particle's surrounding meson cloud. The massive particle favors the creation of virtual rho meson pairs. Because of the skewing of the electrical and magnetic fields, a calculable number of rhos should escape reabsorption and decay into pions plus photons, before the pions are reabsorbed. And there are other decay processes, which I have diagrammed here. But that photon should be *visible* in the stability experiment; it should leave a distinctive signature."

"Where does the energy come from?" Lasky demanded. "You're saying the I-particle effectively charges the vacuum. You don't do that without paying the energy debt."

Peter said, "Cosmic rays. The density is lower in the tropics, granted. The stability experiment has kept a faithful record of every cosmic ray hit for the past year. A year ago there wasn't much supposed 'holy water' in that little plastic tub; now there's a respectable amount. But the *density* of I-particles has remained constant, the ratio of

I-particles to protons. Again—it's a very low number. But statistically there should have been a couple of dozen times in the last twelve months when the energy from an incident cosmic ray or a normal radioactive decay in the nearby environment kicked an I-particle into an excited state." Peter turned to the board, striking at it irritably. "Look at *this* decay mode, and *this* one, and *this*. You get an energetic cosmic ray hit, you get an excited I-particle, you should see this pattern, or this one, or this one, with your photomultipliers." He turned back to his audience. "I've got the whole year's data in my office. If there are I-particles in that soup, I should have between twelve and fifty flash patterns corresponding to one or more of these modes. I've got none."

"And if the I-particle were not stable?" Lasky asked.

"In that case, the events couldn't be counted, because you'd have an explosion on your hands," said Peter. "But Brownie, please, that's what I'm coming to next. I want to emphasize that all I'm talking about now is the I-particle everybody but me believes in, the innocent stable I-particle. It's not there."

"Negative data," said Edovich, as if to dismiss Peter's discussion. "You assert a situation for which there is no supporting evidence, then you expect us to be surprised? Why should we? These are your private fantasies."

"No, Martin, no," said Lasky insistently. "Don't you see? These are not his assumptions—they are yours!"

Umetaro Narita interrupted, from his shadowed corner. "Who took the real holy water?" he demanded.

"I'm not a detective," said Peter. "I don't know who took it. But I think I know what it can do. And that's why I'm here to plead with all of you—to shut down this experiment before it destroys the ring, and possibly kills someone else."

"Yes, yes, Peter, that's very noble, certainly," Lasky said, putting warmth into his words, "that's very convincing, really; and I, for one, am now prepared to accept the hypothesis that the stability experiment may actually have somehow been, uh . . . "

Ishi looked at Lasky expressionlessly. Lasky looked back, took a breath, then continued: "Assuredly we have a security problem, in case we didn't know it already. That you've certainly made clear." He paused and pulled at his lower lip, glancing at Edovich. "But Peter—granting the positively brilliant work you've done to get us this far—it still remains to convince a reasonable man or woman that I-particles are in fact dangerous. A stray photon here or there is hardly out of the ordinary, you know."

Peter looked up at the Feynman diagrams on the board. "Maybe we don't need these? I'll get on to my second point, then." He rolled back the first panel of the chalkboard, revealing a second set of diagrams, even more thickly packed. "All right, here's what the real stuff can do," he said strongly.

This time there were no groans from his audience, only a worried silence.

36

"Chauncey! What are you doing here?" Greta held the heavy oaken door of the Manoa Valley house open wide, steadying herself by leaning against it. The man was a silhouette against the outside light. "Nothing's happened to delay Martin, I hope? Oh, do come in, don't stand there waiting for an invitation." She swung her arm wide, beckoning with her martini. "Join me for a little *apéritif.*"

Greta didn't wait for an answer. She turned and wobbled toward the living room.

Tolliver stepped into the cool dim hallway and closed the door behind him. He stood quietly for a moment, listening, then followed Greta down the shallow stone steps into the shadowed room. Along one side of the room tall Gothic windows overlooked the terrace, with a view through masses of shadowed foliage to the far ridge of the valley, cool blue in the darkening afternoon.

"Dark in here already," Greta murmured. "In the tropics we had to find a house as dark as a cabin in the north woods." She piloted her martini to a safe landing on the closed lid of the Wurlitzer piano, then groped for the chain of a floor lamp. Swirls of warm colored light from its flower-shaped glass shade fell on the walls and floor.

She moved with deliberate steps to the bar, an elaborately inlaid Italian piece, converted from its former function as an upright secretary. A half-full pitcher of martinis rested on its open shelf. Greta swung wide its doors, which were decorated with cameos of half-clad classical maidens; shelves full of expensive spirits and liqueurs glinted like jewels in the eccentric light. "Help yourself, Chauncey."

She turned to him. "Cat got your tongue?" She peered at him, leaning awkwardly forward. "Chauncey, my friend, forgive me for saying so, but you are not your usual impeccable self." She giggled, and turned to retrieve her martini.

Tolliver glanced down at his soiled suit. "Yes, you're right," he said in a low voice. Abruptly he crossed to the ornate bar and selected a bottle of Glenlivet. He pulled its cork with a savage twist of his big strong fingers and splashed a quantity of the smoky liquid into an old-fashioned glass. He knocked off half the glassful, neat, with a toss of his head.

Watching him, Greta giggled again. "And now you're being naughty, Chauncey," she teased. "You don't want to be *too* naughty, dear little boy of mine. After all, my husband will certainly be home any week now. . . ." She put her fingers to her lips and grinned coquettishly. "Ooh, I meant, any *hour* now."

"Have you heard from him?" Tolliver asked hoarsely.

"Nooo, no, no, no. When do I ever?" Greta sighed theatrically, then made for the divan. She sat down and patted the cushions beside her. "Come, come, Chauncey, sit down and talk to me."

"I'm too restless to sit down, Greta." Tolliver walked to the tall leaded windows and stared out at the twilight, twisting the thick glass in his fists.

"Have it your way," she said airily. "Whatever did you

do to your suit? You've got dirt all over your trousers. And did you . . . ? You tore the arm out of your nice jacket! Have you been mountain-climbing, Chauncey?"

"Greta, I have something to tell you," said Tolliver, facing away from her. "It's a very serious matter. I can trust your discretion, I know."

"Chauncey, dear . . ." She left the rest unsaid.

"Yes." He nodded, acknowledging her loyalty. "Greta, in the interests of our country's security I've been forced to do something terrible." His voice was resonant. "I don't feel at all good about it—I'm obviously very upset, as you can see."

"Of course you are, dear—"

"I've killed a man."

"Ough!" Gin slopped over the edge of Greta's glass, down the front of her low-cut print dress. Gasping, she held the half-empty glass away from her and dabbed at her alcohol-chilled skin. She laughed merrily as she got up and hurried to the bar for a towel. "Chauncey, you can't possibly expect me to believe anything so preposterous of *you,* of all people," she said, smiling as she patted herself.

"I don't think you know me well, Greta," said Tolliver, turning away from the windows to peer at her.

"Oh, my," she said hoarsely, her smile fading. "Perhaps I don't."

His body was as straight as ever, but it held a coiled tension quite unlike the awkward stiffness Greta was used to seeing in him. He said, "It was an accident, but that hardly matters. The point is, I did it to save Martin. Because—" He paused. "He knew about you and me, Greta."

She stared at him, horrified, after deducing his obscure meaning. The incident in Hamburg had been brief and pathetic, though unfortunately indiscreet. She suspected Martin knew about it and had forgiven them long ago. "You *killed* somebody for that?" Was he lying to her? Or had Hamburg meant something to Chauncey she'd never suspected? He'd always been a lonely boy. . . .

He stepped toward her and she reflexively backed away, bumping the bar. The bottles and glasses shivered. "Who did you kill, Chauncey?" she asked, hugging herself tightly. In the slanted light from the floor lamp her face looked drawn, aged.

"The reporter, Gardner Hey," said Tolliver. "You met him. As I said, it was an accident, but once it happened . . ."

"What do you need, Chauncey? Do you want . . . ?" She jerked her head distractedly. "God, what could you need? Not money—"

He looked at her sadly, his eyes watering. He blinked and turned to the window. "I've frightened you, Greta. I'm terribly sorry for that. I would never do anything to hurt you, in any way." He sipped at his Scotch and made a face.

"God, I can't think." Greta pressed her palms to her temples, then rushed to the couch and sank into its cushions, drawing her feet up. Tears trembled in her eyes. She avoided looking at Chauncey; through distorting tears she saw the objects in the dark paneled room, the Japanese prints, the Oceanic carvings, the European antique furniture of burnished wood and marble, all the detritus of a cultivated life.

She'd known of murders in her lifetime, not only from the newspapers but with second- or thirdhand knowledge, friends of friends—victims of terrorists, desperate addicts, one woman the victim of her own daughter. One did not live fifty years in contemporary society without compiling a personal list. But she'd never known the murderer, never been the object of confession. To think of it made her joints weak; she sensed the thin white bones inside her own arms, the dark viscera inside her abdominal cavity, the layers of muscle, the rubbery veins and arteries, the stringy white nerves, the whole fragile structure of her body which could so easily be punctured, broken, ripped apart by a bullet, a bomb, a sharp knife, a strong man's hands.

"Greta, I never killed anyone before, and I never want it to happen again. What I want now is to get away from here without being caught. I can't go back to the office or to my house. There were witnesses. They probably saw my car. . . ."

Greta made an effort to hear what he was telling her. Her fear and confusion were partly a result of her drunkenness, she recognized that; the alcohol made the thought of death sadder, less distant.

". . . I know I'll be caught anyway, before long. But I want to choose the place, the people who arrest me. I want to put myself in the custody of men who can keep their mouths shut. Most important, I want to keep Martin and you out of this completely. Unfortunately I can't do that without your help."

"Anything, Chauncey, anything," she whispered, watching him.

"I doubt that Martin has told you about the special relationship between him and me," said Tolliver, and once more that peculiar resonance crept into his voice, that sense of importance.

Greta peered at him, determined to regain sobriety. "Not in so many words, Chauncey," she said carefully. "But of course I know there's always been a—connection with the Defense Department." Her head swam and her stomach swayed, but she was beginning to think more clearly now.

"Yes, well—" He turned his head in her direction, looking past her toward the hall. "That's really why I'm here—"

When Peter Slater really started to roll, the words poured out in long, well-formed sentences, back to back, linking to construct tight paragraphs. But the concentration required for this feat produced side effects: Peter paced restlessly back and forth in front of the board, picking up bits of chalk and crumbling them to fragments between his fingers without ever using them, and he tended to keep his eyes fixed on one face, Lasky's in this case, with an intensity that was frightening, and not wholly conducive to intellectual contemplation.

" . . . The common wisdom tells us we shouldn't expect to see X bosons this side of ten-to-the-fourteenth proton masses, which means we'll never see them directly. But is that all we have to look forward to? Sidney Drell called that the 'theory of the desert,' the implication that there's nothing between the interaction quanta we've already seen and the interaction quanta we can never see. I for one believe there *are* bosons in the desert, and that the decay of the I-particle will clearly demonstrate their existence." Peter said these last words with a ferocity that made Lasky flinch. "For convenience I'll call these hyperweak vector bosons 'exotic light Ys,' or just Ys—they affect only particles with integer inwardness, that is, particles containing one or more i quarks. So obviously protons and neutrons are immune to Y decay."

Peter stopped pacing, stared fixedly at his series of Feynman diagrams. The diagrams mapped the decay of the I-particle by various routes. In each case, however, the key intermediary, the wiggly line that effected the transformation, was a virtual particle labeled "Y," a bundle of energy which flashed in and out of existence too briefly to be observed directly.

Peter started pacing again. "The Y can be charged positively, negatively—in whole units—or neutrally. The mass of the Y-minus is close to three hundred and sixty GeV, with a lifetime of ten-to-the-minus-nineteenth seconds. I believe the i quark typically decays into a u quark via the Y-minus interaction with a half-life of about four or five days, producing a copious amount of negative pions, muons, electrons, positrons, neutrinos, and subsequently a shower of gamma radiation, by these routes." He whacked at the board without slowing down. "Alternately, a Y-plus can convert an entire I-particle into gamma rays via meson annihilation, but for various reasons I think that's a less likely interaction. The data gathered at the explosion site make the first mode look like the villain—the I-particle turns into a neutron, and all that vast amount of excess mass/energy eventually ends up as electrons and gamma rays."

"There's our electromagnetic pulse," Narita said.

"Not from single particle decays," said Lasky. "There's got to be some kind of chain reaction working, and with these I-particles so spread out I don't see how you get it."

"Density is important," Peter agreed. "But critical density is much lower than you'd expect. And the way Martin's collector is designed, the mix just keeps getting richer until it's unloaded. What happens is this: one I-particle goes; these mesons steal ninety percent of the interaction energy—they're traveling at practically light speed—and they drill all the way through what is a pretty rich medium of oxygen nuclei. Many of them are absorbed before they decay. Protons turn to neutrons, and nuclei blow to pieces. Any other I-particles in the neighborhood get excited, and once that happens, they don't have to wait for a Y to come along out of the vacuum, they'll flip." Peter was pacing again, once more fixing his gaze on Lasky. "I can't overemphasize the kind of energies we're talking about here—it's in the tens of GeVs per pion. Those nuclei will crack like pea pods."

"Martin," said Brownie Lasky slowly, "I believe you should be taking this very seriously."

Edovich had slumped far down into the corner of the couch and seemed barely awake. He rubbed his hand over his eyes and yawned before responding. His words were low and mumbled: "A wonderful fiction, Peter. But there is not a scrap of evidence."

"I don't understand how you can say that, Professor," Narita said impatiently. "This explains the observed effects, even the mild residue of radiation from light isotopes. The anomalous gamma in your own machine . . . " The sentence dangled.

"He's right, Martin," Ilse Friedman said.

Yamamura had the presence of mind not to say anything at all, merely watching Ishi with a carefully expressionless face. Ishi stared at Edovich and puffed at his cigarette.

Finally Edovich pulled himself upright on the couch. "Who stole the holy water, then, Professor Peter Poirot?" he asked hoarsely. "You claim you are not a detective, but isn't that why you've called us all to this little drawing-room scene?"

"Martin—forgive me, I have only the greatest respect for you—but I don't understand your obstinacy."

"All your fine diagrams and your Y-particles come to nothing if there was no theft. Y-particles indeed!"

Peter stared at him, the color rising in his fair cheeks. He looked down at the remains of a piece of chalk in his fingers, laid it on the rail, and vigorously slapped his hands together, trying to clean them of chalk dust. He stepped away from the board to the window. The late sunlight was orange, intensely bright; reflections glittered from distant traffic at the start of the rush hour. "All right, Martin, I'll tell you what I think," said Peter. "I think at least two members of your team were involved. Cyrus Sherwood was one of them. Every night since the collector's been operating he'd been replacing the glass ampoule of I-particle fluid with a duplicate containing plain water. He made the exchange at the circuit breaker outside the steel door. Later he or someone else could recover the real fluid from that drop point. The night of the explosion he must have fumbled the switch. Either he didn't secure the vial, or perhaps he even dropped it into his cuff or sleeve without noticing it. Dr. Harper has told investigators that he was perceptibly weak, and that he was doing his best to hide it. The autopsy revealed he had lung cancer, an advanced case. However it happened, the ampoule dropped to the floor. It appears that Sherwood spotted it there a moment later, stopped his cart, and started to go back for it."

"It is a simple thing to speak ill of the dead, but a cowardly thing," Edovich said sadly.

"You said two people were involved, Peter," Narita reminded him. "Why couldn't Sherwood have done it all himself?"

"He could have," said Peter. "I have different reasons for suspecting the other man. Professor Ishi?"

Ishi nodded. "He is here." Miss Sugibayashi got up and opened the door to Ishi's office. She nodded to someone inside, then stood aside to hold the door open.

Peter watched Edovich. The man's expression remained stern, but a curious flicker of interest, then surprise, crossed his prominent features.

The young man who came into the room was pale with shame and fright.

"Watanabe Hiro!" exclaimed Yamamura, gripping the edge of the table, his face a mask of anger.

Watanabe bowed deeply to Yamamura. "I am unable to express my shame, sensei Yamamura-sama," he said in rapid Japanese.

"Please sit down, Dr. Watanabe," Ishi said quietly, indicating an empty chair near the blackboard.

Watanabe jerked at the sound of his name, and bowed deeply to Ishi. "Sensei!" he exclaimed loudly. Then he scurried to the chair and sat down, staring at the floor between his knees.

Ishi nodded at Peter, almost imperceptibly. His eyes were cold.

Peter was chagrined that he was called upon to play the prosecutor as well as the inspector, but he'd foreseen the crux of Edovich's counterarguments and prepared himself to meet them. There had always been men like Edovich who, despite all their intelligence, their great human gifts, were totally blind to any but the bluntest of arguments against certain cherished assumptions.

Human testimony, however, might move them. Peter said, "You visited the stability experiment this morning, Dr. Watanabe. You took a printout of the data for the last several days. Can you tell us what you did with that material?"

"I did nothing, Dr. Slater," the miserable young man replied. "I have it in my office still. I confess I intended to give the information to the reporter for *Science Weekly*, Mr. Gardner Hey." Watanabe spoke in a low voice, rushing his words. He continued to stare at the rug. "But this morning, after Mr. Hey so viciously attacked sensei Ishi in public, I became outraged and refused to keep my appointment with him."

Peter was startled by the response; he'd expected Watanabe to admit he knew the phony I-particle fluid in the cave could give itself away, and that he was hoping to think of a way to doctor the data. Watanabe's confession came as a complete surprise; briefly Peter recalled the saying once current at Lawrence Berkeley Laboratory, that "watching people is like watching atoms—use a big enough quantum and they just scatter."

Martin Edovich had come up off the couch. "Did you let that reporter in yesterday?" he asked Watanabe in disbelief. "*You* were the one who sought to undermine the efforts of your colleagues? *You* let that irresponsible fool loose at the scene of the attack?"

Watanabe would say nothing. He refused to look at Edovich.

Edovich glared around the room, his eyes bloodshot, his red hair standing out in disordered patches from the sides of his head. "How *could* you do that? You are the lowest sort of creature! You are a traitor, in fact—I do not hesitate to call you that. Where now is the vaunted loyalty of your people?"

Matsuo Ishi said quietly, "Dr. Watanabe has too many loyalties, I think. For whose sake did you betray Professor Edovich, Watanabe?"

"For my sensei," the miserable Watanabe whispered.

For a moment the room was silent with confusion. Then Yamamura moved his chair back from the conference table. "For me, yes," said Yamamura gruffly. Abruptly he stood up and bowed deeply in Watanabe's direction. "Watanabe-san, you have done a service not only to me, but to your country. This militaristic barbarian would involve us all in the manufacture of weapons of war," he said, glaring at Edovich, who understood not a word of Yamamura's impassioned speech in Japanese. "With many respects, Ishi-sama, Watanabe was right to do what he could to stop this man."

"At your direction, Yamamura-san?" Ishi asked, in English.

Yamamura gave one sharp nod of his head.

"Then, Yamamura-san, perhaps you will kindly tell us what has become of the missing I-particle fluid," Ishi gently suggested.

"I have no ideas on the subject," said Yamamura, in English.

"You refuse to tell us?" Ishi asked wearily.

"I don't know anything about it," said Yamamura firmly. "*I* have not been stealing the fluid. You have not been doing that, have you, Watanabe?" Watanabe shook his head. Yamamura continued: "I did request Watanabe's cooperation in finding some way to expose Edovich's practices to the world. That is all. Of the rest I have no knowledge."

Edovich laughed bitterly. He looked at Peter, sourly triumphant. "All this vast expenditure of mental energy to uncover a news leak! How sad for your theory, Dr. Slater."

Peter knew he had lost his opportunity to persuade Edovich; now it would be necessary simply to override him. "The facts remain, Martin."

"The facts!" Edovich sneered. "Stupid rumors. Petty betrayals." He turned to Watanabe. "I don't want to see your face again." Then he turned to Ishi. "Now we can end this charade, can we not?"

Ishi reached for his package of cigarettes. His hands were trembling, whether with fatigue or some other emotion it was impossible to tell from his controlled expression. He started to speak, but before he did so, a stifled gasp escaped Watanabe. The young man began to sob uncontrollably. He stood up, looking about wildly, his stricken gaze avoiding the eyes of those assembled in the room. *"Eraiyo, eraiyo,"* he cried, and bolted from the room.

Peter's breast ached for the man. *The pain is unbearable,* he'd said, and Peter found it hard to imagine a more painful episode for Watanabe than this public shame. A century ago he might have been on his way to commit ritual suicide; in this case he was probably rushing off to get drunk, after which he would write an eloquent letter of resignation. Still, it was not an amusing situation; Watanabe would find it difficult to get another job worthy of his abilities, and Peter was directly responsible for his loss of face.

Ishi broke the awkward silence. "The unfortunate young man must resolve his own difficulties. You asked me a question, Professor Edovich, and I am constrained to answer you. You must shut down your experiment. I had hoped you would join the rest of us in that plain conclusion, but the matter is too urgent to allow time for persuasion. Please see to it immediately."

"I will not do it," said Edovich, his red face set in lumpy determination.

"We will do it for you," said Ishi wearily. He turned to Miss Sugibayashi. "Please ask Mr. Tolliver to come in now."

"Sir, I am very sorry to report I have been unable to locate him," she said in a breathless whisper. She was standing in the door to Ishi's office, where she'd gone to answer the phone shortly before Watanabe's precipitous departure.

"Call one of his assistants, then, please," Ishi said. He turned to Umetaro Narita. "Doctor, please personally supervise . . ." He paused and looked back at Miss Sugibayashi, who had not moved. "Miss Sugibayashi?"

"Ishi-sama, I sadly inform you that the Honolulu Police

Department has just telephoned to report the death of the reporter, Mr. Gardner Hey."

There was a moment of silence. The news was upsetting, but it seemed much beside the point.

"They called here?" asked Ishi.

"They are seeking information from Mr. Tolliver. They asked personally for Mr. Tolliver."

"Ne," said Martin Edovich, staring past her. "Pardon me, I must telephone . . ." He shouldered his way past the startled Miss Sugibayashi.

Ishi rose to his feet. "Dr. Narita, see to the termination of the experiment. Dr. Friedman, please stand by in central control should your assistance be required. I will notify the accident investigators of our findings."

"Sir . . ."

"Yes, Dr. Slater?"

"Perhaps you'd better notify the FBI too."

"Why is that necessary?"

"The stolen fluid. We don't know where it is, or under what conditions it's being stored. But a month's worth or more—all in one bottle . . ."

"Sir," said Narita, "he means it's quite possibly as powerful as an atomic bomb."

Ishi groaned.

"There's some valuable, mm, experimental material, you might call it," Tolliver said to Greta Edovich. "Martin's been keeping it here in the house. It would be extremely unfortunate if it were discovered by the wrong people. For his sake, I need to take it away with me."

"Chauncey—"

"I don't think I'll be caught, if I move quickly," he said. "Even if I am, it's better that I have the material than that it be found here."

"Can I call him?" she asked.

"I wish you could, Greta, but it's just not a good idea," said Tolliver sincerely. He changed the subject: "I'll need some other clothes, something out of character for me. I'll find what I need upstairs. You go down and open the safe, all right?"

"But Chauncey, Martin never gave me the combination."

He looked at her oddly. "Fine," he said, "I'll do it. I know the combination." He placed his empty whiskey glass on a side table. He was almost invisible now, a shadow among shadows.

"Perhaps you'd better not, Chauncey," she said sadly. Though once she'd betrayed Martin with this man—out of boredom, tipsiness, resentment that Martin preferred his work to her, whatever other reasons or nonreasons she'd had at the time—she'd never been tempted to repeat that vaguely unpleasant experience. And now, to allow him to open Martin's personal safe without his permission—well, she was too much the pop Freudian to ignore the symbolic violation. Silly, perhaps; but she would not betray Martin again.

Chauncey was watching her. He said, "Okay, forget it. I'm going upstairs for those clothes."

She listened to his footsteps moving up the stairs. When she'd heard him go down the hall and into the bedroom, she moved to the telephone near the bookcase. As she reached for it she was startled by its loud ring. Her heart pounding, she lifted the receiver from its cradle.

She was puzzled: she heard only the whine of the dial tone, and a soft click. Then she remembered that this morning the telephone company had installed an extension in the bedroom, at Martin's insistence. Chauncey had cut off the incoming call, and left the extension off its hook to prevent her from calling out. Terrified, she gingerly hung up.

She thought about the safe Chauncey wanted her to open. It had been in the house since the house was built early in the nineteenth century, according to plans drawn in Boston or New York. The Yankee freebooters perversely needed to feel at home, it seemed, and demanded cellars fit to store piles of coal, stacks of beer barrels, bush-

els of potatoes, in a climate where it made more sense to
lift the living-room floor up off the moldy ground. But
Martin had been delighted when he saw the deep, cool
cavern under the stone house, and doubly delighted by the
big iron safe set into the cellar wall.

She knew what Chauncey was after. One afternoon
she'd been poking around under the stairs looking for a
bigger flower pot for the euphorbia when Martin, home
early from work, had come clumping down the steps. She
hid in the dark, planning to jump out and scare him. But
when she saw the strange steel cylinder he was carrying,
and noticed his nervous haste, she thought better of revealing her presence. She watched quietly as he screwed
the top off the steel bottle and removed something she
couldn't see clearly, a tiny glinting splinter. He carefully
placed the thing in a padded case he got from inside the
safe; she caught a glimpse of hundreds of shining splinters
nestled in its velvet interior. He snapped the case shut and
put it back in the safe, then forced the steel bottle into his
jacket pocket and went quickly back up the basement
stairs, while she cowered in the dark. She heard him calling her name; she waited half an hour until she was sure
he was out in the yard before she emerged from hiding,
prepared with a tale about visiting a neighbor up the
street.

Now tears sprang to her eyes for the second time since
Chauncey had arrived at the front door. She did not want
to die, but it might come to that—for neither did she want
to betray Martin, and what would become of her if she
tried to stop Chauncey? Or was she merely being drunk
and silly . . . Chauncey hadn't meant to kill the little man,
it had been an accident, that's what he'd said, and he'd
sounded as if he meant it.

She heard his footsteps on the stair. "What have you
decided, Greta?" he asked softly.

She was facing the darkness. The tears were falling
down her cheeks. "No, Chauncey, you can't." Her whisper was a barely audible sibilance in the interior night.

"I'll make it easy for you, darling," he said, his voice rich and soothing.

She could not run, and she could not face him. His hands were around her, passing across her eyes, gliding lower, his fingers pressing into her throat; the last flecks of warm light swam from her vision.

37

As the Land Cruiser approached Kono's house he looked over at Anne-Marie, now riding beside him in the front, and asked her if she was going to tell the police that she knew who had murdered Gardner Hey.

"But I *don't* know, Dan," she replied weakly. She'd said nothing to the police about Chauncey Tolliver, for the more she thought about her suspicions the less reasonable they seemed. What possible motive could Chauncey have had?

"You know, photographer," said Kono. "That pale bastard has murder in him. It sleeps in him like the eel in the rock."

"I—I can't say what I'll do," said Anne-Marie.

Kono curled his lip disdainfully, but said nothing more. He swung the vehicle across the road onto the ruts of the driveway. The house and yard were deep in shadow; the sun was long gone behind Makapuu Pali. Kono stopped and got out, leaving Anne-Marie to help Ana over the seat.

Luki, invisible until he moved, was waiting on the porch. His white teeth gleamed, framed in his pale face by his skimpy beard. "Eh, brah," he said lazily.

"You jus' happen to be in the neighborhood, Luki?" Dan said.

Luki spread his palms, the picture of innocence. "Eh, Dan, I heard you were out. Jus' wanted to see you were feelin' fine."

"You safe, Luki. I didn't talk to no cops about you. I always take care of my little brah, you bet." Dan pushed wearily past Luki into the house. As the women came along Luki smiled happily, letting his gaze linger obscenely on Anne-Marie. She heard the dog whimpering under the porch and wondered what Luki had done to suppress the eager animal's promiscuous good spirits. As she started up the steps she found Luki's bare knees suddenly in her way, pressing against her legs.

In that moment she understood the nature of the lonely horror in which Ana, for Dan's sake, had chosen to live her life. Anne-Marie could sympathize, but she could not understand why Ana did it; were she in Ana's place she would change her name and steal away, if necessary—rather than live ostracized on the one hand, and on the other hand vulnerable to the sort of perverse violations that went unnamed but were so graphically suggested by Luki's smirk.

She almost jumped over the obstruction, moving so quickly that Luki could not react. She heard his sly laugh behind her. Once inside she said, "Ana, I must go. I must go *now*. I'm going to call a cab."

Ana turned on the lamp beside the couch. She did not protest. "You never get a cab to come out here. We'll take you." Her voice was flat, defeated.

"Ana, I gotta get some rest," said Kono from the hallway.

"I'll take her myself," said Ana.

Luki peered in at the screen door. "I drive you there, beautiful haole girl. Give you nice smooth ride."

Ana turned on Luki furiously. "Get away from this house, you bastard, or I damage your equipment so bad you won't never give anybody a ride again."

Luki laughed gleefully, then saw Dan's hulk emerging into the light of the lamp. Luki made a show of stifling his giggles.

"We'll all go," said Kono sourly. "You drive, Luki. Then maybe you keep your eyes on the road."

Headlights streamed past in the darkness. The Land Cruiser bounced rhythmically over the freeway's buckled concrete seams, and Ana and Anne-Marie bounced with it, facing each other tensely, seated on the hard little fold-down benches in the back. Luki drove with reckless ferocity, cutting and dodging, racing half a dozen private Grands Prix with any drivers who aroused his envy. Dan brooded in the passenger's seat, looking out the side window.

Despite the rush hour traffic, Luki's aggressive driving brought them over the Pali, through town, and to the airport in less than forty minutes. He pulled the Land Cruiser to a stop on the upper deck of the lavish terminal. Dan opened the back of the Land Cruiser, folding the window upward and the half-doors to each side, and Anne-Marie climbed dizzily down into a warm night redolent with the blended aromas of plumeria and unburned hydrocarbons.

"Thank you, Dan," she said, with as much warmth as she could muster. "I'll be all right from here."

The big dark Hawaiian looked at her a moment—he wasn't in a position to charge her with dereliction of duty, and he could hardly blame her for wanting to get away from his odd brother. His eyes betrayed a grudging affection. "Okay, photographer. Come aroun' sometime, eh?"

She turned to find that Luki already had his hands on her bags and was pulling them from the back of the Land Cruiser. Ana got out, and in the moment's confusion, Luki was on his way to the terminal with Anne-Marie's luggage. Ana's eyes flashed in the garish light from the street lamps. "I'll go with you, Ana-Melia," said Ana. "You stay with the car a minute, Dan."

The two women hurried into the cavernous terminal, an echoing geometric maze of concrete and dark metal and illuminated signs designed with such good taste they were hard to read. Check-in baggage counters were arrayed in front of the pneumatic doors; at the nearest, a sun-dried, middle-aged bleached blonde in airline uniform was coping with a crowd of early arrivals. The next flight to San Diego wasn't for an hour and a half, but she was besieged with connecting passengers from planes that had arrived almost simultaneously, among them a family of enormous Samoans, more than half a dozen adults and children, whose baggage included cardboard cartons tied with string, oddly shaped lumps wrapped in palm-fiber matting, a set of drums, a bundle of huge wooden clubs. It was not clear whether the Samoans were intending to invade San Diego or were merely intent on providing that city with an exotic form of entertainment. "I don't care what they let you do on Air Niugini," the clerk was explaining with frayed patience, "we've got to charge you overweight for over two pieces per person."

While the Samoan family tried to decide how they would cope with this setback, Luki watched with interest, straddling Anne-Marie's stylish luggage and eyeing the lethal-looking clubs. Ana rushed up to him. "Now get lost, Luki," she said calmly. "We don't want you here, understan'?" She was determined not to lose her temper, knowing how much he enjoyed that. Luki just looked at her and giggled.

Anne-Marie had learned that the way to deal with Luki was to move quickly. With hardly a glance in his direction she walked toward a police patrolman who stood watching the terminal interior from a dozen yards away. "Officer, a man's bothering me and I'd like you to do something about it," she said when she reached the cop. Only then did she turn and look back to where Luki had been standing in the baggage line. Her boldness had done the trick;

he'd disappeared. Ana smiled broadly at her. She turned back to the policeman. "I guess I scared him off by talking to you. Will you be around this area?"

"I'll be right here, Miss," he said earnestly. He was young, mostly Chinese-Filipino at a guess, and though he looked inexperienced he also looked determined. Anne-Marie smiled her thanks and walked back to the baggage line.

"It's all right now, Ana. Thank you for everything."

"You gonna write me?"

"I promise. You go on now, okay? I don't want to keep Dan any longer than I have already."

Ana reached up and took Anne-Marie's face between her hands, kissing her on the cheek. "Goodbye, Ana-Melia. You come back, please." She had tears in her eyes.

Anne-Marie smiled tiredly. "Maybe I will, when all this wears off." She watched Ana walk away, and turned back to her luggage with a sigh. The line had not progressed; the Samoans were still negotiating. But Anne-Marie felt no rush.

Luki was talking to Dan in an angry voice. Ana couldn't hear what they were saying, and by the time she'd reached the Land Cruiser Luki had suddenly shouted and turned away, dashing down the wide sidewalk into the smoky darkness. At the same moment a police cruiser pulled up alongside the Land Cruiser. "Move it, buddy," said the cop in the shotgun seat. "Loading and unloading only."

"I gotta find my brother," Dan said, exasperated.

"Fine. Move it first."

"I'll move the car, Dan. Go after Luki. He's after Anne-Marie," Ana pleaded.

"Aiee, I wish this day was over," said Kono. He tossed the keys to Ana and set out after Luki. While the airport cops watched insolently, Ana climbed into the high driver's seat, started the engine, and drove away.

Additional airline personnel had arrived to handle the congestion; Anne-Marie gave her ticket to a neatly bearded man and he began the process of rewriting it, which involved much earnest consultation with his computer terminal. Bored, she looked back at the baggage lines in time to see a tall young man arrive, comically costumed in Bermuda shorts, a loud aloha shirt, and palm-frond hat. He had gaudy vanda-orchid leis piled around his neck and was wearing dark glasses.

He caught her staring at him and returned her gaze. She looked away, and at that moment saw Luki lounging in the shadow of a cement pillar, watching her, wearing his rictus grin. Her confidence evaporated.

"Here you are, Miss. Your baggage-claim stubs are stapled to your envelope."

She regarded the clerk blankly and grabbed the ticket envelope away from him. She hurried from the counter to the young policeman. "There he is, Officer, the man I told you about." She pointed back toward the baggage line and the pillar beyond it, where she'd spotted Luki.

"You mean that pale guy in the shorts? The one who's looking this way?" the cop asked her.

"No, not him. A Hawaiian. He was right there by that pillar, near the door."

The policeman looked at her warily. "You coming or going, lady?"

"What do you mean?"

"I mean, are you leaving Honolulu, or did you just get here?"

"I'm leaving," she said, puzzled.

"Good idea," he said, with a brisk nod. "If I were you I'd just go on down to the gate and stop worrying about this invisible stranger, okay?"

"But, really, I was . . . " Anne-Marie paused. She'd made a fool of herself. Or rather, she'd let Luki make a fool of her. Quickly she walked away, her cheeks burning.

She'd go to the nearest cocktail lounge, or to a newsstand where she could browse for a fat, juicy novel that could entrance her with somebody else's problems. She pushed her way through crowds of Chinese, Japanese,

South Americans—people from every corner of the Pacific rim. The bars on the upper level were jammed. She wanted a place that was full, but not unmanageable. If that noxious creep Luki approached her she would just scream. She could scream all the way to San Diego, if she had to. Noise could be an effective weapon—though in truth, at the moment she'd rather have a gun.

What did he want? Just to make her skin crawl? Maybe that was enough to keep his twisted mind happy; he was like a closet sadomasochist who liked to masturbate to photographs of torture.

She descended a gleaming steel escalator to the open lower deck of the terminal and walked past rows of baggage carousels toward the west end of the terminal. Taxi drivers lounged against their battered cabs in the exhaust-filled night air. They watched her pass, whistling and moaning in sensual parody, as insufferable as Romans. Her efforts to ignore them only made her more rigidly aware of her clicking heels, her swinging skirt, her hips moving tightly from side to side.

She dodged traffic and crossed to a cocktail lounge lodged between buildings of the Inter-island Terminal. It was an old-fashioned, disheveled little place with rattan-and-fishnet decor, reminiscent of the terminal that had stood here in the days of *The High and the Mighty*. The bartender was an elderly Japanese-American, and there was only one couple in the place, a short muscular boy with sun-bleached hair, once brown, who was missing his upper front teeth, and a girl with long matted kinky hair; she was wrapped in a length of dingy paisley from her breasts to her ankles. The boy gave Anne-Marie a toothless mind-blown grin. She smiled halfheartedly and went to the bar, where she ordered a gin and tonic; she thought of the couple on the plane a few days earlier, the ones eager to invest in dope. She thought of Luki and his partners.

When her drink came she paid for it, tipping the grandfatherly bartender too much, and took it to a table near the young couple, next to the window that overlooked the concrete pad where the Aloha Air Lines and Hawaii Air jets warmed up, their engines keening in the night.

A man stood in the doorway of the bar, a silhouette against the streetlamps. Anne-Marie's heart thudded against her breastbone. But it was not Luki.

Instead it was that fellow in the shorts and funny hat. He stared at her a moment, then walked directly to her table. Her throat constricted. How had the world come to be so thickly infested with these creatures?

The man sat down abruptly, pulling off his dark glasses, so that her cry was stopped in her throat. "Chauncey!" she gasped.

"How much did you tell them?" he said harshly. He set his overnight bag on the floor beside his chair, and laid the thin leather case he was carrying on the table.

"Nothing," she said reflexively, quickly adding, "Who do you mean?"

"Anne-Marie, I saw you talking to that kid cop in the terminal and pointing right at me. Then you ran away. What did you tell him?" Chauncey's voice was rich, self-confident; Anne-Marie had rarely known him to sound so sure of himself.

"Oh, God," she said faintly, her giddiness returning. "Chauncey, I had no idea you were within twenty miles of here. I was scared, but . . . I was scared because Luki Kono has been following me ever since I got here. I was telling that policeman about Luki, not about you."

"Luki Kono?" Tolliver's tone was unfriendly, skeptical. "Why should Luki Kono have any interest in you?"

"God knows. He's a sadistic animal. Maybe he's just getting his kicks." She laughed feebly, while her thoughts raced. Chauncey could not possibly know she'd been to the Blowhole this afternoon. He probably hadn't known that she'd ever met the Konos. But she couldn't afford to behave as if she had something to hide. "I'm . . . I'm so glad you're here. I don't know how Gardner ever got me involved with these people—I was just along for the ride."

She smiled as winsomely as she could. "Now I don't have to worry anymore. I ran in here to give him the slip—then when you came in, I thought for a second he'd found me." She convulsively clutched at his damp right hand; she noticed that his left tightened around the handle of the leather case on the table. "Oh, Chauncey, I'm so glad to see you."

He watched her more steadily than she'd ever remembered, his eyes seeming to focus on hers through trembling tears. Nothing in his expression betrayed his opinion of her improvised story. At last he seemed to relax, barely perceptibly; he glanced out the windows, listening to the thin whine of the airliners. "Sorry if I seem edgy, Anne-Marie," he said, turning to look past her. "I can't really talk about all the details, why I'm dressed like this, fairly important matters, you know, situation at TERAC, that sort of thing. Don't want you to blow my cover." He laughed, an insinuating, conspiratorial, dry chuckle.

Anne-Marie's eyes widened in what she hoped was a convincing display of admiration. Chauncey was beginning to sound like a parody of himself. "You mean you're . . . you really *are* a secret agent, Chauncey?"

"Thought sure Peter'd given me away by now. But that's the case, yes. Though I shouldn't really admit it." Chauncey looked at her shrewdly, then looked away. "And how's Peter?"

"I wouldn't know," she said quietly, honestly. "I haven't seen him." A moth fluttered around the red candle on the table.

Chauncey's expression softened. "Have you gone and burned yourself again, Anne-Marie?" The moth dodged away, randomly.

She looked at him from hooded eyes. You evil, sanctimonious bastard, she thought, it's my humiliation that gets you off. You love it when the rest of us are as miserable as you. After all, there's not much difference between you and Luki, evil Chauncey, despite your airs.

Anne-Marie nodded dumbly at Tolliver, her eyes suddenly filling with tears. Let him think what he would.

"And you're going home to Charlie now?" he asked tenderly. She nodded. He said, "I'm so very glad. I can't tell you." He paused. "Listen, I'll change my flight." His voice was sticky with enthusiasm. "San Diego's just as good as LAX, where I'm headed. I'll see you right back to Charlie's door."

Her stomach threatened to reject the gin and tonic, which now seemed poisonously sweet. She smiled at Chauncey through her tears, saw him staring back at her through his watering eyes. With cold fingers she squeezed his clammy hand.

Yamamura wandered the shadowy gardens of TERAC, afraid to drive home to his barren apartment in Wahiawa until he had succeeded in calming his agitated nerves. He could not have been more sincerely frustrated. It was only midafternoon in Tokyo (tomorrow afternoon, if one insisted on seeing it that way), and after much bullying of aides, secretaries, and MITI functionaries at half a dozen levels, he had succeeded in reaching the deputy minister himself by telephone. Such men were not like Yamamura; they were of the old school, meticulously trained and initiated into the mysteries of etiquette demanded by their roles in the bureaucracy—it was said that the highest posts were virtually hereditary. The deputy minister had been distantly polite as Yamamura excitedly related his tale of perfidy and impending disaster. The news was most distressing, the minister agreed.

The deputy minister went a step further: he solemnly announced his determination to see that the ominous implications of Professor Slater's novel theories were studied most thoroughly. And he was profuse in his appreciation of Yamamura's counsel. Yamamura had certainly been correct in his assessment of Ishi's injudicious management, for example, not to mention the devious behavior of the American Edovich. Yet for his own part the deputy minister found some small comfort in the fact that MITI, after all, had had very little to say about the day-to-day operation of the laboratory—notwithstanding Yamamura's efforts to the contrary.

Then Yamamura understood: the deputy minister had already learned of the past hour's events from others, perhaps indirectly from Ishi himself, through informers placed in the Office of Science and Technology. Already a policy position had been drawn up and ratified, without consulting or even paying the slightest attention to Yamamura. Indeed, the delays Yamamura had encountered when trying to reach the deputy minister had no doubt been deliberate, intended to exclude his advice from consideration in the agency's counsels.

The decision, plainly, had been that MITI would dissociate itself from the events at TERAC. And thus from Yamamura himself.

As he walked along the darkened paths he gazed up at lighted windows in the black towers that he now knew he would never, in any sense, call his own. Cloud-filtered moonlight reflected from myriad leaves of the massed foliage; a pale ginger flower gleamed in the darkness. He was reminded of tea with Ishi, and of his betrayal. . . .

Odor of ginger, raindrops on fevered skin—Yamamura weeping.

Frank McDonald was waiting on the control platform; he wore jeans and a plaid flannel shirt, having put the customary lab coat aside. "Everything's set, Ume. That switch will stop the condensor transport. You've got to do it on your own, though."

Narita looked at the scorched control panel. "That's very Japanese of you, Frank. As long as I do it, you're not being disloyal, eh?"

"Something like that. I've known Martin a long time, Ume. He's been wrong a few times, but never about anything important."

"This is important." Narita flipped the warped plastic

cover off the T-bar switch, hooked a finger under the crosspiece, and flipped it up. He heard a faint clicking of relays, noted a few small red glass indicator bulbs light up.

"Damn, look at that!" McDonald exclaimed.

"Did it work?" Narita demanded.

McDonald glanced at him. "Oh, yeah—the transporter's stopped. I was looking at these sensor circuits I just replaced. I just got another big gamma burst."

"Inside the machine?"

"Well, it's hard to tell. We didn't think so before. Penny Harper was working on it, but frankly . . . " He let the thought die.

Narita looked at the warped and burned instruments. "I was thinking, Frank—what if this collector isn't one hundred percent efficient? What if little drops of holy water have been clinging to the channels in there, accumulating for weeks?"

"What of it? Might be worthwhile cleaning it out, when the ring goes down."

Narita's gaze wandered to the bulging steel door on the other side of the cold, echoing room. He shivered. "I think we got this machine turned off just in time, Frank."

"In time for what?" McDonald sounded skeptical.

"To save the ring, maybe. If Slater is right, that gamma burst you saw just now was the disintegration of an I-particle."

"*One* I-particle? Slater thinks they do that?"

Narita nodded. "Yes, he does. Come on, Frank, I'll buy you a drink. It's cold down here."

The space-weapons division chief was a rotund shadow in the moonlight as he walked up the flagstone path toward the big adobe house. The Los Alamos lab director opened his front door before the chief knocked. "Thanks for coming, Hank. Sorry to drag you away, but I'd like to keep this meeting quiet." The director took the chief's Pendleton jacket and hung it on the heavy Spanish rack in the hall. "Coffee?" the director offered. "Something stiffer?" The chief shook his head.

A large, fit-looking man with closely cropped gray hair stood before the log fire whose flames provided the only light in the living room. The man wore a well-tailored brown wool suit and sipped whiskey from a heavy glass, which he set on the mantel as the others came down the steps to the red-tiled floor.

"Hank, you know Tommy Elbert," said the director.

The chief said, "General," and held out his hand.

The general took the hand and squeezed it. "No formality, Hank. I can't express my sorrow at the loss of your fine people."

"Thanks, Tommy." The chief cleared his throat. "Barosz could be a cantankerous old son of a bitch, but he knew his business."

The general stared at the chief a moment longer, his dark brown eyes set in a tanned, sun-wrinkled face. The three men shared the solemn moment. None was a stranger to violent death, although the lab men's experiences were perhaps more remote than the general's. The general gave the chief's hand a final squeeze, and released it.

"It's late," said the director. He waved at suede-upholstered armchairs, and the three settled themselves. "I've already briefed Tommy on our findings, Hank, and he's prepared to share some information with us that up to now hasn't been in the need-to-know category, from our standpoint. First he'd like a little of your insight."

The general said, "You're pretty sure you've pinned down the cause, then, is that right, Hank?"

The chief shrugged. "There hasn't been time to do a thorough literature search, but even so we've dug up a few theoretical papers from a year or two back suggesting that I-particles could behave like this. Fellow named Slater."

The lab director said, "Of course, the results Martin's

been getting seem to pretty completely disconfirm that prediction, so we wondered . . ."

"The question is, how good are Martin's results," said the chief bluntly. "I don't think we have any other candidates."

"Well, they are and they aren't," said the general. "I'm authorized to tell you this by the undersecretary himself, Hank, but we mustn't have it going any further."

The chief shrugged again, allowing his massive body to slide lower into the soft chair.

"In a sense, there may not actually have *been* any reliable results," said the general. "The fact is, Billy Barosz was getting Martin's stuff. Part of it, anyway. There's no other supply."

"TERAC?" The chief glanced at his boss. "The problem they had out there yesterday?"

The director said, "That's one of the reasons we wanted to talk with you, Hank."

The chief hunched down between his massive shoulders and stared up at the leaping shadows on the beamed ceiling, the wavering red and black shapes of heavy vigas and the herringbone-patterned latillas above them. After a moment the chief looked sidelong at the general. "I'd say you'd better call up Martin right this minute and tell him to put the rest of that stuff at the bottom of the deepest hole he can find."

The general looked uncomfortable. "Just like that?"

"Yes. I don't know *how* it works, but I can show you what it just did." The chief hauled himself erect in his chair. The general started to speak, but the chief interrupted him, continuing: "And it occurs to me we'd better get something going upstairs in our respective agencies."

"My gut reaction would be just the opposite," said the general quickly. "Let's try to contain this, Hank, not start the weak sisters running for the exits."

"That's up to you, Tommy," the lab director put in. "But Hank has a point."

"My point is, if TERAC can make I-particles, any industrialized nation willing to spend the money can make them." The chief stared at the general. "Now if I were in your shoes, General, I would consider it my duty to convey that sort of intelligence to the policy-makers, ASAP."

"Well, I'll take the suggestion under advisement," the general said stiffly.

"Let's try to get in touch with Martin," said the director. "The phone in the den's equipped, Tommy, if you want to use that one."

"I will. Thank God it shouldn't be necessary to bother Martin personally," said the general, getting to his feet. "We have a man on the spot."

They left Anne-Marie's half-full glass beside the red candle and walked out of the cocktail lounge. The cloying night air assailed her. She was dazzled by the headlights of circling cars and taxis. Chauncey's right hand on her elbow hurried her along, across a busy sidestreet with no crosswalk, toward the main terminal. Taxis roared past, lurching and squealing, drag-racing each other the last half block of straightaway to the cab stand to get a better place in line. Crowds of pale bewildered tourists stood on the sidewalk in front of the baggage-claim area, and from among them emerged a pale bearded face, a tall thin body striding toward them, suddenly blocking their path.

Anne-Marie shouted, "Chauncey, watch out!" But the glittering knife in Luki's hand was aimed at her; she felt the seam of her cotton shirt snag and rip as Chauncey threw her to the side. She fell to her knees on the concrete sidewalk, too shocked to be afraid. Her hand went to her side, but the blade had missed her skin, had left only a tear in the fabric. She scrambled away.

Tolliver's right hand swung sideways into Luki's belly as the knife arm went past, but without enough strength to do damage. Chauncey had time to drop the bag and case he carried in his left and wheel to meet Luki.

Luki paused, assessing Tolliver's defenses: the man

looked as if he knew what he was doing. "I told Dan she gonna turn us in," he said, talking to distract Tolliver. "An' she went right for you. Had a little meeting all set up, didn'—" He sprang without completing the sentence, but Tolliver was faster and smarter than Luki had calculated.

Tolliver took the knife hand in both his own, wheeling in and to the left, carrying the knife arm past and down, easily launching Luki over his right hip. Luki shouted and threw out his arms, landing badly, losing his knife. The black-handled clasp knife spun into the street. Intent upon the knife, Tolliver moved toward Luki, whose shoulders were off the curb. A taxi swerved away, its tires skittering. Luki rolled back on his shoulders and kicked at Tolliver, but Tolliver easily stepped aside. Luki jumped to his feet, staggering backward. Another taxi came to a halt with a squall of hot rubber; Luki fell against its grille. A third taxi swerved to avoid the second, its driver shouting angrily and leaning on his horn. Luki's sense of direction was reversed—he pushed away from the grille of the stalled cab and walked directly into the path of the speeding one; it smashed into his pelvis and tossed him aside. He flopped on the pavement, screaming in agony.

Anne-Marie was hurrying against the flow of foot traffic, of people running to watch the fight. She didn't care what happened, she only wanted to be away from both men. The police would find them now, thank God. But Luki had almost done it; if Chauncey hadn't been so quick, he might have gotten them both. . . . Her fingers went involuntarily to the hole under her arm, the bare skin exposed there.

A hand came from behind and clamped her arm, jerking her to a stop. "Aaaah," she groaned in terror, frozen, anticipating the blade.

"Photographer, what you running away from?"

"Oh, Dan—" She was weak with relief, but suddenly anger flared in her. She twisted away from Kono. "They're trying to kill each other. I hope they do."

Kono jerked his head to the west, where headlights blazed and horns blared. Cars and taxis and jitney buses were jammed fast in the narrow roadway, and a crowd of gawkers jostled like carrion birds around a road kill. Kono ran toward them.

Anne-Marie crept away, exhausted. The shadows flickered around her like silent Furies crying vengeance for the death of Gardner Hey.

38

Peter lost sight of Edovich's Mercedes in the clotted traffic of downtown Honolulu's rush hour, but he was already sure of the man's destination. It was dark when he parked the Triumph in front of the tall stone house on Manoa Road.

The front door was open. "Martin?" Peter called. "I'd like to come in." He heard nothing. He walked into the house. A single floor lamp shone in the dark living room; what Peter could see of the rest of the ground floor was completely deserted. Feeling very much the intruder, he walked slowly up the wide staircase to the second floor.

Warm light spilled from an open bedroom door. Low voices carried into the hall, the words unintelligible. "Martin," Peter said loudly. "I must see you."

There was a moment's silence. "Come in here," Edovich said gruffly.

Peter walked to the door. Greta Edovich lay in bed, staring at Peter with dark, makeup-smeared eyes. Edovich sat on a chair close beside her, holding both her hands in his. "What's happened, Martin?" Peter asked.

"Tolliver did this," said Edovich. The cords stood out in his neck; his face was fiery red.

"He said he wouldn't hurt me," said Greta in a hoarse whisper. "He was very gentle, really. He only wanted to keep me from calling."

"Is the ambulance on the way, then?" Peter asked.

"I won't let him call one," said Greta. "I'm not hurt." Greta turned to Edovich. "Darling, I want rest. Then I'll be fine."

He looked at her silently, then bent to kiss her. Reluctantly he freed his hands and stood up. She smiled. At the window the poinciana rustled in the night breeze.

In the hallway Peter said quietly, "If there's any sign of concussion she shouldn't be allowed to sleep. We should get her to a doctor."

"There's no concussion. Tolliver knows how to put people out with his hands alone, without leaving a mark. He could tear either of us to pieces, my boy. Come, let's talk in the living room."

Edovich poured himself a glass of rye at the bar, then set it aside. "I'm forgetting my manners," he said. "You take Scotch neat, if I recall."

"Martin, really—"

"Here it is. Don't drink it if you don't want it." Edovich left the glass of dark liquid on the shelf of the open secretary and walked to the windows. He glanced at the empty glass on the side table. "That'll be Chauncey's. It's evidence now, I suppose."

"You knew, Martin. As soon as you heard."

Edovich sighed. He turned, looking frankly at Peter. "I suspected someone might follow me. I'm glad it was you. I thought a good deal about everything you said, while I was driving here. I thought about the way I behaved." He broke off, then walked to an armchair and sat. He sipped his drink. "This tastes good," he said, smacking his lips lightly, studying the glass. "After a hard day at the office."

"Martin—"

"Be patient, my boy. I'm a Catholic, you know. Not that I believe in the old man with the beard and all his saints, but I'm a Catholic anyway; my parents were Catholics—they died for it—and I was bundled out of Yugoslavia by the sisters, so I live because of it. Confession is good for the soul, Peter, but I insist on the ritual. Forgive me, Father, and all that. That's the way we Catholics do it."

Peter said nothing. He lifted the glass of warm Scotch off the secretary and carried it to the piano. He sat on the piano bench, waiting for Martin.

Edovich chuckled sadly. "But I don't think I'll be able to forgive Chauncey. I forgave him once. What he did that time was half my fault. But to kill a man. To put his hands on Greta that way." He looked up at Peter. "I will not tolerate violence."

Peter said nothing. He thought of the bombs the man had designed, the clever remote-controlled instruments of mass destruction. Did he think they destroyed only steel and cement? Well, that was his business. But his sanctimoniousness was hardly appealing.

"I see your thoughts, Peter, your superior moralistic judgments. What I have done I have done for the country I love. I am proud of those terrible creations, precisely because their terror ensures they will never be used. No, I have nothing to confess on that score. Without me, there would be no TERAC, do you know that? Without the confidence of the generals and admirals and members of Congress, that I will give them something for their money, something to contribute to the defense of our nation, you would not have the privilege to daydream in your pretty tower."

"There's a bomb out there somewhere, Martin," Peter said impatiently.

"*Yes!*" Edovich said angrily. "You are in such a hurry, Father, are they lined up outside the door of the booth?

Yes, Father: *I knew not what I did.*" He looked defiantly at Peter. "There you have my confession. I believed totally in the stability of the I-particle. I tried to read your papers, but I could not understand your peculiar reasoning, and no one else agreed with you. It took a man's death to make you speak plain English."

"I regret Mr. Sherwood's death. Am I to blame for it?"

"Decide for yourself. This is *my* confession." Edovich took a swallow of his drink. "Yes, I have shipped vials of holy water to the laboratories that can use it. Its properties are helpful in beam weapons. Yes, I have deliberately kept it out of the hands of the Japanese. Who can trust them? Besides, I have no monopoly—if they are interested, let them make their own."

"Where is it, Martin?"

Edovich pretended not to hear. "Soon I could have proved its worth as a beam medium. Soon we could have developed *factories,* holy-water factories, batteries of explosive-powered accelerators, bulk processing plants. Of course they would consume huge amounts of energy, but the results would be more than worthwhile. I know better than to have faith in secrecy, Peter my boy—but I have faith in a good head start."

"I wouldn't know about those things, Martin. All I know is, you've been a thief and a liar. And if I hadn't been such a snob, I could have seen it sooner. Hey was shouting it in my ear, but he was one of *them.* You were one of us; one of the best of us."

"Your penance is bitter, Father," Edovich sneered. "You throw my own fatuousness in my face."

"I've had enough of this playing with words, Martin," said Peter, getting to his feet. "Do you intend to help us find Tolliver, or are you stalling to give him time?"

Edovich stared at Peter defiantly, his emotions visibly contending. Suddenly he looked immensely weary; his jaws opened slackly, his eyelids and bushy brows drooped to shade his eyes. "He has taken every drop of it with him;

it with him; he thinks I will protect him for its sake. I will not. . . . "

Tommy Elbert, the intelligence general, gripped the handset harder. "Dammit, Sergeant, what the hell does that mean—a 'mechanical interruption of service'?"

The security-service operator replied, "Sir, I think they mean the phone line's been cut."

"What's going on out there?" The general's desperate words came out in a squeak. "All right, we need some people on the ground," he said, recovering the voice of command. "Get me Major Trent at PACAF."

He hung up and turned to find the lab director watching him from the door of the den. "Can't reach the fellow I'm after," said the general, "and Martin's phone is—out of order."

"I think I can shed some light on that," said the director. "I've just been on the other line with some people from TERAC."

The general ran a nervous hand through his short gray hair. "Go ahead, shoot. You can't embarrass me—I've got egg on my face already."

"Do you know the public information officer at TERAC, fellow named Chauncey Tolliver?"

"Yes, I certainly do."

"Thought you might." The lab director took a step closer. "The way I hear the story, an hour ago Martin was sitting in a meeting at which a bright character named Slater—same who wrote those papers Hank dug up—had just told everybody that a person or persons unknown had stolen all the I-particle fluid accumulated in the past year, and moreover, the collector was about to blow itself up. Then they get the news that Tolliver is being sought by the police for questioning in a murder. Whereupon Martin jumped up and ran out of the room. Matsuo Ishi—he's the lab director out there—apparently he's already talked to the FBI."

The general stared at the director, pained, speechless.

Quietly, the director said, "Don't you think it's time we kicked this upstairs, Tommy?"

The phone rang before the general could answer. "Elbert here. What? Just a minute." He fumbled with the scrambler. "Okay, okay. Major, just tell me this: how well do you get along with the FBI out there—?"

At 12:30 A.M. Mountain Time, Brigadier General Elbert called a major general in San Antonio, who some minutes later called a general of the Air Force in Washington, D.C. Some minutes after that, the Air Force Chief of Staff called the Chairman of the Joint Chiefs (it was the Marines' turn to hold the post), and he in turn informed the Secretary of Defense.

Word had gotten to the Secretary of Energy through separate channels. The two men called each other, virtually simultaneously; one had a background in international finance, the other was on leave from a lucrative Washington law practice, its specialty corporate taxation. After an amiable chat the two men decided not to wake the President just yet. They and their advisers needed time to give the matter more thought.

To the Energy Secretary was left the unpleasant task of smoothing ruffled Japanese feathers. Meanwhile, the Federal Bureau of Investigation could cope with the problem of locating Mr. Chauncey Tolliver on its own. No need to burden them with useless additional information.

The telephone rang yet again, and Ishi took it from Miss Sugibayashi. "Yes, Dr. Slater?"

"I regret to say I have more bad news, Professor."

"I wish I were surprised, Dr. Slater." Ishi's polite voice betrayed his weariness.

"Sir, it seems that Chauncey Tolliver has stolen the fluid and may be on board an airplane leaving Honolulu. As the plane reaches altitude, the cosmic ray bombardment will intensify, and the chance of an explosion will increase."

Ishi could see the lights of Honolulu International Airport, thirteen miles away as the crow flies, through the wide windows of the conference room. The landing lights of approaching aircraft hung like shimmering baubles in the velvety night. "How unfortunate for those people," Ishi whispered.

"Worse than that. I can't predict the size of the explosion. If by any chance the vials of fluid were to be brought too close together, so that the explosion of one, instead of dispersing the others, were to set them off—" Peter's voice faltered. He resumed in a more technical tone: "One characteristic effect of this type of explosion seems to be a strong electromagnetic pulse. If Dr. Narita is there he can explain it better than I."

"No need. I understand this pulse interferes with electrical systems?"

"Microcircuitry is particularly vulnerable, Professor. Even at great range. A large I-particle explosion anywhere above the horizon could cause a great deal of confusion. But I was thinking particularly of the nuclear plant control systems, Professor."

Ishi paled. He studied the concerned faces of the advisers who were near him in the conference room. Then he said, "We will shut down TERAC immediately, Dr. Slater. Do you have anything else to say?"

"I can't think of anything right now, sir."

Ishi silently invoked whatever gods were in charge of these matters to ensure that Peter Slater would not discover new scenarios of disaster. "Goodbye, Doctor." He hung up.

Slater put down the phone. He became aware that Martin Edovich was describing for at least the third time the case Chauncey Tolliver had taken from his safe: " . . . a backgammon case, pebbled dark brown fake-leather finish, brass clips, locking clasp. Inside, the halves of the board lift out. Underneath, three hundred and eighty slits in velvet-covered Styrofoam. Full glass ampoules in approximately two hundred and nineteen of them. . . . "

Edovich, Slater, and two FBI men, Linka and a dark compact man named Changia, were sitting in a bare windowless room in the Federal Building. The room was equipped with a recorder, a remote video camera, three telephones, and a computer terminal with direct access to airlines reservations lists and other useful sources of information. Linka was interrogating Edovich, while Changia worked with the terminal.

Changia looked up suddenly, interrupting his partner. "I've got it, I think. He could have boarded one of four mainland flights. One's still at the gate. One's on the taxiway. Two are already in the air. How do you want to handle this?"

"What do you say, Slater?" Linka curtly demanded. "How dangerous is this stuff of yours?"

"Most of it's plain water by now, but the rest . . . If you want to assume the worst—it could go off anytime. The explosion could be huge."

"What's huge?" Linka demanded.

"I just don't *know,*" Peter said edgily. "As big as a fission bomb. Not that big. Bigger."

Linka and Changia stared at him. They would have thought Peter crazy, had not the identities of these two who had blundered into their office already been confirmed. Linka looked up at the lens of the watching video camera. "We need help. Round up some people to augment the force of marshals at the airport."

Changia answered a ringing phone. "For you, George—the Air Force again."

Linka grabbed the handset. "Major, it's a bad time. Call back in ten minutes, will you?" Reluctantly he listened to the rapid words on the telephone. "Yes, we've narrowed the possibilities, but we haven't taken action yet, so . . . all right, we'll think about it. Now I have to hang up." He put the phone down. "They want us to let him get to the mainland, land at Edwards, out in the desert. They'll take charge of Tolliver."

Changia said, "The Honolulu DA will be lucky to see him back here on murder charges once the Defense people get hold of him."

"Let them fight it out," said Linka. "Gets *us* out of it, anyway—maybe the farther we get those planes from Honolulu, the better."

"You can't fly that stuff around, you've got to get it underground," Peter shouted.

"Look, Doctor . . . " Linka said soothingly.

Peter had paced two steps in the cramped room, then turned and paced two steps back. He stopped, staring over Linka's head. "If Tolliver is already in the air, tell the pilot to fly as low as he safely can. Keep the other planes on the ground. Can you find a shielded vehicle somewhere, lead-shielded? Or iron?"

"Could be the Air Force will come in handy after all. We'll see," said Linka. "What about nabbing Tolliver?"

"I can't think of anything he could do that would improve the situation," said Peter. "I can think of several things that would make it worse—like trying to pour the stuff down the drain. It could get trapped and concentrated."

"Okay, we don't let on," Linka agreed.

"We've got to find him first," Changia reminded him.

"Search the manifests, the ones in the air," Linka told Changia. "I'll stop the ones on the ground with some dumb FAA regulation or other—I'll get them to claim their PA system doesn't work."

Linka picked up a telephone as Changia tapped the keys of his terminal. Names moved jerkily up the screen, glowing in green angular letters. "Shout if you spot an alias, Professor," said Changia.

Martin Edovich leaned closer, peering at the screen. Peter looked over his shoulder, curious to see what Tolliver would call himself. Edovich had told him that Tolliver had passports in the names Calvin Talbot and

Charles Taylor; Chauncey really had no imagination, thought Peter.

Peter could still remember the night they'd met, a warm September night at a dorm counselor's welcoming party for freshmen on the Old Campus. Sophisticated eighteen-year-old Peter Slater had watched contemptuously as boyish Chauncey Tolliver had made himself nauseatingly drunk on cheap sherry. Peter had helped Chauncey's roommates get him into bed, had in fact introduced Chauncey to the efficacy of aspirin taken before drunken sleep. Chauncey's gratitude had proved boundless. Somehow, over the years, Peter had provided many other opportunities for Chauncey to make a fool of himself, and Chauncey, driven by God knew what sense of connection between them, had availed himself almost every time.

Then Peter's gaze was caught by a name in green letters: "PHELPS/A-M, MRS." "God help her," he whispered.

"What's that, Slater?" Changia demanded.

"On the San Diego plane. I know that woman. She was Gardner Hey's photographer. Tolliver set up the assignment for her."

"She could be in on this?"

"No, no," he said impatiently. "But she knows Tolliver. She can identify him. If he's on that flight she could be in danger of her life."

"If he's on that plane, she's not the only one in danger," said Linka.

Chauncey climbed the stairs to the 747's lounge, feeling more like himself—his new self, that is.

Everything he'd done since leaving the Edoviches' house had resulted in increasing his confidence. He'd been faced with numerous checks and setbacks, and he'd emerged from each in a better position than he'd gone in. He'd even escaped that encounter with Luki Kono easily enough—Luki had provided the perfect diversion, lying there on the pavement making such an appalling noise.

Chauncey had taken the precaution of ducking into the

men's room to change into the blue seersucker suit he'd bought off the rack at the Ala Moana Center. He'd planned to change later, on the plane, but it made no difference—and besides, getting out of that ridiculous costume cobbled together from items in Martin's closet had given him a psychological boost.

The biggest boost of all came when he saw Anne-Marie ahead of him in the line to board the San Diego plane. He'd been late to the gate, and he'd half feared she'd run away, but she'd stuck to their plan after all.

He caught a glimpse of her ankle disappearing up the lounge stairs as he got aboard. His last-minute flight change had the disadvantage of sticking him with an undesirable seat in the middle of the plane's wide center section, where he found himself surrounded by sunburned dermatologists and their spouses returning from a convention. But once the plane was in the air Chauncey summoned a flight attendant and went through the necessary paperwork to trade his ticket up to a first-class passage.

He reached the top of the half-spiral stairs and stepped into the lounge. He knew the floor plan of the plane almost instinctively; earlier in his career he'd been forced to memorize the layouts of all commercial aircraft engaged in major overseas routes, and this was one of the standard 747 interior arrangements, with swivel chairs to starboard and boothlike settees to port. Chauncey knew where the food trolleys were stowed, where to find the elevator behind the galley, where the diplomatic mail locker was concealed. In one of the swivel chairs, her back turned to him, sat Anne-Marie, chatting with an older woman.

Chauncey walked to her, smiled at the older woman—who paused in the middle of her sentence—and bent to say, "Don't mind me, dear. I just wanted to let you know I'm safely aboard."

The woman who looked up at him was not Anne-Marie. She was as tall and as tan as Anne-Marie, and her hair was as dark and soft, and she was wearing a denim skirt and a cotton top—not really all that similar, on close inspection—but her lips were lush and red, her eyes big and dark brown, and she was not the same woman at all.

Chauncey was stunned. "I—I'm terribly sorry. I thought—I obviously mistook you for someone else." He backed away.

The woman smiled her forgiveness. "Please don't worry about it." Her wide smile seemed amused, and her gaze lingered long enough to let Chauncey know his interruption had not, perhaps, been completely unwelcome.

He nodded, speechless, and hurried to find an unoccupied seat. He chose one behind a partition, forward and on the opposite side of the lounge. He sat down and wiped hastily at his eyes, which suddenly were watering again, and took a deep breath. He laid the backgammon case on the table in front of the settee and put both his big hands on top of it, and slowly recovered his calm.

Had Anne-Marie betrayed him after all? He restrained the urge to leap up and run downstairs to search through the hundreds of passengers in tourist class, to make sure she was—or wasn't—somewhere on the plane. But he persuaded himself to sit very still, not to make a scene. What would it prove if she wasn't there?

Assume the worst, that she knew what he'd done, that she'd phoned the police. Did it really make a difference? The coded telegrams he'd sent had already made sure he'd be met by his own people in San Diego.

What about Martin? If Martin had had the sense to keep his mouth shut, he too would get clean away. Greta hadn't been hurt, and she was in a perfect position to blame everything on Chauncey, which was just fine—everybody always did.

So some fast talking might be necessary to convince his people that killing Hey was really necessary—perhaps on the basis that Hey knew all about the theft of the holy water and was about to publish?—but no one could contradict him. In the end they'd give him a new name, maybe even a new face, and send him out of the country for a few years.

As Chauncey pondered these matters his confidence returned. Paradoxically, he felt a sense of liberation, of new potential. His life history could be described in terms of the relationships he'd mishandled, the crossed signals he'd broadcast: managing to chase away the people he cared about—his father, Peter Slater, at last even Martin Edovich—through an excess of affection, while managing to refract his strong attractions to women through complicating male friendships. Did he really like Charlie Phelps all that much? Or was Charlie just a convenient way to keep him from risking a direct approach to Anne-Marie?

Chauncey decided that the answers to these questions could easily be foregone—they were less important than the realization that he could start over again, here and now, and refuse to make the same mistakes. He was a new man. He was confident, in control, possessed of secret knowledge, possessed in fact of a secret elixir whose power exceeded anything known. . . .

Chauncey forgot that he'd had similar feelings before: when he became a secret agent for the Air Force, for example, while still posing as a serious scholar of Asian history, or when he became a public information officer, and secretly remained a spy. But each time he'd assumed a new role he'd used it to justify the human failures of the old one. Now, in this newest part, that of the master agent licensed to kill, he'd even managed to justify manslaughter. . . .

The urge to find Anne-Marie returned. He owed it to her, as well as to himself, to make sure she did nothing to risk giving the game away, if it weren't already too late. He unsnapped the loose seatbelt and started to get up.

"Excuse me, is that backgammon you've got there, by any chance?" It was the woman he'd mistaken for Anne-Marie, bending toward him.

He paused, kept his seat. She was beautiful; she had the features he'd always admired, the long dark lashes, the bold gaze, the expressive mouth. And he was a new man, remember?—free to talk to this woman, to weave a web of shared confidences without worrying about what others thought. "Yes," he said. "Do you play?"

"I do," she said, "I confess I'm a bit of an addict. And it's a long trip to California." She laughed. "I'm impossibly rude, I'm sure that's what you're thinking."

"Not at all. Please, sit down. Perhaps the attendant will be along soon and I can buy you a drink." His voice was deep, assured; the new man was firmly in control. The new man thought it would be an amusing experience, rolling dice on a board worth a third of a billion dollars—

The woman slid into the seat beside him. "My name's Stephanie," she said.

"I'm Calvin," he replied, after an instant's thought—he'd used the more dashing of his assumed names when giving the flight attendant the phony credit card. He snapped the brass clips on the case and opened the board onto the table in front of them.

Stephanie smiled at "Calvin," and—without quite looking her straight in the eye—he smiled back.

With Changia somewhere behind them in his official sedan, agent Linka allowed Peter Slater to drive him to the airport in his Triumph; the FBI man had reluctantly allowed Edovich to go home to his wife, but he needed Peter to identify Chauncey Tolliver. Peter wasn't a bad driver, but he wasn't good enough to drive the way he did, red-lined all the way, on a freeway choked with the island's notoriously lousy motorists. Linka arrived at the airport pale and shaken.

They left the car at the base of the tower and rode the elevator to the control room. Shadowy figures hunched over green radar screens. Blue and white lights outlined the runways beneath the windows: close in, the old runways merged with Hickam Air Force Base to the west, and a mile farther out the broad Reef Runway occupied landfill in what had once been a shallow lagoon. Aerial traffic was heavy.

The tower supervisor huddled with Linka and Slater.

"You wanted a guy named Calvin Talbot, right? He's confirmed on the San Diego flight—"

"We know that already," said Linka irritably. "Have you talked to the pilot?"

"That's right, we have," said the supervisor, in a voice well practiced at calming nervous pilots. "He's reversing course, descending to minimum legal altitude, and he's taking the usual precautions with respect to the passenger. . . ."

"They know who he is?" Peter demanded.

"Why yes, sir, they certainly do," said the supervisor. "They've made no indication they suspect anything, as you folks ordered. But they're prepared to deal with him if he decides to make trouble."

"What about Anne-Marie? Miss—Mrs. Phelps, I mean?"

"We can't confirm she's on the flight," said the supervisor.

"You mean she isn't on it?" In its fierce haste, Peter's hope sounded like anger.

The supervisor shook his head. "It's uncertain. She checked in and was issued a boarding pass, but the attendants haven't had time to match her with a seat on the plane. They do have other things to think about—"

Peter turned away, shutting out the man's excuses. Through the tower's clear glass windows he could see downtown Honolulu, four miles to the east, and Waikiki's blazing lights another three miles farther along. If Peter had turned around, almost 160 degrees, virtually the opposite direction, he could have seen the dim lights of TERAC gleaming at the crest of the island, thirteen miles away. But instead he watched the landing approaches, the floating lights in the sky, the bright novae of safely closing airliners.

Chauncey had won two out of three games, on luck alone. The woman played well, and she knew how to keep the game spicy, doubling and redoubling at crucial moments.

They'd ordered brandy and talked awhile, after all the others had turned out their reading lights, and the lounge had grown almost dark. Somehow his arm had gone around her shoulders, and she'd gotten sleepy, and now she was dozing against his side. She was so warm. Her fingers rested lightly on his stomach, the tips of her nails just reaching beneath the placket of his shirt to brush the skin. And perhaps she wasn't really asleep—at least not completely.

As he'd gotten to know her he'd almost completely put Anne-Marie out of his mind. Too bad it couldn't go any further. They would exchange telephone numbers, and promises, when they got to San Diego. But of course the number he would give Stephanie would be fake. They'd never see each other again, unless he could come up with something—there were several hours left to think about it.

Gently he leaned across Stephanie to look out the half-shaded window. Below the plane the moon paved the blue black sea with silver.

The waves were too close. And the moon's path . . . What time was it? He carefully freed his arm, pushed back the sleeve of his slightly oversized shirt, looked at his watch. Still early.

He understood instantly. The plane was flying west, not east; he should not be able to see the moon at all from this side of the plane.

They knew about him. And this mincing caution meant they must know what he was carrying. It was not Anne-Marie who'd betrayed him. Martin, or more likely Greta, had talked to the wrong people.

He twisted his head to bring his lips close to the ear of the sleeping woman. "Stephanie? Stephanie, I'm sorry, but I've got to excuse myself—"

She nodded sleepily as he slipped away; he was bold enough to plant a quick kiss on her smooth brow. He folded the backgammon board without bothering to gather the chips and dice. He collected his overnight bag from the rack and took both pieces of luggage to the lavatory, clicking the door shut behind him. Just before it closed he saw the flight attendant in the galley at the aft end of the lounge looking toward him, wide-eyed but otherwise expressionless.

A fluorescent light flickered into life. He sat on the toilet seat and rummaged in the overnight bag until he found the bottle of after-shave he'd taken from Martin's cabinet. He unceremoniously dumped the contents into the stainless-steel basin on his left. The cramped cabinet was suddenly rank with the sharp odor of citrus and alcohol.

He snapped the game board out of the backgammon case and set it aside, revealing rows of tiny glass ampoules nestled in black velvet. He picked out the first with his fingernail. He unscrewed its threaded plug and poured the thin fluid into the neck of the empty lotion bottle. He leaned over, the velvet case on his knees, and held the empty vial under the spigot with his right hand; with his left he pushed down to open the tap. Cold water flowed. He had to rap the cylinder of crystal sharply against the basin to dislodge an obstructing air bubble.

He recapped the ampoule, now full of water, and replaced it in its slot. The entire operation had taken more than ten seconds. His speed would increase with practice; nevertheless, he had over two hundred ampoules to go. Being realistic, that meant over forty minutes minimum—and he had no idea how long the plane had been flying since turning back.

He would save as much as he could.

The "occupied" sign on the lavatory door glowed steadily. The flight attendant peeked from the galley curtain at the lighted latch. She whispered into the intercom, "He's been in there almost half an hour, Captain. He must know."

The captain's voice sounded in her ear, stripped of its

usual resonance: "I'm sending Niels back; he's armed." The attendant saw the curtain leading to the flight deck pushed aside and the big blond engineer step through. He winked at her and patted his uniform jacket, then leaned casually against the stair railing. "The movie will be over in about twelve minutes," said the captain. "I'll make an announcement then—suspected engine trouble, free hotel—the usual. Meanwhile I'm going to try to get us down as quick as possible, so see to it that everybody's strapped in."

"Yes, sir."

"Stay by the intercom when you're done. I'll find out whether these fellows on the ground have any bright ideas."

There were no more lights in the sky above Honolulu. Air Traffic Control had landed all the planes they could, kept departing flights on the ground, warned off approaching flights. Peter Slater stared at the hazy night above Waikiki, above the dimly illuminated slopes of Diamond Head, watching for the solitary glimmer of Tolliver's plane. He realized he was looking straight at the hotel where he'd spent one night with Anne-Marie, although he could not distinguish it within the mass of glowing lights that outlined the beach almost eight miles away. If he ever saw her again, he'd be content merely to see her safely back to earth. . . .

"Dr. Slater?" It was the tower supervisor. "Could you give us some help on this? Seems the captain wants to know if he should do anything about the fact that this man Talbot has locked himself up inside one of the toilets."

"What?" Peter struggled to assimilate the odd fact; then the meaning struck him. "Oh, no, he's trying to . . . Let me talk to the captain." The supervisor handed him a microphone. "Captain? Captain, this is Peter Slater. The name is *Slater*. I think Tolliver—Talbot, that is—will talk to me. But you've got to get somebody to *tell* him that right away. You've got to explain to him what's wrong.

I mean, tell him *I'll* explain what's wrong. . . . " The horror tumbled over Peter, scrambling his words. He paused, speechless, as he saw the white lights flare in the distance beyond Diamond Head; the plane had just turned on its landing lights.

"Captain, you can't do that," Peter whispered inaudibly. "You can't come down right there. . . . " He turned on the tower supervisor. "What's he doing, coming in like that? Doesn't he know he's a flying bomb?" His words were shockingly loud in the murmuring darkness of the control tower.

"We thought he should land on the old runways, nearest the tower," said the supervisor, "so the bomb-control people could get to him right away."

Wild-eyed, Peter watched the glistening lights of the approaching airliner. He brought the microphone closer to his lips and started talking as fast as he could: "Get away from the beach, Captain, and tell the man in the lavatory that he mustn't spill any more holy water. He mustn't spill any more holy water, and you must get your airplane away from the beach, do you understand me? Fly out to sea, and tell the man in the lavatory . . . "

Hiro Watanabe was among thousands of late-night revelers prowling Kalakaua Avenue. The fancy boutiques were dark now, but the restaurants and saimin stands filled the warm air with the smell of hot grease and spices. From the bars floated the twang of electric guitars and the flat, amplified voices which accompanied them. Gaudy souvenir shops vied to dazzle the eye, displaying chunks of coral spray-painted pink and blue and copper, and ranks of spring-mounted hula dolls wiggling their grass-skirted bottoms.

Watanabe weaved a little as he made his way down the wide sidewalk, humming a tuneless chant, intermittently breaking into a couple of dance steps before dodging nimbly away from an imminent collision with another pedestrian. He'd left his wife at home after a wretched disagreement—the foolish woman would not understand that they were *ruined*—and he did not want to think about yesterday, or today, and especially he did not want to think about tomorrow.

Watanabe hadn't seen the approaching airplane yet, and out on the beach the lovers, and second-honeymooners, and the kids telling tall tales and scoring dope and trading dreams talked in whispers and wiggled their toes in the warm sand and ignored the plane whose lights hung like a distress flare over Diamond Head.

Then Watanabe heard the shrill scream of jet engines directly overhead and glanced up in time to see the lights of Waikiki reflected from the white belly of the low-flying 747. Even as he watched, the plane banked and turned out to sea, its engines thundering in the night. Watanabe thought of the pale owls he'd watched as a child, swooping like ghosts in the torchlight of the Nara shrines.

Enraptured, Watanabe gazed at the turning, diving plane.

The 747 ruptured and was instantly swallowed in a sphere of intense light. Hiro Watanabe never saw those few fragments which described their flaming arcs toward the ground, for in the first instant he'd been struck blind.

39

The chief surgeon froze, his gleaming scalpel poised above Luki's spine; the clustered lights overhead flickered and threatened to go out. But somewhere flywheels engaged with a rumble, and circuit breakers clacked open and shut: the hospital's old, bulky emergency generators shouldered the burden as the city's grid failed.

Luki would not benefit from their dependability. From the moment the taxi had smashed his pelvis and severed his spine, he had been dying; an hour later even the angry surgeons would admit it and turn to other tasks, more hopeful if even more desperate.

The glare washed through Penelope Harper's room at Tripler Army Hospital, six miles away. Through the room's white curtains, through the thin gauze that layered her face, her tender eyes registered the untimely brilliance. In her sleep, drugged against pain, she murmured dreamily: "The light like bones . . . so beautiful."

345

Martin Edovich, material witness to various and sundry felonies, sat in his crumpled clothes and watched his wife's troubled sleep, timing each of her sibilant breaths. On the bureau near to his hand stood an almost empty bottle of slivovitz. Outside, he knew, a pair of federal marshals sat in their drab car, keeping watch over his house and grounds.

Light penetrated the bedroom window, inflaming the poinciana, throwing the dark beams of the ceiling into high relief. In his alcoholic stupor Martin Edovich immediately knew the light for what it was; had not the young genius Peter Slater predicted disaster?

Edovich's time sense dilated. He peered at the smeared empty glass he clutched in his thick fist: it glowed like a crystal chalice in the unearthly light. Slowly, expanding from the deep, a wrenching sob welled up in his breast.

Matsuo Ishi stood before the tinted plate glass of the darkened conference room, watching the landing lights of the lone airplane as it descended over the shimmering haze of the city more than sixteen miles away. All his advisers had gone home, their duties completed. Below him the great ring lay shadowed by moonlight. A blue light on a telephone call box, the orange glow of a streetlamp, only served to emphasize TERAC's emptiness. For the second time in four days its proton and antiproton beams had spilled into yielding rock. The ring was dead. The nuclear reactor which had fed its ravenous appetite for power had gradually been brought under mechanical control, its fuel bundles withdrawn from the core, the reactor's heat carried off by coolant.

From the ponds of TERAC hot wet vapor billowed into the night sky, livid sign of entropy.

Matsuo Ishi had directed his team to prepare for the worst, and it came. The dark glass barely softened the apocalyptic panorama: for a moment Ishi saw himself in the window as if in a mirror, hunched in surprise and terror, clearly reflected against the starkly illuminated ring below. Above all the horrors that were to follow, Ishi would remember that moment when his own ghost came rushing like an emblem of shame to superimpose itself upon the image of the great work he had labored to complete, and which somehow, incomprehensibly, he had brought to dishonor.

Pablo Tabilang, fisherman, witness to murder, sat on the bare wooden stoop of his Waimanalo shack, sipping happily from a tumbler of sour red wine and listening to a portable radio, while he considered the betting possibilities for the weekend's schedule of clandestine cockfights. Three of his fishing buddies were sprawled on the steps below him, all of them quietly eyeing the surf across the road. They'd retold the day's extraordinary events to one another so often that the novelty had drained off. Suddenly the sky above their heads seemed to wash away, as if the full moon had doubled in intensity.

The stringy old fisherman grunted. "Seen dat befo, you bet. Dem dumb sailors at Pearl musta blew 'em anotha ammo dump, like inna war. Kill plenty dat time." Tabilang reached to turn up the radio, but it crackled and hissed at him, and in front of his house the icy blue streetlamp fizzed and went dark.

Dan Kono and Ana Apana never saw the strange light. Hours earlier they had followed the ambulance to the emergency room of Honolulu General Hospital. A harassed intern had eventually told them that Luki would be in surgery for several hours more; Dan had decided to take Ana home and return later, by himself.

When they walked into their dark, bare house they realized their solitude was, for once, a blessing. There was no elation in their homecoming, but the need they felt for each other was intense. Their lovemaking was dark, slow, and grievous; they made love as if on mountaintops, in sea caves, among the moon-shadowed canyons of clouds.

Above the ridge of Makapuu Pali a great light bled the sky of stars, and went unnoticed by them.

"He's down!" the controller said, incredulous. "Oh God, he went down." Six miles from the tower the blip left the scopes.

From the tower Peter saw the blue white flash eat the night away in an instant. His analytic mind never stopped functioning, running on a track of its own, recording details with interest and precision: the plane low, fleeing the city, wheeling out to sea; the Wall of Waikiki rendered stark as chalk; the light everywhere, reflecting from sea and sand and glass.

And with another part of his mind he had a vision. Expanding shells of light radiated from the center of the Pacific Ocean, and where they skimmed the surface of the globe they left flames—the seamounts and archipelagos, the lush islands, the continents themselves, blazing into char—and soon the lumps and masses of cinders merged and crumbled into one. It was as if Peter had seen the Ancient of Days reach down with blazing compasses and with a backward flip of his wrist send the world tumbling into formlessness, into the void.

And darkness was once more on the face of the deep.

Peter thought he was blind. The details of the moment—the city, the controllers at their consoles—were printed on his retinas in negative, black on angry red. He stood stock-still, afraid to move, horror and panic rising in him as he began to assimilate what had happened.

Then he realized that his vision was returning, at least at the edges, though a darkly coruscating purple blotch superimposed itself wherever he turned his gaze.

The radar screens in the control tower were dead. Radios and telephones were useless. No lights marked the airport runways. In the distance the city was dark, and flames licked at the sky.

Peter himself was suddenly useless; worse than useless, he was in the way, and a symbol of horrid failure to those around him. In the eyes of those who must now cope with disaster, he was one who had helped create it. He stumbled blindly down the stairs, past the main control rooms where red emergency lights now throbbed like coals in the wind.

Before he reached the ground floor he stopped, leaning weakly against the wall as running men moved up past him. Tears streamed from his burning eyes. Anne-Marie . . .

When the light came she was sitting on the bed beside an open suitcase, toying with her diamond rings. She saw the light first in the depths of the largest stone.

She'd returned to the little hotel and gotten the same room back—a perfectly nondescript room, but it was no man's land. The henna-haired desk clerk had been thrilled at the hope of scandal, but Anne-Marie had not evaded her curiosity; instead she'd confronted it: "Perhaps you can help me. I'm looking for a job and a place to stay, and I really don't know that much about the island."

An extraordinary transformation had swept over the lonely clerk; shocked out of her cattiness by this cry for help, she was warmly eager to be of use. "Why, my dear, let's see what we can do. You're a good photographer, I've heard that. I'm sure I can help you find someone who . . ."

And now Anne-Marie sat pondering the impulsive decision, testing her resolve. There were dark circles under her eyes, eyes of a grayer blue than Peter had known, for she'd put her contacts aside. Despite her exhaustion, she found she was calm; she'd taken a first step at a new angle from the old path, a step away from the roles others had created for her, the hollow roles she'd created for herself. There was no elation in the wordless feeling of rightness, but it seemed to grow stronger with the . . .

Then the diamond ring flared and the light beat through the window. The curtains seemed transparent; a sheet of smoke boiled up and curled away, but the combustion was snuffed out in a blast of air that shrieked through the open louvers. Glass slats cracked and flew inward, to be entangled in writhing curtains.

She half rose, turned to face the imploding window. Her hair blew across her eyes.

Downtown Honolulu was a midnight ghost town, haunted by hundreds of running shapes which materialized in headlight beams, then disappeared again into the night.

Sirens howled. Cars swerved to avoid ambulances and fire trucks heading for the only sources of light, the billowing flames of Chinatown, the old neighborhoods behind the canal, the crowded wooden houses of Kaimuki.

Multistoried wooden tenements were ablaze; adults and children leaped from balconies that collapsed under them in cinders. In the streets, fire trucks collided, and firemen groped for hydrants by the lurid light of the spreading fire. The smell of pineapple syrup spread thickly along the air as the cannery burned.

In the valleys the homes of the wealthy were shielded from the blast and heat by the mountain walls, but great winds swept toward the ridge, tearing branches from the trees, scattering roof tiles, strewing the streets with flowers.

Lower down, the same winds hurled cars through the streets, left power lines in sparking tangles, ripped the roofs off buildings which had withstood the blast. Near the harbor the winds picked up the tangled debris of factories and boatyards and tossed steel beams and sheets of corrugated iron like chaff. The winds flung people from their hotel balconies, sucked them out of their rooms; it plucked them from the sidewalks and left them in heaps in the angles of concrete towers.

The blast had pushed a hole in the sea, baring the white sand bottom of the long sloping beach. A thirty-foot wave washed over Kalakaua Avenue and spilled over the banks

of the canal, leaving sailboats stranded on the Ala Wai
golf course as it receded into the seething ocean.

Where homes and cars were intact, radios and televi-
sions buzzed incoherently. Phone lines left standing by the
wind were nevertheless dead; mobile radio transmitters
were burned out. Thrown back on word of mouth, emergency services responded in scattered groups to the places
where need of them was most obvious, west of Bishop
Street, east of University.

Thousands wandered unaided in Waikiki, unknowingly
abandoned, some burned, some blinded by the primary
flash. Ten thousand windows lay in shards; beneath the
gutted, blackened towers the streets glittered terribly in
the moonlight. Moments after the great light had come
and then vanished, leaving them in darkness, the desperately burned sought relief in the salt surf, crying for help
that was long in coming.

No light penetrated the cold filing drawers of the county
morgue, wherein lay the well-inspected remains of Cyrus
Sherwood and Gardner Hey.

40

Ferdinand Kawaiola and his men from TERAC had been assigned to Waikiki, once it was apparent the conflagration in Chinatown was under control. There they worked to extinguish the fires that had sprung up almost capriciously among the wooden bungalows clustered along the canal. The neighborhood was a remnant of the old Waikiki that had somehow survived the building boom of the last two decades; what survived of it now owed its existence to the shadow of the tall concrete hotels, which had absorbed the heat and blunted the force of the wind and waves from the sea.

They worked hard and efficiently, though all of them believed themselves dead. They thought Honolulu had been the target of a nuclear bomb, and that they would eventually fall victim to radioactive poison. Because they, of all the firefighters on the island, knew most about the dangers of radioactivity, they had the least hope.

By morning most of the fires had been extinguished or had burned themselves out. Kawaiola was thankful that it had been a calm night with no natural wind to fan the flames, that the burning buildings had been separated widely enough to forestall a self-feeding firestorm, that the waters of the canal were near at hand. Nevertheless the old fireman had exhausted himself fighting the blaze; he sat on a pile of spent oxygen bottles in the shade of a charred, decapitated palm tree, and stared wearily into a paper cup of orange juice a medic had given him.

Across Kalia Road the Army had established a field hospital in the park. Sometime in the night the military had restored essential communications, using runners, semaphore systems, wire telegraphs, and any miscellaneous pieces of electronic gear which by accident or design had been shielded from the peculiar electromagnetic pulse of the explosion. By dawn the authorities had begun to quantify the disaster, structure it, organize its relief. Massive aid was already beginning to arrive from the mainland, so Kawaiola had heard, and the monotonous roar of jet cargo planes landing one after the other at the airport reached his ears even at this distance.

Kawaiola glimpsed health-physics types snooping about through the wreckage down by the beach, their counters probing sand and metal and concrete. Every once in a while one of the hooded investigators would stoop to pick up a sample of soil or debris and deposit it in a sealed plastic bag. One of his firemen had told him the good news, still a rumor—it couldn't have been an A-bomb, because there was hardly any radioactive debris. Kawaiola didn't know whether to believe it or not; true, their chirpers and badges hadn't warned them of danger, but what besides an atomic bomb could have produced the devastation he saw all around him?

He would give it more thought later. His eyes closed and the empty paper cup slipped from his weary fingers to fall silently on the scorched grass. He was almost asleep when he heard the curious mewling sound, *mizu, mizu, mizu,* repeated monotonously. His eyes flew open. At first he thought it was a sick animal—the sound came from a nearby hedge—but then he realized it was a distorted human voice.

He stumbled toward the bushes and yanked the branches aside. A young Japanese man lay on the ground, his arms outstretched. He turned his face toward Kawaiola.

The fireman recognized the bright red skin of a third-degree burn; what made him sob in anguished surprise was the open wound of the mouth, the lips dissolved in burst blisters—and the eyesockets, open but empty, the melted fluid streaking the man's cheeks.

"*Iesu Kristo,*" whispered Kawaiola. "Man, let me help you."

The horrid mask bobbed on the stalk of neck, twisting to seek the source of Kawaiola's voice as a morning-glory seeks the sun. The mouth hole contracted: "Hwata, hwata," the man said, the shapeless murmurings of an involuntary ventriloquist.

At first the big Hawaiian didn't know where to grab him, but he put his hands around the man's waist and hauled him erect, grimacing at his stifled cry. "Come on, walk across the street with me, brah—that's all the farther you got to go."

As they approached the hospital tent Kawaiola saw that his charge was only one of dozens, perhaps hundreds, who lay on cots and blankets near the entrance of the big canvas shelter, while more burned, blinded, and lacerated converged on the emergency aid station, and the ambulances came and went in a steady shuttle, their sirens silenced, redundant.

"Rest here, brah, I'll get you some water." Kawaiola helped the man to the ground, still a dozen yards from the tent. He glanced once more at the ravaged face before he left, and could not help wondering if he'd seen the man before.

Watanabe and Kawaiola never recognized each other. Not that it made much difference to either of them.

"Hwata," said Watanabe, as Kawaiola hurried away. He had no eyes to cry.

Japanese eyes followed Peter Slater to the elevator; Japanese eyes followed him when he got off at the top floor and walked toward Ishi's office, led by Miss Sugibayashi. Only one desk in three in the building was occupied, and those only by Japanese. No phones rang, no typewriters rattled; the silent stares were unmitigated by sound effects. "Why are they here?" Peter asked her in Japanese.

"They don't know where else to go, sir," Miss Sugibayashi replied.

Ishi's office door stood open. Peter went into the empty room and waited until Miss Sugibayashi reluctantly followed him inside. It seemed to him indecent that the abandoned office should stand exposed; he closed the door behind her.

"When did you last see him?" he asked.

She spoke rapidly, tonelessly: "After the accelerator was shut down he dismissed the staff to their homes. When the explosion occurred he directed the emergency services personnel to place themselves at the disposal of the Honolulu city government. He stood watching the fires for a long time—then he attempted to call Tokyo, but the phones were not working. He said he would try again, when it was morning in Tokyo. He told me he would rest until then, and that I should do the same; there is a little cot in my office closet. I brought it out—at first I could not sleep, but suddenly it was morning, and—" The young woman paused and looked up at Peter. He'd often found her chubby round face and rosebud lips faintly comical, but the dark eye makeup smudged on her cheeks gave her a distracted, unfocused appearance, hardly amusing. "He wasn't there," she said.

He knew what she feared. She must have known Peter would understand, and that as a foreigner he might be willing to interfere.

"Perhaps I am not a good Japanese," she said, apologizing.

"Surely you are right to be concerned for him," Peter said impatiently. He looked around the room, with its bookshelves and its spare, well-crafted furniture. In the center of the desk lay a notebook with a black paper cover. He picked it up, flipped the pages from right to left, found the diary's last entry—bold calligraphy down the middle of the page:

Know when to stop
And you will meet with no danger.
You can then endure.

Peter stared at the graceful, vigorous characters. The quotation had the flavor of the Tao about it, the economy of expression characteristic of Lao Tzu. "When did he write this?"

Miss Sugibayashi shook her head dumbly. Never would she have examined his most private papers.

If it was a suicide note, it was one of uncompromisingly bitter irony. He set the book down, looked quickly around the desk top, the shelves, the tables. He rummaged in the desk drawers, finding only a few items of even mild interest: a set of nail clippers, a pair of spectacles he hadn't known Ishi used, an exquisitely carved netsuke in the form of a mischievous monkey spilling a bucket of water, a smooth brown horse chestnut of the same size, polished by frequent rubbing.

Peter looked absently at Miss Sugibayashi, who hovered beside the closed door. Where would he have gone? A devout Japanese might have visited one of the island's many Buddhist temples, but Ishi had never struck Peter as conventionally religious. Indeed, he had always seemed eminently practical.

What had Miss Sugibayashi said? They don't know where else to go. . . .

"Wait here," he said to her, "I'll contact you as soon as I can."

The nearest entrance to the ring was in a service building behind Dirac Hall. The tunnel ran close to the surface, this far from the mountains; Peter skipped quickly down a single flight of metal steps and came to a steel door. It was wide open.

As he stepped into the tunnel he felt the caress of cool air flowing from the heart of the mountain, three curving miles away. The tunnel was quite empty. He turned to his left, for no particular reason other than that it was Ishi's left foot that was twisted.

The hard leather soles of Peter's moccasins slapped against the concrete tunnel floor, sending ringing echoes away in front and behind. He walked energetically, in long, swinging strides—for as long as he walked briskly in circles, he could put thought and feeling out of his mind.

Those last moments, wheeling in the night sky . . . God grant she never suspected, never woke up, never sensed a thing. Not so many years ago Peter would have been prepared to demand a great deal more from God. By now he'd lost even Einstein's feeble hope that God was not malicious.

He stopped then, and stood still. The whisper of far-off exhaust fans, the faint buzz of the green fluorescent lights, the gurgle and wheeze of distant pumps infiltrated the deserted tunnel. Peter closed his eyes and let the tears well up behind his lids, hot as his blood. After a moment he walked on, still crying, following the tunnel's gentle curve easily enough, though its image wavered and flowed.

He crossed one deserted experimental hall and at length traversed another sixty degrees of empty tunnel. The tears dried on his cheeks. His head was pounding, though his sense of pain was somehow dulled by the phantasmagoric perfection of the curving tunnel. The air grew much colder.

Then, in the instantaneous interval between one footstep's dying echo and the hard slap of the next, he heard another human sound. He paused, and soon, by the rhythm of the footfalls, he knew he'd found Ishi.

Without thinking, Peter retreated before the oncoming footsteps, until he came to a storage alcove, its door recessed in the tunnel's inner wall. He pressed himself into the shadows and stood still. Before long the old man appeared in the distance, a dark speck, rocking from side to side as he came on.

Ishi was talking to himself. The Japanese words, garbled at first, distorted by echoes, soon came clear: "... then elder brother came to visit me again. He revealed that it was the Prime Minister's uncle who had saved me from the factories when I was a boy. . . . I agreed to meet with him. It was cold in the garden; the winter sun gleamed from the bare stalks of the pampas grass. . . ."

Peter held his breath, terrified now of discovery. Ishi passed him by without a sign.

"... only I could bring the feuding parties together. Remembering the words of my father, who taught me that the most honorable thing is to give without thought of reward, I accepted the directorship. . . ."

Peter peered from his hiding place as the lame man walked on. It took a long time for the tiny dark figure to vanish around the subtle arc of the subterranean chamber.

Peter hurried along the tunnel in the opposite direction. He came to an experimental hall: Hall 30, the den of the I-particle collector, now quiescent. He clambered down steel stairs, pushed through a steel door in a concrete-block wall, dashed to the elevator.

High on the slopes of central Oahu he walked dizzily into the sunlight. Fields of green cane bent and rippled in the gusty breeze. Farther away, a cane rig lumbered out of a burned field, its driver intent on earning his day's pay as long as there was earth beneath his wheels. The trailer was stacked twenty feet high with burnt stalks like a pile of bones. Peter could see the red mud the rig was shedding in its wake; he could almost smell the charcoal and molasses.

In the distance the city stood gleaming. Only when he looked closely could Peter see the rising threads of smoke.

Unlike Ishi, Peter found no words at all to voice his despair. The shimmering beautiful surface of things, the cutting edges of the distant breakers glittering with the sun's reflected fire, all this was a sham, a trick of vibrating fields which, unobserved, possessed no independent existence, held no meaning, no savor, no hope. The world had vanished overnight.

Anne-Marie woke groggily; it took her some seconds to realize that she was safe and well, lying in her bed amid the shambles of her room at the Diamond Head Crater Hotel.

She remembered it all in an instant. The lower floors of the hotel, well shielded from the blast, had served as an emergency shelter. Those among the hotel staff and guests who'd escaped serious injury had volunteered what help they could to the team of Air Force medics who ran the shelter.

It was dirty work, carrying off bloody clothes and linens to a growing pile on the beach, wiping up the spills, the vomit, holding agonized wounded in their beds. Sometime before dawn an Air Force nurse had ordered Anne-Marie to sleep. By then she was only half conscious with fatigue—she'd managed to sleep well into the next night.

A hundred things she had to do flooded her mind. She realized that the news of the terrible explosion and fire must have been communicated to the whole world by now; she had to reassure her child, her friends, her husband. And she thought of Peter . . . but as yet, she didn't even know what had really happened.

Before all, she absolutely had to have something to eat.

Later, in the tangled mess inside her room, she found her clothes and her cameras, undamaged. But she never learned what became of her contact lenses, or of Charlie's diamond rings.

ONE YEAR LATER

*There is no excellent beauty that hath not
some strangeness in the proportion.*

—FRANCIS BACON, *On Beauty*

SEN. BUCKLER: . . . we have heard very disturbing testimony here this morning, Dr. Slater, indicating that you have given out national security secrets to the whole world!

PROF. SLATER: Those secrets were never secret, Senator, except to the ignorant. The theoretical papers have been circulating for years. In the forties, we tried to hoard the so-called secret of the atomic bomb, in the fifties we thought we could monopolize the hydrogen bomb. For decades we've wasted our treasure on brute force and trickery. That's over, ladies and gentlemen. Annihilation is easy now.

SEN. BUCKLER: The point is, you made statements to the press . . .

PROF. SLATER: Excuse me, Senator, but do you think this bottle on my desk looks like cough medicine? (Witness indicates a small bottle with labels, filled with clear fluid.)

SEN. BUCKLER: Is this supposed to be some sort of . . . ?

PROF. SLATER: The fluid in this bottle happens to be chemically identical to the fluid which produced the fifty-kiloton explosion that destroyed Waikiki.

(Loud commotion within the chambers.)

PROF. SLATER: (shouting) It's plain water. Water, that's all.

SEN. WHITE: Order! We'll have silence or I'll clear the chambers. (Order is restored.) Go ahead, Dr. Slater.

PROF. SLATER: Of course, there are no I-particles in this water—but if there were, no one could easily have detected them. If there were I-particles in this water in the same proportion as in the fluid which destroyed Waikiki, and if this bottle exploded in my hand at this moment, it would leave a crater three hundred feet deep and a thousand feet wide here where the Capitol now stands. Washington would be wiped off the map. I repeat, you could have done nothing to stop me from bringing it here. Not only are there no more secrets, Senator, there is no more defense. . . .

Peter closed the little Government Printing Office booklet which contained the transcript of the hearings. He hadn't done too badly on that one; he was beginning to get the hang of it. The stunt with the bottle had even managed to steal some of the thunder from the bomb boys with their neat columns of radius-and-area versus death-and-injury, their maps with the concentric circles around ground zero, all the devices that made the destruction of a city seem rather like a particularly bad traffic accident.

He turned to the last pile of mail on his dining-room table, the hand-addressed cards and envelopes. He no longer looked forward to reading most of his fan mail; too much of it was frightening. But his eye was caught by a note card with an inscription in blue ink, drawn by a strong feminine hand.

He read the note, and his heart leaped.

Jennifer Phelps grunted and splurted and crawled rapidly forward half a yard before collapsing on her belly. With back arched fiercely and head held high, she peered myopically at the immense promontory rising at the edge of the blanket in front of her: Peter Slater's knee.

Peter looked at her thoughtfully, then looked up at her mother. Anne-Marie was watching him. Her skin was even darker now, with only an underlying blush of rose. Her chestnut hair hung in shining braids over her bare shoulders. She was so beautiful she made him nervous.

"Don't stop talking, Peter," she said. "I want to get caught up."

"Your daughter is fascinating."

"Tell me that after you've changed her diapers two hundred times," she said. "So—you were telling me why you were never in when I called? Something about Washington?"

"A lot of testifying. I think congressional committees must be like a lecture circuit—once you're a star, all the chairmen want you. And you can't say no. The Defense Department is very unhappy with me."

"Does that bother you?"

"A couple of years ago I would have thought of it as a regrettable inconvenience. Now it seems more like a compliment." He sipped his wine, eyeing the baby. "How come you never left a message?"

"At least I called. You never did."

Too vividly he remembered their last conversation, the night she'd asked him to help Gardner Hey. Someday he'd have the courage to ask her if she held him responsible for the reporter's death. "I feel foolish around you, even now. You went by your hunches, or your stars, or whatever—and you were right."

"I don't want to hear that you're a convert to astrology," she said. "I gave it up—much too reductionist." Her gray blue eyes sparkled with humor; she'd also given up her colored contact lenses, permanently.

"I haven't really changed," Peter said. "Maybe I pay more attention when someone calls me a snob."

Jennifer had changed course and charged again; her fitfully churning arms and legs got her as far as the blanket's edge, where she immediately grabbed a fistful of rank grass and tried to carry it to her mouth. The grass was tough and refused to tear; she pulled her nose into her fist instead. "I read an article you wrote," said Anne-Marie, "in the *New York Review*—of all places. I liked what you said."

"I was talked into that by a Berkeley friend," Peter said ruefully. "It made me infamous. I get hate mail from my colleagues."

"You're serious?" Resting a hand on her daughter's back, she steered her toward the center of the blanket.

"Oh, I get fan mail too," said Peter. "The hate mail comes from the bomb freaks, the fan mail from the Luddites. My fellow theorists are only faintly embarrassed by my bad taste, but science writers love me. Good old Peter Slater, always good for a quote. That article's from the speech I made, the day after . . ." He looked away, swallowing. "I thought you were dead. It was days before I would believe you really weren't on the plane. So I was drunk when I made the speech. I was surprised I held the audience—they got an earful of what I thought of Martin."

"What's happened to him?"

"He's back at Los Alamos. They keep him out of the news, but he hasn't suffered any. You know, I'm still trying to come to grips with that—a man like him, who's so completely lost the capacity for wonder that he'll go ahead with a cynical scheme because he thinks he can't be surprised, that nothing *new* could possibly upset his plans."

"His wife must have suffered. And he didn't get the Nobel Prize."

"That's some punishment, I suppose. But Greta's probably fairly content. Santa Fe's a nice town—great scenery, good restaurants, good opera, lots of ex-Easterners in Pueblo drag writing novels and throwing pots . . . "

"Peter!" She was laughing. "You really are a snob."

"Sorry." He grinned, unrepentant. "Oh, and the company's not bad in Los Alamos, either."

"If you like physicists."

He raised an eyebrow. "Some do."

She smiled. "To their peril." She watched him a moment in silence, then dropped her gaze. She changed the subject: "What's it like out there? Has anything really changed?"

"I guess not. We were picketed for a couple of months. We almost lost the Japanese participation altogether—the shame of the thing. But TERAC is still the world's premier research facility, and people are pragmatists in the end. Jobs got shuffled, that's all." His words trailed off. He looked away from her. "How many thousand dead, Anne-Marie? I should have memorized the figure by now, but somehow—" He laughed bitterly. "And the irony is, Honolulu was lucky. Chauncey had enough of that stuff to level this island, if he'd put it together a different way. We know that from theoretical studies. That's the kind of theory I worry about, these days."

"Peter—" She reached out her hand to touch him, but her daughter lunged with a fierce cry and clutched her forefinger.

Peter laughed. "Can I pour you another glass of wine? Give you something more to eat? Get you to tell me the story of your life?"

"All of the above," she said, gently freeing her encumbered finger. She held out her clear plastic cup and he filled it with cold Chardonnay, which he lifted from a sweating bottle-brick. She sipped the fragrant wine and looked at the distant horizon. The sea was a deeper blue, the clouds a purer white than a year ago. The stones of the ancient heiau seemed less menacing, though no less fraught with power. Was the mana of the ancient Hawaiians as morally neutral as the strong nuclear force? Or had the old gods exacted their revenge?

"As for me, the legal garbage takes up a lot of my energy." She sighed. "Charlie's being a complete . . . well." She took a breath and started again. "He wants to keep Carlos, and he's trying to get Jennifer too. I haven't seen my son since before I came here, the same day I met you. I can imagine what he thinks of me. Since the day after the explosion I've talked to him twice on the phone, Christmas and his birthday, and even then Charlie was listening in on the extension. But I've got a lawyer I trust. On my good days I think I have a chance of working out something reasonable."

"What do you call reasonable?" Peter sawed into a baguette with a Swiss army knife.

"I want—Carlos to live with me, at least during the school year. I'd settle for that."

"What about the other way around?" Peter handed her a chunk of bread smeared with soft cheese.

"Maybe," she conceded. She took the bread and cheese and stared at it. "The point is, I want him to know there's a choice—he doesn't have to grow up to be a wheeler-dealer."

Peter watched her eat. "Nor should he have to run away from it." When she brushed the last crumbs from her skirt he asked, "And Jennifer?"

"When she's old enough, Charlie's welcome to visit." Her voice was cold.

"Tough on him," Peter remarked, looking down at the infant, who was now trying to chin herself on his knee. He put the cheese out of her reach.

"He was tough on me," said Anne-Marie.

"I'm not defending him. I don't even know him."

"No, you're just defending the ex-husbands' team. That's okay. But don't expect me to take your advice."

"Never," he said solemnly. "Not my department. Salami?" He handed her another hunk of bread, stacked with slices of pale pink salami.

"Love it." She bit, and watched him as she munched. Her daughter, with unquenchable determination, continued to climb onto Peter's thigh. "This is good," said Anne-Marie. "Why am I always hungry? So, Peter—I've told you the rest, haven't I? I've got a nice tiny sublet in Kahala, been there eight months and hoping the man who owns it goes native east of Java or somewhere—he's the type. And after a couple of months of really being scared I got a good job. I do PR photos and copywriting and odd jobs for this little boutique ad agency. They're good people. They didn't freak out when I took off to have Jennifer, and they pay me more than I'm worth."

"You'll turn that around soon enough."

"I'm working on it. I've brought them some interesting clients already. You don't really want me to talk shop, do you?"

"I don't give a damn," he said. "I just want to watch you."

"You're so sweet to say so." She leaned forward and gazed deep into his eyes. "You won't mind my telling you that my daughter has just made a large wet spot on your classy whipcords." She grinned.

He looked down, startled, but had the presence of mind not to grab the baby. Instead he capped his tan, long-fingered hand over her tiny bulbous skull. "You really don't know me that well, sweetheart," he said, Bogart-fashion. "But I wouldn't mind changing that."

"Is that a truly terrible pun?" Anne-Marie asked, her eyes wide. "Or a sincere offer?"

"I'm not too proud to display my ignorance," he replied. "Where do I start?" Gently he wrapped his hands around Jennifer's tiny smooth body and lifted her, wiggling, into the air. As he brought her close she grabbed at his nose and hooked a sharp thumbnail in his nostril, but he smiled through his grimace and planted a loud wet kiss on the bare stretch of tummy that showed between her diapers and her undershirt.

Halfway through the strange new task Peter paused. "Is this going right?"

She'd been staring at the horizon, at the rustling palms and the plum trees glistening in the sun. She turned and answered him seriously. "This isn't an occasional game with me, Peter. It's a real basic part of my life. And so is my son. I hope you'll meet him soon. And neither of them is all my life—I'm myself, too, with a place I go to work, and a place I live. . . . "

"The point's taken," he said. "Don't be so terrified that I'm going to try to fit you into a mold. I still love you. I never stopped."

"Dammit." She was crying, the tears falling freely onto her lap. "You disappeared. I *made* you disappear. And now you're back."

"Yeah—ouch, shit, I got myself in the thumb—you all right, Jenny?" When the baby splurted at him vigorously he proceeded, reassured. "Yeah, anyway, basic law of particle physics: all things have to disappear. Out of the void, new forms appear. And here we are, all of us; pretty bizarre set, right?—There, kid, that's got you." He raised his hands away from the newly diapered baby, as if he'd just produced a dove from a silk scarf. "Not bad, eh?" He reached down and turned Jennifer over on her stomach. Within seconds she was crawling for the grass.

Peter looked on, crestfallen. "She crawled right out of them."

"Don't worry," said Anne-Marie, kissing his cheek. "You can come around sometime and practice. If you come around I'll *make* you practice."

He turned his face and kissed her mouth. After a long moment, he said, "There will have to be problems, you know."

"You figured it out," she said. "And I love you, too." She'd never said that to him before, never said it before to anyone and meant it. The palms whispered to each other, echoing his amazement.

The man and woman kissed a long time. The half-naked baby girl made it three feet into the field of grass before they reached to retrieve her.

Matsuo Ishi's elder brother let him have the use of a farmhouse in the mountains behind Osaka. It hovered near the edge of a village of some twenty thatch-roofed houses, near a clear swift stream. Dark cedars stood behind it, and on the shadowed hillside where moss could be grown there was a clearing big enough for a teahouse and a tiny garden.

Ishi and his wife lived alone, seeing no one except the farmers who leased their fields of indigo. Each morning Ishi walked in the woods and fields, searching for evocative rocks for his planned garden, or for promising juniper saplings to create the small shaped trees he would plant there.

In the afternoons, when the sun reached into the main room, he knelt on the polished boards in front of the open screens and wrote in his diary. The day's events took only a line or two to record. He augmented his diary with essays and observations, small treatises on the classics, both Western and Chinese. Zeno was a favored author, as was Lao Tzu. But he read further afield also, works he'd avoided in his youth. One day he copied these words he'd found in Sun Tzu's thirteen chapters on the art of war:

> There are five qualities which are dangerous in the character of a general.
> If reckless, he can be killed;
> If cowardly, captured;
> If quick-tempered, you can make a fool of him;
> If he has too delicate a sense of honor you can calumniate him;
> If he is of a compassionate nature you can harass him.

Now these five traits of character are serious faults in a general and in military operations are calamitous.

The ruin of the army and the death of the general are inevitable results of these shortcomings. They must be deeply pondered.

In his hatred of war Ishi had paid too little attention to its cruel wise lessons, so dearly bought. It seemed to him now that all human endeavor, by whatever name one might call it, was a struggle to achieve a moment's understanding amid ceaseless confusion and night.

The wind sighing in the cedars, the warm sunlight on his face, the black ink flowing from the brush onto the white paper—allowing symbols of meaning to rise from the void—these evanescent things had been bought at the cost of great sacrifice and striving. And yet, they were fine things, were they not?

Sighing, Ishi put down his brush. His eyelids were heavy. Peacefully, he dozed. The world went busily on.

Sources Quoted or
Referred to in the Text

Werner Heisenberg, *The Physical Principles of the Quantum Theory,* trans. Carl Eckart and F. C. Hoyt, University of Chicago Press, 1930.

Harold G. Henderson, *An Introduction to Haiku,* Doubleday, 1958.

Lao Tzu, *Lao Tzu, Tao Te Ching,* trans. D. C. Lau, Penguin, 1963.

Joseph Needham, *Science and Civilization in China,* Cambridge University Press, 1956.

Rainer Maria Rilke, *Duino Elegies,* trans. C. F. MacIntyre, University of California Press, 1965.

Sun Tzu, *Sun Tzu, The Art of War,* trans. Samuel B. Griffith, Oxford University Press, 1963.

Lewis Thomas, *The Medusa and the Snail,* Viking, 1979.

Steven Weinberg, *The First Three Minutes,* Basic Books, 1977.

Frances A. Yates, *Giordano Bruno and the Hermetic Tradition,* Routledge and Kegan Paul, 1964.

Hideki Yukawa, *Creativity and Intuition,* Kodansha International, 1973.